MP

Praise for Ba

"Barbara weaves a fantastic tale of myste~~~
enmeshed in gothic elements of the old style that
you'll feel you've picked up a masterpiece from the
'60s."

—*Goodreads* on *Darkening Around Me*

"Just the right atmosphere of gloom, chills and
ghosts. Great!"

—*Goodreads* on *Darkening Around Me*

Praise for Jane Kindred

"This gothic-inspired modern romance is built on a
supernatural base that drips with intrigue, mystery
and some deliciously dark humor."

—*RT Book Reviews* on *The Lost Coast*

"This complex and wickedly decadent dark fantasy
bombards the reader with its sensuality and
heartbreaking reveals while building to an explosive
ending."

—*RT Book Reviews* on *Master of the Game*

LEGENDARY SHIFTER
&
SEDUCING THE DARK PRINCE

BARBARA J. HANCOCK
AND
JANE KINDRED

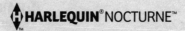

Recycling programs
for this product may
not exist in your area.

ISBN-13: 978-1-335-24999-9

Legendary Shifter & Seducing the Dark Prince

Copyright © 2018 by Harlequin Books S.A.

The publisher acknowledges the copyright holders
of the individual works as follows:

Legendary Shifter
Copyright © 2018 by Barbara J. Hancock

Seducing the Dark Prince
Copyright © 2018 by Jane Kindred

HARLEQUIN®
www.Harlequin.com

Printed in U.S.A.

CONTENTS

LEGENDARY SHIFTER   7
Barbara J. Hancock

SEDUCING THE DARK PRINCE   307
Jane Kindred

Barbara J. Hancock lives in the foothills of the Blue Ridge Mountains, where her daily walk takes her to the edge of the wilderness and back again. When Barbara isn't writing modern gothic romance that embraces the shadows with a unique blend of heat and heart, she can be found wrangling twin boys and spoiling her pets.

Also by Barbara J. Hancock

Harlequin Nocturne

Brimstone Seduction
Brimstone Bride
Brimstone Prince

Legendary Warriors

Legendary Shifter

Harlequin E Shivers

Darkening Around Me
Silent Is the House
The Girl in Blue

Visit the Author Profile page
at Harlequin.com for more titles.

LEGENDARY SHIFTER

Barbara J. Hancock

For the warrior in us all. Because she rocks.

Prologue

All he could do was watch and wait.

He found pleasure in it, surprisingly enough. Anticipation made the torment sweet. Elena Pavlova's mother had slit her wrists to protect her daughter ten years ago. Her sacrifice hadn't kept him from visiting her daughter's nightmares with delicious visions of the future they'd have together. He couldn't physically have Elena, yet. Her mother's blood had bought her a reprieve. But the protective power of the spilled blood was running out.

As a witchblood prince of the Dark *Volkhvy*, Grigori was used to getting what he wanted. He was part of the royal family in a culture that condoned Darkness. He stood just inside the open window of Elena's bedroom and watched her toss and turn in her sleep. The soft sounds of her fretful sighs were mere whispers compared to the noises she would be making in the nightmare that disturbed her sleep. Because he was in control there, unbound by her mother's rough folk magic.

What a shocking surprise that had been.

The voluminous curtains on the window billowed outward to brush against him, stirred by a midnight Saint Petersburg breeze. He'd seen the girl dance. He'd decided to have her. But her mother had been raised to believe in the old ways. She'd died so her daughter could live.

Or so she'd thought.

The curtains continued to flutter around him like white wings on either side of his tuxedo-clad body. When he was finished here, he would make other clandestine appearances throughout the city. He was a royal among Dark *Volkhvy* circles and the Dark *Volkhvy* ruled from the shadows. Their power was rising, bubbling to the top of a world rent by betrayal and hunger.

The mother's blood had run out before he was bound forever. At best, she'd bought her daughter time. Time to be stalked. Time to be hunted, night after night in her dreams. Elena had been a lovely swan as a teen. She'd only grown more graceful and more alluring as she'd aged into a prima ballerina. His anticipation had grown with every passing year. Every time she donned the pristine white feathers and pirouetted across the stage.

Then an injury had interfered with her dancing, and her vulnerability had inflamed his desire to even greater heights. He had fought against the binding. He'd done everything to try to break it, to no avail. She still had a grandmother who lived and watched over her with all the old folk magic most modern-day Russians had forgotten. He could only send more violent and vivid visions to Elena each night, fueled by his frustrated passions.

Finally, her grandmother had died and he'd sensed the

power of Elena's mother's blood fading. She'd sacrificed every last drop to fuel a protective barrier spell around her daughter, but it wouldn't last. She might have known some of the old ways, but she was no *Volkhvy*. Lately, he'd been able to approach Elena and speak to her. He'd added to the torment of the visions he sent to her nightmares by telling her that they were true.

She would be his.

When the protective spell her mother's blood had created ran out.

Grigori watched his delicate swan whimper in her sleep. He couldn't even approach her bed to get a closer look at the rapid rise and fall of her chest, the flush on her porcelain cheeks, the heat rising off her sweat-dampened skin.

Love was abhorrent to him. The residual love of her grandmother was infused into every object in this house and, combined with her mother's sacrifice, continued to hold him at bay…for now.

Power was everything to one of his kind. Once a witch turned to darkness, the taint was passed down through the generations—growing stronger with every birth. And his family was the oldest and darkest of all the Dark *Volkhvy*. He gloried in subjugating innocence. His conquest of Elena would be more satisfying because it hadn't been instant. Her fear and his anticipation fed the dark taint in his blood, making it—and him—stronger.

The breeze from the window must have soothed her. She quieted as he watched, and he knew it was time for him to leave.

But soon. Very soon. He would be free to make her nightmares come true.

Chapter 1

Wind blew stinging clouds of icy dust from the jagged gray rocks on the side of the mountain. The snow was so white the exposed rock glistened darkly against it in the fading light of the sinking sun. Every surface was coated with a fine sheen of ice. Elena Pavlova had only been outside the full cab all-terrain vehicle that had brought her this far for a half an hour, but in spite of the preparations she'd made—her ski suit, insulated boots, gloves and scarf—the protective clothing didn't prevent her face from feeling as cold and hard as the frozen rocks.

Mountain tours never came this far in winter, but it had been imperative that she get as far as possible before she sent prying eyes away. She'd insisted that the driver leave her, but only a substantial bribe had finally persuaded the man, who obviously thought she was on a suicide mission.

And maybe she was.

Night was falling in the Carpathian Mountains in Romania and she would never survive the elements if she didn't find the shelter she sought. Refuge. Redoubt. Haven. Her eyes teared against the biting wind and the moisture froze on her eyelashes until her lids were heavy and her vision obscured.

She'd heard the tales since she was a child. She'd listened, rapt, as her grandmother had read from the worn but beautiful book Elena currently carried in a small pack on her back. Her childhood had been two things: dancing and the Slavic legend of the Romanov wolves. Bloody toes and even bloodier stories of the fight against evil.

Hundreds of years ago, the Light *Volkhvy* had chosen a younger son of royal blood to stand against their dark brethren. They'd spirited Vladimir Romanov away to become their champion. He'd been given enchanted wolves and a castle enclave deep in the Carpathian Mountains. In return, he'd been bound to an endless fight. Grim fairy tales to read to a child, but, looking back, Elena realized her grandmother had been preparing her to fight the darkness herself. The old ways were wise ways, but knowing them wasn't only a defense. Playing at the edges of *Volkhvy* power by telling the tales and practicing the small hearth magics with charms for luck and wellness ran the risk of attracting the attention of true witches. Ones from the dark as well as the light.

Too much dabbling could lure an ordinary person into a *Volkhvy* world they weren't prepared to face. *Perhaps her family remembered the Old ways too well.*

Elena was living proof. She was stalked by a witch-blood prince and her fascination with the legend had turned into a call she couldn't ignore. She'd been pulled across thousands of miles from Saint Petersburg to Cerna, and the call only became stronger the closer she came to the mountains.

It was almost physical now. In spite of the cold, she was aware of a strange pulse beneath her skin that compelled her onward. Her choice had seemed so clear—heed the call or stay within Grigori's grasp.

By the time she came to the pass, her lungs hurt with every frigid breath and her weak knee was on fire. She wouldn't have made it this far over the ice and rugged terrain if she hadn't spent years pushing past physical pain to achieve the optimum performance from her muscle, sinew, heart and will. Prima ballerinas weren't born. Or made. They were forged in the fire that was the Saint Petersburg Ballet Academy.

Elena paused. She wiped her eyes with gloved fingers, but they weren't so hindered by icicles that they missed the castle she'd come to find. She couldn't see it because it wasn't there.

She'd chased help that only existed in a book of legends. No more. No less. She'd followed landmarks in the illustrations and carefully tried to sleuth her way to the right place. But her beautiful book crafted of intricate, hand-painted and cut designs that leaped from the page in three-dimensional depictions of a castle, the Romanovs and their enchanted wolves was nothing more than a storybook.

Her grandmother had blamed Elena's nightmares on the book, but ten years of bad dreams hadn't prepared her for the true horror of the witchblood prince who stalked her. She'd been haunted by the loss of her mother, only to learn her death had been a heroic sacrifice and not a suicide. Her mother had spilled her own blood to protect her daughter from a Dark *Volkhvy* prince. Her blood had fueled earthy folk magic. Nothing compared to the power it faced down and held back, but her mother's fierce love had strengthened it.

He had stood out from the other patrons even before he spoke—tall, lean and beautiful to the point of being unnaturally perfect as if he was a mannequin, not a man. Not a hair of his glistening gelled hair had been out of place. There hadn't been so much as a speck of lint on his tailored tuxedo. He'd moved like oil into her path with a flow to his gestures that was less grace and more fakery. His appearance was a charade. One meant to obfuscate his true nature. Yet one that revealed all, if you looked closely enough.

The sun was almost gone. Suddenly the white glare of ice and snow turned russet as it reflected the orange glow of the sky. Elena had nowhere else to go. The guide in his all-terrain vehicle was gone. He had taken his money and followed her orders: *Don't wait for me. I won't be coming back.* The dire economics of the region precluded any squeamishness over what she might do once he drove away.

It was true. She would freeze to death rather than go back and give in to Grigori's demands even though she hadn't found the help she'd hoped to find.

You'll be utterly mine. Your mother only ensured I would require even greater satisfaction from our time together because of the delay.

A sudden sound dispelled the ice in her veins. A long, echoing howl—both mournful and triumphant—filled the air and conquered the wind as the king of sound on the mountain. Adrenaline rushed lifesaving vigor to her limbs. Her heart pounded. Her breath poured from her lips in vaporous puffs of fear and hope. The call that had brought her all the way from Saint Petersburg seemed to respond to the howl. It rose in her throat as if she should cry out a reply.

But her head was more rational than her heart.

Freeze or fangs?

Probably both, yet the possibility that the legend was true sent her scrambling farther along the pass in spite of her terror and the pain in her leg. The Romanovs controlled powerful wolves that were trained to fight the Dark *Volkhvy* witches. The alpha wolf was her last, best chance to defeat the witchblood prince. Another howl swelled up and out from the unseen chest that gave it birth. Paired with the decreasing light, the howl seemed to raise hungry shadows to consume the world. She hadn't brought a flashlight. Or a tent. She didn't own a weapon of any kind. Weapons were useless against the witchblood prince, and mortal shelter would only protect her from the elements long enough for him to find and claim her.

Perhaps she'd been seeking death after all. If the call that had drawn her here was a lie, death would be preferable to a life spent as Grigori's captive.

Even sleep hadn't given her peace in years. Every night she suffered horrible nightmares in which she was caught by Grigori and unable to escape. She'd thought they were only nightmares. Now that she'd seen her tormenter in real life, certainty had settled into her bones. Death wasn't the worst fate she could suffer. As his stalking had escalated, so had her resolve to escape.

The snow was deeper and softer where drifts had accumulated in the protected lee of the pass between mountainous ridges. Her legs weren't very long. At twenty, she was thin and graceful, petite and powerful. In spite of her knee, her body responded to the desperate pounding of her heart. *Go. Go. Go.*

She was all muscle, tendon and sinew. It didn't matter that the ligament in one knee had required surgery to repair. All the rest made up the difference, fueled by adrenaline and fear. But if the howl had spurred her on, the sight of the creature who had opened its maw to create the sound caused her to freeze in place. A white wolf had climbed to the top of the ridge on her left. He was immense, larger than any wolf nature could have made. He stood on the peak, a ghostly silhouette against the darkening sky, and he howled again.

Elena's legs—her stock and trade, the one thing between her and oblivion—gave out beneath her. She collapsed to her knees in the snow. She cried out when her right knee made contact. An unnoticeable deformity in the shape of her femur had caused her to land from jumps with incorrect form. Over the course of a decade, after millions of repetitions, her knee had been stressed by the imperfection. She'd recovered well from surgery and spent over a year in physical therapy, but the snowy hike had aggravated her injury.

Another howl answered the first. On the left peak directly across the pass from the white wolf, another wolf appeared, as russet as the sunset had been moments before. Even if she could get to her feet, she would never outrun them in the deep drifts of snow. There was no castle. There were no Romanovs. As hard as she squinted against the icy wind, she could see nothing to refuel her hopes. There were only two giant wolves whose echoes sounded hollow and hungry as they bounced off the icy walls of the pass. *This is better than Grigori*, the blood seemed to whisper as it rushed in her ears. The ice on her eyelashes had melted as fresh hot tears filled her eyes. They shimmered there, making the gloaming world mercifully indistinct, but even now she refused to let them fall. She closed her eyes to will them away, but then it was an effort to lift her lids against her weighted lashes. She did it anyway. If she had to meet a grim fate, she would do it with her eyes open.

Only her nightmares made her cry. On waking, when she was alone with no one to see, she often found her cheeks damp. She'd grown to be terrified of enclosed spaces and the sound of frantic, fluttering feathers—the two elements of her nightmares that never changed. She'd never cried over bloody toes or aching muscles or the harsh practices meant to perfect the curve of her arms and spine. The nightmares were far worse than any real-life trials. It had been horrible to discover that Grigori was real even more so because it meant that he had witnessed the tears she'd thought were shed in private. He'd seen her weak and terrified. That knowledge and his pleasure in it caused bile to rise and burn her throat. She wouldn't cry now that she'd found only a part of what she'd been looking for, even if the wolves turned out to be her salvation in a darker way than she'd intended. She wouldn't season their meal with tears.

The illustrations in her book hadn't done the wolves justice. They were more monstrous. Far above her, she could see the power in their limbs and the glint of their eyes. She could also see the flash of white that indicated deadly teeth against their damp fur.

It was only the movement of the wolves' attention from her to elsewhere that caused her to lower her attention from the ridges back to the pass. She blinked against icy lashes as an approaching form swam into focus. A tall, muscular man clothed all in black walked purposefully through the deep snow. He came out of the swirling white clouds of flakes as if he materialized before her eyes. He wore a cloak with a fur mantle that covered his broad shoulders. Its voluminous folds whipped around his powerful strides. But it was another sight behind him that caused her to gasp in stunned surprise.

Before she'd fallen, there had been nothing but ice and snow on the cliffs of the pass. Now, in the last hazy hint of twilight, ramparts and towers seemed to solidify from the shadows high above. Behind the man, the castle had appeared as if the mountain itself had decided to morph its rocks into the shape of a king's home. Around the highest tower, ravens circled in and out of storm clouds that clung to its pointed peak. The structure was surrounded by a stone wall that enclosed the entire keep and a small village around the foot of the castle. She could see thatched rooftops peeking over the wall. Wind swept over her in a new way. The sudden appearance of the castle and the enclave its walls created had diverted the air. This new breeze rushed over the man, and his long, tousled hair was blown into a riotous black mane around his face.

He held a lantern in his hand. Its light suddenly flared to life and its glow illuminated the man's face. The world fell away—castle, mountain, wolves and snow—until only his face shone before her. The call had brought her to the right place and the right time. The compulsion to come here hadn't been a lie.

"Romanov," Elena said. Her lips were stiff with cold. Her voice was muted by the wind. The white of her breath dissipated in wisps blown away from her face, taking most of the sound with it. The snow had claimed all feeling from her legs, and the numbness climbed steadily up her hips to her waist.

He heard her. He stopped and lowered the lantern so its light shone in her eyes and on her face, leaving his in shadow.

"Whoever you are, I'm not the man you seek," he said.

The wolves had leaped down from the peaks on either side of the pass while the castle and the man had distracted her. Their large, powerful forms had eaten up the distance much sooner than ordinary canines might have done. They came to the man—one on each side—and he chided their eager prancing without taking his attention from her face. She'd been right about the wolves' size. Both came to their master's chest, and he was no small man.

The wolf she'd come to find would be even larger.

She needed larger-than-life legends to help her escape Grigori's clutches.

"I'm not here for a man. I'm here for the wolves," Elena said. The wolf she needed was the alpha of the Romanov pack and he would be as black as midnight. The old legends said that only the alpha wolf could defeat the strongest of the Dark *Volkhvy*.

The creatures paced toward her, but the man called them back to his side by name.

"Lev. Soren. Heel." Though his face was shadowed, she could see the stern set to his lips and jaw. "Then you have come for nothing," he said to her bluntly.

He gestured and the two wolves churned snow as they spun around to rip back toward the castle in the distance. Oddly, she felt abandoned rather than spared. Her stomach hollowed within her as if she'd fallen from a great height. The cold reached relentless icy fingers into her heart. Its thumping had slowed as if the muscle that pumped her blood was beginning to freeze.

"You risked your life," the man said. "For nothing." He didn't follow the wolves. He stepped closer. His clothes were fashioned with tooled leather and thick stitches. The wool of his cloak was thickly woven and the fur of his mantle blew this way and that in glossy chunks. There was a richness of texture to his entire appearance that made her frozen fingers twitch. Though she'd come for the alpha wolf, a being more fantasy than reality, this man looked solid and strong. Against the backdrop of ice and snow and plain gray rock, he was sudden, vigorous and very alive.

Far from *nothing*.

Only his eyes kept her from reaching out to him. They were green. A frigid pale green. Ferocious and intense. Bright against his black hair and the deepening darkness, but also intimidating.

"I risked my life to escape from a nightmare. I've accomplished that. At least for now," Elena said. His words had caused the pulse beneath her skin to fade. She was left on top of a mountain in a snowstorm with nothing to anchor her there. No certainty. No song.

"You won't find escape here," the man said. But he knelt down beside her. Elena was so cold, the heat from his lantern seemed to warm her, or maybe it was the heat of his large body so close to hers.

This was the right place. She wasn't mistaken. Even with the physical pulse of the compulsive call to climb diminished, her instincts to trust the old legend wouldn't fade. She was here for a reason. The book in her bag had shown her the way. Her grandmother had told the old tales as if they were true. They might have fueled her nightmares, but they might also prove to be her only hope against Grigori once the protective binding her mother had bought with her blood ran out.

"I won't go back," Elena said.

Her body was done. Frozen. If he refused to help her, she would die. But it was force of will, not bodily exhaustion, that caused her to take a stand even as she knelt in the snow.

"Not tonight anyway," the man said. "The storm is only getting started. I won't leave you here to die." She cried out when he reached to pick her up, but she quieted when his hold turned out to be surprisingly gentle for such a large man. He stood easily, trading his lantern for her body in one smooth, easy move. "But this isn't an invitation to stay," he continued.

"You are a Romanov," Elena murmured against his windswept hair. He turned to walk back through the deep snow. The ache in her knee throbbed in time with the thudding of her heart. Her weight in his arms didn't slow him down and neither did the drifts of snow. He left the glowing lantern behind them, so every stride carried her closer and closer to the dark where his wolves had disappeared. She'd seen his face earlier. She'd recognized his features—the square jaw, the sculpted nose. She'd seen their like in the book that had brought her here, but her book's illustrations had been fanciful compared to the actual man.

"I am Ivan, the *last* Romanov," the man replied. "You came for a refuge, but you found nothing but cursed ground."

When she'd fallen to her knees, Ivan Romanov wanted to rush forward to her aid. That very human reaction had slowed his response. It wasn't the fall that caused his heart to swell and his chest to tighten with concern. It hadn't been the pale blue of her lips or the porcelain of her skin or her thick dark lashes crusted with a dusting of white. Her sapphire eyes, vivid against the blowing snow, and the stubborn light that intensified in them even as darkness fell, had compelled him forward. Whatever had driven her up the mountain in winter hadn't faded with the fall or the intimidating appearance of the wolves.

She would rise.

She would press on.

And if he didn't do something to prevent it, she would die at Bronwal's great gate. Her eyes revealed a different person than her slight form suggested. When he picked her up, she weighed nothing in his arms. He had trained for centuries, but it wasn't until he felt her delicate, mortal burden that he had the insane idea he had trained for just this moment.

For centuries.

She reached to hold around his neck. In spite of the stubborn light in her eyes, her arms surprised him with their strength. Only the wisps of respiration that came too quickly from her lips betrayed her fear. She was bundled in insulated clothing of a make and design he'd never seen. It had been many years since anyone other than the *Volkhvy* had ventured close during the Romanov materialization. The glimpses he'd seen of the modern world as it progressed had created an incomplete picture in his mind, always changing.

Her clothes told him little about the woman who wore them, but her determined journey through the pass should have alerted him. Her size was deceptive. Her eyes and tight hold as well as the tension in her body against him—those things revealed the woman to him.

Her limp did not define her.

She wouldn't be frightened away. Not easily.

"You can shelter here for the night out of the storm, but when it passes, you leave," Ivan said. He'd left the gate open. Lev and Soren stood on either side to guard the entrance. He'd seen them do so thousands of times before. The momentary electricity that had claimed his limbs when he'd lifted the woman in his arms drained away. He recognized the numbness as it returned. He was beyond weary. More worn by the years of coming and going from the Ether than he'd ever been worn by battle.

His father, Vladimir Romanov, had betrayed the Light *Volkhvy* queen centuries ago. He hadn't been satisfied to be a champion. He'd wanted to rule. The queen's punishment had been unrelenting. She'd cursed Bronwal and all the people in it to be bound to the Ether for eternity. Every ten years, the castle materialized for one month. It was taken into the Ether after the month was over, again and again. Each materialization, fewer survivors materialized. His father had been the first to succumb.

The quickening Ivan had felt in himself when he'd rushed to the fallen woman wasn't respite. It was torture. The years had piled on until his soul was crushed by too many losses to bear. And yet there was always one more.

Not always.

His enchanted blood had prolonged his life as had Vasilisa's curse.

But he wasn't immortal.

He said a prayer of thanks for that small mercy before he carried the woman inside.

Chapter 2

Even though she had the snowstorm and the frigid mountain pass for comparison, she didn't find the great hall of the castle welcoming. It was nothing like the illustrations in her book. Dark, gray, unlit by torches or firelight, it seemed more a massive cave than a place where people would gather. A fireplace several times larger than any she'd seen before yawned cold and dark. Wind whistled down its chimney like a banshee. A frozen banshee.

In the shadows, the elaborate tapestries hanging on the walls were lifeless and dull. In her book, they were painted with vivid detail that never seemed to fade. Romanov had carried her through the outer keep without greeting or comment from a dozen or so dreary-looking denizens going about half-hearted work. The gamboling of the giant wolves had seemed cruelly vigorous in comparison. The wolves were playful when all else was doom and gloom. They must have been protected from the gloom of the villagers by their simpler, animal comprehension.

Something was wrong with Bronwal. The wrongness permeated the people and the atmosphere, including the man who held her to his chest.

Inside, the great hall was deserted. Elena tried to speak, but her teeth chattered together and shivers racked her body. The trembling meant her nerves hadn't been frozen, but the pain of her skin coming back to life caused her to moan.

"We have no accommodations for visitors. Not anymore," Romanov said. He turned around as if he was looking for somewhere to put her that wasn't dark and damp.

"I s-see th-that," Elena replied. Welcome or not, she was here. She'd made it. Once she warmed up enough to face the challenge, she would find the alpha wolf even though this last Romanov was determined to send her away. She'd be much better off facing this man's determination not to help her than she'd been facing Grigori in Saint Petersburg alone.

"Fetch Patrice. To the tower room," Romanov ordered. The russet wolf jumped to attention. He stopped his leaping and stared at his master for several seconds as if his wolf brain had to interpret the command. Then he was off. The white wolf sat on its haunches and looked at them.

"I know there are plenty of empty rooms. Don't look at me like that. Anyone who would have an opinion about where best to put her is long gone," Romanov said.

He tightened his arms when she tried to press her palms against his broad chest for release. He didn't place her on her feet. Inside the castle, even in the lofted great hall, he seemed much larger. He was well over six feet with muscled arms and legs that matched his intimidating frame. His hold was overwhelming. His embrace swallowed her petite body. He held her close against his chest. Odd, since he had ordered her to go away. His heartbeat was clear and strong against her cheek.

Suddenly, he was too real. Her respiration quickened and her fingers curled into the damp material of his cloak. He felt her increased tension and paused. His whole being became alert. She could sense the intensity of his attention on her face. Her focus was on the fur of his mantle, but she forced her gaze from that safe haven to more dangerous territory.

In the shadows, his eyes were lighter than his dark brows and hair, but they were hooded against her. She couldn't read his emotions before he looked away. He betrayed nothing of his inner feelings yet she sensed them beneath his stiff demeanor. She noted his tightened hands and his unwillingness to meet her eyes. They waited for a long time, made longer by her fatigue and fear.

Finally, at some unspoken signal, he turned again and headed from the room in a decided direction. They came to a circular stone hall that eventually changed to stairs. She held him as he carried her up and up the never-ending climb. She was accustomed to athletic artists and dancers. Sophisticated and polished businessman and patrons were her usual companions. She wasn't used to storybooks come to life from legends that originated in the Dark Ages.

Romanov's scent was one of wind and snow, leather and fur. His hair had enveloped her with stinging strands outside on the mountain. Now it dried around his face in a riot of damp waves. By the time they came to an open door at the top of the stairs, Elena had seen Romanov's face by the light of a thousand torches. The impact of his appearance wasn't diminished by the increased time to study him. His face was as bold as the rest of him, with a strong brow and patrician cheekbones. His lips were sculpted and sensual against his hard features and there was a shadow of beard growth on his jaw that only served to highlight its perfect, sharp angles. The contrast of his green eyes continually startled her against his dark hair and pale skin.

Not that he looked at her again. He kept his gaze on the stairs. He didn't have to look. She could feel his attention zeroed in on her every blink and sigh. She'd followed a call she couldn't define to a strange place she'd only heard about from a storybook, but she was afraid she might have found more danger than she'd left behind. The wolves had been terrifying, but Romanov was in some ways more intimidating than his pets. In trying to escape Grigori had she placed herself in even greater danger?

The glow of a small fire met them when he stepped inside the room at the top of the long, spiraling stairway. A round woman in a faded apron bustled around and the russet wolf stretched out by the fireplace, soaking up what heat it provided in its infancy. Romanov had carried her up into the tallest tower she'd seen from far below in the pass. The windows were obscured by ancient stained glass, wavy and dense with imperfections. Occasional shadows seemed to swoop by, hinting that the ravens still circled outside. The room was furnished sparsely with a plain wooden bed draped in thick velvet textiles against the cold. There were two sturdy chairs on either side of the fire. There were no lamps or electric outlets. No technology of any kind.

Had she expected modern amenities in a castle made by magic hands centuries ago?

The woman didn't speak. She quietly straightened a woven throw on one of the chairs by the fire and Romanov responded by placing Elena on it. The move was hurried, as if he couldn't wait to put her down, but also gentle. He was being careful with her leg. His size and strength and gruff manner made his courtesy that much more surprising.

"It isn't a new injury. My name is Elena Pavlova. I'm a dancer. The stress of the climb aggravated an ACL condition I developed from my years in ballet," Elena said. "I'll be fine with rest and another knee surgery." She didn't tell him she'd never dance again. An additional surgery might give her a greater range of movement, but she would never reclaim the grace she'd lost.

She could no longer focus on dancing. It had been a necessity to help support her family. It had saved her when her mother died, but now all of the drive she'd used for the dance needed to be focused on survival. Never mind there was an empty place left by the loss of her dance deep inside of her. It had given her purpose for so long even though it had been a cruel taskmaster more than a heartfelt occupation. The call had seemed to fill the void for the last several days, but she tried to ignore it now. She was here. Why did it still seem to compel her toward something she couldn't see?

"Thank you," Elena said to the woman, who tucked another throw around her legs. Patrice didn't reply.

"It's been several Cycles since she's spoken. You spoke of the wolves. You must know of the curse that binds us. The Queen of the Light *Volkhvy* punishes us for my father's betrayal of her trust. Every ten years, Bronwal materializes from the Ether. At the end of the month, we disappear into the Ether once more. We all change each time we're lost in the Ether," Romanov said. "When the enclave dematerializes, we're left with an awareness that makes the Ether a purgatory. It drains our souls away, little by little, time after time. For some there's a sudden vanishing. For others, a slow fading away. Vladimir Romanov hasn't been seen since the first Cycle."

The legends about the Light *Volkhvy* champions had always seemed magical and romantic to her, filled with heroics and daring. She hadn't known about the curse. No wonder there seemed to be something wrong with her storybook castle and all the people she'd encountered in it. The thaw she'd been experiencing seemed to pause as ice reclaimed her heart, but if Romanov noticed her chilling realization he betrayed nothing. Elena slowly shrugged out of her backpack as her host ignored her, and Patrice took it from her only to drop it on the floor as if she wasn't aware she had taken it. The chubby woman had crinkles around her eyes and merry red cheeks, but her silence negated who she'd once been. Her features seemed to indicate that she'd once been a jolly soul, but she wasn't fully with them. Her eyes were distant and her movements were automatic. It wasn't only that she didn't speak. She didn't seem to hear them well. The backpack landed near the russet wolf and the giant creature nosed it and then ignored it as if it had proved of no interest.

"You're here after all this time," Elena said. She'd come looking for champions. She'd hoped to find enchanted wolves and their masters. She'd never imagined she'd find the original Romanovs themselves. "You're the oldest son of Vladmir Romanov. One of Queen Vasilisa's champions. Fully awake and aware." The heat from the fire began to warm her again. Her shivering had stopped. Her teeth didn't chatter. Romanov filled the room with his restrained energy. He'd let her go, but she could still feel his hold. He was powerful, but his power wasn't merely physical. There was no way he had faded from what he had once been. Why did he want her to think otherwise?

"In time I'll fade away too," he said. "In one month, Bronwal will go back to the Ether. Maybe this time I'll stay there, vanished, like the rest of my family." He shrugged, but the light gesture didn't match the shadows that haunted his eyes. *He's not sure what each materialization will bring. Who will remain and who will be gone forever.* Elena's body was beginning to adjust to the heat from the fire, but Romanov's circumstances left her heart permanently chilled. It must have been torture through the decades to lose his loved ones, one by one.

He sat in the opposite chair and stretched his long legs out in front of him in a deceptively relaxed position. The white wolf, Lev, had found them. He came into the room reluctantly and slumped at his master's feet as if he had grown unused to such comforts. The russet wolf, Soren, stretched out on the other side. Without saying goodbye, Patrice left the room. Would she wander the halls aimlessly until the castle went back into the Ether? Would she even exist during the next Cycle or would she be lost to nothingness, never to be seen again? Elena had come looking for help against Grigori, but she had found more darkness here than she'd expected.

"I need the alpha wolf. My grandmother said he was the Light *Volkhvy*'s greatest champion. Are you his master? Will you help me find him?" Elena asked. It made her nervous to see her bag so close to the subjects of the book inside of it. It might seem childish to Romanov

even though it had served as a lifeline to her. But her
knee throbbed and that was the more pressing problem.
She stood and leaned to unbuckle her boots. She carefully took them off without jarring her knee. Then she
reached to unzip her ski suit and pull it down. Beneath
its down-filled pale blue polyester, she wore simple white
silk thermals. Gooseflesh rose on her skin at the sudden
rush of air against the thin material. Finally, with some
painful maneuvering, the damp suit was peeled away.
She draped it over the back of her chair and she sat again,
free to massage her troublesome knee. There was a scar
where the first surgery had extended her use of the knee.
Without that repair, her walk through the snow would
have been impossible, not merely excruciating.

It wasn't until her pain eased that she noticed the tension in the air. Elena stilled. The fire had caught and it
blazed brightly, bathing her in a flickering spotlight. She
understood her mistake even before she lifted her eyes.
Romanov wasn't a modern man and she had basically
stripped in front of him. She was a ballerina. Her body
was an instrument, a tool. Her every movement was a
deliberate placement of everything from her spine to her
toes, but she was completely disconnected from the sensuality of her lithe limbs. The theater had no patience for
modesty. They hurried to change from one costume to
another in hallways amid a rush of similar nude forms.

But this man wasn't a dancer. He didn't even belong
to this century at all. He'd been born in the Middle Ages.
Her book was very old and it told a tale much older than
its pages.

She'd always thought of the Romanovs as legends.
Larger than life and not quite human. But this Romanov
was a man. One she didn't know, from a time she couldn't

understand. And he was a man tortured by a cruel curse. When she did look up and her gaze collided with his, he looked stunned, as if shedding her wet clothes in front of him was more shocking than his cursed castle, monstrous wolves and disappearing people. He also looked even more real. The leaping flames reflected in his eyes seemed to reveal the emotion he'd tried to hide before. His glance dropped to sweep her body. There was color in his cheeks and his lips had softened. Her stripping might have surprised him, but he was appreciative of what she had revealed. His lingering perusal made her cheeks heat. The flush was a tingling pleasure in the cool room.

In time, he might fade as he predicted, but he was fully here now and she must seem nearly naked to his old-fashioned standards. He didn't look away, but he did raise the direction of his gaze from her breasts to her eyes.

"You won't find help here. Loss. Despair. Resignation. Those you will find. But not help," Romanov said. His hands had grasped the arms of his chair with a white-knuckled grip and his voice was strained. His accent was exotic to her ears. His vowels and consonants were slowly uttered with deeper inflections as out of place and uninfluenced by current civilization as his leather and furs. He must have had contact with the outside world each time he materialized. She could understand him, but it was as if he was a time traveler speaking a language that wasn't his native tongue. It was a visceral experience to have to listen to him so carefully and watch his eyes and his lips move as he spoke. She had to attune her entire body to him in order to communicate.

Elena trembled again, but not from the cold. She didn't see resignation in Romanov's eyes. The waves of black hair around his face were highlighted by a halo of firelight. From that glowing frame, his green eyes shone with repressed passion…and anger. Beneath his dramatic brows and offset by pale skin, the emotion in his irises caused her heartbeat to kick in her chest and her breath to quicken.

He didn't want her here.

In her nightmares, she had wings, but they were always clipped. She was flightless. Caged. Kept at the whim of Grigori for reasons that caused her to beat against the bars of her cage until her white-feathered breast was stained with blood. She'd danced Odette many times—the swan tormented by a sorcerer. Her performances were as prophetic as her dreams. Grigori had seen her dance as a young girl. He'd vowed to have her. Her mother had used every last drop of her blood to bind him away from her daughter.

She'd never known why her mother had killed herself. Only a few months ago, Grigori had revealed the truth. Her mother had traded her life for her daughter's and it had only bought Elena's safety for a limited time.

"I've had my share of despair and loss," Elena said. "Resignation? Never."

She wouldn't be frightened by his anger. Or not cowed by it anyway. She had done nothing but search for a way to survive. She was going nowhere until she found it.

Suddenly, over Romanov's shoulder, she saw bars on the door to the tower room. They were artistically twisted in patterns of vines and flowers, but they were iron bars nonetheless. Romanov had drawn his legs back and he'd straightened. His wolves had also straightened to sit at attention by his side.

Three sets of eyes stared her down.

She had nowhere else to go, but that didn't matter. Not

if she was trapped in a tower of a cursed castle and kept from finding the alpha wolf she sought.

I am the last Romanov.

He hadn't said it in a tone of resignation. He'd said it like his soul stood rooted in its last stand for eternity if need be. Had she disturbed his lonely vigil? Was that why he was looking at her with anger in his eyes?

This man ruled here. There were no councils or committees. He was a king and she was a trespasser. For some reason, he had decided to stand between her and the alpha wolf she needed to find.

"The Romanovs were given great power by the Light *Volkhvy* to fight against the dark. You were given powerful enchanted wolves to fight by your side. A Dark *Volkhvy* is my enemy," she said.

Romanov stood. She wasn't certain if it was a conscious move or if it was an automatic response to her mention of the Russian witches who had cursed his family.

"My father betrayed the Light *Volkhvy*. He wasn't satisfied with leading a pack of champions. He wanted Vasilisa's crown. His actions brought the curse down upon us. There are no champions left here. Only the dishonored and the walking dead. My father doomed himself and all of his people to this endless punishment. You've wasted your time," he said.

"You're not dead yet," Elena whispered. He was anything but dead. He shone with life. That was what captured her attention when lantern light, torchlight or firelight illuminated his face. She'd seen many dancers glow on the stage, backlit by spotlights and painted scenery. With only the gray of his cursed castle's backdrop, Romanov glowed—with anger, frustration and restrained passion—but he was definitely alive.

"All I ever held dear are dead. Gone. Vanished into nothing. My time will come. It *must* come. And soon," Romanov said.

His hands were fisted. This man was part of the legend she'd sought, but he was also more—more human, more fallible, more tortured than the tales had led her to believe. She'd been an innocent child fascinated by the three-dimensional paper images that had popped up from the pages of her grandmother's book. What had she known of love and loss? Since then, she'd lost her mother and her grandmother. And, finally, she'd lost the dance. Everyone she'd ever loved and her lifelong purpose. But that didn't mean she was ready to give up. She'd been called here for a reason. She refused to be turned away before she understood the tingling in her veins that said this was where she was meant to be.

If he wouldn't help her find the alpha wolf and fight Grigori, she would have to find the wolf and face the witchblood prince on her own. Romanov was a living, breathing legend, but he was finished. Fed up with the love and loss of this world and all the people in it. He wanted her gone because he wanted to die.

She jumped up when he turned toward the door. She couldn't be caged. It was too much like her nightmare. But instead of running for the door, she rushed to her backpack. She unzipped the top and rummaged until she pulled her precious book from its depths. Instinct drove her now as instinct had driven her to follow its stories into the mountains. Her grandmother had been a wise woman. She'd treated the legends with respect. Romanov was at the door when she turned to show him the book. He needed to be reminded of what his family had been in the fight against the Dark *Volkhvy*. Of what he could be still.

"Stop," Elena commanded. She held the book toward him and opened it as if she was the witch casting a spell. But in this cold, dark stone fortress, the book had lost its magic. It seemed small. Its colorful pages were more worn and faded than she remembered. It opened on her favorite scene. A lush forest of dozens of paper trees popped up from the page, and from between the trees three wolves ran. The white. The red. And the black. But they paled in comparison to the real wolves in the room, and they were so crumpled from use that they didn't leap from the page as they had when she was a child.

Romanov looked from the book as the trees fluttered in her trembling hands up to her face.

"This is what brought you here?" he asked. The whole hollow castle seemed to still around them. His soft, pained voice echoed down the quiet stairs.

"My grandmother's stories brought me here. She told them while we looked at this book," Elena explained. The book itself wasn't as impressive as her grandmother had been. In the same room as the last Romanov and his wolves, it wasn't impressive at all.

But she couldn't explain the pulse beneath her skin that had drawn her to his castle as if it were magnetized and she was raw ore dug up from the earth by an unseen hand.

He turned away again, from her and the legend, and Elena closed the book and dropped it onto her chair. She wouldn't be locked in the tower. She would fight if she had to. The wolves led the way. They disappeared down the stairs in front of their master. Romanov's large body blocked the door. He turned back to face her when he crossed the threshold. He slowly reached for the door to swing it closed.

"No. Wait," Elena said. She rushed forward, but he shut the door too forcefully for her to prevent its closing. The lock clanked home as her hands gripped the iron vines. She pressed her face to the space between the bars. Romanov stood inches away from her, separated by the thick oak of the bottom of the door and the scrolling iron at the top, but also by centuries of experience that had left him jaded and untouchable.

Roses. She saw them closely now. Dozens of iron roses "grew" along the vine-shaped bars. The door was an ancient artisan's masterpiece and a horror at the same time. She was trapped. The only thing that kept the scream from rising up from her gut was the absence of bloody feathers. As long as she was still herself, she could fight.

"You can't keep me in here," Elena protested.

Romanov leaned down. The firelight illuminated his face once more. He leaned so close that his raven hair brushed her cheek through the bars. He was older than she could imagine, even though he looked barely older than she was. He was more savage than anyone she'd ever encountered with his leather and furs and several white jagged lines from battle scars on his face, but he was also fiercely handsome. His rough, masculine beauty caused her to gasp at the sudden intimacy of his closeness. The door was between them but it felt like nothing at all.

She'd come looking for a legend, but he was *real*. She breathed in the scent of wind and snow held in his hair. And then she held her breath to keep from appreciating the wild bouquet. Of its own volition, her gaze cataloged every scar, every dark eyelash that lushly rimmed his eyes and the oddly vulnerable swell of his sensual lips.

His eyes were hooded and hard, but the tenseness in his jaw eased when he noticed her catch her breath and hold it. He must have seen her sudden surprise at the physical attraction she felt for him in spite of her desperation. His gaze tracked over her face. She held her body still. She bit a lip that suddenly tingled because his were so kissable and so close. His attention dropped to her lips and then to her tight-knuckled grip on the bars. When he spoke, his voice was quiet.

"I'm not locking you in the tower, Elena Pavlova," he said softly. His voice still vibrated against her even though they weren't touching. It was deep, low and raw with some restrained emotion she couldn't name. He looked back up, into her eyes. His gaze held her for long moments so that when he lifted an iron key scrolled with tiny vines and roses that matched the bars, she released her breath in surprise. The key dangled from a delicate silver chain and it bumped her hand again and again through the bars while he waited for her to move. She released the bar to open her hand for the key. Her fingers were shaking. Rather than dropping the chain, he lowered it slowly down into her palm to pile on top of the cool key in a slow, lazy coil of precious metal. For several seconds, his large hand rested over hers. His touch was light and warm. He stilled her trembling. She'd thought she knew his story, but his tale was still unfolding right before her eyes. She'd become a part of it, and it was a tale rife with danger.

She'd responded to the call. She'd come to the mountains for a legend and his wolves.

She'd found a man.

"The tower is for your protection. You hold the key while you're here. Don't be fooled by your pretty book.

This isn't a fairy-tale castle. Bronwal is cursed. Those who come and go from the Ether are forever changed and even while we're in this world the Ether isn't fully dispelled. Whatever you do, don't consider this a refuge. The *Volkhvy*, both Dark and Light, aren't to be trusted *and neither am I.* The Romanov curse is real…and deserved. Don't forget that while you're here," Romanov said. He was warning her away. He wanted her to keep her distance. But he uttered the warning only after he'd leaned down until their lips were even closer together— nearly touching—between the iron bars. The door was nothing. It didn't seem to exist at all. She looked up into his eyes and rather than repel, they caught and held her more thoroughly than any cage.

Perhaps it wasn't the castle that was the magnet.

She'd been wrong. He was worn, not jaded. And he was touchable. Very touchable. It took all her self-control not to touch him now when he seemed to invite it.

"Sometimes the month passes in the blink of an eye and sometimes it stretches on in an endless trial. But however our time passes, it ends with a *Volkhvy* Gathering. If you came here to escape a *Volkhvy* prince, it was a mistake. They all come to dance on our graves. Or wasn't that bit a part of the tale you were told?" Romanov whispered. "The *Volkhvy*, Dark and Light, are drawn to power. And Bronwal glows cruelly and seductively with power to their eyes. You'd do well to stay locked in this tower until the storm passes and you're strong enough to leave." His voice had dropped even lower and one sigh would have brought her to the taste of his lips. She held very still. She didn't move. He dared her to greater intimacy, but she refrained. Because she could see that he was only torturing himself. He had no intention of kissing her. She wondered if he knew how much he tortured her too. His body was pressed to the outside of the door and hers was pressed against the inside. She could have sworn their body heat mingled even as they were kept apart.

"When you've caught the attention of a witchblood prince, there isn't any place safe on earth," Elena said. "I thought I was looking for refuge, but I'm not. I'm looking for a fighting chance."

She straightened back from the bars and lifted her chin. She hadn't come here to tempt a legend to kisses. She'd come to find a wolf and she didn't intend to give up.

Chapter 3

Elena placed the key's chain around her neck and let her means of freedom dangle down between her breasts like a pretty bauble. She couldn't leave the tower immediately to hunt for the black wolf. She didn't want to follow Romanov and the other wolves down the stairs. After the moments of intimacy through the bars of the door, she thought it best if she avoided the alpha wolf's master. He wanted her to go away…and he didn't at the same time. His actions didn't match his words.

She found herself wanting to prove to Romanov that he was still alive. As if he could be woken from his stubborn vigil of despair by a kiss or a touch or an embrace. She hadn't expected to find that sort of temptation at Bronwal. Romanov was a dangerous distraction she couldn't afford. The pain in her knee was also a distraction she couldn't afford. She always carried supplies to deal with her injury. In her backpack, she had first-aid cold packs, pain medication and a neoprene sleeve to offer support when she overdid.

Mountain climbing definitely qualified as overdoing.

She needed to treat her knee before she tried to do more. The strange compulsion that had called her to Bronwal now seemed to urge her on the hunt. She needed to resist that compulsion until she was sure that Romanov was farther away from her room.

Patrice surprised Elena before she could pull on the orthopedic sleeve. She opened the door with a key on an iron ring that hung from a braided leather belt around her waist. She led the way in front of a haphazard team of servants. They carried a large hip tub and a seemingly endless supply of steaming pitchers and pails full of hot water. Two large men in mismatched livery placed the wooden tub beside the fire. They both nodded in her direction before they left the room. Patrice gestured and the other servants walked forward one at a time to pour the water they were carrying into the tub.

Observing the procession was like watching time pass before her eyes. The people had hair and garb from varying centuries and all of them looked worse for wear. Elena's chest tightened in sympathy. The curse had punished all of the Romanovs' people, from the head of the powerful family to the tiniest chambermaid. It looked as if anyone who was able chipped in to do the work that had to be done even if it hadn't been his or her original specialty. The liveried men had obviously been something other than maids in the past.

Once the tub was filled, Patrice pulled a corked vial from one of the numerous pockets in her shabby apron. When she opened the vial and upended it over the water, a light, fresh scent filled the air. Mint. Elena breathed deeply as the aromatic steam rose.

"That'll warm your bones, Miss," a pretty young girl said. When she smiled, a dimple graced her cheek alongside a sprinkling of freckles. "If you need anything while you're here, they call me Bell." She was last in line and emptied her chipped pitcher with a nod of accomplishment before turning to leave the room. Her dress was nicer than most. It had been patched and mended. And her brown curls were clean beneath a faded cap. The cap and her boots looked like she'd borrowed them from a boy twice her size. Elena supposed there was no one left to protest if a maid chose unconventional attire.

As before, Patrice didn't say a word. She followed the last servant toward the door.

"Thank you. Thank you all," Elena said.

She was surprised when the older woman paused at the door to look back over her shoulder. There was a crinkle in her forehead as if Elena's thanks and the steaming tub confused her. Poor Patrice. Not all there, but still present enough to perform old duties long expected of her. She must have been a housekeeper to the Romanovs before the curse descended. Elena ached for her confusion, but then the puzzled look eased and Patrice turned back to walk out of the room. She closed the door behind her and the lock engaged.

So if the lock on the door wasn't to protect her from Ether-addled servants, what did it protect her from? The *Volkhvy*, the Romanov wolves…or Romanov himself?

Elena reached up to grasp the iron key Romanov had given her. She closed her fingers around it, easily remembering the brush of his hand and the closeness of his lips as he'd warned her to stay locked in the tower of her own volition.

Those that come and go from the Ether are forever changed.

She'd seen dishonor walking with the witchblood prince. Romanov seemed its opposite in every way. Yet she couldn't help if an insistent thrill of fear electrified the blood in her veins. He wasn't what she'd expected. He was cursed by a dark enchantment she couldn't imagine having endured for so long, but he was also undeniably attractive. Her urge to hunt that wouldn't ease might well be blamed on the memory of the almost-kiss. He'd seemed so hungry for contact and so determined not to succumb. Still, she had to focus on the black wolf, not his master. She could fight Grigori without Romanov, but she couldn't win without the alpha wolf.

A wolf hunt loomed, but Elena's knee throbbed and she was cold to the marrow of her bones. She released the key and ignored it and her memories of Romanov's nearness as she took off her long underwear. She was alone. The door was locked. She couldn't resist soaking her whole body, including her knee, while she waited for the right time to leave the tower. There was no doubt that she would. She had come to Bronwal for a wolf champion. She wouldn't leave without finding him first.

It was probably not wise to wander around a strange castle after midnight looking for a witch-eating wolf. Sometimes wise wasn't an option when you were hunted by a witchblood prince and running out of time.

Elena had dried herself with rough towels the servants had left near the tub. She'd pulled on the one change of clothes she'd packed—underwear, jeans, a T-shirt and

a loose-knit sweater. Soft-soled sneakers completed a
look that was practical and completely out of place. If the
servants had presented a hodgepodge of passing centuries that had briefly influenced castle life, she was fairly
certain she would be the first person to walk Bronwal's
halls in jeggings.

Even after the bath, her body was exhausted. She
might have opted for a quick nap before she left the tower
to refresh herself if it wasn't for the possibility that her
sleep would be disturbed as usual by nightmares.

She wasn't a swan.

She was a woman.

And hiding in a tower wasn't going to solve her problems.

Her knee still ached, but she washed several pills
down with a bottle of water she'd also packed in her
bag. Patrice hadn't thought to offer her food or drink and
Romanov hadn't returned with a tray. Thank God. She
couldn't handle another tête-à-tête with or without bars
between them. Eventually, moonlight filtered through the
wavy glass that must have been an extravagance when it
was installed in the narrow tower windows. Had it been
placed by magic before Vladimir's betrayal? The whole
castle was evidence of enchantment later darkened by
the curse. The wavy stained glass glowed beautifully by
the light of the moon while hungry ravens circled per-
petually outside.

When Elena decided it was relatively safe to leave the
room, she pulled the chain over her head and used the
key to unlock the door. The sound of the tumblers moving in the lock echoed down the stairs with loud metallic
clinks. She placed the chain back around her neck while
she paused to wait for a reaction. No one came to stop

her. From the top of the winding stair, she could only see torch-lit shadows flickering on the walls. Distant sounds came to her ears. Singing and sighs and soft sobbing from somewhere far away. The castle didn't sleep. The atmosphere was one of restlessness and regret. Patrice wasn't the only one who wandered. Romanov had warned her that it wasn't safe. She risked running into Light or Dark *Volkhvy* or humans caught up in the curse and driven mad by their endless returns to the Ether.

Yet it was running into Romanov again that she most feared. His magnetism was at least as strong as the original pull that had drawn her to the mountains, but the curse had changed everything. She had to be careful about the darkness she'd found, in Romanov and in his castle. He was right. She had to resist her attraction to her host, but she also had to find the alpha wolf. Her resolve to resist Grigori was useless with no power to back it up.

Elena Pavlova would leave tomorrow. The training courtyard was the emptiest, most hollow place he had to endure during a Cycle and tonight it was rapidly becoming covered in a frigid blanket of snow. Nevertheless, Ivan had trained in it for hours. He rarely wasted a Cycle with sleep, but this time his restlessness had another cause. He would be haunted by her small, perfectly formed breasts for the rest of his days on earth. Her nipples had been hard from the cold and damp. Their rosy darkness had been vivid against the thin white silk of her unusual undergarments. He'd had to force himself to look away. And now he needed the snow and exertion to keep him sane.

She had been completely innocent of her inadvertent seduction. Not in the manner of a child, but in the manner of a woman who had more urgent matters than seduction to attend to. She had said she was a dancer. It showed in her every move. Even her limp was graceful, a careful shifting of weight and form. He was captivated by her manner of movement and her urgency. She'd flushed when she'd noticed his reaction to her disrobing. It had been a simple, practical removal of wet clothes not intended to shatter him completely.

But it had.

And then to pile torment on top of torment, she had paused in her desperate bid to ask for his help to tremble and stare. Her eyes had widened. She'd held her breath and captured the soft swell of her lower lip in her perfect white teeth. He'd been alone for a long time, but he knew the signs of desire when he saw them. Especially when he was burning with it himself.

First, she'd looked at him like she was searching for something he could never be. Then she'd looked at him as a woman looks at a man, and he'd wanted to respond to the hunger that had risen in her eyes.

He'd been blissfully numb before she came. He couldn't remember the last Cycle where he'd felt anything but the growing wish to fade away. He'd gone through the motions. He'd cared for Lev and Soren. He'd endured the "honor" of the *Volkhvy* Gathering that was, in fact, a celebration of his eternal torture and the aura of power released by the Ether every materialization. But it had all been done in a haze of endurance as if he ran a marathon of epic distance with one stride more, then one more, then one more before the final finish line.

His haze had been cruelly lifted.

He struck again and again at the scarred oaken practice figures in the moonlit courtyard with the sapphire sword. The gem in its hilt was flat and plain. It was an enchanted sapphire, but it was only moonlight that occasionally caused its surface to glow. The Light *Volkhvy* queen, Vasilisa, had given the sword to his father as a gift for his mate. When Ivan's mother had wielded the blade, the power in its gem had been dazzling. Now it was dulled by the curse.

The dead stone was doubly cruel because its moonlit dark blue reminded him of Elena's serious gaze leveled on him with expectation and hope.

He couldn't help her. He couldn't revive the sword. His blows rained down on the oaken cross that had once been used to train the Romanov guard. Clouds of white burst into the air as every blow shook the wood and kept the snow from settling. They were all gone now. The Ether had eaten them. *A devora.* It had taken his father first. Perhaps justly, for it was Vladimir Romanov who had tried to betray the Light *Volkhvy* queen, Vasilisa. It hadn't been strictly a political betrayal. It had been a betrayal of the heart. Ivan's mother had been killed by the Dark *Volkhvy* king. Afterward, his father had become Vasilisa's lover. But his father had craved more power. He hadn't wanted to be a mere champion. He'd wanted to rule.

In retribution, Vasilisa had punished him and his offspring and all of his people.

Sweat poured down Ivan's face like the tears he'd never allowed himself to shed as a teen when the weight of the world had fallen on his shoulders. Steam rose off his heated skin as the salty moisture hit the night air. He'd been raised to fight the Dark *Volkhvy*. As the oldest, he'd assumed leadership. He'd become the alpha. Even as a teen, he'd already been a battle-scarred warrior in those days. But he'd been unprepared to fight against dishonor, nothingness and despair. He'd carried on. For years, he'd tried to earn redemption while one after another after another of his people and loved ones faded away, Lev and Soren by his side.

He hadn't been able to hold back the darkness. The Ether won, again and again. The curse was triumphant. Bronwal had been under siege for centuries and it wasn't until Elena arrived that Ivan had realized, for him, it would never be over.

Because in that moment, at the door of her room, he'd known he had no intention of succumbing to the beast as his brothers had done. Neither would he vanish quietly into the Ether. He was the last Romanov. He would stand. Alone. Forever. *To ensure that the curse ended with him.* If he allowed himself to disappear into the Ether for good, the castle, the wolves and the sword would be undefended against anyone who might try to claim them when they materialized each Cycle. His brothers, Lev and Soren, had given up their humanity to escape permanently into their wolf forms. Either they couldn't remember how to be men or they didn't want to. The shame of their heritage was too great.

He would never abandon them, but would never join them.

He wasn't free to help Elena Pavlova in his wolf form because he had to maintain his control and his human faculties. He had to defend Bronwal and keep possession of the sword. Until his unnaturally long life finally came to an end in death and dust.

He also wasn't free to be a man with Elena. He had to resist the mutual attraction that had flared between them. The only way to break the Romanov curse was to guard against passing it on.

The cross he attacked with powerful blows finally disarmed him. With one last swing, he buried the sword too deeply to retrieve and he released its hilt. The dulled sapphire seemed to mock his resolve in the moonlight. Snowflakes immediately began to adhere to its surface now that it was stilled. Let it be there, buried deep in the oak, when the Dark *Volkhvy* came to try to steal it. Every Cycle, they came. And he was always ready. This time would be no different.

He was the alpha wolf that Elena Pavlova sought. But he wasn't free to be wolf or man with the woman who needed his help.

Chapter 4

The lighting in the castle was as haphazard as the servants who had helped her the night before. With servants influenced by their time in the Ether, it was no surprise that jobs such as maintaining torches and lanterns went undone or half-done. The entire castle had an air of hushed neglect, but there was also a sense of expectation as if dust and cobwebs and candles waited and waited for care that never came.

Elena walked quietly on her sneakered feet. She placed her weight on her toes, unconsciously tiptoeing down gloomy halls. There had to be hundreds of empty rooms. She explored them, one by one. But the weight of what she found settled heavily on her heart. Her chest constricted and her breathing turned shallow. Again and again she found knitting laid to one side and never taken up again. She found dusty books marked with faded ribbons. There were chessboards waiting for next moves that would never come and clothes laid out that would never be worn. Toys abandoned.

And paintings of generations of Romanovs lost to the Ether.

The curse had been a terrible punishment and a horrible fate for the legends she'd loved as a child. Ivan Romanov lived in a haunted home. Bronwal was a majestic graveyard filled with the discarded remains of lives interrupted never to resume.

Finally, Elena came to a large portrait hall lit only by the scant light of sunrise filtering through heavily draped windows set high in the stone block walls. The scarlet of the thick velvet drapes gave the light a reddish glow. She moved along the edges of the room, avoiding the center of the floor filled with a forest of sheet-draped statuary.

Instead, she looked at the people. Especially an oversize painting that dominated the room. The subject of the painting was Ivan Romanov and his family—mother, father, and two younger brothers. She stepped close to the base of the portrait to stare. There was warmth and familial affection captured by some long-gone artist's deft hand. Ivan stood behind and between his younger brothers with his hands on their shoulders as if he held them still. She could see the twinkle in the boys' eyes and the patience of a wiser older brother in Ivan's. The younger Romanovs weren't identical twins. One favored his father with reddish brown hair. One favored his mother with pale, unblemished skin and platinum blond hair. But all of them had the Romanov nose and the tall, fine forms of aristocratic warriors.

Had he lost them all to the Ether?

His mother had leaned toward all three of her boys.

Her body language conveying that she preferred their company to her husband's. The eldest Romanov looked more proud than warm, but she was certain it was her knowledge of his failures that diminished him in her eyes.

She'd come for the alpha wolf, but she couldn't help being drawn to the Romanov tragedy, as well. No matter what their father had done, the boys had been innocents caught up in the curse through no fault of their own. Elena had to force herself away from the painting. It was too easy to be transfixed by the younger Ivan and the warmth and ease that was now absent from his green eyes.

She saw the shapes first beneath large sheets in the center of the room. She walked to each and pulled them off, first one and then the other. She found stone carvings of the two wolves she'd already met—the red and the white.

But there was one larger covered form behind them.

Its sheet came off in her hand in a sudden flourish and dust filled the air with motes that rained down over the black marble she'd revealed. The alpha wolf was the size of a great stallion. It wasn't a pet of the Romanov family. It was the greatest champion just as her grandmother had said. Its purpose was evident in every stone sinew and in its marble teeth.

Where had the alpha wolf gone?

Surely he hadn't disappeared into the Ether. Not the largest and strongest of them all. She looked into his ferocious maw and her flight instinct kicked in. The sheet dropped from her numb fingers and her breath came quickly.

She risked her life in this place where'd she'd come to try to save it.

Hunting such a creature without its master's blessing was as suicidal as climbing up the mountain looking for a fantasy castle. She should leave as Romanov advised and never return.

Elena lifted her hand and her fingers hovered near the black wolf's face. She noted the tremble of her digits and forced herself to touch the cold stone. She cupped beneath the great snarling mouth as if she held the wolf's head in her hand. She couldn't leave. The hollow place inside of her where the dance had been wouldn't allow it. She was here for a reason she didn't yet understand, but the search for the black wolf was a part of it.

Her silent communication with the statue was interrupted by a clicking sound behind her.

She recognized what made the sound even without turning around.

Slow, stalking claws click, click, clicked on the tiled floor. They approached her from the way she'd come. Elena didn't turn around. She looked into the alpha wolf's stone eyes. They were as black as the rest of him, but the midnight glinted in the soft glow of filtered sunlight. Even as her heart pounded and her spine froze, the sculpture's eyes seemed compelling.

She braced herself. The clicking came closer and closer from two distinct directions. One to her left and one to her right. When the massive creatures she'd met earlier came into her peripheral vision, flanking her on either side, she had the crazy sense that the two other wolf sculptures had come to life. Of course they hadn't. These were the wolves from last night. And this time their master wasn't around.

There was no one to call them off.

"You know where I can find the alpha wolf. Take me

to him," Elena said. Her voice didn't waver. She spoke firmly. The flutter was hidden from view deep in her stomach and her knees. The wolves moved to stand beside the sculpture of the alpha wolf, on either side. They loomed over her and they were no longer acting like gamboling giant puppies. Their eyes blazed with predatory intent. Had they been hunting her while she searched the castle? Had they followed her from room to room at the bidding of their master or for some hungrier cause?

"I came for the alpha's help," Elena said. They weren't ordinary wolves. Perhaps they would be able to understand. "A Dark *Volkhvy* stalks me. A witchblood prince. No friend of yours. Help me against him," she urged.

She had no idea if they understood her words, but she had to try. She hadn't come this far to stay locked in a tower.

First the russet and then the white stepped toward her. Elena lowered her hand from the marble wolf's jaw. The trembling in her fingers was more noticeable, the better to show the wolves the terror she tried to hide. It was the russet wolf with coppery eyes who lowered his head to her hand first. She cried out softly, certain he would bite off her hand, but then the silky hair on the top of his head tickled the palm of her hand. The white wolf stepped forward to lean and lower and nudge her other hand until it too rested on a monstrous wolf's head.

"Does this mean you'll help me?" Elena said. "Will you lead me to the alpha wolf?"

The courtyard was churned into ruts and packed dirt by frequent use. Considering it was only materialized a month every ten years that meant the sweat that ran down

Ivan Romanov's half-naked body had been well-earned time and time again.

The wolves hadn't understood her after all.

They'd led her to their master. A betrayal for sure, but she couldn't blame them. Especially when she was grateful that they hadn't eaten her for breakfast. They left her and bounded onto the field, chasing each other beneath the rising sun. It was cold in spite of the sun. Snow drifts lay all around. Elena wrapped her arms around herself. The castle walls protected the inner courtyard from excess snow accumulation, but Romanov's practice field was dusted with white and edged by icy foliage on evergreen bushes. It glistened and dazzled her eyes because they'd grown used to the dimness inside.

Ivan lowered his arms. He'd left a sword embedded in the cross-shaped practice form. It was buried deep in the scarred wood. So deep that she wondered at the force required to leave it there. He didn't turn around. She could see streaks of sweat on his muscled back and his labored breathing as his broad shoulders rose and fell. A leather cord wrapped the wild hair she remembered from the night before. The thick queue hung midway down his spine.

She didn't like his hair bound. She wanted to free it. The crazy urge took her by surprise, as did the sudden feeling that everything she'd been looking for was here, in this courtyard, for her to see.

She hugged herself tighter as she waited long heartbeats for him to turn and face her. He expected her to leave today. She hadn't found the alpha wolf. Grigori would find her, alone and defenseless. There was nowhere she could hide from him. Ivan Romanov couldn't be her only hope because he was a man who didn't believe in hope. Not anymore.

"Did you send the wolves to find me?" Elena asked.

Though she'd braced herself, she wasn't prepared for Ivan to suddenly turn around and pace toward her. She backed away several steps from the ferocity that tightened his face before she stopped herself and stood her ground.

"You weren't in the tower," Ivan said.

He came close enough to touch her, but instead he reached for the key between her breasts. He didn't pull it from her neck. He only held it in his large, calloused fingers. She looked from the key up to his eyes. He loomed over her, but it wasn't fear she felt at his sudden nearness. No. The thrill in her veins and the rush on her skin was something besides fear. Awareness. Expectation. In the meager sunlight, she noted that his irises were brighter than the snow. His pupils had retracted, allowing lighter green and gold flecks to glow. The lightness softened his otherwise forbidding expression. His hair had been loosened around his face by his exertions, and glossy chunks of it threatened to come free from the leather cording.

If he sought to intimidate her, he succeeded, but only because she was intimidated by his accessibility. Why did she notice indications of softness that were probably a lie? And why did she feel as if she was missing a truth she needed to see?

"You gave me the key. And I chose to unlock the door," Elena said. She still didn't mention the call that made it impossible for her to hide. There was something here she needed to find. Something more than a man and a wolf, but they were part of it, she was sure.

"I can't decide if you're brave or foolish," Romanov said. His gaze was intense. His hold on the key between her breasts was tight. She couldn't back away. She was caught and held—both by his hand and his eyes.

"Careful and brave rarely go hand in hand. Brave is doing what has to be done, no matter the risk," Elena said. "My mother was brave. She gave her life to call forth an ancient binding spell so that I could live free. I'm only just learning how to be brave for myself."

He leaned slightly, bowing his head toward her face. At the same time, he pulled the key slightly toward his chest. It was an infinitesimal movement. But the chain definitely tightened against her neck. Her neck and his hand were engaged in a silent tug of war that mimicked the tug of war she was battling between the magnetic pull of his broad chest and her trembling body.

Why did the courtyard seem like the final destination in the long journey she'd taken? And why did she look for softness in this legendary man? Because she wanted him to tighten his grip on the key and tug harder. He was powerful. He could narrow the gap between them without her permission. It would absolve her of the bad decision she suddenly wanted to make.

Because in spite of the talk of being brave, all she could do was lower her attention from his angry eyes to focus on his mouth. Somehow, the truth was there for her to see. The swell of his sensual lower lip belied his talk of her foolishness. He wanted her here. He wanted her close. Deep inside, a liquid tightening coiled and a hunger rose. She wanted to kiss him. Never mind that he was an angry warrior who claimed he wanted her to stay locked away until she could leave. He held her for a reason. He stood tense as their bodies paused in the nearly touching position. Her breasts were inches from the warmth of his chest.

She lifted her gaze quickly to see what he would do. But his eyes were shadowed now by a thick fall of wavy black hair that had escaped its confinement. His irises glittered with an emerald sheen behind those snow-dampened locks. But his expression was obscured. She could only take in the rise and fall of his chest—it seemed slower than it should be, as if he controlled his breathing or even…did he hold his breath? Her own breath was shallow and quick. Her body held still as she waited to see what he would say or do.

"You are brave. Braver than I hope you'll ever know," Romanov said. It was almost a growl, uttered past a tense and tightened jaw.

"What is it I should be afraid of? What could possibly be worse than being captured by the witchblood prince who stalks me?" Elena asked. She closed her eyes and willed away the hot moisture that threatened to rise behind her lids. She'd already betrayed too much of her vulnerability to him and he refused to be moved. She wouldn't give him her tears too.

"I don't know the prince of whom you speak. And I know many monsters. Some man, some truly beast. The Ether claims more of my humanity with every Cycle. And you ask what you should be afraid of as if a threat doesn't stand before your very eyes," Romanov said. His voice had dropped to a low, agonized whisper. It seemed confessional. Yet he told her nothing she didn't already know. He was dangerous. She could sense it. She could see it. But he was also so much more. Compelling. Alluring. Seductive. More attractive to a civilized woman than he should be.

"I will not give up. I will not go away," Elena insisted. A sudden persistent pull on the silver chain caused her eyelids to open quickly. They were closer. There was only the slightest brush of contact between them, but the tips of her breasts burned. She did hold her breath then because respiration caused an agonizing allure of friction she couldn't resist.

But she didn't pull away.

And she didn't close her eyes again.

There were no tears now. Only a giddy heated pleasure radiating from her distended nipples to the rest of her body. The glittering intensity of his gaze was locked on hers, but he must have known the chain was indenting the nape of her neck because he allowed the silver links to go slack. Now it was up to her to stay close or move away. He no longer held her in place.

She stayed.

And the attention of his eyes fell to the key in his hand. She watched him as he focused on placing the key against the hollow of her neck. The heat of his hand had warmed the iron. Nevertheless the contact sent shivers down her spine, especially when he allowed the key to fall. It slid down until the hollow of her cleavage caught it. The warmed iron between her breasts caused her to gasp. But then when he lifted his free hand to touch her, the sudden weight of his calloused fingers and palm cupping the back of her neck was so much hotter. Her gasp became a trembling sigh and then a whimper when his fingers brushed under the chain as if to soothe the mark it had left on her skin. He was moved, but she wasn't sure what to expect. She suddenly feared she'd woken a sleeping giant, one that might consume her body and soul if he decided to stay awake.

"I won't send you back out into the snow. But you won't find what you seek at Bronwal. There are no champions here. Only heartache and defeat. Only darkness and danger," Romanov warned.

Elena breathed freely now. Her whole body burned and she didn't care. For so long she'd been harassed and harried. She'd been injured, physically and emotionally. Plagued by nightmares and loss. Desperation hadn't been the only thing that drove her to climb the mountain, but it was desperation—a different kind—that caused her to lift her arms. She placed her palms against Romanov's sweat-dampened chest. She felt the thudding of his heart, his powerful muscles and his heat. He jerked at the contact. *But he didn't jerk away.* He stilled as she slid her hands up inch by inch, measuring his height and his solid reality, until she held a broad shoulder in each hand. She didn't understand what had called her to Bronwal, but she understood this.

Her hands had been trained to be a graceful expression of her art, but in that moment they were strong. They held a legend. And he was the one who trembled beneath her fingers. His mighty form reacted to the delicate intimacy of her touch.

His hand tightened on the back of her neck. She was held again. And she didn't mind. For the first time in a long time she focused on pleasure instead of pain. It was warm and immediate and all else fled from her thoughts.

"One word and I'll let you go. I'm not so Ether-addled that I have no self-control. I will be a man, not a monster, for as long as I'm able. For now, I'm able. Walk away from me," Romanov said. But as he spoke he pulled her close and it was gentler than she could have imagined. He didn't crush her against him. He pressed and her curves complied until they were melded together.

She tilted her chin to meet his descending face. And

still he paused. Their lips were only millimeters apart. His warm breath tickled her slightly open mouth.

"I'm a dancer. I've spent more time as a swan than as a woman," Elena said softly. The tears were back, burning her eyes. She ached to kiss him. And more. He was big and powerful, and when his other arm came up to press against her lower back the sensation of being held, safe, away from all that had come before, left her light-headed. But she was at a loss off the stage. She didn't know how to claim a new life now that her old life was over.

"No. I'm holding the woman. Without a doubt, it's the woman's mouth I'll taste," Romanov said.

Elena drew a shuddering breath of air as he traversed the last distance left between them.

Their lips touched and his mouth moved with eager hunger against hers. In nightmares, she'd endured depravity. This was pure, human and real. She tightened her hands on his shoulders as her stomach swooped and soared and her legs went weak. She also opened to the masculine seduction of his rough, slick tongue teasing between her lips.

Living off the stage was more instinct than practice. She swooned into the kiss without thought to form or precision. Romanov was all heat and pleasure and he consumed her easily. The thrill that rushed beneath her skin echoed the call she'd followed up the mountain. She couldn't separate the sensations. She'd wanted his hair unbound because she wanted this wildness. He'd seemed to offer it with every glance, with every move, even though he'd withheld it.

Her tongue hungrily licked past his lips and twined with his. He held her tight as if he hadn't been offering to let her go seconds before. She didn't want to go anywhere.

Her search seemed to be over. The call was silenced because it had been answered, somehow, someway, by his lips and teeth and tongue.

"You risk much. This woman is protected by her mother's spilt blood and claimed by Grigori, the witchblood prince. You might be Vasilisa's plaything, but that won't stop him from torturing you for eternity if you despoil his prize."

Romanov tore his lips from hers and whirled around to face the interruption. A man had entered the courtyard from the keep. Elena immediately found her footing as she was shoved behind the warrior she shouldn't have been kissing.

Her life wasn't a life free to indulge in sensual assignations. Especially with the legendary master who refused to help her engage the help of the alpha wolf.

The man who had entered the courtyard cautiously approached them. Of course, he was no man. He was *Volkhvy.* And judging from his intimate knowledge of her tormentor, he was Dark, not Light.

"You've come for the Romanov blade, but you'll find it buried deep in a cross purified by generations of my honorable men. It won't come to you easily, and the sapphire has long lost its glow," Romanov said. He'd placed himself between her and the *Volkhvy.* But he had no weapon in his hands.

The Dark witch was dressed in black leather from head to foot. He shone like obsidian in the winter sun. His white hair was braided in a thousand plaits and piled on top of his head, and his movements were young and quick. He was at least as tall and strong as Romanov himself. Elena's heart pounded, overwhelmed with the rude transition from passion to fear. The wolves would come. Surely, the wolves would come.

"Grigori will kill you for taking the taste he hasn't been able to take himself. He will cut out your bold tongue," the man said. He laughed when he said it. And he attacked.

Elena was startled by another sudden shove that sent her sliding backward in the snow away from Romanov as he pushed her several feet before he and the *Volkhvy* collided. She didn't fall. She kept her balance as only a woman with years of physically demanding training could have. Her knee screamed, but it didn't give way. Her arms flew out to automatically aid her equilibrium, and anyone watching would have thought she had merely been landing from a smooth pirouette.

"You grow weaker with each materialization, old man. The stone can be recharged. I'm not sure the same can be said for you," the witchblood man said.

"Try and try and try again. But always empty-handed in the end. Right, Dominique?" Romanov taunted in return.

"You know this man?" Elena asked. She'd immediately recovered and gone to a weapons rack where practice swords and daggers were hung in a rough array.

"Him. Many others. They're all the same to me. They come for the sword Vasilisa gave my father," Romanov said. "They leave without it." His blows connected powerfully with the *Volkhvy*'s abdomen, chest and jaw. The witchblood man recovered from each blow much more quickly than a mortal man would. But after one particularly hard connection, he did spit blood into the snow. "Sometimes they don't leave. Perhaps it's your turn to die, Dominique."

"Romanov!" Elena shouted. She threw a short broadsword high into the air. It flew in a wide arc and then down into Romanov's hand. She grabbed two daggers for herself, but as her hands closed over their hilts, something drew her attention across the courtyard. Her eyes fell on the sword Romanov had buried deep in the scarred practice form. Her feet carried her closer to it of their own volition. One step and then another. The sapphire didn't look that dull to her. It seemed to sparkle in the sun.

"No. Go inside," Romanov ordered. She ignored him. The *Volkhvy* had drawn a blade from a sheath on his back. His leather trench coat whirled around his legs as he brandished it. It wasn't jeweled, but the metal itself glowed in his hands.

Elena had gone for the easily accessible weapons because that's where she'd ended up when Romanov had shoved her away. Now she tucked the daggers in her back pockets and went for the more powerful blade. It was buried deep in the wood of the cross. So deep that it held her entire body weight, such that it was, when she grasped its hilt and tried to pull it free.

"I'm not running away. Not anymore," she said through clenched teeth. She refused to let go even when the hum of power in the sword caused her arms to go numb. Romanov was wrong. There was power left in the blade. It hummed like bees beneath her skin, vibrating her body as she pulled. She braced her feet against the practice form. Her knee screamed, but she used all of her strength to push with her legs and pull with her arms at the same time.

"It won't matter. Running, hiding, making a stand. He'll have you in the end. There are many that claim to be *Volkhvy*, but only Dark *Volkhvy* royals can trace their lineage back to Baba Yaga herself. The witchblood prince won't be denied. Oh the pretty tales he's told about his future plans for you, my pet. Or I should say *his* pet," the *Volkhvy* said. His laugh was cut short by a sudden fierce attack by Romanov. The powerful warrior hacked and hacked until the muscles on his back stood out in bunches and the witchblood man was driven to his knees. The *Volkhvy*, Dominique, parried as many blows as he could, but others connected with him until his white hair was painted with crimson flecks of blood.

"You should have given up. This will be your last attempt," Romanov said.

Elena suddenly fell to the ground as the Romanov blade came out of the practice form. She cried out as the fall jarred her knee and she closed her eyes against the pain, but she didn't drop the sword. She landed on her back with the sword grasped in both hands. It took long seconds to catch her breath and regain her feet. Seconds Romanov didn't have. As she opened her eyes and stood, the *Volkhvy*'s hands glowed. His blade had been knocked from his fingers, but he looked prepared to unleash some kind of spell against the man she'd been kissing minutes before.

"No," Elena shouted. She ran toward the men with the sapphire blade held high.

But there was no time for spells or the Romanov blade. Romanov plunged the dull practice sword into the *Volkhvy*'s chest. The rusty metal must have penetrated the witchblood man's heart. Thick black blood bubbled up from the wound and from between the man's lips as he fell to the snowy ground.

Romanov fell to his knees beside his old adversary and grasped him by the lapels of his leather trench coat.

He jerked him up toward his face. Elena stopped dead in her tracks and lowered the Romanov blade before the gruesome scene.

"Take Grigori a message. Tell him Elena Pavlova belongs to no one but herself," Romanov said. "And that Bronwal is defended. For eternity."

Elena started and dropped the Romanov blade when the bleeding man hazed before her eyes and disappeared leaving nothing but a puddle of steaming black blood on the ground. The sword fell with a solid thud that caused Romanov to rise to his feet and turn as if he was prepared to face another challenger.

"It's a defense mechanism. *Volkhvy* fade back to their home when they're gravely injured," Romanov explained. There was black blood on Romanov's sculpted cheek. From it a slow curl of steam rose in the air. His hair was loose now. It had come unbound during the fight. Long black waves framed his face. His hands were clenched. His chest rose and fell from the exertion of defeating a magical foe. But it was his eyes that caught her attention. They tracked from the sword on the ground to the practice form, to her face and back again.

"You tried to bring me the Romanov blade," he said.

"You warned Grigori away," Elena replied.

He stalked toward her looking battered and bruised, but the confident look in his eyes and the puddle of *Volkhvy* blood on the ground made him seem invincible. Why had she been so desperate to help him when he had refused to help her?

The answer came from the things he'd said to the witchblood man.

She thought he would pick up the blade she'd dropped, but he stepped over it instead. He'd already recovered.

His breathing was no longer labored. As she watched, the black blood completely evaporated from his face. He ignored the sword and came to stand directly in front of her, his attention fully on her. His penetrating gaze caused a flush to rise as she remembered her hungry response to his kiss.

"I'm no longer Vasilisa's champion against the Dark *Volkhvy*. I'm no one's champion. But I am the last Romanov and I stand to defend Bronwal. Forever. I warned Grigori away for that reason and that reason alone," Romanov said.

"Why didn't the alpha wolf...or any of the wolves come to help you?" Elena asked. The courtyard was empty. The sunlight was hidden behind clouds that had drifted in sometime during the fight. New snow fell in soft silence. Fluffy white flakes contrasted against Romanov's dark hair for brilliant seconds before they melted. The black waves released from his queue grew damp once more.

Romanov laughed softly and the snow globe the world had become suddenly crystallized and warmed at the same time. Elena hugged herself to keep from reaching out to him because his laugh was hollow rather than happy.

"I don't need wolves to fight a *Volkhvy* of Dominique's degree. Only the lesser witches come for the Romanov blade in its current state. Its power has faded. It holds no attraction or appeal to greater witches," Romanov said.

"Grigori would never fall to a common sword. Even if it pierced his heart," Elena guessed. Deep down she'd already known. That's why she'd sought the help of the alpha wolf.

"This blade is far from common. But it is also far

from what it was when it was given to my father," Romanov said. He turned away to bend and retrieve the jeweled sword. The sapphire in its hilt winked dully in the cloudy light.

Elena reached to touch the sapphire. She wasn't sure why. The dark gem was cool and damp beneath her fingers.

"It's very old," she said.

Romanov had frozen and she was reminded of her first glimpse of him last night. He stared at her face as if he saw something in it that caught his attention and wouldn't let him look away. The snow was falling more heavily and it swirled around the place where their bodies kept it from the ground. But when she looked from the gem up to his eyes he was no longer a legendary figure come to life. He was a complicated man. One who swore he was no hero while at the same time warning her greatest enemy away.

"It isn't age that diminishes the stone. It's dishonor," he said. "It wasn't meant to be brandished by a traitor."

Elena withdrew her hand and Romanov blinked and looked away from her face. He lowered the blade until its tip pointed to the snowy ground.

"You've carried the weight of your father's mistake for a long time," Elena said. "But I can also see that you aren't bowed beneath this burden. You might doubt that you're still a champion, but your body knows. You don't fight like a man with nothing to lose. You fight like a man with everything to lose. I can see that the stone doesn't shine," Elena continued as she turned to walk away through the accumulating snow. "But I can also see that you still do. You shine. And you could help me if you would."

He didn't reply and she didn't pause. She left him and his dishonored blade in the whiteout of falling snow. She wouldn't kiss him again. She would avoid him while she sought the alpha wolf. The ferocity of his unexpected needs drew her, as did the skin-to-skin electricity between them. But she hadn't climbed the mountain to find a seductive lover. She'd answered a call that couldn't be denied and she'd come to find a way to defeat the witchblood prince.

Chapter 5

She'd tasted like honey cakes and her scent had been feminine and minty sweet. The combination had gone to his head like a mead brewed for maximum potency and pleasure. Romanov sought out his rooms and the cold comfort of a bath to wash away the remnants of his long training session and his battle with Dominique. He used a rough cloth to sluice icy water over his skin. Crazy that he should kiss her. But it was a crazy inspired by sizzling attraction that clouded his thinking and burned in his blood. She should have been frightened away by his brothers, by the castle, by his tales of Ether-mad people wandering the halls.

Instead, her body had melded against his chest in his arms. She'd reached for him. She'd held on tight. She'd eagerly welcomed the thrusting of his tongue. She'd tasted him. She'd moaned and sighed as if her body craved more intimate contact with his than could be had in a courtyard in the snow.

The cold water was useless against the onslaught of sensations his mind insisted on recalling—one by one in slow, torturous succession. He hardened with the memory and he was glad he'd filled his own tub. He didn't need an audience for his body's reaction half an hour after Elena Pavlova had allowed—nay, participated in—an embrace and kiss that shouldn't have happened.

Once again, he'd been surprised by how powerfully muscular her seemingly delicate dancer's body could be. He'd wanted to rip her clothes away so he could explore and appreciate every taut line, every smooth curve. Not to mention the soft, full breasts that contrasted with her spare frame and the warm, hidden crevices he could only imagine.

Oh damn, how he could imagine them.

Many Cycles had come and gone since he'd been alive enough to feel like this. And even more since he'd been foolish enough to act on the feelings. He was cursed. He wasn't free to crave and savor and…

His body was reddened from its rough washing when he stood to allow soapy cold water to run off his skin. He wouldn't indulge his erection. He left the bath instead, wrapped in a sheet that was tattered and faded. No one had been prescient enough to mend or replace linens in a long time.

He walked to the window and pressed open the stained glass that had been added centuries after the castle was constructed. Throughout the castle there was evidence of the passage of time. People had tried to carry on. Some still did. The window's iron hinges protested, but the cold air rushed in, bathing his moist face and chilling his body temperature. He needed the blast of winter air.

Dominique wasn't dead. A normal blade would never kill a *Volkhvy*. His bold message would be delivered to Grigori. He'd told Elena he wasn't a champion. He'd told her the alpha wolf wouldn't help her. Both of those things were true. But he was a defender of his family's enclave and he would be here when Grigori came for the dancer he had claimed.

If he assumed wolf form to fight the witchblood prince, he might lose himself to it as his brothers had. Bronwal would be deserted and the Romanov blade would be up for grabs. The Dark *Volkhvy* might gain a foothold that couldn't be dislodged without a clearly sentient person to stand against them.

He couldn't risk the shift even for Elena Pavlova.

From where he stood he could see the ravens that circled around Elena's tower. They soared like feathered shadows around her room. It seemed a dark foreshadowing of what was to come.

His only option was to force her to leave Bronwal.

Cruel that he should continue to taste her and recall with perfect clarity the bold strokes of her tongue.

He wasn't sure how he would drive her away when everything in him wanted her to stay.

But he had no choice.

She'd fallen to the ground when she'd pulled the Romanov blade from the practice form in the courtyard. It had been a hard, bone-jarring fall. The blond waves of her hair had tumbled into her face and her eyes had closed. She hadn't seen what he'd seen as her body flew backward. It hadn't been the weight of the blade or the momentum of her jerk that had sent her to the ground.

The dormant, fading sapphire in the hilt of the Romanov blade had flared in her hands. A powerful force had radiated out from the awakened gem. It was that force that had sent her petite body to the ground.

The stone had dimmed immediately after and it hadn't glowed again when she rose to her feet and picked it up. But it hadn't been his imagination. The sapphire had reacted to Elena's touch. He shouldn't be surprised. He'd felt the same awakening in her presence. Not to mention what her touch did to him. An hour later, and the blood in his veins still thrummed from the fleeting kiss they'd shared.

As the ravens swooped and soared, he lifted his hand to feel his lips as if he would be able to feel the ghost of her heat on his mouth as well as he did within.

The wolf he kept buried howled deep in his chest, but not as deep as it had been before Elena arrived. She tested his control. She tempted him to give in to the passions he'd denied for so many Cycles with ease.

He had no choice but to send her away when the weather allowed it. He'd almost shifted when Dominique had taunted him in the courtyard. He couldn't risk what he might do if Elena was still at Bronwal when the *Volkhvy* came to gloat at the Gathering.

Almost as if he'd willed it to show its face, the sun burst from behind the storm clouds that had eaten its light earlier in the day. The mountains were covered in snow, but the clouds were gone and no more flakes fell from the sky.

He couldn't help remembering the stories of how the Romanov blade had chosen his mother. He remembered her as a ferocious warrior well able to wield it, and yet she'd died with the blade in her hands in spite of its power. She'd fallen against the Dark *Volkhvy* king.

Vasilisa had created the blade for the alpha's mate.

He refused to accept what its wakening in Elena's hands might mean.

The curse changed everything. It twisted all of the old enchantments. He was doomed to stand alone forever. The sapphire's glow only illuminated his pain.

Chapter 6

Evening came early as the sun set once more behind the rocky ridges of the snow-capped mountains. Elena figured out how to open one of the stained glass panels in her room so that she could see the brilliant red sphere as it sank. It turned the entire world to crimson and gold, while ravens continued to lazily patrol the skies around her tower. After the kiss and the fight, she'd retreated to the tower. She'd slammed the door and turned the key. But no one had followed her. She was alone except for the ever-present birds. Their constant revolutions occurred silently, with only the occasional flutter of wings.

Once the sun went down and the world went dark, Elena took one last deep breath of the fresh air and then closed the window against the night. With the snowstorm clearing, it was only a matter of time before Romanov decided to send her away. She didn't have long. The unwound clock in her room didn't tick. It didn't have to. She felt the seconds counting down with every heartbeat in her chest. The call beneath her skin had become a continual sense of urgency rather than a pulse.

It compelled her to be brave. She didn't have much time. She unlocked the door and left the tower to search for the alpha wolf. The long winding stairway was deserted, but when she left the tower to travel into the main part of the castle, she wasn't alone. Lev and Soren appeared behind her. Romanov had ordered his wolves to stalk her. Their claws could be eerily quiet when they wished. But not as eerie as how loud they could be seconds later. The *click-click-click* that occasionally sounded behind her caused her heart to pound. She bit her lip so often against the fear that her lower lip became swollen and sensitized.

She was already more conscious of her mouth than she'd ever been.

She'd been kissed before. She'd enjoyed it. That pleasure was pale in comparison to what had flared between her and Romanov when their mouths had come together. He could have crushed her, easily. His arms were massive and not in that showy way that bodybuilders attained. Romanov had real, ropey muscles that flexed and released when he moved, in the same way that a dancer's muscles stretched and released. Not for looks. For utility. It so happened that muscles built for utility were the most attractive of all. Her stomach went all molten liquid when she remembered his embrace—his calloused hand on the back of her neck, his other splayed on the curve of her lower back. He'd pulled her close, not as if she needed to be held, but as if he was hanging on for dear life.

She'd felt solid and necessary. So real and seductive because he seemed to crave her warmth and solidity.

And all because a man kissed her. Not a mere fantasy. Ivan Romanov was a legend, but that wasn't all he was.

The stories were dust, blown away by muscle and heat and friction and the hungry penetration of his tongue.

Elena Pavlova belongs to herself.

His words had been echoing in her head for hours. He was wrong. She had never belonged to herself. The dance had owned her for two decades. She'd loved her grandmother and her mother, but the dance had ruled her world. Every move she made from dawn till dusk had been to serve the dance. All of the masters who had driven her to try to achieve perfection had demanded her obedience and her complete dedication, but it had been the ballet that they'd all served.

Back in the apartment she'd shared with her grandmother, dozens upon dozens of pointe shoes hung from their ribbons on nails driven deep into the wall. They were dingy pastel satin, stained with years of her blood, sweat and tears. They were also prize trophies that proclaimed her servitude, not her independence.

What did the servant do when the master freed her from obligation?

Elena shivered as she continued her self-guided tour of Bronwal.

Even if Grigori had never seen her and never claimed her as his own, she would be in crisis now that her career was over. She was a prima ballerina, but an injured athlete's future wasn't guaranteed with surgery. At best, retirement could be held off as a dancer was forced to accept lesser and lesser roles. Where she went from there was always going to be a question she had to answer.

Lev and Soren seemed to have infinite patience with her wanderings. Only the occasional sound of their claws on tile interrupted her thoughts. The clicks were discordant against the ticking clock of her heart.

She'd wanted to dance and the dance had consumed her. Now she longed for a chance at something more.

Elena Pavlova belongs to herself.

There was a possibility that Ivan Romanov, the last Romanov, had voiced her true desire. If she survived Grigori, she would be free for the first time. It would be up to her what she decided to become with her freedom.

The castle seemed to be utterly empty except for her lone human form followed by two giant wolves. Only distant sounds indicated that her solitude was a lie.

As Elena searched for the alpha wolf, she thought about Romanov's lips. She'd kissed him even though she shouldn't, but it felt like the first real choice she'd ever made. She'd been driven to dance by a natural affinity, but the dance had subsumed all of her passion years before it ruined her knee. It had stopped being a choice and become an obsessive obligation. She danced because she had to. To provide for her grandmother. To honor her dead mother's memory.

Seeking the alpha wolf was also something she had to do. It wasn't a choice. It was survival.

But kissing Ivan Romanov had been *her* decision. He had given her ample opportunity to run away. She had to take responsibility for the consequences. The weakness in her knees. The warmth in her belly. The heat of shame when she acknowledged she would make the same choice if she could go back and relive that moment again, even though the kiss had been a mistake.

She hadn't gone back to the tower room to flee Romanov. She'd fled from her desire until she could be certain that she would come out only to seek the alpha wolf and not her host.

The castle was as poorly lit as it had been before. She walked by the sparse light of flickering torches and a small flashlight she'd packed in her bag. On the walls she caught occasional glimpses of the wolves in the form of hulking black shadows. She'd grown up with tales of these wolves. Their shadows were very like the paper cutouts that leaped from some of the pages of her grandmother's book. Ferocious yet lovely. Mysterious yet beloved and familiar.

"My, what very big teeth my childhood stories have," Elena said. Her voice echoed down the empty corridor. It also trembled. Because no matter how nostalgic she was for her grandmother and the old tales she knew, the wolves that trailed after her were deadly and real. They didn't walk by her side as friends. They followed suspiciously and cautiously as she searched their home for the alpha.

And their master ignored her desperate efforts.

She was glad he was nowhere to be seen.

Once again she roamed from room to room. She didn't expect to suddenly turn a corner and run into the alpha wolf, but she did hope for a clue to his whereabouts. The Dark *Volkhvy* and his talk of Grigori had only increased her sense of urgency. Before the witchblood prince found her, she had to have a champion to face him down. If Romanov wouldn't help her, she had to help herself.

Her chest grew tighter and tighter with every room she searched. Every breath seemed to require more and more effort to take.

It wasn't only time constraints and her failure to find

the black wolf that caused emotions to knot around her heart and crowd out her lungs. It was the fate of the people who had once called Bronwal home. She'd yet to encounter a single soul wandering in the halls. She heard them far off—laughing, crying, calling out the name of a loved one again and again with no reply. She braced for a possible encounter around every corner, behind every door.

But she found only dust and desertion.

She was a living trespasser rifling through the belongings of the lost. She tried not to disturb personal effects. She limited her search to books and papers. Some bit of knowledge about the alpha that might add to what little she'd learned from her own book of Slavic legends.

There was nothing. The people of Bronwal had lived with legends. Their personal tales had been told over tables and cook fires. On dance floors and battlefields. The books they'd kept on shelves had nothing to do with the *Volkhvy* or the legendary wolves. The dusty papers were love letters or ledgers. Diaries about mundane daily events. Not tomes devoted to the alpha wolf's summoning.

Lev and Soren paced restlessly when she paused in a room and then they followed her on to the next. They didn't make a sound until she stumbled upon a large chamber that had obviously been a family suite.

Elena pushed the heavy door open wide and walked into the room. One of the windowpanes had cracked. Snow had disturbed the sanctum created by abandoned neglect. It swirled icily when she opened the door. Her breath fogged from her parted lips in the unheated air. The bed was a curtained masterpiece of carved mahogany. But it wasn't the snow or the bed that caught her attention.

There was a small cradle beside the bed. The winter breeze from the broken window caused it to sway with the tiniest of creaks, a sad and empty sound far from what must have been ages ago when a mother rocked a sleeping infant in his or her comfy bed.

Elena's eyes burned. She walked toward the cradle even though the tightness in her chest had spread all the way up to her throat. She grasped the flushed skin of her neck with a trembling hand when she was close enough to see the crumpled blankets and an abandoned toy on the floor.

She knew what it was before she bent to pick it up. It was grayish in the dim light of her flashlight, but she recognized its shape. It was Lev. Or a hand-sewn likeness of the great white wolf made from a fluffy white cloth that had grown dingy with neglect and age.

It was the first evidence she'd found of the wolves beyond the sculptures in the portrait gallery.

She turned the toy wolf around and gasped when she saw the finely rendered face. Blue embroidery thread had been carefully employed to represent the wolf's eyes. This had been the baby's toy and it had been left behind when the baby—disappeared into the Ether for the last time?

A tapestry hung behind the cradle, softening the cold stone wall with muted colors. She raised her flashlight to illuminate the intricately wrought piece of art. Then she gasped. How had someone created so much life and movement with a needle and thread? The compulsion that had brought her to Bronwal suddenly became a thrill of recognition. Thousands upon thousands of tiny stitches glimmered beneath her flashlight's beam. They composed a portrait of a woman dressed in medieval style, but she wasn't some simple maiden. Over her long dress, bronze thread had been used to depict a breastplate, and she wore a matching bronze helmet. From beneath it, a riot of red hair swept out from her face and shoulders in a wild halo created by an unseen breeze. The expression on her face was both ferocious and serene. Purpose was evident in every line of her body and in the sword she lifted into a sewn sky filled with embroidered clouds.

She didn't recognize the woman, but she recognized something in her—an emotion she felt within her own breast.

At first, Elena mistook her sword for the sapphire blade, but once she pulled her eyes from the fascination caused by the woman's seeming serenity in spite of whatever unseen danger she faced, she realized her mistake. The stone in the hilt of the sword wasn't a sapphire. It was a blood-red ruby. The massive tapestry seemed an odd choice to hang over a baby's bed, yet Elena could almost imagine the woman in the portrait watching over the tiny baby as he or she slept. With that thought, it suddenly didn't seem out of place at all.

She held the toy wolf in one hand and the flashlight in the other, but she reached with the hand that held the flashlight to gently touch the gem on the sword with one extended finger.

A low growl suddenly interrupted her fascination with the tapestry.

Elena whirled toward the hall, wildly painting the walls with an unsteady beam of light. Once her eyes could focus, she saw the wolf toy's living likeness blocking the door.

One of her wolf shadows was no longer content to follow in her wake. He'd come forward. And he didn't seem happy at all. He was much more ferocious than the toy in her hand. As her flashlight steadied and her beam illuminated the doorway, Lev's legs were braced and his hackles were bristled along his giant back. Worst of all, his teeth were bared in a snarl. The trembling in Elena's hand returned and transferred itself to her entire body in an instant. If the wolves had been suspicious of her before, that suspicion had transformed into outright aggression.

Lev paced one stiff-legged stride toward her and then another.

"I mean no harm. I didn't mean to…disturb the baby's room," Elena said. And it was true. She wished she'd walked by this door. It was too horrible. Her understanding of the torment that must have plagued these people was complete. Here had been a tiny baby only beginning his or her life, but now gone. This was worse than death. A baby ceasing to be. Had the mother gone first or had she followed later? And what of the father? Had he mourned, had he grieved? The *Volkhvy* divided themselves by Dark and Light, but this curse had been the work of the Light *Volkhvy* queen. Which meant there was really no distinction between Dark and Light at all.

Elena turned slowly and carefully to place the wolf toy in the cradle. Lev growled louder, but she withdrew her hand to show what she had done. She raised her empty palm toward the wolf that had allowed her to pet him before. He didn't seem soothed. In fact, he took another step toward her while Soren stood tense at the door.

"I'm sorry, Lev," Elena said. She meant for everything. Not only that she'd disturbed the chamber, but for all the loss and the pain. She was sorry that her presence disturbed the entire castle. Bronwal was a tomb. Every footfall in the dusty passages was a desecration. And yet it was a desecration she must commit to survive.

Soren had disappeared. But the distant castle and the room suddenly hazed as her perceptions narrowed down to her and the lone wolf that remained. She was alone with the white wolf and he seemed seconds away from tearing her throat out. Elena edged back inch by inch until the cradle was between her vulnerable jugular vein and Lev.

"I need the alpha wolf's help. I can't stop looking. I won't. But this room is obviously off-limits. I understand. Let me leave and I won't disturb the baby again," Elena said. Even as she said it, she was glad she'd seen the tapestry. There was something important about the warrior woman. Her senses tingled with potential revelations that seemed just out of reach. Something about the tapestry captured her. She'd been searching Bronwal to unlock the secrets of summoning the alpha wolf. The tapestry seemed to hint there was more to the legend than she'd been told.

With a start she noticed that Lev's giant paws were already in the snow that had come in the cracked window. His breath came in white clouds between his bared teeth. She wouldn't be able to fight him off with nothing but a flashlight. She was trapped as she was trapped every night in swan form in her nightmares. Her only consolation was that Grigori wasn't here to see her die. He would get no more pleasure from her pain. The trembling in her body transferred to the light in her hands. The beam wavered on the floor. She faced her death. She wasn't sorry she'd tried. She didn't regret listening to the call that had brought her here. If anything, the discovery of the tapestry made her fiercely glad. She didn't cower. She braced her legs and waited for the white wolf to pounce.

"Lev," Romanov said from the doorway.

Elena's attention flew from the shivering light to the man who had suddenly appeared from the shadows.

He didn't shout. He didn't have to. His firm tone rent the silent, chilly air as commanding as it needed to be without him raising his voice. Romanov was part of the mystery. He, too, caused a thrill in her like the tapestry on the wall. Even in danger, she recognized the pieces coming together—Romanov, the missing alpha, the warrior woman, the swords.

The white wolf froze. His breathing was labored as if he expended great effort to halt his attack midspring. Sure enough, his haunches were compressed as if his master had interrupted seconds before he left the ground.

"I didn't mean to upset him…" Elena began.

"You can't possibly understand what you've done," Romanov said. "Lev. Leave. I'll take her away. She won't bring you here again. She didn't know."

"You weren't always his master," Elena guessed. "This was his family."

"He isn't a dog. Or a pet. He has no master, Elena. He's never had a master. But, yes, this was his family," Romanov said. His tones were raw and subdued as if his chest was as tight as hers.

"I'm sorry," Elena said.

The white wolf blinked as if he'd been woken from a berserker trance. He backed away from her until he bumped into Romanov's legs. Then he yelped as if he was startled. Romanov reached and placed his hand on the side of the great wolf's face. But Lev jerked away and ran into the corridor. Elena watched as the wolf disappeared. Soren, who must have gone to fetch Romanov, stood in the hallway. He blinked at her several times, slowly. Then he ran after his companion.

Elena's face was wet. She stumbled away from the empty cradle toward the door.

"You wander a cemetery looking for salvation. Yet nothing exists here beyond invisible bones," Romanov said. He stopped her at the door with two large hands on her upper arms. He held her at arm's length and looked down into her eyes.

"Is the alpha wolf gone? Is that what you're not telling me?" Elena asked. She searched his gaze, but her flashlight was pointed at the hallway and they were left in cold shadows.

"You'll never find him," Romanov replied. "He isn't gone, but he's buried. That's all you need to know."

He was wrong. She needed to know much more. She needed to understand. She'd been compelled to come here, but she was confused by all she'd found. Elena pulled away from her reluctant host. Romanov was a mystery, but she understood one thing: Grigori was coming. He was ten times as dangerous as Lev.

"Then I'm cursed, as well," she said. "Lost like all the people of Bronwal. Without the alpha wolf, I'll die."

He didn't go in search of his brother. Lev would have run far from the castle to try to escape the grief he wasn't able to leave behind as easily as he'd left his human form. His memories might be muddled. So hazy that he'd followed Elena as Ivan had ordered without knowing he would step into a room that would penetrate the senses of the beast he'd allowed himself to become.

It must have been like losing Madeline and Trevor all over again.

He hadn't thought that far ahead when he'd ordered the wolves to trail after the woman he had to avoid himself. There were portions of Bronwal he refused to visit even though he didn't allow himself the luxury of retreating into wolf form. Near immortality was a heavy weight to bear. He couldn't blame Lev for running away. Not now. And not when he'd given up his human form for good.

Elena didn't understand the forces she tampered with or the simmering pain she threatened to unleash. He clenched his fists against hundreds of years of love and loss. He stiffened his spine against the weight of it. Lev would recover. The farther he ran, focusing on the churning of his powerful legs in the snow, the better he would be able to fully become the white wolf again. He would forget. Ivan didn't have that luxury. He could only endure.

Perhaps Lev's pain would at least serve a purpose.

Elena had been terrified. It had been a fresh hell to see her in danger and frightened. When Soren had come to his rooms to find him, he'd understood his brother's unspoken urgency. But he hadn't expected to find Elena in such dire circumstances after the red wolf had led him to her. Lev might have killed her without completely understanding what he'd done. Ivan had interrupted just in time.

He'd warned her that the castle wasn't a safe place. Now she'd seen for herself. He should be glad.

Instead, it was torment to recall the fear in her eyes.

In his wolf form, he was much bigger than his brothers and much more savage. He was the eldest brother and the leader of their enchanted pack. And the black wolf was so close to the surface of his skin this Cycle that its ferocity was a part of him even when he walked on two legs. He hadn't needed to assume wolf form to defeat Dominique. He'd done it with human hands.

Lev wasn't the only danger to the determined dancer.

Bronwal was no haven for Elena. It was a monster's lair.

Lev had terrified Elena, but her fear was nothing compared to Ivan's horror as he'd seen the white wolf stalk the woman he'd kissed hours before. The scene had seemed like a premonition of what might occur if he gave in to the alpha wolf clawing its way out of his heart.

But it had also been a revelation.

Whether she knew it or not, she'd held the flashlight in the exact same way that his brother's wife, Madeline, had held the ruby sword in the tapestry on the wall behind her. Elena had been frightened, but she'd also been magnificent. In her simple modern clothes, she'd seemed as much of a warrior in her own way.

He cursed the fickle universe that would bring him a potential mate now, when he was doomed and disgraced. The sapphire might flare for her. The Romanov blade might come to her hand. She might be a warrior at heart, all determination and perseverance and steadfast resilience, but the time when he might have gloried in discovering her was long, long past.

He would never bind her to his horrible fate.

The Light *Volkhvy* had chosen the Romanovs as champions. They had gifted the Romanov sons with the ability to shift into supernatural wolves that could stand against the dark. And they had crafted the swords to aid in the fight. Lev's wife had claimed Lev's sword before she had claimed his heart. She'd fought by his side from the first day they'd met, and it had been obvious the sword had chosen her as its mistress.

But he couldn't allow the sapphire blade to choose Elena Pavlova.

Chapter 7

On the way back to the tower, Elena was puzzling over the tapestry when she ran into Bell. The young servant was struggling to pull a trunk up a flight of stairs. Her burden was bigger than she was, and Elena paused to watch as the other woman doggedly refused to give up. Her lack of makeup and her size had caused Elena to misjudge her age the first time they'd met. This time, Elena could see that she was curvier than she'd appeared while she'd been carrying water. She probably wasn't much younger than Elena herself, and that wasn't even taking the curse into account.

A shock shivered down Elena's spine when she acknowledged that the young woman might look eighteen or nineteen years old, but she'd been born centuries ago.

Bell paused and stood against the trunk so it wouldn't slide backward. She used her weight to hold it while she straightened to stretch her back. Elena wasn't sure how many more flights she had to tackle, but she was only halfway up this one and the brown curls on her forehead were damp with sweat from her exertions.

"I can help," Elena offered. She was sorry she spoke without clearing her throat when the other woman dropped down in a defensive crouch as if she braced against an attack. The move allowed the trunk to slide back one jarring step with a loud boom that echoed off the stone walls of the stairway.

"I'm sorry," she apologized as she stepped forward to place her weight against the trunk too. "I didn't mean to startle you."

"Can never be too careful in Bronwal. Not now. You never know if someone Ether-addled or worse is going to come at you without really seeing who they're attacking," Bell said.

"Someone or some *wolf*," Elena agreed.

"There's only one wolf you have to worry about at the moment. Soren would never hurt you," Bell said.

"You don't worry about the black wolf?" Elena asked.

Bell had leaned to pick up the end of the trunk she'd been tugging before, but this time Elena leaned to pick up the handle on the other side. They hoisted together and, even though it was heavy, they were able to climb up the stairs without much trouble.

They were both stronger than they seemed.

"I worry about everyone and everything in Bronwal. It would be a mistake to lower my guard. But the red wolf is usually not far when bad things happen. He keeps an eye on those of us left behind," Bell said.

"Isn't the black wolf a guardian too?" Elena asked. She

followed Bell's lead from the top of the staircase down a short hall and up another flight of stairs.

"Romanov is our guardian," the other woman said. She acted as if she'd answered Elena's question even though she hadn't. Where was the black wolf? Had it disappeared into the Ether or was it wandering around the mountain like Lev, Ether-addled and dangerous?

After several more flights of stairs that left even Elena winded, they came out of a narrow door and onto the ramparts of the castle. Bell was probably used to the view, but she paused to take in the endless stretch of craggy mountains anyway. They must be too spectacular to ever become commonplace and maybe she missed them when she was in the Ether. Enough to need to soak in the view when she could.

"The Mountains of the Sunset…you need to come up one evening to see the colors. I never tire of it when we're materialized," Bell said. She really was surprisingly pretty. Her hat shadowed her face and hid her good looks until her bowed lips and dimple flashed when you least expected it. "That's why I've made my room up here. And because no one wanders up this high. Romanov was right when he said you should stay in your tower. To survive, we have to be careful, all the time."

Bell tugged on her handle to show Elena which way she wanted to go. They wound around the main body of the castle on a walled walk with openings that allowed a person to see for miles. Elena supposed the openings had once been intended for guards to keep watch. Now, she took advantage of them to gauge the weather on mountains as they walked.

No snow fell. The sky was clear.

Finally, when her arms seemed like they would scream

in protest, they came to an abandoned aviary. The stone structure was circular with a high, domed roof made of copper. The scrolled iron cage that had once surrounded the aviary on one side was in rusty disrepair, but the mews was intact. Someone had lifted the top fastening window shutters and propped them open so that they fanned out all around the aviary. There were no birds inside to keep contained. Instead of birds, the floor had been swept and mopped clean and covered with colorful rugs. There was a bed and several chairs, as well as shelves full of books. There were other bits and baubles that shone or sparkled throughout the room so that Elena revised her opinion.

There was one bird who inhabited the aviary—a cheerful magpie just over five feet tall.

"Thank you for your help. It's been a while since anyone has lent me a helping hand," Bell said.

Elena was glad to set her side of the trunk down when Bell indicated the spot where she wanted it placed at the foot of the bed.

That's when she turned and noticed the russet fur that covered one of the rugs near the door. Did Soren keep vigil between the door and the bed when Bell was sleeping?

"But not so long since someone lent a helping paw?" she asked. She leaned over to pick up a strand of red hair and lifted it to show the other woman.

"I don't sleep a lot while we're materialized. I hate to waste a minute. But needs must, and sometimes I can't help myself. Once, last Cycle, a Dark *Volkhvy* found me here in my aviary. They're always a danger, but they usually confront Romanov. I don't know how or why one came for me. But Soren intervened," she said. "He saved me."

She opened the trunk while she spoke. Nestled inside was a jumble of clothes and possessions. Elena noticed that the clothing was meant for a man. No doubt more practical than some of the clothes made for women when the people of Bronwal were born.

And Bell did seem to favor practical clothes. Her boy's hat was always placed firmly on her head.

"He seems to do that a lot," Elena said. "He fetched Romanov and saved me from a very angry Lev a half an hour ago."

Bell dropped the lid of the trunk and straightened.

"Was Soren okay? I worry sometimes that Lev will turn on him. He's so far gone," Bell said.

"He was fine. The last I saw of him he was chasing after Lev and he didn't seem frightened," Elena said. "You grew up with them?" she asked. She already knew the answer. Bell was younger than Elena but not by much in actual physical years, although the curse had doomed her to "live" much longer.

"I came to Bronwal when I was a baby. I've never known any other home. But I wasn't always a servant. That happened after the curse, when more and more servants disappeared," Bell said. "I was put to work and I didn't mind. Not when the Romanovs had taken me in and given me a safe place to live."

"What happened to your parents?" Elena asked.

"They were killed in one of the last battles between the Romanovs and the Dark *Volkhvy.* I don't remember them. Sovkra was the mountain village where I was born. It was decimated. Vladimir Romanov found me in a field of burning bellflowers. He carried me out of the village as a wolf would carry a pup."

"And he brought you home," Elena said.

"Yes. The nanny and servants who cared for his children raised me. They all called me 'Bell' because of the scorched flowers I clutched in my hands when the gray wolf lifted me from the flames. I was clothed and fed and basically allowed to run wild until I had to take up the tasks of running the castle myself," Bell said.

"If Vladimir had taken you elsewhere, you wouldn't have been caught up in the curse," Elena said. Bell had been an innocent babe rescued by the Romanovs when she'd been orphaned.

"I wouldn't change a thing if I could go back and if I had that power. This is my home. These are my people," Bell said. She stood tall and squared her shoulders. In spite of their serious conversation she still had a hint of a sparkle in her eyes. It might be moisture. It might be determination. Elena couldn't be sure. "One day the curse will be lifted and the Romanov brothers will be free. I won't lose myself before that. I want to be here to see…their faces."

Elena had the feeling there was a particular face that Bell might be pining for, but she shied away from further questions. There was no way to know if Ivan Romanov's brothers would return from the Ether where they had disappeared, but she had too many of her own foolish hopes to dash Bell's.

"I'd better go and find Soren," Bell said.

Elena took one last look at the view. It was a fairy-tale setting, but this was a dark, dark tale indeed, especially now. The snow that had bought her time to search for the black wolf had stopped falling.

* * *

Her book was tucked in the backpack she'd left in her room. The familiar object came into her hands as if her fingers were made to flip its pages. She'd looked through it so many times. It had been an escape from the dance when she'd thought it was a fantasy world. Later, after her mother's death, it had been a comfort. Then, later still, once Grigori revealed himself and his plans, it had been hope. But she hadn't turned to the book for comfort or hope this time.

The binding fell open to her favorite illustrations: one of the castle. One of three Romanov wolves running through a wintry wood. One of Vladimir. She paused on the illustration of Ivan's father. She traced the square angle of his jaw and the sharp line of his nose. So very like his eldest son's.

Ivan Romanov and his brothers weren't pictured. His mother was only shown on horseback with indistinct features. As she looked closely at each intricately crafted three-dimensional image that rose from every page, she scanned for something she'd never noticed—swords with enchanted gems on their hilts. The artist had created a complex world completely out of paper. The movement of the pages caused the paper to fold up and out and each image was seen as a silhouette against a backdrop of shadowy black.

There were battle scenes. There were many ordinary blades. None with the jeweled hilt she was looking for, but she thought to scan the vines and flowers, the skies and borders and all the other places in the book that had become so familiar to her that she barely noticed the details they contained.

That's how she found the sword from the tapestry. Its

ruby was unmistakable once her eyes and tracing finger separated it from the leaves of the great oak in which it was hidden. After that, she redoubled her efforts to find Ivan Romanov's sapphire blade, but it eluded her notice. Page after page held birds and roses and scrolling designs, but no Romanov blade. Until finally she found another sword. This one was hidden in the twining briars of a wild rose that climbed the side of the castle's wall. Except the gem in its hilt winked with an emerald sheen.

She'd held the sapphire hilt in her own two hands. She knew she would find its like in the book. She'd seen the ruby sword in the tapestry. Now she knew there had been at least three Romanov blades. One for each brother?

But it hadn't been Romanov's brother wielding the sword in the tapestry. Who then? The missing brother, the abandoned room, the empty cradle… Elena closed the book before she'd found the sapphire sword. Her throat was tight and her eyes burned. The warrior woman in the tapestry had seemed so at home with the sword in her hand. Had she been married to one of Vladimir Romanov's sons?

She'd never known her favorite childhood story was a tragedy. She wondered which brother in the portrait she'd seen had disappeared with his entire family into the Ether. Had they all gone at the same time or had some or one been left behind?

There was so much she didn't understand. She didn't know if she'd have time to delve as deeply as she needed to into the past and the facts behind the legend in order to summon the alpha wolf. It was all much more complicated than she'd expected. She'd wondered if the legend would prove to be true. She'd never expected to have to search for a reluctant champion once she found Bronwal.

It was late. Most of the distant sounds in the castle had quieted to murmurs and indistinct scrapes and sighs. Bronwal never slept. But it did experience lulls in activity. Elena's stomach had growled for the hundredth time. Her encounter with the white wolf hadn't faded in her mind, but her hunger couldn't be ignored any longer. No one had brought food to the tower, and her energy bars were running out. She was forced to abandon the book and go looking for a kitchen.

This time she bumped into several servants on her way down to lower floors in the castle. Each time they barely acknowledged her presence. Each time she was struck by their eclectic manner of dress. There were many different periods represented, as if coming and going from the Ether was a kind of time travel. Often they were disheveled and threadbare, as if they didn't have the cognizance necessary to take care of simple matters of hygiene and personal appearance.

One man tried to stop her. He grabbed her arm and yelled nonsense questions in her face. His bloodshot eyes rolled around in their sockets and his clothes were nothing but rags that hung on his emaciated body.

"I'm sorry. I don't understand. I can't help you," Elena said. She pulled away with all her strength and the man fell sobbing to the floor. She backed away as she finally recognized some of the syllables he was rolling together.

"Mywifemywifemywifemywife."

She had to leave him. There was nothing she could do. She couldn't break the curse or end his suffering. The inhabitants of Bronwal were wanderers. Drifting in and out of existence every ten years. Her heart beat rabidly in her chest as she continued down more flights of stairs. She noted many others she passed had similar wild eyes and uncoordinated, shuffling steps. For the first time, she wondered if Romanov had ordered Lev and Soren to follow her as guardians rather than spies. Alone, she encountered many more of Bronwal's mad inhabitants. Now that she didn't have the wolves' protection, how would she ever find the alpha wolf when she had to dodge the angry white wolf and navigate crowds of desperate, zombie-like people?

This was Ivan Romanov's world. How had he managed to stay sane for so long?

And what of the alpha wolf? The curse affected the people of Bronwal, but now she'd discovered that it affected the wolves, as well. The white wolf's statue was smaller and less powerful than the black wolf. The alpha was larger in her book's illustrations too. If she found him, he might be more savage toward her than Lev.

When she reached the lower levels, the smell of freshly baked bread filled the air. It was a welcome change to dust and unwashed bodies. She hurried forward, propelled as much by her stomach as by the need for cheer, any cheer, especially the kind found in a warm kitchen on a cold night.

She didn't expect to find Ivan Romanov leaning on a scarred wooden table where Patrice worked. The older woman's arms were up to her elbows in dough.

"I thought you might make your way down here," he said as Elena hurried into the room only to stop dead in her tracks.

Unlike the rest of the castle, the kitchen wasn't deserted. There was a fire in the large hearth, and the ovens built into the stone on either side of it were filled with baking loaves. Besides Patrice and Romanov, there were several other servants bustling around. Elena recognized some of them as people who had carried bathwater to the tower her first night. Several were busily sweeping up the flour that Patrice didn't seem to notice she'd dusted all over the floor.

"Nothing like the smell of breakfast to get you out of bed," Patrice said. It was well past noon. Breakfast would have been hours before if Bronwal kept to a regular schedule. Elena had eaten nothing but protein bars since the light meal she'd bought in Cerna after her long journey south from Saint Petersburg to Romania. Her stomach gurgled audibly and Romanov straightened. He motioned her forward to a stool beside him. In front of it was a plate filled with freshly sliced bread. Near that was a stone crock of pale yellow butter and a wheel of fragrant cheese.

"The kitchen is the last living place in Bronwal. You can always be sure of finding someone here," Romanov said.

Why would he offer her comfort if he was determined she should go away?

She'd sworn to keep her distance from her host, but Elena couldn't resist the bread or the warmth of the fire. She tried to tell herself there was nothing else drawing her near him. Her hands were like ice from the chilled corridors and stairways. She stepped forward and perched on the stool. The scent of the bread and cheese caused her to nearly swoon, and her mouth watered as she used a knife to dip up and spread the thick, churned butter. It flaked in rich chunks beneath the knife's blade, as only real butter would do.

"I was going to bring you a tray," Patrice mumbled as she continued to knead and roll and punch the springy dough.

"Actually, I was," Romanov said.

He reached for a piece of bread from her plate and lifted it to his mouth. He took a bite as she bit into the piece she'd buttered. They both chewed slowly. As the butter and bread dissolved in Elena's mouth, she was light-headed with relief. Better that she'd come to the crowded kitchen than to have Romanov come to her room alone. But her relief was short-lived because a smudge of butter from the bread had smeared on Romanov's lower lip. Her mouth went dry and she couldn't tear her focus away. She watched the butter as he chewed. She stared, transfixed, as he swallowed and licked his lips clean. His enjoyment of the fresh bread was evident. His pleasure caused her to tighten and tingle, then liquefy in places best ignored in his presence. She had to force herself to swallow past the sudden paralysis in her jaw and throat as tingling desire rose up, refusing to be ignored.

It was torture to be physically attracted to the man who was standing in the way of her desperate goal. She'd never allowed sensual distractions in her life, even when her situation hadn't been life or death. But the chemistry that assailed her whenever she was around Romanov didn't ask for permission. In fact, it seemed to be heightened by her desperation.

How could he ignore her predicament when he obviously couldn't ignore her?

His large body leaned against the tall table closer to her than it had been before. She was certain he had imperceptibly shifted while she'd been focused on his lips. When she forced her gaze up from his mouth to meet his eyes, his intensity caused her breath to catch. His eyelids lazily hooded the gleam of his irises, but his interest was anything but lazy. Although his posture was relaxed, his body was taut. He radiated a heat that competed with the oven. He was gauging her reactions. He was tuned in to her response. He'd noticed her quickened breath and her focus on the mere flick of his tongue. And judging from the intensity of his interest he liked the way she had instantly kindled from such a simple, innocent move.

The liquid in her belly and lower seemed to bubble in response. She'd been famished for food, but now she was hungry for whatever his dark green eyes seemed to promise as they looked into hers.

"You say you want me to go away before the *Volkhvy* Gathering, but then you offer me warmth and comfort. The snow is piled high outside, but it's no longer falling," Elena said. She couldn't indulge the heat between them with flirtation or niceties. She needed his help to find the alpha wolf. She didn't need this desire that flared between them. Kisses wouldn't save her, even though her body lied and tried to tell her they would.

"We move toward oblivion with every passing second," Romanov said. "I can offer you a meal before you have to leave." He didn't back away. In fact, he reached to toy with strands of hair that had fallen free of the messy bun she had hastily created with her heavy blond waves before coming downstairs. Again, it seemed as if he tortured himself. His body was tense. Did he want to plunge his fingers into her hair and pull her into his arms? His powerful hand shook. *He would rather devour than toy.* That thought did nothing to help her ignore the heat that had radiated out from her bubbling stomach to claim her entire body. His hand might shake, but its trembles were contagious. Her whole being quaked. Her breath came quick through dry lips. And she held herself back with only the most determined control.

"Your oblivion will not save me. I have to stay here and fight. There's no escape but the one I make," Elena said. "I can't run away. Ultimately Grigori is going to find me. I need the alpha to fight by my side."

"And what if the alpha devours you instead? What then?" Romanov asked.

Suddenly, the kitchen was quiet. All the servants had disappeared. The only movement was the flickering flames in the fireplace and abandoned dough rising on the table beside them. And the rise and fall of their chests as they both breathed in and out. Hers was rapid. His was slow and deliberate. She watched as his broad chest expanded and then fell as air exhaled through his lips. Was it a calming meditation? Or was he inhaling the mint fragrance he released as he continued to gently play with her hair?

The slight movement of his hand turned out to have purpose and consequences. Her hasty bun was loosened. Little by little, he freed her hair from its confinement until it tumbled down over her shoulders. She watched him as the waves came free. His eyes darkened. His lids lowered. And she still kept herself still beneath his touch. Even when he slowly threaded his fingers into the loosened waves to cup the side of her head, she didn't move beyond her shaky breaths and her trembling body.

"You ask for more than it's in my power to give you. I can't control the alpha wolf. I can't call him to fight by your side. I can only hold Bronwal. Do you understand? This place and all its people. Their ultimate fate is my responsibility," Romanov said. But his hand tightened so that he held her even as he spoke of holding his people's cursed universe on his shoulders, alone.

"Then I have to hope the alpha wolf will choose to help

me of his own accord. Without your call. Without your permission. Lev wanted to tear me apart for disturbing the baby's room. But Soren ran for help. He could have looked away. He could have left me to die. He didn't. There's a champion deep inside of him still. I have to believe the alpha wolf will be the same," Elena said.

"The alpha hasn't been a champion in a very long time. He's nothing but an abandoned savage. I'm afraid he'll turn his savagery on the world if he's called. And, unlike Lev, there's no one stronger to remind him of what he used to be," Romanov said.

Elena's spine stiffened. She drew her body back from the man who heated her bones and chilled her heart. Surprisingly, in spite of his tension and his powerful grip, he eased his fingers to let her go. She left the stool to step back from the table and from Romanov's heat. Her leg hurt. Her body was exhausted from lack of sleep and from her battle with the elements. But she wasn't weak. She never had been. Not even in her nightmares when she was reduced to frantic, fluttering wings.

"I'm small, but I'm stronger than you know. *I* will remind him," Elena said.

Romanov's hand had fallen to his side. He flexed his fingers open and closed as if he couldn't quite believe he'd let her go.

"The alpha could easily crush you with only one bite," Romanov said. "He's an enchanted monster driven nearly mad by a relentless curse." He stepped after her suddenly, and she was too startled to back away. He reached for her again before she could widen the gap between them. His body was only inches away. His hands clasped her shoulders and pulled her even closer, until their bodies touched in a full-length press that shocked every cell from her head to her toes. "You fear being captured by the witchblood prince, but you should fear death."

"You endure a fate worse than death. And yet it isn't the Ether that you fear. It's the materialization. What new loss will each one bring? Loved ones? Your own faculties? The idea that the Dark *Volkhvy* will claim what you've defended all this time. I don't fear the alpha wolf's teeth because my future with Grigori will eat away at me little by little. I prefer death to that."

Romanov's chin rose as if he'd been slapped by her words. But he didn't let her go. If anything, his hands tightened on her shoulders. Her breathing was shallow and quick, yet his scent enveloped her along with his heat. He'd been in the kitchen long enough that the scent of fresh baked bread clung to his skin, but it was the scent of the mountain that rose from his hair. It was a wild and snowy scent with the slightest hint of evergreen.

"You're wrong. It's the freedom of oblivion that I most fear. Because its call is more seductive than any I've ever experienced," he said. "Until now."

She wasn't prepared for his hands to slide from her shoulders to her back. Instinctively, she raised her hands to brace against his chest, but somehow she ended up with fistfuls of his faded linen shirt in her hands. Its lacings hung loosened and open at the neck, and when he pulled her closer she ended up staring at the pulse that throbbed at the base of his throat.

The heat of the fire was nothing compared to the heat that radiated from his body to hers. His hands burned on the small of her back and when he spread his fingers to actually hold her waist, the burn traveled to all her intimate places. Suddenly, Grigori was the last thing on her mind. Her nightmares were replaced by fantasies.

If she kissed the pulse of his jugular, it would be a mistake, but it would be one she chose to make.

The thought was all she needed to urge her forward. She went up on her toes. She leaned. She captured his hot, salty skin between her lips. She meant the taste to be a slight indulgence, an exercise in free will. But his fierce groan, the jerk of his entire body in response and the sudden desperate clasp of his hands caused her to open her mouth to taste him more fully and bathe his pounding pulse with a flick of her tongue.

"My God, Elena," Romanov said. His hands rose from her waist to her face, but he didn't push her away. He pressed her closer, groaning as she responded with a nip of her teeth and suction. His skin was so hot. His pulse so strong. His passionate sounds rumbled deep in his chest and vibrated against her breasts. He was wild winter wilderness, but he melted for her. He stood alone, but she held him and pleasured him and he wasn't alone anymore.

"You don't want to die. You want to live," Elena murmured against his throat.

"I crave respite," Romanov countered. His hands stopped her kisses, but he didn't push her far away. With the slightest pressure of his palms on each side of her head, he only made enough distance between them so that he could look down at her face. She opened her eyes. Her body was languid with desire. It pulsed in time with the heartbeat she'd tasted.

"That's not what you crave," Elena said. "You don't want to disappear into the Ether. You want to feel again. You want to connect."

"How can I resist? You awaken me. You refuse to keep the door locked against me," Romanov said.

"I won't be caged. I'd rather face my fears than hide from them," she replied.

"Then you admit you fear me?" he asked. His whole body stilled as if he braced for her answer.

"I think you want me to fear you. If I'm afraid, if I run away, then you can be as numb as you have to be to stay standing," Elena said. "But it isn't only my kisses that wake you. It's my cause."

"I have all the cause I'll ever need to stay standing, Elena Pavlova. I stand for my family. Not the Light *Volkhvy*. I don't stand against the Dark. I stand against the Ether that has eaten everyone I've ever loved," Romanov said. It was a hoarse confession. One that burned her eyes. "I'm not a champion. I'm a survivor. And there's a hungry wolf at my door. I fear him. As should you."

She drew in a startled breath when he swooped to claim her mouth, but her breath wasn't deep or long enough to keep her from going light-headed when his lips pressed against hers. This time he chose to kiss her. Not to relieve the torture but to intensify it. He groaned as his tongue found hers and the vibration traveled with velvet licks to the V between her legs.

Elena let go of his shirt and slid her arms up, way up, and around his neck. She appreciated his height and breadth even as she held on for dear life. Her head was light. Her knees soft. But his body was solid and hard against her. There was no interruption this time. He explored the depths of her mouth fully with practiced ease that nevertheless caused his body to shudder against hers with the pleasure he found.

His lips were gentle and sensual even though they were firm, moving hungrily to devour her every gasp. His tongue was flavored with honey and wine. The stubble on his cheek and jaw was pleasantly rough against her skin.

He held her face in place for his kiss for a long time, but when he dropped his hands to lift her shirt and find her skin she cried out into his mouth at the heightened sensation of his warrior's calloused fingers on her bare midriff.

Her cries caused him to pause, but only for a second, as if he caught himself waiting for her permission or denial, and then pressed on. She whimpered when his fingers dipped into the waistband of her pants and this time he didn't slow or stop. He jerked her forward and she found herself straddling his bent knee. He pressed her against his leg and she whimpered again because the pleasurable pressure and friction took her by surprise.

She rocked her hips to increase it and he groaned, but he also helped her move with his powerful hands cupped around her bottom. The thrusting of his tongue matched the rhythm of her hips and she felt the rise of his erection beneath his leather pants against her right thigh.

He called out her name when she reached for him to press and measure and pet the hard length of him through the leather. His heat and size and obvious pleasure caused her to rock harder against the leg she rode, and suddenly his head fell back and their lips parted. She looked down at his face and realized he had lifted her up and braced his hips against the table until she was above him.

Romanov's eyes were slits. His lips were swollen. His hair was a wild tumble around her face and shoulders. He looked passionate, disheveled and very touched. She continued to rub his hard shaft and move her hips and he watched her face as the ultimate pleasure finally claimed her. She cried out as she came. Her legs clenched around his muscular thigh. And his hands tightened on her, pulling her as close as she could get against him as she pulsed with the orgasm achieved while they were both still clothed and standing in the kitchen.

She collapsed against his broad chest and he held her there, not speaking, as time passed. The fire crackled. The dough hardened, neglected and forgotten. Distant sounds finally penetrated her consciousness once more.

"A long time ago I feared losing dance because it was all I had. I didn't know what else I would do once I couldn't dance anymore. But now I only fear Grigori. Because I'll find my way given the chance. My purpose is in me. I only have to remain free to find it," Elena said softly. While she spoke, she thought about the resolve in the woman's face on the tapestry. Her expression echoed an untapped feeling in Elena's heart. Something called to her. The discipline and dedication she'd learned in service to dance had only been preparation. There was something beckoning to her on the horizon that nearly overshadowed the dread of Grigori that permeated her past.

"Where is the sapphire sword and how do you protect it when it's not with you?" she asked. She also wondered what had become of the ruby and emerald swords, but she didn't want to talk about the loved ones he'd lost.

Romanov straightened and placed her limp body on the stool nearby. Even with the fire, she felt chilled as he moved away. This had been another mistake she would make all over again if she had the chance. But she was fairly certain Romanov wouldn't. His brow was furrowed and his fists had clenched as soon as he'd placed her to the side.

"If you call the black wolf, you'll face something darker and hungrier than your witchblood prince." Romanov stood several feet away from her. He ignored her question about the sapphire sword. He looked tall and powerful even in a simple linen shirt that had come partially undone and scuffed leather pants. He wore no armor or furs now. He wasn't armed. His strength was all in his honed muscles and large frame. Still, the determined set to his jaw and the planted placement of his riding boots would cause his stance to be intimidating to any adversary. Yet as he spoke of the wolf, his eyes were haunted, shadowed by real trepidation.

His concern was contagious. Elena's heartbeat quickened and her post-orgasm languor fled. Her body stiffened and she rose from the stool to face him.

"I'm not afraid of the dark," she said.

It was true. She wasn't afraid of darkness. Only of being trapped. Only of having her free will taken away.

But she wasn't blind. She could see that Romanov was genuinely afraid for her, and that knowledge caused gooseflesh to rise on her skin.

"Is there no chance, then, that the alpha wolf will choose to help me rather than hurt me?" she asked.

"He may have no choice. Like Lev, he may have been driven mad by his time in the Ether. He might no longer be a rational creature. He was always a beast that was almost impossible to control," Romanov said. She watched his fists clench and unclench as he spoke. With his mussed hair and fire-lit eyes, he looked nearly mad himself.

But his lips were still swollen from her kisses and her mouth still tingled pleasantly with remembered sensation of the passion they'd shared.

"You don't want me to summon the black wolf, but there are other reasons you want me to stay in the tower,"

Elena said. She stepped lightly toward him. He didn't back away. Because there was nowhere to go or because he secretly wanted her closer? Liked her closer? Would take her as close as possible if her quest for the wolf wasn't standing in their way?

"Every day you spend in Bronwal is potentially deadly. You court disaster every time you leave the tower," Romanov said.

"Do I court disaster by leaving the tower or by searching for the alpha wolf and finding you instead?" Elena said. She knew the answer. They had kissed. She'd experienced an earth-shattering orgasm. And yet there was so much more that could happen between them. It would be a disaster to allow the attraction between them to take them where it wanted to go. But she would choose to follow it if she could because it would be a glorious disaster she had chosen for herself after years of following a course set by others.

She'd narrowed the gap between them. He could have turned away to leave the room. He hadn't. He had watched and waited as she approached. His eyes were bright and his wild hair made her fingers twitch. But he was also simmering with a rising emotion that tasted like anger in the air. There were clouds darkening his expression, and his body appeared so tense and tight that his tendons might snap if he deigned to move an inch.

Elena, the deceptively delicate swan who was made of mercilessly trained muscle and bone rather than feathers, continued bravely until her toes stopped inches from his. She tilted her chin to meet his thunderous gaze.

"I'm lost. I can't be found," Romanov said. "You think you have found me instead of the wolf you seek, but you've found nothing. No one. A castle full of ghosts."

"It wasn't a ghost that pleasured my body moments ago," Elena said. She didn't reach for him. She wouldn't force herself on him. But there was more to his resistance than fear for her safety. He protected Bronwal, but he also protected himself. He'd lost too much to care again.

Her body trembled at his nearness. She vibrated with need. His body must do the same. That's why he held himself so still and tight. Because the pull between them was elemental and fierce.

"We're snowed in. Trapped together. But the *Volkhvy* Gathering comes closer every day," Romanov said.

"I will find the alpha wolf before the Gathering," Elena warned him. "And I will either be devoured or I will gain his trust."

"Trust moldered to dust in this place many years ago," Romanov replied. "Lev and Soren guard the last blade. They will sound the alarm if Dark *Volkhvy* appear. The other blades disappeared into the Ether and never returned. It's best you forget they ever existed. In time, the sapphire blade will disappear, as well."

Romanov finally broke away from the invisible magnetism that seemed to hold them together. He walked around her to the counter, picked up the remainder of a loaf of bread, then strode out the door without another word. Elena more slowly and thoughtfully followed suit. The bread was cooled, but still delicious, and she needed to keep herself fueled.

Imaging the sapphire blade winking out of existence caused her insides to hollow in spite of the bread she consumed. She wasn't sure why. But she had an instinct that the blade must remain in Bronwal in order for Romanov to survive. The blade was a part of the puzzle here. One she was determined to solve. One she was compelled to solve the same way she'd been compelled by the legends from the time she'd first heard her grandmother's tales.

Maybe the blade could help her against Grigori whether or not she was able to summon the alpha wolf.

Lev and Soren guard the last blade.

The last bite of bread she chewed was hard to swallow past the sudden lump of fear that closed her throat. She would have to face the red wolf…and the white in order to approach the sapphire sword again. And she wouldn't be able to stay away. Suddenly, she was certain that all her questions would be answered if she could hold the sapphire sword one more time.

For the few seconds she'd held the blade in her hands, she'd felt something in the cool wash of adrenaline that had flooded her veins. She'd heard something in her pounding heart. Then she'd fallen backward and the blade had slipped from her fingers and the feeling was gone.

But the memory of it remained.

And she'd seen the echo of it in the eyes of the woman on the tapestry in the baby's room.

He had failed to resist their connection. In fact, he'd done the opposite. He'd gloried in her passion. He'd soaked up every noise, every reaction—from the salty perspiration on her upper lip to the powerful thrust of her petite hips. He'd helped her achieve a shuddering climax, and the surprisingly supple bottom he'd kneaded while she clenched and came had almost sent him over the edge himself. Not to mention the heat of her against his leg and the curiosity of her fingers as she'd measured him through his pants.

It had been heaven and hell.

Heaven because her taste and touch had enflamed him

faster and hotter than anyone before. Hell because he'd wanted to tear off her clothes and taste more than her lips. He'd wanted to feel her heat intimately with nothing in the way. He still did. His imagination had been given more fuel to work with and it had already been torturing him, day and night.

He was hard and ready. His mind filled with images of her spread beneath him. She would open. She would be slick with passion. She'd already shown him her hunger. He wanted to stoke her pleasure higher than he'd been able to with only the pressure of his thigh. He wanted to play her with his hand. He wanted to lick and tease until she begged him to join with her.

He'd watched her orgasm, but he'd never seen her bare breasts.

With her blond hair, blue eyes and porcelain skin, he could picture rosy nipples to match her rosy lips. He ached to see and suckle them. He was in a frenzy to explore for other rosy treasures, as well.

He went for the practice field. There was nothing else he could do.

Nothing short of a full-on shift would scare her in the face of her determination, but how could he loose the wolf when what he wanted most was to be a man in her arms? How could he purposefully frighten a woman who was obviously drawn to the sapphire blade?

Because, in the end, he would have no choice. She had to leave for the good of Bronwal and for her own good. He couldn't allow her to bond with the blade. He'd have to risk a shift to scare her away. She thought she wanted to find the black wolf, but once she saw him she would change her mind.

The enchanted monster inside of his soul howled with

glee at the idea of freedom. He hadn't run beneath the light of the moon on four massive paws in decades. Since long before he'd seen the last glimpse of Soren's human face. His desire for Elena wasn't helping. It only made him feel more desperate to make her leave before he lost control. If she didn't want him in return, he could more easily ignore his need to claim her. But her obvious hunger for his touch shook him to the core.

Only he could guarantee that she made the right decision. She couldn't be allowed near the sword again. Of that, he was certain. Beyond that, if marauding *Volkhvy* and Lev weren't enough to force her away, he would have to take matters into his own hands.

Elena had come to Bronwal to seek help from the alpha wolf. But it was the alpha howling inside of his chest that had to frighten her away.

Chapter 8

Elena knew it was crazy. She should make sure to stay as far away from Lev as possible. It was madness to go looking for the red and white wolves in order to find the sapphire sword. The power in the gem wasn't hers to tap. It would probably be no more useful than an ordinary blade against Grigori. But even though logic told her it was silly to seek out the sword, her heart told her otherwise. When she'd been in the courtyard with the blade, she'd felt as if she'd found everything she'd been looking for, even though the black wolf hadn't been there.

She still hoped to find the alpha wolf. She hoped he would become her champion against the Dark *Volkhvy* who stalked her. But she couldn't stop thinking about the woman in the tapestry. She'd held the ruby sword as if she needed no other champion but herself.

It was only an hour before sunset. The castle was darkening by the second. She wasn't sure where Romanov had gone after their time in the kitchen. She had let him walk away. His resistance made her passionate capitulation more embarrassing. She had held nothing back in her response to his touch. She had been decadent in the way she had ridden his powerful thigh to take her pleasure.

What was worse, she still wanted more.

The idea of his bare, hot skin between her naked legs caused her breath to hitch and her sensual abandon to seem like a permanent result of her time here in Bronwal. God, he was so powerful and he maintained such control. Even while she was crying out with release, he was watching and holding and helping her reach the peak. He had denied himself surcease. And it had tortured her because she wanted him to give in to the pleasure she could give him, as well.

Her imagination could well envision his powerful body completely naked and shuddering beneath her touch. She had tasted the skin of his neck. She wanted to taste more. She wanted to trace every inch of him with her tongue and watch as he lost all control.

For her.

But what frightened her most was that part of her desire was hinged on the idea of waking him and bringing him back to life. He so obviously didn't want to wake. He was determined to resist the attraction between them and she was bound for disappointment.

She'd gone back to her room for the daggers she'd taken from the practice field. They were tucked in the back pockets of her jeans. She couldn't imagine using them, but she would if she had to. Against the white wolf or against one of the shuffling souls in the dark hallways of the castle, if either tried to harm her. She would defend herself. Elena reached to reassure herself that the hilts were within easy reach again and again. The daggers reassured her, but they didn't call to her in the same way that the sapphire blade called.

More than her fight against Grigori had brought her here. Hadn't she always been fascinated with the Romanov legend? She'd begged for the stories again and again. She'd been obsessed with the book long before she'd known she was in danger.

The key to the tower room hung around the chain on her neck. There was a hideaway available to her. She could duck her head in the sand. She could lock herself away. But that would solve nothing. It would be a temporary redoubt. Nothing more. She had to move. She had to strive for answers.

She couldn't ignore the sword. It called to her with a subtle song. One of enchantment, but also one of discipline and determination. She came to the main hall where Romanov had first carried her. This time the massive fireplace was lit. Shadows danced on the walls cast by the leaping flames.

The woman in the tapestry had been a warrior, but Elena had recognized the expression on her face and the passion in her eyes. She'd had the face of a prima ballerina. Her own face carried that look. She'd seen it reflected in the other dancers in her troupe. What were they if not warriors? They were graceful, but hardened. They faced a battle against fatigue and weakness and age every day. They fought against every soft, human failing and mercilessly trained it away.

The white wolf rose to his feet when she came into the room. His movement drew her eyes from the shadows on the wall. The red wolf was there, as well. He was already standing. Beside him, the sapphire blade rested across the arms of a throne. A larger throne stood beside it. They were carved from some massive, dark wood streaked even darker with generations of soot. She hadn't noticed the thrones when the hall had been unlit by firelight before. They were in a raised, recessed alcove that had been black as midnight the evening she'd arrived. Now, the firelight revealed the sword and the thrones and painted them all with shifting darkness that highlighted rather than concealed.

The thrones were as empty as the rest of the castle. And yet they weren't abandoned. The wolves stood watch, and as Elena stepped cautiously forward the details carved into the wood of the thrones became clear: wolves. There were wolf heads carved on the arms of the larger chair and on the back of the smaller one. Three wolf carvings in all. Their mouths were open wide, and each tooth had been painstakingly crafted, along with each strand of hair in the pelts on their heads.

The red wolf and the white wolf watched her approach.

The sword was on the smaller throne. The wolf head carved on its back was the largest of the three. The alpha wolf watched over the smaller throne and the sword. Elena didn't know what that meant. The head wasn't carved as a lifeless trophy. It was snarling and vital. Ready to defend and protect?

"In wood the alpha wolf helps you protect the sword. Where is he in life? Surely he hasn't faded away," Elena said.

The red wolf moved when she spoke. The white wolf stood planted in place, but his haunches trembled. Soren paced in front of Lev. He put his body in between his white companion and Elena.

The problem was that both wolves were in between her and the Romanov blade.

Now that she'd seen it, she was even more certain that it had called her here. It wasn't the wolves that made her heart pound and a thrill like anticipation suffuse her skin. But she needed to hold the sapphire blade again to be sure. She needed to claim it. The tableau of empty thrones and waiting sword and protective wolves wasn't in her book of legends. Her grandmother had never mentioned the swords. Or the thrones. Yet Elena took another step forward. And then another.

This was a part of the legend she felt rather than re-membered.

Somehow this was her part, even though she was a modern woman visiting a castle kept separate from the passage of time. She was no mere visitor. She'd been called. And the call had begun many years ago when she was a young girl listening to stories on her grand-mother's knee.

"I'm here because I'm meant to be," she said. Her voice was soft but firm. It echoed in the cavernous room, but it wasn't swallowed or weakened. It was magnified. Lev whined and Soren blinked. Neither moved out of her way.

The daggers in her back pockets were there should she need them. She was pretty sure they wouldn't faze the giant wolves that protected the thrones. Even if she knew how to wield them.

"I came here for help, but I'm beginning to think that you're the ones who need my help instead. You're los-ing this battle. You've almost lost him. He's more than ready to fade away. It seems as if the alpha wolf is already gone," Elena said. "Let me have the sword. I won't take it away from Bronwal. I'll use it against Grigori. I'll use it to help you stand."

Soren listened to her every word. She was sure of it. He met her eyes. He blinked. And then he pressed back against the white wolf's trembling body. Lev allowed himself to be pushed out of the way. He stepped back, pace after measured pace, until she had a clear path to the sapphire blade.

"It isn't my imagination, is it? I need the sword. And you need me to have it," Elena said. "I've been distracted by my search for the black wolf. This is what I was meant to find all along."

She moved carefully closer to the thrones. She made no sudden gestures. She placed her feet softly on the floor. She kept her eyes on the sapphire. It winked darkly in the shadows of flames. Lev whined when she passed, but Soren stood, stalwart, in his white companion's way. Elena was terrified, but she didn't pause. It shouldn't be easy to claim the blade. This was a test for her to pass in order to prove she was worthy of wielding the enchanted sword.

She should have known that *Volkhvy* enchantments were more complicated than a human could understand. Slavic peasants had practiced simple hearth magic for centuries. But royal craftsman had carved the thrones for the Light *Volkhvy*'s champions, and Vasilisa herself had conjured the blades and enchanted the stones.

Elena might have felt the call of the sapphire blade since she was a child, but only the alpha wolf could approve or disapprove of her quest.

The rumble began in the soles of her shoes. It radiated upward through muscle and bone. It vibrated her chest until it rose to her ears and she finally heard the audible sound that had begun as a resonate, deep-chested hum.

The growl caused all the blood to flow from her face and arms, leaving them numb. It seemed every drop of life-giving fluid settled in her stomach, where a heavy knot formed as the first growl rolled into another without ceasing.

The light from the giant fireplace and the leaping flames were no longer the only shadows. A hulking darkness fell over her and the wolves. It climbed up and up to paint the entire wall. The darkness coalesced into a shape that engulfed the entire throne alcove.

As she tried to remember how to breathe, the shape became the black-as-midnight shadow of a wolf. The alpha wolf. Materialized out of the Ether to eat her alive. Or so it seemed in those seconds that she tried to remember why Grigori had seemed like any sort of threat at all.

Soren and Lev tucked their tails and retreated behind the thrones. Elena shook and shivered and tried to straighten out the signals from her brain that were alternately telling her to run, faint and stand as still as stone. When she saw the previously ferocious muzzles of the red and white wolves show up beneath the thrones, she was finally able to move.

She turned to face the black wolf.

He wasn't her alpha. She wouldn't cower and quake. If she died, she would die with daggers in her hands. They were there, suddenly, even though she had no memory of drawing them from her pockets. And they were steady in her palms. Her tremble was gone.

If Soren and Lev were as large as ponies, the alpha was as big as a draft horse. The doorway into the hall was an arched one, double and grand, and the powerful shoulders of his black body filled it. He stood with paws planted and his teeth showing sharp and white against the black snarl of his muzzle. Had she caused him to materialize from the Ether because she'd come for the sword? Perhaps his instinct to champion had left him, but his protective instincts were more powerful.

"I came for you, but I found the sword. You don't have to help me against the witchblood prince, but I must wield one of the Romanov blades. I feel the sapphire's call. Surely, as its protector, you recognize that?" Elena reasoned. "The woman in the tapestry wielded the ruby blade. I'm not trying to steal this sword or take it away. I'll use it against Grigori, but it will also be in defense of Bronwal. I promise."

She didn't cry. She didn't run away. She reasoned with a monster. And he listened to every word. Like Soren, he was more aware than an ordinary beast. Hope flared in her breast. The knot in her stomach eased. The daggers in her hands dipped down, and she almost sheathed them back in her hip pockets.

Except, unlike the red wolf, the black wolf's teeth were still bared against her. He stepped forward, not from animal instinct and rage, but for clearheaded, rational reasons she couldn't understand. Who could interpret a beast's reasons for determining enemy or friend? She'd tried. He might understand her words, but he refused to bow to the sapphire's call.

Her knees softened as fear reclaimed her.

Romanov had warned her that the black wolf was deadly. Her hope might have sealed her fate. But there was still one last chance she could grab— The sapphire stone had flared. She'd seen it from the corner of her eye. Even the black wolf had turned his face toward the vivid blue flash. It hadn't been firelight. The flame's glow was completely shadowed by the alpha wolf's body. *The stone had lit from within, in the same moment that she'd promised to defend the castle.*

The flash hadn't soothed the black wolf. In fact, it seemed to be the sudden light in the sapphire stone that had set his paws in stalking motion. He paced toward her and one of the wolves under the thrones whined. Soren or Lev? In sympathy or in anticipation?

"You won't kill a woman the sword has chosen," Elena said. But she had no idea if her supposition was correct. How long had the alpha been hidden in the Ether? And what did he care about an enchanted sword's preferences?

There was nowhere to run. Nowhere to hide. Even if she'd wanted to flee to the tower, the black wolf's powerful legs would catch her before she made it out of the room. From the corner of her eye, she saw the red wolf wiggle out from under the chair. He stood staring at her and the alpha wolf as if he wasn't certain what he should do. But when Lev also came out of hiding and aggressively tried to move her way as if he would stalk her too, Soren stopped him. The red wolf knocked the white wolf to the floor and placed one paw on his neck to keep him supine.

She'd been distracted. When she turned her full attention back to the black wolf, he was only a few feet away. She started, but she didn't back away. She stood her ground, a tiny, ineffectual dagger in each hand. The alpha wolf stepped closer and closer until his nose was above her head and between the small blades she clenched in her fists. She could do damage with them if he decided to attack. She could hurt him before she died. But the daggers wouldn't defeat him. At best, they would buy her seconds of time. As she tilted her chin to look into his emerald eyes, her hands were stilled by what she saw there. Intensity burned bright in the gem-like gleam of his irises.

It was an intensity she'd seen before.

"Romanov?" she whispered. Her fingers went limp and the daggers clattered to the floor. The black wolf flinched for all his size and strength. But he didn't lash out. He didn't growl or bite.

Ivan Romanov wasn't the master. He was the wolf. Her search had been over as soon as he'd materialized in front of her on the snowy mountain pass. Answers to so many of her questions suddenly crystalized in her mind.

"You've been in front of me all along. What haven't you told me?" Elena asked. In spite of the deadly teeth, she reached to touch the bottom of his jaw. She cupped his monstrous face in the palm of her hand. Her book of legends had shown her the Romanovs and their wolves. She hadn't understood. *The Romanov brothers are the Romanov wolves.* The russet, the white and the black.

The alpha wolf was stiff with emotion. He didn't relax into her hand. How could he? She had woken him. She had disturbed him from the deep sleep in which Ivan Romanov had buried him in order to maintain his stand as the last Romanov. His brothers were gone, but not permanently into the Ether as she'd supposed. They had shifted and either they had chosen to stay in their wolf forms…or they had been trapped in them unable to return as men.

Soren whined again and Elena looked toward the red wolf. Suddenly, she understood Bell better than she had before. The other woman longed to see Soren's *human* face. The clothes in the trunk and the hat Bell always wore…had they been Soren's long ago? He still had more understanding than an animal would have. He still remembered the man. Lev had forgotten. Would Soren forget eventually too? And now that Romanov had shifted to let the alpha wolf free, would he lose himself too?

"What have I done?" Elena said.

More pieces of the puzzle came together in a painful picture in her mind. Lev, the white wolf, had also been a man. The tragedy she'd stumbled upon in the baby's room became clear. Romanov had said he wasn't a pet. He'd never been a pet. But the family who'd lived in the room had been *his*.

Hot tears filled Elena's eyes.

"Why didn't you tell me?" she asked.

She looked back at Romanov, the alpha wolf, and found him staring beyond her head. Not at his brothers. His focus was on the thrones. She followed his gaze to find that it fell on the gleam of the sapphire stone.

"Lev's wife wielded the ruby Romanov blade," Elena whispered.

Romanov had shifted to keep her from the stone.

Sympathy had hollowed her gut, but pain caused it to tighten as if she'd been stabbed. Cold ache suddenly burned away and in its place came a sharp stabbing heat. He was here to protect the blade from her. He didn't think she was worthy of it.

She lowered her hand and clenched her fist. It took every ounce of her strength not to use it to strike him. To share the pain that tore her apart.

"You don't have to want me. Or accept the blade's decision. But I won't be frightened away. Don't you know that by now? The blade knows. I'm a warrior. Whether you fight by my side or not," Elena said.

Before any of the wolves could react to her decision, Elena pirouetted. She used her good leg to hold her weight and it spun her as it always had, tried and true. Then she ran and leaped for the dais, even though there were no strong arms there to catch her. She landed gracefully in spite of the pain in her injured knee. And she reached for the blade. None of the wolves tried to stop her. In part because Soren still stood on Lev's neck, holding him down.

Her hand closed around the hilt of the Romanov blade and the sapphire flared once more. A vision of another woman filled her mind. She recognized Romanov's mother from the portrait in the hall. Vladimir Romanov hadn't only betrayed the Light *Volkhvy* queen. He'd betrayed the memory of a woman who had pledged to protect Bronwal by his side when he'd betrayed her queen. Elena clenched her teeth as she felt a glimmer of what the other woman must have felt. Maybe it was better to be rejected before you fell in love, not after.

She turned with the blade in both hands. She'd never been trained, but it seemed more comfortable in her grasp than it should, as if it had been made for her. She would learn how to wield it even if Romanov didn't approve.

The alpha wolf stood in front of her. Raised on the dais, she was able to meet his eyes. From her better position, she could see the midnight shine of his wild black fur and the epic proportions of his shoulders. There was no doubt that he was Ivan Romanov. The tale had finally pieced together in her mind from the legend and everything she'd learned since she'd come to Bronwal.

Her spine tingled with the impossibility of a man being able to become a beast, but she couldn't unsee what she'd seen in the black wolf's eyes. She'd climbed a mountain to find a legendary castle and this wolf. She thought she'd found his master, but he'd been here, hidden before her very eyes, all along. She held the sword up between them, but she could have easily been pledging her loyalty to him and his cause rather than taking a defensive posture. Her heart pulled her in both directions.

As she'd told Soren, the Romanovs needed her. The sword had somehow known it. It had called her across time and great distance. Now that it was in her hands, she wouldn't let it go. Not only because she felt safer than she'd ever felt, more ready to take on her evil magical stalker, but also because the pale blue glow of the sword's gem seemed to illuminate a path she'd been looking for.

"I've always longed to be more than a dancer. That's why the book of legends called to me even before I heard the sword. Let me help you. The sword has spoken. See how it fits in my hands? Help me to learn how to use it. Let's stand together against Grigori and the Dark *Volkhvy*. After the Gathering, I'll leave. I'll walk away. I'll let you and the sword vanish back into the Ether without me if that's what you want. But, for now, teach me how to fight," Elena said.

Soren whined again. Lev had gone limp. He panted on the floor beneath his brother's paw from his exertions to get free. Did the red wolf think he would have to rescue her from the alpha too? It would be pointless for him to try to intercede. If the black wolf decided to attack her, his much smaller brother wouldn't be able to prevent it.

But the eyes she gazed into weren't an animal's eyes. Ivan Romanov had risked the shift, but his beast hadn't swallowed him whole yet. There was a man's reasoning and a man's soul in the black wolf's giant body. Elena faced him and waited for him to decide if he would flee or teach her to fight. Because that was his choice. He could give up and let the black wolf's savage nature take over, or he could accept her as the warrior called to carry the sapphire blade.

She refused to believe that Romanov, even in his black wolf form, would attack her and try to drive her away if he was still in control. So she stood. She waited. She held tightly to the hilt of a blade she hadn't been trained to use. And she prayed she wouldn't have to try to kill the man she'd kissed only hours before.

Chapter 9

The standoff seemed to last for hours. Elena's arms protested the weight of the blade. For all her fitness, the particular muscles needed to brandish a sword hadn't been developed. Sweat dampened the waves of hair on her forehead, and her lower back screamed. Finally, because she had to, she made a decision. If he attacked, she would die before she had to admit she'd been wrong.

Elena lowered the sword. She released it with one hand and used the other to deliberately place its point on the floor beside her. The black wolf trembled in reaction to her movement. His entire body was stiff with tension, but he vibrated with energy as if one wrong move would cause him to leap. She lifted her free hand anyway. She placed it on the side of Romanov's great wolf head.

She wasn't sure if it was her shivering or the alpha wolf's she felt.

"You won't attack me. Not as long as you're in control," Elena said. The black wolf blinked, but he continued to shudder beneath her hands. Was that Romanov seeking to maintain control? Or was it Romanov trying to let go? Standing her ground and reaching out to the alpha wolf was the bravest thing she'd done. It was also the most dangerous. She'd seen the fatigue in Romanov's spirit. She'd seen all of his loss and pain. She had to trust that he would continue to stand and fight even though she had seen so much evidence that he should choose the contrary.

The black wolf rumbled low in his chest. Her body jerked in response and the tip of her sword came off the ground. But it wasn't a growl. It was vocalized pain. The great beast backed away from her touch. The rumble built and built until once again she felt it in the soles of her feet, but when the alpha wolf threw back his mighty head and released the sound in his massive chest as a ululating howl, it was that devastating call that shuddered her bones.

She had magnified Romanov's pain.

She couldn't undo it. She couldn't drop the sword or retreat back down the mountain. Not without giving up her freedom and the newfound sense that her purpose was here. As a dancer, she'd had to learn to press through the pain, to push past it. Romanov had been nearly consumed by it for too long. Maybe it was time for him to face it down.

"Come back to us, Ivan Romanov," Elena urged as the howl trailed off to nothing. The black wolf's nose came back down and he looked at her from where he'd retreated across the room. "Come back to us and help us fight."

Soren and Lev had howled along with the alpha. Their

smaller voices had joined with him in expressing grief and frustration. Lev had leaped to his feet and Soren had allowed it, but the white wolf didn't attack her. He followed the example of his alpha wolf.

"I want to be ready when Grigori comes," Elena said. "I thought it was the wolf I sought, but I was wrong. It was the blade…and the man who can train me in how to use it."

The black wolf whirled around and ran away with powerful strides. Lev yelped and followed after. Soren stopped to look at her for several seconds before he followed his wilder brother.

She was left alone.

The Romanov blade easily took her weight when she leaned against it. Her legs suddenly felt insubstantial as if all her muscle had turned to smoke beneath her skin. She'd faced down an enchanted creature who might have eaten her in several gulps. Her head had told her to run, but her heart had told her to stand her ground.

She still wasn't certain which had been right.

She might have seen the last of the wolf and the man. They might disappear into the Ether and leave her to face Grigori alone.

As the legendary black wolf, Romanov ran through the snow. His great paws churned icy clouds into the air, and as they fell down all around him he was dusted with a fine coating of white. It glistened as the sun rose, dazzling his eyes. The airborne ice particles stung his nose and weighted his lashes.

Still, he ran.

Soren and Lev howled behind him. The hunt was on. There was a stag. Its blood pumped, warmed by the chase.

It would have been natural to run the prey down. To take its life to fuel his own and that of his pack.

But something told him he'd better hold on to more of his humanity than that.

His hold was tenuous.

There was a powerful thrill in the idea of letting go to become a simple-minded animal driven by instinct. He wouldn't. He couldn't. But this time he wanted to more than ever before. No wonder Lev had escaped into the white wolf form when his family had disappeared into the Ether. Romanov understood that decision better than he ever had.

He crested a rise and looked down at the stag as it raced desperately across a clearing between patches of evergreen below. It was difficult, but he reined in his instincts and he let the animal reach the opposite side. It paused, as if startled by the possibility it could escape the giant, hungry wolf. Its head lifted, and white billows of respiration puffed from its flared nostrils. Its sides heaved and it stomped one of its front legs. It dared to try to warn him away?

That defiance was almost his undoing. The alpha wolf tried to wrest control from the shreds of his humanity. It almost succeeded. But then the stag must have scented his hunger on the cold breeze because it startled and turned to plunge into the woods.

He let it go.

Soren and Lev caught up with him. Even Lev respected his pause on the ridge top. His brothers didn't race around him as they once would have to nip submissively at his chin and heels. He hadn't been the alpha around them in a very long time. They were afraid. Both crouched at a distance. Watching and waiting to see what he would do.

Back at the castle, there was someone else waiting for him to choose, as if his choice hadn't been made the moment she'd materialized out of the snowstorm on the pass. The sword had known. For how long? How powerful was Vasilisa's magic? Could it really have found his intended mate across so many decades and miles? Or was this another cruel aspect of the punishment she'd leveled against the Romanov family?

Loss and love. Love and loss. The cycle seemed as endless as the Cycle of the curse.

He wouldn't accept the sword's decision. He wouldn't court the same devastation Lev had faced. He wouldn't ensnare Elena in the Romanov curse. But he would reclaim his human form. He would honor her decision to wield the blade. That much he could do without risk. He could help her learn to defend herself against Grigori now that the sword had chosen.

The Gathering approached, as did the Ether.

He didn't have much time to ensure that her stalker wouldn't enslave Elena before he and the sapphire blade disappeared. The risk wasn't in the blade, because he would die rather than bind her to the Romanov curse. The risk was entirely in the shift.

Because he would give in to the wolf rather than allow her to suffer for the witchblood prince's pleasure. He would save her from the Ether and from Grigori even if it meant all else was lost.

Chapter 10

Elena had to improvise a gym. She'd discovered in her standoff with the black wolf that her arms needed strengthening. Her searches throughout the castle hadn't led her to any modern amenities when it came to weight-lifting, but she remembered the training courtyard and the equipment there.

She might not have weights, but she knew how to use them, and there was a whole rack full of heavy training staffs carved from oak.

She'd go insane if she waited for Romanov to return even if she didn't fret over how he'd return, as man or wolf. He'd been gone an entire day and night. Instead of useless worrying, she swallowed her discomfort over pilfering for clothes appropriate for the training courtyard. She passed over numerous wardrobes full of dresses until she found a long-sleeve tunic to shield her from the cold mountain air. She paired serviceable fur-lined boots with her own jeggings. She did take a long red cloak from a trunk that she knew had been meant for a formal occasion. It was lined with black velvet and embroidered along the edges of its hood and hem with thorns and roses. It was a cold day and she didn't want to try to transport the equipment to an indoor location.

She thought it was a good decision when she stepped out into the sunshine, but once she'd chosen a hefty staff that seemed the appropriate weight to begin to build her strength, her exertion and repetitions didn't fill the courtyard as Romanov had filled it.

At one time this place had been filled with soldiers.

Elena looked around. Snow had covered much of the ground, but she could see the depressions in the dirt where Romanov and others had performed the repetitive movements necessary to build muscle and skill, dexterity and endurance.

She'd been backstage alone before. She'd been in empty halls with deserted dressing rooms. Practice studios were always a little echoing and haunted. But they filled again. Dancers and want-to-be dancers returned. Instructors and music would come. They always came. In a perpetual rhythm of practice and performance.

This was different.

The people who had trained here would never be back.

Even Romanov might be irrevocably lost.

The idea tightened her throat and dried her mouth. The area behind her eyes burned with unshed emotion. How could she care so much about a man she'd just met? The answer was in the legend. She'd always cared, but more than that…he mattered. His story mattered. His tragedy, his pain, his cause. Even if she accepted that she would never be more to him than what she was now, it mattered if the man was lost.

The heart that beat in his chest was Bronwal's heart. Even if it would never be hers.

"I return only to find Little Red Riding Hood in place of the swan," Romanov said.

Elena lowered the staff she'd been lifting like a hand weight with one outstretched arm. Its tip disappeared in the snow, but then it hit solid ground and it held, straight and tall. She gripped it with white knuckles, relieved that she had support to keep her from buckling in relief. Part of her had thought she'd never see him again. Another part had assumed the wolf would return rather than the man.

"I had to borrow some clothes. I packed too lightly. I'm not sure I really believed I'd find you here," she replied. She didn't tell him she'd had to have the cloak when she found it because it seemed fitting to have a red hood when surrounded by wolves. And then there had also been the thorns and roses, very like the ones on the tower door and its key. The cloak seemed to have been left for her, even though she knew that wasn't possible.

"You're welcome to it. And whatever else you need. No one will miss anything you take. They're past the point of caring," Romanov said.

He'd shifted from wolf form, but his hair was windblown and damp. His cheeks were flushed with cold and exertion. His clothes were much like the ones he'd worn when they'd first met. Leather pants. Tall riding boots. A long-sleeve linen shirt covered in a leather jerkin and topped with a fur-lined cloak. The fur cape on the cloak capped his shoulders and made him appear even larger than he was.

He was untouched by this century.

But even though he seemed a savage warrior she knew now that his touch was gentle and his kisses were seductively passionate, with a mix of hard and soft that she'd easily come to crave.

"We have two weeks before the *Volkhvy* begin to arrive. Both Dark and Light will come. Are you certain you want to wield the Romanov blade against them? If you do, they will try to kill you. You'll have more than Grigori as your enemy," Romanov said.

"From where I stand I see no difference between the Dark and the Light. They both torture. They both kill. I'll gladly stand. If you'll teach me how," Elena said.

"It isn't the standing I'll need to teach you. You stand on your own. I'll simply show you swordsmanship. I'll show you how to use the blade. I see that you're trying to strengthen your arms. You're already fit. We'll only enhance what's there," Romanov said.

"You're going to help me?" Elena asked.

"We'll help each other and then I'll be gone. Do you understand? The Ether will take me and the Romanov blade. No matter what damage we do to the *Volkhvy*. The curse cannot be broken. I will disappear," Romanov said. "Alone."

She gripped the staff tighter. He'd already rejected her. This was simply a reiteration. One that cut her, but she wouldn't allow the pain to consume her. There wasn't enough time.

"Agreed," Elena said softly. She braced her spine and jerked the staff up from the ground. She tossed it to him and turned to grab another. She would train, tirelessly. She would fight with all her heart because it wasn't wanted elsewhere. And once Grigori was defeated, she would leave this place stronger and wiser than she'd been before.

The sword had proclaimed her a warrior. If she had to let it disappear into the Ether, she would still be the person it had called. That knowledge gave her a purpose she'd never known before. The dance had always been something she did. It hadn't fit in her heart, only in her muscles and her mind. The sword seemed different. It fit with all of her, in and out. Where it led her after Bronwal would be up to her own feet and free will.

That she would never forget Ivan Romanov was a given. She would simply have to survive losing him the way she'd survived other losses.

The courtyard would never seem empty to her again. For an entire week, she and Romanov filled it with sweat and blood. Her tears, as usual, were stored up for night-mares that never came. When she finally collapsed at night, there was only the sleep of exhaustion.

It was more brutal than any training she'd endured. But her body responded like the fine-honed tool that it was. Oh, she had to resort to the neoprene sleeve to support her injured knee, but in every other particular she grew stronger. She was athletic and graceful. As a dancer, she was an expert in copying motion, in replicating genius. And her instructor in this was brilliant as only time and enchantment could make.

There was pain. In varying ways. Physical pain from overexertion and constant demand. Emotional pain from Romanov's touch and his constant nearness paired with his continued rejection.

He pressed close behind her to position her arms and legs and hips in the appropriate offensive stance. His wild wintry scent engulfed her. Heat radiated from their bodies to mingle in the cold air around them in an aura just shy of steam. She held her breath. He continued explaining what she should do to disarm an opponent as if there was no attraction vibrating between them.

It was torturous. But it was a sweet torture she grew to anticipate every morning.

Her cloak's hem grew stained. The muscles she used to dodge and parry and block grew harder and stronger. Her endurance increased from what had already been prodigious levels.

The training became a dance between them. His touch on her, professional and impersonal. Her response in perfect symmetry with his instruction. In spite of his large frame and solid build, he was incredibly graceful. The power in his muscles enabled him to easily move—to spin, to lift, to turn, to hold.

Oh, the holding.

Even as she became certain that she could stab the Romanov blade into Grigori's heart without hesitation, she soaked up the pleasure she felt from Romanov's touch. If she survived, the memory would have to last her for the rest of her life. She wouldn't be welcome back in ten years' time, and she wouldn't be able to handle it if she came back to find him forever gone.

"You aren't concentrating," he said. And he was right. At least in so far as he knew. She had allowed herself to become lost in sensation rather than follow-through on the expected deflection.

She would have been dead if he hadn't halted his own strike by dropping his sword on the ground. Instead of a strike, he jerked her forward with a ferocious hold on both of her wrists. They stood face-to-face with arms above their heads and their bodies pressed together.

They'd been breathing heavily from exertion. The friction of her breasts sliding against his chest caused her breath to catch. But holding her breath wasn't enough to stop the electricity that arched between them.

And, this time, Romanov didn't fool her.

He was affected too.

She tilted her chin and met his hooded eyes. He searched her gaze and his eyes widened when he noted her desire was barely held in check. The hands on her wrists eased. His attention fell to her lips as she moistened them with a dart of her tongue.

"It doesn't matter what our bodies want," Romanov said quietly. His voice vibrated against her, deep and low. "The Ether can't have you. I won't let it happen."

"You think if you kiss me, I'll be drawn into the curse? You've kissed me before. What harm is there in another?" Elena asked. She knew the harm for herself. That she'd become even more hopelessly addicted to a man she could never have.

"You're assuming I could stop with kisses," Romanov said. "That's no longer true. If I kiss you again, we'll go further than we can go and still maintain your freedom."

It was true in more ways than he understood. It would be hard, even now, for her to ever be free of his impact on her life. Having free will and being free from entanglements were not the same.

"And now you've ensured that I want your kiss more than before," Elena said.

He jerked. His whole body was tense and hot against her. But then he held more still than she thought possible. A hair couldn't have floated between them, but he held his position. Not coming closer or moving away. Then his eyes closed and he breathed in, long and deep. And she knew what he was doing because she'd been doing the same thing all week. He was soaking up the sensation of her body trembling in his arms. He was trying to feel all that he could allow himself to feel.

No more. But no less either.

She trembled because *this* with Romanov shook her more than actual lovemaking had with another man. Perhaps it was best if they couldn't consummate their relationship. Standing with her arms held high and their bodies barely touching slayed her senses and her emotions. Especially when she watched him take what pleasure he could take in it. Actual intercourse with this man might destroy her.

A cacophony of angry barks sounded from inside the castle.

They'd been training with practice swords. The sapphire blade was in the throne room guarded by Lev and Soren.

"I hoped the burgeoning power in the stone might warn them away," Romanov said. He let go of her hands and turned toward the castle. He left the practice sword on the ground. Instead, he walked purposefully to the entryway and reached for a much sharper blade kept on a rack sheltered from the elements just inside the door.

Elena lowered her arms and followed. She still kept the daggers in her hip pockets, but she didn't pause for another weapon. The sapphire sword waited for her. She would use the very thing they sought to steal against the invaders who had infiltrated the throne room and disturbed the wolves.

Lev and Soren continued to bark, but now their

alarmed noises were interspersed with sounds of fighting—snarls and growls and the occasional high-pitched yelp. At the sound of the first yelp, Romanov picked up speed and Elena followed suit.

They ran into the throne room, side by side, their movements already coordinated by their time spent training together.

There were two men and one woman in the throne room. They were wearing modern tactical gear, but they fought with their bare hands—the greenish glow of power emanating from their fingers seemed to be their only weapon. As the woman held Lev away from her throat, the green light flared and the white wolf fell back as if he'd been shocked by an electrical charge.

"The waking sapphire has called more powerful *Volkhvy*, Elena. Be careful," Romanov warned. He waded into the battle his red brother was waging against the two men. Soren still had cagey human intelligence at his disposal. He hadn't attacked blindly. He led the two male *Volkhvy* away from the thrones so Elena could get to the sword. But Lev was already back on his feet. Human intelligence or not, he was an enchanted wolf created by the Light *Volkhvy* queen to fight this enemy.

The female intruder cried out when the white wolf leaped on her back and drove her to the floor before she could steal her prize. Elena leaped over their writhing figures. She needed to claim the sword for herself before the *Volkhvy* managed to get to the blade. But as she leaped, her injured knee didn't bring the foot on that leg far enough up and away from the woman's glowing fingers. The Dark *Volkhvy* grabbed her ankle and pulled her down.

She barely managed to catch herself with outstretched

arms before she landed hard. Breath was forced from her lungs as the marble ground suddenly compressed her abdomen. Yet it wasn't the struggle to breathe that kept her down. It was the arcs of painful power flaring from the woman's hand to her leg.

Her entire body quaked as every nerve fired and every muscle jerked out of control.

Grigori had never been able to touch her. The blood her mother had spilled fueled a protective hearth spell that kept him away. That this lesser *Volkhvy* physically harmed her now was evidence that the time her mother had bought her was waning. Fear of Grigori suddenly blossomed anew inside of her chest. He wasn't here. It didn't matter. She'd dreamed of what he would do to her when he could finally touch her. In a flash, she recalled every unwanted caress.

Lev helped her. He clamped down on the woman's forearm and she shrieked as she was forced to let Elena go. Her body stopped quaking as suddenly as it had started. Elena collapsed and eagerly gulped air as her lungs began to work once more. She wasn't sure if Lev's help was intentional or not. As she struggled to her feet, she was grateful all the same.

She moved much more slowly this time. All three intruders were occupied. Their curses filled the air. Their black blood mingled with red. Too much red, but she couldn't pause. She would be worthless without the sword. Elena limped up the stairs to the thrones. This time when she reached for it, she held the sword in an appropriate grip. Her training had been professionally absorbed and now implemented. She pivoted back around, strengthened by the power in her hands. The blue glow from the stone was pale, but unmistakably brighter in reaction to her touch.

All the Dark *Volkhvy* paused to look up at Elena on the dais.

"The sapphire blade is mine," she proclaimed. "I will defend it."

Her figure was petite. Her voice was firm, but quiet. The wolves and the man who also defended the blade should be much more intimidating, but the sapphire's glow spoke of the sword's opinion. She was the warrior the intruders should fear. Her touch bonded with the blade and called Vasilisa's power inherent in the gem to life.

And there was nothing Dark *Volkhvy* respected more than power.

"Go. Warn all your brethren, Dark and Light, that Bronwal is defended," Romanov ordered. He didn't support her claim on the sapphire sword. He wouldn't. But he didn't deny it either. Both of the men he fought had been injured badly. Their black blood stained his sword and curls of steam rose from its sharp edge. But Romanov bled, as well. She could see scarlet slashes on his face and chest.

And that's when she knew.

It was too late for her to choose to walk away. Not because of the blade, but because of the man. Anger rose like bile in her throat. Fury heated the blood that pumped through her heart. How dare they defile this already besieged man?

As Elena gathered her muscles beneath her to jump into the fray, the three Dark *Volkhvy* became hazy and indistinct in front of her eyes, then disappeared.

"Dominique wasn't capable of Ether manipulation.

These three were definitely more powerful than the usual thieves. Powerful *Volkhvy* can disappear and reappear at will from place to place. Possibly from time to time," Romanov said. He cleaned his sword on the edge of his cloak, but it was a habit more than a necessity. The dark blood had already disappeared, as well as the witches it had come from.

"And they were afraid of me?" Elena said shakily. Knowing that magic was real and seeing it manifested in front of your eyes were two very different things.

"The power in the sapphire could kill them. There's nothing a nearly immortal creature fears more than death," Romanov said.

"It's frightening for a mortal creature, as well," Elena said. Now that the adrenaline rush had fled her body, she was left shaking in reaction to her instinctive stand against the intruders. She might have been called to wield the sapphire blade, but that didn't mean becoming a warrior was easy. Her legs shook, and without thinking she sat on the nearest seat available.

The room grew quiet.

Lev and Soren stopped smoothing their ruffled fur and licking their injuries. They stared at her instead. And Romanov walked forward slowly one steady step at a time.

She was on the smaller throne. The one with the alpha wolf carved onto its back. The wolf carving was above her head. She didn't have to turn and look up at it to remember every tooth, every hair.

"You brought me here that first night. I couldn't see the thrones. There was no fire. The alcove was invisible in the darkness. You stood with me in your arms rather than set me down," Elena said.

"No one has sat on that throne since my mother died,"

Romanov said. His intense gaze was trained on her with some unwavering emotion she couldn't name.

"The larger one was your father's," Elena said. She looked beside her where the larger throne stood. "It's yours now."

"I'm the last Romanov. The throne is mine, but there's nothing to rule here. Bronwal is an abandoned place. We do nothing but linger and languish at Vasilisa's pleasure," Romanov said.

Elena placed the Romanov blade across her knees. The sapphire had dimmed, but they'd all seen it glow. She settled more fully into the throne.

"Perhaps that's our problem. You're prisoner to Vasilisa's pleasure and I've been prisoner to Grigori's. We have existed to serve their needs instead of our own," Elena said.

"I won't allow my needs to place you at risk," Romanov said.

"And I'm not allowed to determine what I will risk for myself?" Elena asked.

Once again, she sacrificed much to open herself to rejection. He hadn't asked her to be his queen. He never would. To him, she was as much an invader as the ones they'd vanquished, no matter what the sword said. She'd destroyed what little peace he'd found in his lonely duties. She'd brought all his pain to light.

"You don't know what the Ether is like," Romanov said. But as he spoke he stepped up the stairs of the dais, one by one. Elena rose to meet his approach. She held the Romanov blade down by her side. He stopped at her sudden movement. He stood only a few feet away.

"I know what your kisses are like. I know how your body feels between my legs. How your shoulders feel in my hands," Elena said. "I know if Grigori captures me tomorrow I'd be happier to have the memories of your touch to sustain me through my imprisonment."

"To join with me is to court a curse more horrible than you can understand. Ask Lev if his wife was happy to lose her baby to the Ether once Vasilisa's judgment fell. We were her chosen champions, yet she showed no mercy. No one was spared, not even a newborn child. Madeline was a warrior who fought by Lev's side for Vasilisa. It didn't matter. She and her baby disappeared in the first Cycle," Romanov said. He stepped nearer as he spoke, as if proximity would convince her. He fisted his hands.

Down on the main floor of the hall, Lev slipped away into the dark hallway beyond. Soren whined and ran after his brother. Neither had wanted to hear the tale.

"How long did he last once she was gone?" Elena asked.

"I haven't seen Lev's human face since the first materialization that Madeline didn't appear. He shifted to search for her. *Volkhvy* use the Ether to travel the world. Lev thought Madeline and Trevor might have materialized somewhere else. In our wolf forms we're nearly tireless. For a century of Cycles he searched the world for her. Until he forgot how to be human again," Romanov said. "Until he seemed to forget his pain."

"He shifted for her," Elena whispered. "Not to run. Not to hide."

"He used his enchantment to try to save her," Romanov said. "But he failed."

Elena didn't shed tears for herself. But for Madeline and the great love Lev had felt for her and the baby, she cried. Her cheeks were scalded with hot, liquid emotion.

She didn't call attention to them by wiping them away. Besides, Romanov's green eyes seemed brighter, as well.

"And you think it would have been better if they hadn't been together at all," Elena said.

"Soren lost much, but not as much as Lev," Romanov said.

"And you? You're so much better off because you're determined to stand alone?" Elena said. She refused to draw closer to him even though his pain beckoned.

"I won't share my burden with an innocent," Romanov said.

The curse was horrible, but much of Romanov's pain was self-inflicted. He'd lost too much to risk new connections. He was determined to suffer alone. Yet she'd been called to this place. She'd found it when others had failed. She was here for a reason.

This time Elena wouldn't leave her sword in the throne room. She stepped forward to pass by Romanov, but she paused when she reached his side. Their hips were parallel. She didn't face him, but she did look up to meet his eyes.

"You sell me short. The blade has spoken and I believe it's spoken well," Elena said. "Because I wouldn't fade away."

She had some pride. She didn't completely bare her heart. She didn't tell him she would brave the curse for him as long as she knew he would be waiting on the other side when they materialized again. She'd only just acknowledged it for herself.

She hadn't gone for the sword in order to protect it from the Dark *Volkhvy* intruders. She'd gone for it in order to help Romanov and his brothers repel invaders. And not even magic had been able to stop her.

But her insides were in a tumult and her legs were numb, especially the one that had channeled the *Volkhvy* woman's power into her body. That leg was a reminder that Grigori would touch her soon if she didn't stop him.

As she paused to speak to Romanov, she swayed on her feet. His eyes widened and he reached for her. His large arm wound around her back and his warm hand braced her hip. The move placed his entire body against her side, not pressing, but supporting. Elena could have jerked away...if she wanted to prove her fortitude by falling on her face.

Something was wrong. The Dark power the *Volkhvy* had used to hurt her was still jolting through her body making her muscles weak.

"You're hurt," Romanov said.

He didn't wait for her to confirm what he could see with his own eyes. Instead, he bent to scoop her up the way he had when she'd collapsed in the snow. She was flooded by thoughts of other times she'd been in his arms. The kisses they'd shared. The pleasure. The pain. She had a sword in one hand. She couldn't wrap her arms around him. She had to be content with one hooked around his neck and the other held down by her side to keep the edge away from his body.

Now that he'd made his feelings clear, she should keep her distance but she preferred not to faint. The power had found its way into her head and her vision had gone blurry. Her equilibrium was gone. The room spun around them as Romanov stepped down the stairs.

"She needs to rest. Fetch Patrice," Romanov ordered.

He seemed to speak to his brothers from a great distance. Down a long tunnel. One that spun in a kaleidoscope of shapes and colors. Elena closed her eyes against the dizzying whirl. His chest was the only solid thing besides the sword in her hand in a world gone mad. She leaned her face against it. Without intention, she found his heartbeat beneath her cheek. It thumped steadily while she hoped hers did too, in spite of her detachment to its feel and sound.

The Dark *Volkhvy* had used great force to break through the last of her mother's protective spell. Maybe such negative power coursing through her was more than her mortal body could take.

Elena held on to Romanov and the sword. They were all she knew as he carried her up to the tower room. She didn't note the passage of time as he hurried on the stairs or the change of light as he laid her on the bed and turned to throw open several windows. She didn't feel the cool rush of wintry air on her flushed skin or the soft blanket beneath her. She reeled when his hold disappeared, doubling the ferocity of her grip on the hilt of the Romanov blade. When he returned to her side, she cried out because he reached to move the sword and she thought he was trying to take it away.

"I only want to position the sapphire against you, Elena. It's glowing. I think Vasilisa's power might help you recover," Romanov said. His voice was nearly a growl.

She allowed him to move the sword. He pressed the cool stone against her chest. She grasped it with both hands then. She held the hilt between her breasts. Its long shaft lay on top of her, from her lower ribs to her knees.

At first she felt no improvement. Her head swam. She was afraid to open her eyes. But then almost imperceptibly the breeze tickled across her face. The numbness that had tried to claim her began to recede. Finally, she felt her heart beat inside of her chest. There was no noticeable electric current from the sword. Not like there had been from the Dark *Volkhvy*'s touch. Vasilisa's power was more of an emanation that her body soaked up. Like heat. Like the rays of the sun.

"I brought mulled wine. I thought it might fortify. Also cheese and bread," Patrice said.

Elena recognized the housekeeper's voice. She couldn't speak to thank the woman for responding to her distress. She couldn't thank Soren and Lev for obeying Romanov and going for help.

"This is my fault. The black wolf could have easily dispatched them," Romanov said. "They hurt her because I avoid the shift."

"Better *them* hurt her than *him*, I say. That black wolf can't be trusted. I've seen the Ether in his eyes," Patrice said. Elena wanted to protest. She wanted to say that the black wolf hadn't hurt her. That Romanov was in control. But her lips wouldn't open no matter how she willed herself to speak.

"I am the black wolf, Patrice. You know that," Romanov said.

"I'm not as Ether-addled as you think. I know who and what you are. And I know it would destroy you to hurt this one. Best not risk it. Best not risk it," Patrice replied. Her voice faded as she must have left the supplies she carried to wander back the way she'd come.

"You…wouldn't," Elena managed to utter. Sensation returned to her little by little. She could feel her body again. Her legs were no longer numb.

"You misplace your optimism," Romanov replied. Elena's lashes fluttered when she felt the slightest brush of calloused fingers on her cheek. He sat nearby. He must have pulled a chair closer to the bed. His caress was incongruous, a butterfly's wing from a man who could crush someone with his bare hands. But it continued. She wasn't mistaken. He outlined the whole of her face, softly, as if he memorized her repose or the color returning that signified she wasn't near death.

"Not…optimistic. An optimist hopes," Elena said. "I know." She swallowed and licked her lips. It felt a triumph especially when it was followed by the ability to slit open her eyes. He was only a blur leaning over her. But he was a welcome blur. One that encouraged her to blink and try to regain her focus.

She had been afraid of the black wolf. She had even entertained the possibility that Romanov would cede control to the beast and allow it to consume her. But his fear of the same caused her to fully believe it would never happen. He had enough doubt in himself for both of them. She was suddenly fully confident that he would never harm her, even if it meant sacrificing himself.

"I am the black wolf," Romanov said. "Its instinct and savagery are a part of me, and with every Cycle as we tire of holding on to our humanity the wolves take greater hold."

"A wolf would never harm its mate. I'm not afraid," Elena said. She closed her eyes again. Immediately regretting the claim. It was a groggy thing to say. Once the words were out of her mouth she wished her lips hadn't begun working again at all.

"No," Romanov whispered.

His voice was close. Very close. Warm lips pressed against the corner of her mouth. No, she wasn't his mate? Or no, he would never harm her? Her head went light again at the possibility of the latter promise and also because he slid his lips from the corner of her mouth to the center. She was awake. She was alive. All sensation had returned. His slightly open tasting of her lips proved it. As did the gasp he inspired when he boldly teased her with a flick of his tongue.

Elena released the hilt of the sword. She was able to lift her hands to cup the sides of his face. Thank God, because he might have pulled back if she hadn't stopped him. He might have moved away. She wasn't strong enough to hold him in place, but her touch caused him to pause long enough for her lips to open and her tongue to twine with his. He responded by sinking into her and the kiss as if her taste and touch saved him from a dark abyss. As if he was the one who had been near death, but her kiss had woken him from despair.

"You won't harm me," Elena murmured between deep, tender delvings into the velvet recesses of his mouth. His only response was a groan of pleasure that may or may not have been conceding her argument and then the repositioning of his body on the bed beside her, which seemed like the truest concession.

The sword was between them, but it didn't keep them apart. They merely accepted the danger of its sharp edges, carefully, as part of their embrace, its unyielding presence nothing of a deterrent when compared with greater obstacles they still had to face.

He kissed her until she was light-headed again. This time from want of his touch, not dark magic. She allowed her fingers to wind their way into his wild hair. Heat rose from his scalp in spite of the open windows. Their twining tongues stoked flames hotter than the remnants of the fire behind the grate. A raven's hoarse cry reminded her of the birds that constantly swooped and soared around the tower, but their movements couldn't compete with the whirl of desire Romanov caused in the pit of her stomach.

He paused when she tried to press closer. The sword had finally become too much of an impediment. Their lips separated and Elena was afraid he would pull away. She forced her fingers to loosen in case he did, but instead of breaking away he only edged back far enough to take the sword from between them. He carefully moved the blade to the other side of her body and then he stilled.

Elena watched as his green gaze tracked over her rumpled hair and her flushed face. She licked her swollen lips and a slight smile curved one corner of his sensual mouth. His lips were swollen too. Paired with the untamed black waves of his hair and his pale skin, his passion-darkened mouth was more than enticing. She allowed one hand to slip from his hair down to his lips. She extended one finger and gently traced his full lower lip. By the time she'd traveled from one edge to the other, her finger trembled in reaction.

The masculine vulnerability of his well-kissed mouth sent a delicious curl of hunger to her stomach and lower. She melted as he allowed the caress. She pressed her thighs together to keep from spreading them and begging for his touch.

But she didn't have to.

He felt her movement. He let go of the sword to cup her hip with that hand. He gauged her tension and he kneaded her muscles to ease it. Of course the motion of his strong fingers so close to her need only made her tension worse.

"Romanov," she said. It was nearly a moan. He looked up from his hand to her eyes. What he saw there made his gleam with appreciation. His smile hadn't faded with her touch. It increased with her moan, tilting his lips beneath her trembling touch. "If you're going to leave this bed, do it now. If not, prepare to be kept here till morning," she warned.

"You need to rest and recover. If I stay, there'll be less resting," Romanov said. He was teasing her as if they weren't toying with a *Volkhvy* curse. What had changed? Why wasn't he leaving her here alone behind a safely locked door?

Her question must have shown in her eyes.

"I should leave. But I can't. You were gone. Before my very eyes. First, in the *Volkhvy*'s grip and then in reaction to it. And the only thing I could think was that I hadn't touched you when I could. I hadn't appreciated every inch of you while we were together," Romanov confessed. "I will leave this room only if you want me to leave. If not, we will steal this time together and you'll still be free. I will never make you my wife. I'll never chain you to my name or to the curse."

Elena understood he was making an honorable pledge, but her newfound connection to the sword made it particularly poignant to hear his determination to set her free. Freedom was what she'd wanted above all things, but she'd wanted the freedom to make her own choices. Now, it seemed as if Romanov prevented her from fully embracing the sword's call because he wanted to protect her. That, in addition to the idea of lying with him and then losing him, made her hands tighten on the nape of his neck.

She pulled his lips back to her so he could make no more horrible promises she didn't want him to keep. She would take this stolen time he offered to share with her. Later would be soon enough to regret it.

He took her move as an invitation to stay. His mouth

met her open lips and their tongues danced and delved again with an eagerness neither of them tried to subdue. Her whole body welcomed him, softening, opening and melting against him. He was a big man. When he half leaned over her and nudged one of her legs to the side so that his warm thigh slid between hers, she gloried in his weight. His broad chest mashed against her sensitized breasts and she hooked her leg around his waist to encourage him even closer.

But he pulled back instead. He broke their kiss and dropped his lips to trail down the side of her jaw and then farther down still to the throbbing pulse at the base of her throat. His mouth was soft and firm. He kissed her skin as thoroughly as he'd kissed her lips and he teased her with occasional moist licks of his tongue.

"You're so deliciously delicate and yet so strong. I tremble at the thought of harming you in any way, yet you have proven time and again that you aren't afraid," he said. The whisper of his words against her neck caused a thrill to shiver down her spine.

"I'm only afraid I'll startle you with my hunger," Elena said. But she hesitated for only a moment before the press of his lips along her collarbone caused her hips to rise in response. She pressed her heat against his hard, muscular leg. The sensation was even stronger than it had been before, when he'd pleasured her in the kitchen, because this time she knew there would be more.

"I want your hunger," Romanov said.

He had continued to knead her hip, but now he lifted his hand to the neckline of her tunic. It was linen and crafted simply and loosely. It was gathered and threaded with a string that tied at the neck, and the knot had already loosened with her movements of the morning. His fingers easily flicked the tiny bow free and he slowly parted the material, which opened all the way down to the middle of her chest.

The lace of her bra and the swell of her breasts above the modern undergarment were exposed.

"Brace yourself," Elena breathed. "Because I'm very hungry." Her chest was rising and falling quickly with her respiration. Her hands gripped his shoulders. But even that steady anchor didn't stop her body from jerking when he trailed the warm pads of his calloused fingers along the top of the lace he'd uncovered. She followed his intent gaze down to his caress. Her nipples had swelled and hardened. They peaked rosy and pink, begging for his touch beneath the translucent white lace.

"I can see that," Romanov said.

In a move that made her gasp, he reached to twist her bra free. The plastic fastener in the center of the lace cups didn't slow him down. A flick of his strong fingers caused the undergarment to part. And the elastic on either side pulled the lace off of the swell of each breast to reveal her hardened nipples. Her pale skin was flushed with pleasure as blood rushed to his touch, but that pink flush couldn't compare to the darkening of her areolas and nipples as his teasing fingers found them.

"Oh," she cried out as his large hand went from teasing to encompassing. His touch was hot as he weighed and lifted the globe of one breast, but its heat didn't compare to the moist fire as he leaned to take the entire tip of her breast in his mouth.

He suckled and her hips bucked. Her hands clenched and pulled, ripping his tunic instead of bothering with his ties. She didn't allow the sound of the rent to slow her. In fact, the sudden give and tear spurred her on. She pulled harder until the fabric came away from his torso in her hand. She threw it to the side all while he caused her to rock and toss her head back and forth with the suction of his mouth and the velvety friction of his lathing tongue.

"Elena," he groaned, loudly, breaking his suction and moving his lips down her body.

Now that his chest was bare, his skin burned against her everywhere it brushed. He kissed and licked until he came to fabric. She muttered a protest as he stopped, but he only paused long enough to pull the tunic over her head. She lifted her back and arms to help him. He slid the straps of her bra off her shoulders as well, and tossed both garments to the side. Then he looked down at her. His eyes gleamed in appreciation.

She was suddenly reminded of the legend and the wolf. He was a man in her arms but he was also every bit the wild alpha. She reached for him, afraid he might be too wild for her to keep in the bed long enough to mate.

To remove her shirt, he'd crouched between her legs. Her hands dropped to hold either side of his hips. His supple leather pants were tighter than they'd been before. She could see the bulge of his erection. She could see where the cock she'd explored before was long and thick and curved to the side. It barely missed showing over the top of his waistband. She could see where the damp head of it pulsed, waiting to be freed.

His stomach was lean and hard. He sucked in air as her fingers reached for the crisscrossed ties that held his pants in place. This time she slowly worked the leather lacings free. Allowing him the anticipation of her obvious intent. She made sure to brush against his erection again and again as she worked the lacings free.

"Your hunger is nothing compared to mine," Romanov

said. Sure enough, his warning was a growl and his body trembled beneath her touch.

Elena was still half-reclined with her legs spread around his knees. When she had unfastened his pants and spread the leather, the white of his undergarment was loose and easy to pull down. His erection came free and jutted out toward her with a heavy bounce.

She needed him to fill her. She had gone to molten liquid, but she didn't want to rush their time to completion. Instead of falling back and begging him to rip off her jeggings, she reached for him. She held his erection in both of her hands. He cried out at her touch. He thrust into the tight grip she made with her fists end to end. But when she urged him closer and rose up enough to tease her tongue across the swollen head of his cock, he held perfectly still.

Was she too bold? Had her hunger finally been too much?

"Elena," Romanov moaned. She looked up to see his head thrown back. His knees had spread and braced on the bed on either side of her body. She moved one hand off his shaft to make more room for her mouth to engulf him. He wasn't still then. His hips jerked and she enjoyed the friction of her suction and his thrust.

His hands threaded into her hair as she worked his erection with her mouth. He was hot and salty and sweet. And so hard against her tongue she couldn't help but fantasize about how he would feel when he finally thrust inside of her. She throbbed between her legs. She was dewy with heat. But more than anything since he'd brought her to orgasm with nothing but his hard leg and a kiss, she'd wanted to pleasure him in return. Every thrust of his erection between her lips and every cry of her name gave her as much pleasure as he received until it was Romanov who stopped her.

His hands tightened. He gently pulled himself out of her mouth. She opened her eyes to protest, but he silenced her with a deep, hot kiss made even hotter by the taste of him they shared on her lips.

As he kissed her, his hands left her hair and fell to her jeggings. She was glad she wore the simplest stretchy denim. But he took her by surprise when he gripped her hips instead of pulling her pants down.

"I want you every way that a man can take a woman, but I don't want to hurt your knee. Help me gets this off without jarring your leg?" he requested.

And this was the man who had feared he would shift into a giant wolf and devour her?

Elena lifted her hips and worked the denim down her hips. He pulled her borrowed boots off her feet, first one and then the other. Then he helped her with her pants, slowly and gently.

She was left wearing nothing but a scant lace panty when they were finished. Romanov's eyes darkened when he saw the dampened, dark curls between her legs, but he leaned to kiss her scarred knee first. His touch as he held her leg for the gesture was softer than she could have imagined such a large man capable of. He killed with those hands. He'd defended Bronwal for centuries with them. For her, they were so careful. So considerate.

But then they scorched as both hands rose up the top of her leg without breaking contact with her skin. Elena watched his touch caress closer and closer to the juncture of her thighs. When he reached the lace that covered the curls that drew his attention so intensely, he was suddenly not slow at all. He grabbed the elastic of her bikini briefs and slid them down to her midthigh. Not slow, but still considerate of her knee. The move allowed him access to her while still keeping her from spreading her legs.

He touched her then.

Large, calloused fingers dipped into her curls and she cried out when he found the sensitive flesh he sought. She tried to spread her knees, but the lace caught and held her in place. She could only burn for more while he teased. His hooded gaze watched her frustration as it warred with enjoyment. His exploration wound her tighter and tighter. Her hips moved as he began to gently and softly thrust along her moist crevice.

"Please, please," she begged. She'd never needed release as badly as he caused her to crave it. But it wasn't only an orgasm she wanted. She wanted to mate with this man. She wanted him joined with her. She wanted him as close as she could possibly take him.

Instead, he gave her the teasing thrust of his middle finger, thick enough to make her cry out and jerk her hips up to meet it. She grabbed his arm and he allowed it. He allowed her to encourage a harder and deeper thrust of his hand.

"What do you want, love? I'm afraid to hurt you. You'll have to show me," Romanov said. He sounded as if he was teasing, but he wasn't. He was still afraid he would hurt her even now when she bucked under his touch, crazed with desire.

She came then around his thick finger with soft, jerking sighs.

"Elena," he breathed as her inner muscles fluttered against his touch.

But there was still hunger and his mere touch wasn't enough.

Elena pushed his arm back and he allowed her to move him. He patiently waited for her to direct their actions even though his erection was massive. As he watched, she pulled the lace from her legs and threw it on the floor. Then she boldly pushed the legendary warrior back until he lay supine on the bed.

She wanted him in every way a woman could take a man. She wanted to show him that her knee wouldn't prevent their joining. But she had also wanted to take him for days and she wasn't about to let the chance pass without taking full advantage of his offer.

He was incredible. She paused to appreciate the tableau. His wild hair was spread darkly over the white linen on her pillows and his muscular body was intimidating even in repose. His erection lay curved to the side across one of his hard thighs. He was obviously more than ready. In such flagrant excitement, his control of his body was beguiling.

She'd been bewitched by Ivan Romanov long after she had been stalked and he had been bespelled by another.

"I'm not a virgin. I've been with others. But never with anyone who was so strong. Your control is a siren call to my body. I want to make you lose it," Elena said.

"You test my control beyond measure," Romanov said. "But my control is yours. I give it to you because I can give nothing more."

A poignant tug on her heartstrings seasoned the moment. He gave her this because he couldn't give her his name.

Elena mounted her hot warrior. His skin burned between her thighs, but she was slick with expectation and her previous orgasm. He helped her spread her legs and position his shaft. With his hand, he teased the head of his cock against her opening. But she'd had enough teasing. She was throbbing and ready once more.

She lowered her weight onto his erection. Her body stretched to take him inside. Deep inside. She rocked to heighten their mutual pleasure and also to work her folds to open wider and wider to accept his full girth and length.

Her knee did twinge. But she did it to herself with her frenzied movements as she rode him and she didn't care. Not when his head fell back and his eyes rolled. Not when his hips jerked up to meet hers in a fury of thrusts that bounced her breasts. His skin glistened with sweat. She tasted salt drops on her upper lip when she licked them. His hands slipped on her hips.

And still she took him deeper.

Her inner recesses pulsed around his steely member.

She raised her arms high above her head and even without wings she flew.

He pulled out as he pulsed with his orgasm and even that was proof that he cared. About her. About a possible child. Even as he lost control for her, he kept it, as well.

She would never fear the alpha wolf again.

Losing Ivan Romanov was her only concern.

Chapter 11

He navigated the Ether with ease, as did many of his kind. He loved the chill of it against his skin and the vacuum of its hunger as it tried to take his soul. Many said his family was addicted to its constant pull. After all, his ancestral home had been built on the very edge of the world where the veil was most thin, and, even when they weren't traveling, the hunger of the void was a constant thrill they all experienced from infancy.

Grigori never stayed long away from the rush. He had been the witchblood prince of the Dark *Volkhvy* since his conception, but he'd been free to come and go as he pleased. He pleased often. Living on the edge of the Ether was nothing compared to traveling through it from place to place all over the globe.

As the son of the Dark *Volkhvy* king, it was fitting that he rose to prominence as the darkest, most Ether-influenced of all who had come before him. He was too busy taking to worry about the weaker witches who warned him to be careful. He had gloried in every depravity his power would allow until a Russian peasant woman had stood him down.

She'd used love as power. And none of his travels had prepared him for the strength of the shield she bought for her daughter with her blood. Every moment since had felt diminished.

Except the time he'd spent delivering his special promises in Elena Pavlova's nightmares. More thrilling than challenging the Ether's inexorable pull, his time with his swan soothed him. The visualization and manifestation of what he wanted to do to her when she was finally in his power had eased his impatience.

She'd taken that away from him.

Grigori paced the length of his quarters. His rooms had been built on the top floor of a complex that almost seemed to be a part of the cliff from which it jutted, an architectural masterpiece of steel and glass and stone. One entire wall of his loft-like space had been made of glass. It faced toward a canyon abyss that no human could have traversed. No human could have seen the shimmer of Ether either, though Grigori stared at it often. It bisected the canyon in a sheet of nearly imperceptible power. At times, when the light and weather provided the exact conditions, the Ether wavered like the northern lights before his rapt attention.

The Ether's vacuum was the greatest when it was most visible. He'd often been brought to his knees by the pleasure of its hunger. There were times when he'd imagined its hunger had somehow transferred itself to him.

His hunger for Elena was as powerful as the Ether itself. He'd had no way to ease it for weeks. The connection that he'd established to her through her dreams had been severed.

Only now had he discovered why.

Grigori was tall and lean. His muscles wrapped around his bones in corded perfection. The dark power that continually coursed through him burned away all but what was necessary. He had to keep it at a fever pitch to fight the Ether's pull, especially when he was at home. He looked like a devoted athlete. One addicted to Pilates and the ketosis craze.

And right now his spare frame shook with fury.

The witch who had brought him the message from Ivan Romanov was on his knees. His blood poured onto the polished marble floor, black puddles on white. Steam rose all around him. It proclaimed his weakness. If Grigori's blood had spilled, it would have ignited into blue-tinged flames.

Two Dark *Volkhvy* servants held Dominique by the arms. It wasn't necessary. He had nowhere to go and no power left to take him there. But it was more convenient to Grigori to have him lifted and displayed rather than wilted on the ground. The better to lash out at him again and again. Dominique had failed the witchblood prince. He wouldn't do so again.

"She is protected," he whimpered. "She doesn't stand alone."

He had repeated the same phrase even after Grigori had reacted with slicing jolts of power that flayed the skin from his back and chest.

Elena had taken a few lovers before. Grigori hadn't cared. She'd still been his, night after night. His claim had been unchallenged by momentary pleasure taken with mortal men.

But the Light *Volkhvy*'s dishonored champion was no mortal man.

The name of Romanov was still spoken in hushed tones of anger and fear among the Dark *Volkhvy*. There was no creature capable of threatening a powerful witch…except the Romanov alpha wolf and his brothers. The rising of the Dark had occurred in direct correlation to the fall of the Romanov family. And Vasilisa, the Light *Volkhvy* queen, was too wrapped up in her vengeful punishment to care.

"He still stands. Bronwal is defended. And Elena has sought shelter there to seek his help against you," Dominique said.

Grigori didn't wait for his servants to act. He leaped forward and grabbed the bleeding witch. He used Dominique's slashed and bloody body to push open the glass doors that led onto the platform outside. The observation deck had been built to take in the spectacular view. Its edges and its flooring were more glass than steel. Dominique began to scream long before Grigori easily hoisted his body over the rail. His rapidly falling form was soon a tiny speck, but the witchblood prince watched until it hit the Ether and winked out of sight.

Eaten by Ether was too good for the worthless witch.

But at least now Grigori knew.

He'd been to the Bronwal Gathering often as a young man. The power expended to fuel the curse was an incredible lure even for *Volkhvy* who had power to spare. The Dark and the Light were drawn to the mountain every ten years for a decadent ball. What wasn't to love? He'd even enjoyed the dangerous element of being close to the one being who could kill him. They all did. They bated the wolf, knowing full well the wolf was almost gone.

He stands.

Did he though? Did he stand with Elena? Or was he a broken creature barely holding out against the Ether's pull?

Grigori's fury eased. His servants had backed away from him with their heads down and their hands grasped behind their backs. He might have thrown them to the Ether as well, but he didn't. He now knew where to go to collect Elena Pavlova once the power of her mother's blood ran out.

Chapter 12

She bathed by firelight. The water was pleasantly warm against her sensitive skin. This time, rose petals floated around her. Romanov had closed the windows before he went to fetch the bath. He hadn't reappeared, but servants carrying the tub and the pitchers and buckets had. They didn't seem to mind the extra work she'd added to their nonroutine. In fact, more of them seemed to meet her eyes and speak to her and each other as they worked. Maybe their faculties improved the longer they were materialized. Maybe it helped to have something ordinary to do.

Bell made an appearance. She brought rose water in one of Patrice's vials. It sloshed fragrantly into the tub when she opened it and filled the room with its light scent.

"Where is Patrice?" Elena asked. She had wrapped herself in a 1950s-style smoking jacket she'd found in the wardrobe. It was crafted of thick, quilted ebony velvet and it served very well as a modest bathrobe while servants came and went. She was no longer surprised by the evidence of the passage of time she found each time she opened a cabinet or drawer.

"She's around. Don't worry. She isn't going anywhere as long as she's needed," Bell said. "And we make sure she's needed, don't we?" Her hazel eyes flashed from the shadows of her ever-present cap. Elena had reached out to touch Bell's arm and the other woman had responded by hugging her, as if the contact had startled but pleased her.

"Some of us hold on. Some of us don't. It gets harder every time," Bell said into her hair. And then she ran out the door and down the stairs.

Now, Elena bathed and tried to imagine what it was like to fight the Ether the rest of your days. The Ether must be like Grigori. Hungry. Always lurking. Eager to pull you away from the world and everyone you loved. She'd been startled by Bell's sudden hug, but the other girl must crave human interaction from a person who wasn't addled by Ether.

Romanov had resisted its pull for a long time. Even after all his loved ones had succumbed. What chance did she have to convince him to allow her to resist by his side? Regardless of what he'd said when she first arrived, he was still a champion, and champions weren't used to needing help with their battles. Even ones as amorphous as this. The sword had called her, but its call was useless if Romanov didn't accept its decision.

Her body was tender and replete from their lovemaking. She stretched her legs and arms, and, though the cooling water soothed, it also caused gooseflesh to rise on her skin. She had to rise. She had to seek out the man who was still determined to send her away. He'd given her this bath rather than pillow talk because he didn't know what to say. She'd been wrong when she'd thought he didn't think she was worthy of the sword. His rejection was all about protecting her. She was certain he had feelings for her.

If he cared less, he might have let her stay.

Ivan had a responsibility he couldn't shirk. The fact that his Audience with Vasilisa happened to coincide with his need to avoid Elena was fortuitous, not planned. It was both torturous to leave her after their lovemaking and absolutely necessary. Impossible pledges had risen from the depths of thawed places he hadn't even known still existed in his heart, and he'd had to get away.

He couldn't even fool himself into believing that he'd never touch her again.

As long as he was materialized as a man, he would be drawn to her. The cold Ether in all of its infinite power, he could resist. Elena's humanity, he could not. Her warmth and hunger were irresistible; her warrior's spirit completely beguiling.

He should have been bracing himself for his mandatory time with Vasilisa. She required a meeting every materialization. She was ancient. She was powerful. And she was still angry with his family after all these years. She needed to see them suffer. At first, they'd thought it was a mercy that she didn't annihilate them following Vladimir's betrayal. They'd tried to carry on as her loyal subjects during the materializations. But it wasn't long before they realized that death might have been preferable to an eternal purgatory of punishment. She would never relent.

Ivan had borne the brunt of her attention once he'd

taken command. He had to face her every Cycle. If he refused to give her an Audience, she might decide to further punish his people in some horrible way. But he'd long since given up hope of seeing her anger fade or her forgiveness earned.

He strode through Bronwal to the Audience Chamber with no plan or preparation. His thoughts were consumed with Elena. So when he arrived to find his brothers already stationed outside the door, he was startled. He was usually the first to appear.

"I'm not late. You're early," he said to Lev and Soren. Soren was the only one who reacted with a cocked head. Lev only stared straight ahead. He was almost like the statue of himself in the gallery. "Want to come inside?" He held the door open, but neither wolf responded to his invitation. He didn't blame them. Vasilisa's manner of appearing had always been difficult to witness.

The Audience Chamber had once been a chapel; its high arched windows were constructed of intricate stained glass depicting religious scenes and saints. They were beautiful and nearly forgotten, larger-than-life obscure figures that muted the light from outside. All other chapel accoutrements had been removed. There were no kneeling benches or crosses. There was no altar. In the entire vaulted room, there was only a huge Baroque mirror, elaborately crafted of gold-leafed metal in the design of roses and thorns, and a single, tall candelabrum that provided enough artificial light to see.

The candles had been burning for a while. The room was filled with the scent of melted wax, and a fresh molten flow had joined centuries of dried and hardened wax that had flowed before.

Ivan approached the mirror until he was close enough

to see his shadowy reflection in its antique, rippled glass, but he left plenty of room for what was to come.

The candlelight flickered while he waited. He didn't wait long. No matter how many times he saw the glass begin to bow outward in the shape of a woman he was always bothered by the silvery mirror flowing across Vasilisa's face and form. It ran like water sluiced off of a sea creature that rose from the depths, first liquid and then foaming around her moving body. She stepped out of the mirror, which was, in fact, an enchanted portal she'd crafted so she could come and go from their lives at will. She'd used it to visit their father after their mother's death.

What had been crafted for love had been warped for revenge.

She used it now to subjugate the last Romanov. Ivan didn't kneel. He didn't have to. He had no other liege. No one else held sway over the *Volkhvy* power that ran in his veins. It was her power. He'd had a mortal mother, but Vasilisa had also been his creator. She had made him the black wolf.

"Queen Vasilisa, I am still here," Romanov said. He'd greeted her with the same words every materialization for a century. It had never been intended as a pledge of loyalty. It had always been defiance. And the savvy ruler knew it. She had allowed him the luxury up until now. He always wondered, every time he uttered the words, if it would be the last time.

"So I see," Vasilisa replied.

She was older than the castle itself, but she appeared to him as a handsome middle-aged woman. He never knew what fashion from what century she would choose to wear for these meetings. This time she was dressed in an elaborate gown with a nipped waist and an oddly pronounced bottom. It was intricately crafted of brocade silk in jewel tones of violet and amber. Her snow-white hair was piled high on top of her head in coiled curls held in place with gold pins. Her hair had always been white. He remembered the shock of it when he'd been a young boy. Her white hair and unlined face. As Vasilisa came from the glass, the pins in her hair sparkled and Romanov saw the perpetual roses and thorns in their design.

"I never know if it will be the black wolf waiting for me. Have you never thought of it? The black wolf could devour its maker as easily as it has devoured countless Dark *Volkhvy*," Vasilisa said.

"And then what would happen to my people?" Ivan asked. "They wouldn't be freed from the curse."

"No. They wouldn't. That would have been a self-destructive spell for me to weave. Casting my own downfall as their means of release?" Vasilisa walked slowly around the room. Her shoes were anachronistic compared to the rest of her dress. They were high-heeled boots of a more modern design. They flashed as she lifted her skirts daintily over puddles of molten wax on the floor.

"I would have let the black wolf take you many years ago to save my family," Ivan confessed. She already knew it. Saying it aloud only gave him comfort. He distressed her not at all. This was their usual conversation. Vasilisa seemed to need to air her grievances again and again. And he couldn't resist the urge to join her. It was a repetitive battle they waged with familiar accusations and false civility in place of actual blows.

Death by a thousand forced conversations with a being who radiated hatred of the blood she'd made.

"Your mother died at the hands of a Dark *Volkhvy*

king. She died for me. And now her son threatens me with teeth that I allowed him to have," Vasilisa said. This was why she came every Cycle without fail. To condemn him and his family over and over again.

"My mother died for you. She died trying to defend your prince consort when they were attacked by the Dark *Volkhvy*. And you cursed her family. It only seems fair that I would end the curse if I could," he said.

"You know nothing of what your father did to deserve this curse. I respected your mother. She was a fine warrior to carry the sapphire blade. Your father was a savage. He didn't deserve the power he was given. I'm not surprised he was the first to fade," Vasilisa said. As usual, his defense angered her and yet she seemed eager for the emotional release of their verbal thrusts and parries.

"My father betrayed you. You punished him. I won't fault you for that. My mother wielded the blade long after their love failed. When she died, there was no one else to balance out his greed. I was too young. My brothers were even younger."

"You are Romanovs," Vasilisa said. She raised her voice. Her body stiffened. There was the anger he'd always known. It wasn't quick and hot and gone. It simmered, low and forever. As long as he appeared, with every Cycle, she would arrive to rehash the events that had led to their long, arduous demise.

"My father did what he chose to do with the power he'd been given," Ivan said. "The power you gave him. We've only tried to survive the aftermath of his bad choices."

"He betrayed your mother and my consort long before he betrayed me," Vasilisa said.

"Yes. He did. Before she died, he had mistresses. You weren't his first bad decision, but you were the worst," Ivan said. "I'm just glad he didn't pursue you until my mother was gone. She was loyal to you. She believed in the Light."

"Naomi was my warrior. I never would have betrayed her. I never would have betrayed my prince. Vladimir knew that. He waited until they were dead," Vasilisa said softly. "Or he ensured that they would die."

"How would she have felt about what you've done to us?" Ivan asked. He ignored her new accusation. What did it matter if his father was an even worse traitor than he'd realized? But he was genuinely curious about the mother he'd only known when he was a child. He was surprised when Vasilisa's face visibly flinched. Her eyes widened. Her teeth clicked shut. In all the meetings he'd been forced to attend with her, through all the Cycles he'd endured, he'd never seen her betray any emotion other than anger.

Had he gone too far?

"Were you going to tell me about the sword?" Vasilisa suddenly asked. Her reaction hadn't been in response to his words. She'd been responding to a slight sound outside the door. Lev had growled. Now, he whined, a much softer, pained sound. And Ivan stiffened when a familiar voice warned the white wolf to stand down. This meeting was about to take a turn nearly endless repetitions hadn't prepared him for.

"It called her here, but I'm not going to let her stay," Ivan said.

"Do you honestly think who stays and who goes is your decision?" Vasilisa asked, so sweetly that shivers tickled down his spine.

* * *

Her connection with the sapphire had grown stronger. After her bath, she pulled on fresh underwear and jeans. She shrugged into her black long-sleeve T-shirt and tall leather boots. She wasn't sure who had washed the clothes she'd worn, but she was grateful. The energy in the gem on the hilt of the Romanov blade hummed beneath her skin. She wound her damp hair up into a messy bun and belted the sheath she'd found for the blade around her waist. It had taken her a while to find a sheath that was still in good condition. She'd tried and discarded several whose leather was pitted and cracked before she'd found one that had survived the neglect.

She'd found the belt and the boots in the same place. They were sitting together in a dark hallway, as if the person who'd worn them had simply vanished.

The sword belt hadn't been made for the sapphire blade, but it worked. She slid the sword home with a firm hand, and it wedged into a loose iron ring lined with a leather loop. The tip of the blade ended up all the way down by her injured knee, but there was enough give in the construction of the belt to allow her to manipulate the blade out of her way as she walked.

By the time she walked out the door and down the stairs, she felt more like a swashbuckler or a musketeer than a warrior. Or perhaps a tiny dancer playing a swashbuckler? She had yet to prove herself or put the sword's choice to the test, but she had to believe she could and would use it when the time came to defend Bronwal and herself.

And Romanov.

Before Vladimir's betrayal, the Light *Volkhvy* queen had created the swords and the wolves. If she'd intended the swords to choose worthy mates for her wolves, she must have done it for a reason.

Even enchanted champions were stronger when they weren't alone.

She'd climbed the mountain to find a legendary wolf to save her, but the hum of power the sapphire caused beneath her skin suggested that she might be able to contribute to the salvation of them all.

Chapter 13

When Elena found the wolves outside of the door she had been drawn to, almost like a human magnet, she was certain she'd found Romanov. The hum of power beneath her skin made her heart flutter and her skin tingle almost as bad as it had when she'd been "electrocuted" by the Dark *Volkhvy* woman, but it seemed as if her body was adjusting to *Volkhvy* power. Either that or the sapphire channeled it in a way that her mortal form could withstand.

The white wolf snapped out of his nearly frozen stance. He'd been staring straight ahead. When she stepped closer, he became limber once more. He dropped his head. He planted his front paws. He growled. The sound skittered along her spine. It was a clear warning. Soren whined. But he didn't leave his post on the opposite side of the door.

"Romanov is in there, isn't he? I'm going in. If I have to go through you, Lev, so be it," Elena said.

The sword slid easily out of the hilt she'd found. There was barely a scrape of its blade against leather and then a slight vibration along the shaft like a soft metallic song.

She hadn't been training long, but she'd been training all her life. One dance wasn't so very unlike another. Her body easily assumed the stance she'd been taught. And it wasn't a defensive one. She moved forward. Soren whined again. This time his concerned sound was paired with movement. It was the red wolf, not the white wolf, that stepped to block her way in front of the door.

Elena paused. Without thinking, she switched the placement of her feet and her arms to a defensive stance. She wouldn't attack Soren. Not unless she absolutely had no other choice. The red wolf's eyes were still intelligent. They sparkled like warm copper pennies as their gazes connected. He had saved her from Lev when she'd disturbed the baby's room. How could she hurt him now?

"Where is your sword, Soren? Where is the warrior that would fight by your side?" she asked softly. The red wolf only blinked at her. His brown eyes were intelligent but enigmatic.

This time it was Lev who whined. Elena looked at the white wolf. His tail had fallen and he'd tucked it between his legs. His knees had loosened and he'd dropped his belly to the floor. Did he understand her question or had something else scared him?

Her answer came from behind the wolves. The large oaken door opened inward. The overwhelming scent of candles wafted out along with the stronger scent of roses. She'd bathed in rose water, but this scent was more lush and wild. It didn't come from her skin.

"Welcome to Bronwal, dearling. I'm afraid you'll have to come inside to meet me. I'm only allowed in the Audience Chamber before the Gathering," a woman's voice echoed in singsong tones from the candlelit room beyond the door. There was an odd jewel-tone quality to the light that Elena didn't understand until she stepped forward. The wolves parted, one on each side. Soren's hackles had gone high. Lev's belly was now on the ground. He didn't growl when she passed. Before she crossed the threshold, she saw a glimpse of stained-glass windows that explained the quality of the light.

"Elena, no. Walk away. The Audience will be over soon. She'll be drawn back to where she came from until the Gathering," Romanov said.

But Elena wouldn't leave him alone in the room with that threatening voice.

She came forward with her sword still drawn. The hum of power beneath her skin was nearly unbearable. She bore it. She clamped her teeth against the vibration and the pain it caused in her knee.

She didn't expect to see a petite Victorian lady in the middle of the room near a mirror. The mirror's glass swirled like a whirlpool of silvery liquid. The swirl reflected the stained glass causing a kaleidoscope effect on the vaulted ceiling above them.

She knew the identity of the woman she faced before anyone spoke another word. The reaction of the wolves and Romanov's desperate tone gave her clues, as did his use of the term "audience." Only the queen who had made him could require Ivan Romanov to attend her.

Vasilisa wore the colors of twilight paired with the color of the sun.

There was more purple than gold in her dress, as if the gold was fading away.

"Oh, this is such a surprise," the Light *Volkhvy* queen

said. She was between Romanov and the mirror. She had obviously been walking around the big warrior who stood almost at attention. He hadn't rushed toward the door to try to stop Elena from entering. She was fairly certain his verbal warning had been a superhuman effort on his part. This audience was an enchanted one. He had no choice but to be here and be teased and tormented by the queen who had cursed his family.

Elena's hand tightened on the sword. The sapphire nearly burned her hand with its power. But its power had come from Vasilisa. She was almost certain she wouldn't be able to use the Romanov blade against the queen who had made it.

"Where did you come from, dearling?" Vasilisa asked. "I'm impressed that you've woken the blade after so long. The last woman to wield it was a great favorite of mine. She killed many Dark *Volkhvy* to defend the Light."

"I've come from Saint Petersburg," Elena answered. The information came too easily to her tongue. She looked from the violet-clad witch to Romanov. His hands were clenched, but he hadn't turned to face her. Was he compelled to stand there at the queen's pleasure as she'd been compelled to answer the queen's question?

"Don't look surprised. He is mine. And now that you've claimed the Romanov blade, you are mine, as well," Vasilisa said. She came closer to Elena but she stopped well before they came face-to-face. Elena looked down at the floor. The queen had stopped inside the circle of light radiating from the mirror's swirling face.

Vasilisa was tied to the mirror.

"*No.* I'm not going to marry her. I'm going to send her away," Romanov said.

Vasilisa turned to stare at Ivan Romanov. He was vulnerable standing there unable to move, but he was also impressive. Because even frozen in place by the Light *Volkhvy*'s power, he was still taking a stand.

"My enchantments aren't affected by silly mortal ceremonies. The blade has called her and she has claimed it. All that's left is for you to claim her. I suspect that's already occurred, whether you'll admit it or not," she said.

Elena's face burned.

The queen turned back to her and laughed as if she'd sensed her emotion.

"My enchantments also aren't affected by carnal actions. Can you imagine how complicated that would have been with Vladimir Romanov claiming every skirt that walked by? I'm talking about connection and emotion. Mortals might say heart and soul. What say you, Ivan Romanov? Does this warrior claim your soul?" Vasilisa said.

"I stand alone," Romanov replied. Too easily for it to be a lie.

Elena didn't drop the sword. She couldn't. Her hand went cold as the constant vibration of power she'd experienced since she'd picked up the blade disappeared. The sapphire flickered as if it tried to fight Romanov's decision, but then its glow faded away.

"And now I can see another claim on this woman," Vasilisa said. Her arms had fallen at her side and her figure moved backward toward the mirror without any obvious steps. The silvery whirlpool left the frame to reach out toward the approaching queen. "She is claimed by the witchblood prince. His mark is upon her. It rides her shoulders like a shadow she can't escape. The sapphire's power hid her for a while, but now she's exposed." The liquid mirror began to engulf the queen's face and figure. It flowed around her. It ran into her eyes and nose and mouth. Elena couldn't breathe as she watched in horror. "Only the black wolf can stop Grigori. And the black wolf doesn't dare to show itself at the Gathering. I couldn't protect it from all the Dark and Light that will come to the ball, even if I cared to try."

Her last words were gurgled rather than expressed. Elena gagged as the queen disappeared into the glass. Her body had been completely absorbed.

"It's only a portal. She's fine. I doubt if she even breathes air. It's probably vengeance that pumps through her lungs," Romanov said. The tension in his broad back had eased. He turned to her and she saw that his green eyes were his own. His rejection hadn't been a trick of the queen.

She forced her numbed fingers to let go of the sword. It fell with a ringing clank on the flagstones of the floor. Elena looked up at the saints in the windows. They were vivid in their pain, each martyred for one cause or another. Ivan Romanov belonged up there with them. Memorialized in stained glass.

"I told you I wouldn't bind you to the Ether," he said.

"Instead, you would allow Grigori to find me," she said.

"He has to come to the Gathering in order for me to kill him," Romanov said.

"I should be the one to defeat him with the Romanov blade. He is my monster. My nightmare. You can't kill him with your bare hands as you kill the lesser witches," Elena said.

"I will do whatever I have to do to stop him," Romanov said.

"You heard the queen. The black wolf can't take on a whole Gathering alone. They've been baiting you all along. That's why they come Cycle after Cycle. Each one hopes to be the one who can deliver the last Romanov's head to the Light *Volkhvy* queen or the Dark *Volkhvy* king. She created you, and now she will stand back and allow you to be killed if you shift during the Gathering to protect me," Elena said.

"I will do whatever I have to do to stop him," he repeated.

She was left alone in the chapel when he walked away.

"Except give me your heart," she said. The stained-glass saints died as martyrs all around her and they gave her no reply.

Chapter 14

The absence of the sword's hum was a keen ache in her bones. The ache she also felt over Romanov's rejection was overshadowed by concern. He had stood for Bronwal and his lost family for so long. She hadn't realized what risks she would be asking the legendary warrior and his black wolf to face when she'd first climbed the mountain in the snow. Escaping Grigori had dominated her mind.

If she escaped him now at the price of Romanov's life, she would be tortured in a completely different way.

She didn't leave the sword where it had fallen in the chapel. Romanov had walked out without picking it up. He'd left it dull and silent at her feet. She had leaned over and picked it up herself. She'd resheathed it, and it was back at her side. She wouldn't meekly accept his decision. The sword had chosen, and she had accepted its call.

Romanov had rejected her, but what if he decided to

shift to save her? What would that say about his true feelings for her? Would the sapphire sing to life in time for her to prevent his sacrifice?

She had to hope the sapphire understood Romanov's heart better than she could.

But hope wasn't enough. She only had one more week before the Gathering, and in that space of time she had to make Ivan Romanov change his mind. The sword had to be brought to life again before Grigori arrived. Somehow she had to get Romanov to accept her as the wielder of the sword and his mate, in spite of his desire to protect her. She had to risk her pride and her heart for a legendary warrior who might simply be fulfilling his duty. They'd had a fiery connection from the start. The chemistry between them was unmistakable. But the sword required a pledge of the heart, and Romanov might have lost his ability to love long before they met.

Elena in the chapel with Vasilisa had been almost more than he could bear. He'd always hated the Audience. The mirror was a horror. The Light queen had the power to destroy all he had left with the flick of her hand. Even when he'd been treated as a treasured pet as a young boy, he understood she wasn't human and feared her. Her feelings were more volatile and changeable than a mere mortal's could be. When his father had betrayed her and the curse had come down on Bronwal and all connected to it, his fears had been confirmed.

He'd walked a fine line with her ever since.

The Audience was required. He was compelled to attend and held in a paralyzed state while it occurred to ensure that the queen had safe passage. All of that had been a trial and tribulation he endured for his people time and time again.

But up until Elena walked over the threshold of the chapel's door, he hadn't known true terror.

If Vasilisa even suspected he cared for the petite ballerina, she would be lost. Hadn't the Light *Volkhvy* queen taken everyone he'd ever loved away from him? The sword had almost given him away. The sapphire had almost refused to lose its glow. He'd had to let the black wolf totally claim his heart in order to fool Elena and the queen. Once Elena believed him, the sword finally let her go.

He'd felt the sapphire die. He'd felt the cold numbness claim the woman he could have loved. And the black wolf had howled long and loud in the deep recesses of his body. Its savagery had helped him fool Elena, but even the wolf didn't want to let her go.

All the while, he'd stood facing the mirror, unable to turn around. He hadn't seen Elena's face. Worst of all, he hadn't been able to go to her when Vasilisa saw the mark of Grigori upon her. The black wolf did more than howl when the Light queen said that the witchblood prince had claimed Elena. It had clawed and chewed and shredded his soul with its vicious teeth trying to get out.

He had exposed Elena. To protect her from the queen, he'd betrayed her to Grigori. And the only way he could put it right was to loose the alpha wolf to prowl, even if that allowed Bronwal to fall.

Grigori knew where she was.

The afternoon faded into evening, and every second seemed to tick away like a bomb she was powerless to defuse. Her connection with the sword had hidden her from Grigori. Now that the connection was gone she felt exposed. It wouldn't matter if she tried not to sleep. She'd tried that before. She'd used coffee and caffeine pills. More and more until her hands shook and her heart raced. And still she had always eventually slept. He hadn't been able to physically touch her, but he was always there as soon as her eyes closed. One blink too languorous at 3:00 a.m. and suddenly she was gone into a nightmare world she couldn't escape.

And that was when she'd been protected by her mother's spell.

The Dark *Volkhvy* woman had touched her.

Elena remembered the shock of the power flowing through her and the knowledge that her mother's protection was almost gone.

Elena trained for hours all alone in the courtyard with a sword that didn't sing. But once the sun went down, she retreated to the tower room. The key to the lock was still around her neck. She'd recognized the roses and thorns on the mirror in the chapel. It wasn't odd that the Light queen's motif was worked into the construction of Bronwal. It had been built for her champions.

There was no use in locking the door. She did it anyway. Grigori wasn't welcome. She wanted to make that perfectly clear even if her will didn't matter to him at all. He might not need her permission, but it still felt empowering not to give it. Eventually, after hours of waiting as wakefully as she could in a chair, she moved to the bed she'd shared only the night before with Romanov. The sheets had been changed. Patrice or Bell had come and gone. She didn't even have the comfort of his scent on the pillows.

She placed the Romanov blade beside her. It was a

cool comfort, but a comfort nonetheless. Even power-less, it reminded her of whom she had chosen to be. She wouldn't allow Grigori to take that from her even if he hurt her in her dreams. The fear that he might be able to physically touch her now caused her stomach to clench.

But then she heard toenails on the stairs.

First Lev and then Soren appeared at the door. She saw their great white and red heads position themselves on either side like sentries. They weren't as big or as pow-erful as Ivan, but they were here. Perhaps their presence would keep Grigori away.

He found Lev and Soren where he'd ordered them to stand. They were wide-awake and alert even though it was well past midnight. He quietly approached and looked in the door. He didn't try the handle. He needed to believe it was locked against him. One glimpse of Elena asleep on the bed they'd shared made him want to join her there and pull her into his arms.

He didn't.

Instead, he turned and placed his back against the door. He crossed his arms over his chest.

Her whereabouts might be visible to Grigori once more, but if he tried to appear he would face all three of the Romanov wolves.

Chapter 15

She had wings again. They were large and white and beautiful in the moonlight…until they were covered in her own blood. The cage was too small. Smaller than it had ever been. It constricted her movements including her ability to draw breath into her plump, feathered breast. Elena frantically beat against the bars of the cage. It was useless. She didn't care. After weeks of freedom, the confinement was worse. Much worse.

Because Grigori was there.

He wasn't with her in the nightmare as he usually was. He was with her body where it slept in the tower.

"Your wolves won't save you," he said. His voice was sultry and low and so close to her that she realized he was bending close to her ear in real life. She felt his heated breath against *skin*, not feathers. In this nightmare, she was a swan in a cage. In real life, she had fallen asleep and Grigori had found her. He was there. Leaning over her helpless, sleeping form. "I'm only here to remind you that you're mine. You can't escape me. Your wolves are an inconvenience. No more. No less. And no matter what he's done to you, it hasn't erased my mark."

She stilled in her cage. Her tiny swan heart fluttered in distress. She needed to take to the sky. She needed to flee. But she was helpless. When the press of his hot lips came against her cheek, she could only react as the swan. She erupted in a furious, frantic explosion of bloody feathers. She flapped her wings even though they caught against the bars of the cage. She struggled even as she bled. She fought. She screamed as a swan with wordless cackles and cries. And Grigori laughed. He enjoyed her anger and her pain.

But it wasn't his laugh that woke her from the nightmare.

Romanov called her name as Grigori's soft and silky touch began to slide along her helpless arms. Romanov's familiar voice rang out and delivered her from her sleep paralysis.

She sat up. She struggled against a tangle of sheets.

Thud.

The scent of ozone filled the air, but it was dissipating through an open casement window. She had checked all the latches before she got in bed. It was pitch-black outside.

Thud.

Once she was free of the sheets, she ran to the window to latch it again, but that's when she saw the shadowy form of a large raven distinct against the grayer black of the night sky. It circled around the tower, calling and calling.

Thud.

Its call sounded like Grigori's laughter. It hadn't been a dream. The witchblood prince had been in her room. He had touched her. Only Romanov had stopped him from continuing to molest her as she slept, trapped in a nightmare she couldn't escape from by waking.

"Elena!"

The tower room door splintered in a loud crash as Romanov came into the room. He'd used his shoulder against it. She'd heard the thuds, but hadn't processed what was happening. She'd only heard her name.

"He was here. Physically here. He kissed my cheek," Elena said. "He touched my arm." Her insides were hollow. Her heart barely seemed to beat. "He was never able to do that before. My mother's protection has faded away."

It was like losing her mother all over again. The shield had been powered by blood, but it had been love that had strengthened it and made it hold against Grigori. Her mother was gone.

Romanov came to her. He reached for the sword in her hand that she hadn't even realized she'd carried with her to the window. Its stone responded to his touch when his hand closed over hers. The pale blue light rose up and illuminated his face.

Elena stepped forward to press against him. She needed his solidity and his strength.

The stone's glow increased. But Romanov didn't pull away. His hand tightened over hers on the sword's hilt, and his other arm came up to wrap around her back. He held her. He pressed her against his chest. Only then did she feel the trembling that racked her body. It wasn't fear. It was anger. Pure fury that Grigori had dared to touch her. He'd done much worse in her nightmares for years.

She'd experienced every depravity he could think of in her dreams. But nothing was worse than the actual violation of his lips on her skin.

"I will kill him. I'll spill every drop of his black blood," Elena swore.

Romanov didn't argue. He held her while his brothers paced around the room. The large wolves were obviously shaken by the invading presence they could sense had been there.

"I was just outside the door. We thought you were safe. Until you cried out in your sleep. The window should have made a noise. Lev and Soren should have smelled him," Romanov said into her hair.

"They're used to the scent of ravens. And Ether. I've smelled it in the hallways. It's like ozone after a storm. Grigori had never been able to get close enough to me for me to smell it before," Elena said. "But he reeked of it." Suddenly, she buried her face against Romanov's chest. Long locks of his hair hung down. She snuggled into them, breathing deeply of his wintry, masculine scent. His scent drove Grigori's away.

The glow of the stone responded to his reaction to her nuzzling. It grew brighter, bathing both of them in its light. The entire room was lit by the softest haze of blue now. It couldn't be ignored.

"The stone knows what you try to deny," Elena said softly. She pulled back to look up at his face. His eyes held hers in the low light; they seemed a darker green in the shadows.

"I'm not ruled by Vasilisa's blade," Romanov said.

"You'll die if I can't wield the sword," Elena said.

"You'll die if Vasilisa thinks that I care for you," Romanov replied.

He leaned down to kiss her and her lips opened eagerly beneath his. The kiss wasn't tender. It was bruising and angry and all the more sweet because he lost control for a few seconds before he regained it and pulled away.

Elena looked over his shoulder at the crushed tower door. It had come halfway off its iron hinges. The latch hung busted to the side. More evidence of the powerful feelings he wouldn't share.

"This was never a refuge, but it's even less of one now that Grigori has tainted it. I can't sleep here again," she said. She reached for the key around her neck with her free hand. She lifted its chain from around her neck. The key dangled from the silver chain, more useless than it had ever been. She'd never been willing to use it against Romanov. While he watched, she dropped it on the floor at their feet. There would never be bars between them again.

"You can't be alone. This happened even with me and my brothers outside the door," Romanov said. He held her too tightly but she didn't pull away. If his ferocious grip was all he could offer, she wouldn't push him away. "Come with me. The sword will light our way."

He didn't let go of the hand that held the sword. It ended up gripped between them by both of their hands as they walked down the stairs. The faint blue glow spilled over the steps in front of them and they followed it away from the ravens, the key, and the wrought-iron bars made of thorns and roses.

Chapter 16

They didn't stop on any of the main floors. Staircase after staircase wound down through the center of the castle. Romanov had said they would follow the sword, but it was actually his steps that led them, illuminated softly by the gem's light. He paused to enter the door of a large chamber beneath the kitchens. Elena waited outside. It was a room she hadn't explored, and through the narrow opening he'd left, she could see walls lined with books and the foot of a massive bed. She assumed it was his room. The air held the scent of paper, old ink, leather and the slight hint of ash from a fireplace she couldn't see.

When he carried some bedding out of the room, he brought the scent with him. It was pleasant and sensual in a homey way. She hadn't imagined him sleeping or reading or warming himself by a fire. Apparently, legends needed the comforts of hearth and home even when they tried to deny it.

The stone had faded greatly by the time he returned to her side, but once he'd shifted the bedding to one side and clasped her hand, the stone brightened again. It was like a mood ring for their relationship. He refused to acknowledge their connection, but his silence didn't fool the stone.

Several more flights of stairs took them lower and lower until they were below the keep. The polished flagstone roughened into coarser stone until the last stairway was nothing but steps that had been roughly carved out of the mountain itself. They had descended beneath man-made levels into a natural cavern that opened up into a cathedral-like space beneath the castle.

The sapphire gem in the hilt of her sword suddenly flared and Elena paused on the stair. Romanov allowed himself to be pulled to a halt by her stop.

"It's beautiful," she said. The light from the stone filled the cavern with its soft blue glow. Natural mica in the cavern's limestone twinkled like stardust above and around them.

"And cold when you don't have a wolf's coat. That's why I brought the blankets," Romanov said. His breath fogged in the air. "Welcome to the black wolf's lair. It's the one place I could think of where even a witchblood prince would be afraid to follow. I haven't been here myself in some time."

Elena shivered, but not because of the cold. She could imagine the alpha wolf in this place. It was a fitting lair for an enchanted wolf.

"Even Lev and Soren don't come here," Romanov said. He tugged on her hand and she followed him the rest of the way down the stairs. The walls narrowed and curved so that the cavern became a tunnel. The air was slightly warmer. Their breath no longer showed. The tunnel was large enough to accommodate the black wolf, but small enough to be cozier than the cavern. And, when the tunnel curved to end in an irregularly shaped oval room with a depression on its floor, she knew they'd reached their destination.

Romanov spread the bedding out on the smooth stone floor.

Once again, the stone's glow began to fade. The room darkened around them. The stardust on the walls twinkled when she moved closer to Romanov. He'd brought several blankets, furs and a heavy quilt. The nest looked appealing, not the least because the man himself had settled to his knees on the bedding once it was laid.

"Vasilisa isn't here," Elena said as she sank to her knees beside him. She placed the sword within reach on the edge of the depression. When she released the hilt, the gem faded more still. They were in darkness but it was a slightly bluish dark that sparkled around the edges of her vision.

"No, she isn't. We're alone," Romanov said. "Except for the blade."

"The blade already knows," Elena said. She flaunted his denials. She dared him to continue to reject her.

But her bold words turned to a gasp when he reached for her face in the dark. She could barely see him. His expression was shadowed. But she recognized the intensity there. She saw his intention. His strong calloused fingers cupped her face on either side. He tilted her chin and he held her firmly in place. Her breath caught as he slowly lowered his lips to her upturned mouth.

When their lips touched, the sapphire pulsed in time with the throbbing beat of her heart. The strobe effect combined with the mica on the walls caused her head to swirl. She closed her eyes and realized it wasn't the light or sparkle that made her dizzy. It was Romanov's tongue teasing in and out of her lips in time with the beat of her heart. She reached for him and found the heat of his skin through his linen shirt where his leather jerkin had ridden up at the waist. He moaned against her tongue as she tasted his lips and caressed the heated skin she could feel through his shirt.

"Elena," Romanov breathed against her mouth when they paused for air. "I won't let Grigori or the Ether have you. When this is done, you'll be free."

"I thought I wanted freedom, but now I crave something more. I want to fight by your side. Forever or as long as the fight goes on. I won't accept anything less from you, Ivan Romanov," Elena vowed. "You've brought me to your lair. Now let me into your heart."

"She would destroy you to punish me. I'm the last Romanov and she won't rest until I've been completely subdued," he said.

He raised his head away from her lips and his warm hands slid from her face. She held him, but he seemed prepared to pull away. His body had gone stiff beneath her hands. His spine was ramrod straight as they faced each other, knees to knees.

Elena twined her arms around his neck. She didn't grasp him. She only held him. She only pressed the length of her torso against his. She was rewarded by an intake of air and the tilt of his chin as he closed his eyes at the sensation of her full breasts against him.

"Then she'll never rest," Elena said. "The Ether will

never take us. Not when we have this to look forward to with every materialization."

She pressed into him harder and he didn't resist when her weight urged him back on the quilts. She straddled him once he was stretched out beneath her. She reminded him of what they'd shared before with a gentle rocking of her hips. And she was rewarded with a sudden hardening beneath her bottom. It seemed as if all they'd ever have was stolen time, but she'd decided she could live as a swashbuckler after all if Romanov was her reward.

"It isn't only the Ether I'm afraid of for you, Elena." Romanov reached up to cup her face again. His move stilled her hips. She held herself still with her hands on his broad chest. He pulled her down so he could look into her eyes in the soft blue light. "My mother died at the hands of the Dark *Volkhvy* king. She was holding the sword when she fell. It didn't save her. My father didn't save her. Warriors fall even when they have the full protection of the Light. I can't lose you to the Ether *or to the fight.*"

Elena couldn't breathe. She could see the darkness in his emerald eyes. The shadows she'd thought were only Ether taint. He'd been hurt long before the curse by his mother's death. He'd been trying to save Bronwal far longer than she'd imagined. His mother had been killed battling the Dark *Volkhvy*, and he'd had to continue to fight for the deadly queen who had demanded his mother's sacrifice. Suddenly, Elena knew… Vasilisa had cursed the Romanovs by choosing them as champions and enchanting their blood. Ivan saw the sword and the shift as a curse.

Even before the Ether began to devour the castle ten years at a time.

The legend that had enchanted her since she was a child wasn't a legend to Ivan. It was a nightmare from which he could never awake. He cared for her. She was certain. But she was more certain than ever that he wouldn't allow the sword to claim her.

He'd always loved the galaxies that shimmered here beneath the earth. He'd claimed this place a century ago because of the mica in the walls. Now as he saw them sparkle above Elena's head he was glad that he'd found the cavern one wild hunt long ago. He'd been in his wolf form back before there was any danger in it. He and his brothers had been chasing a large hare more for sport than for food. It had darted down a hole close to a crevice that led into the cavern. He'd sought refuge here after that. He would shift and lie beneath his own private stars while his parents fought and his mother cried.

After she died, he would come here to retreat from Vasilisa when she came to see his father. Everyone suspected they had become lovers. The queen's prince consort had died in the same Dark *Volkhvy* attack as his mother. Ivan hadn't cared about his father's assignations with the queen. But he couldn't forgive the "Light" queen for being the cause of his mother's death. She'd been strong and brave and honorable.

And then she'd been gone.

He'd been left with nothing but the demands of his brothers and the harshness of his father. Then he'd been left with nothing but the entire Romanov enclave and everyone in it. Vasilisa hadn't even blinked when she'd condemned her young wolf shifters to hell. He'd endured it alone.

Until Elena Pavlova came.

She couldn't have any idea how tempted he was by what she offered. A mate. A partner. Stalwart support in the face of the endless vacuum that sought to annihilate him. He'd felt its pull long before the curse. After his mother's death, he would stay too long in his wolf form and have to force his way out.

But this time was different.

"I had no say in my mother's sacrifice, but I can prevent yours," he said.

"She died for a cause she believed in. The sword wouldn't have chosen her if she didn't willingly pick it up," Elena said. "Vasilisa is wrong in many ways, but she's right to fight the Dark *Volkhvy*. I've seen the witchblood prince's dreams and desires. He has to be stopped. Not only from tormenting me. Stopped altogether."

"You're a dancer. Not a warrior," Ivan said. He lifted one of her arms from his chest and trailed his fingers along its graceful curve. Her muscles were harder though. He could feel the bulge of her bicep beneath his thumb. They silently proclaimed his words a falsehood.

"I am both. I've always been both," Elena said.

He pulled her closer and silenced her with his lips. She resisted for only a moment before she allowed her body to melt against his. He plumbed her mouth with his tongue, exploring the different textures of silk and velvet while his fingers threaded into the blond waves of her hair. The glow from the sapphire had given the flaxen strands a blue halo. He closed his eyes against a truth he tried to deny. She couldn't be the sapphire's warrior.

He wouldn't allow it.

A faint scent of roses came from her skin, but it combined with her unique energy to create a lighter, fresher scent than the heavier scent of Vasilisa. The *Volkhvy* queen's perfume brought to mind lush, blood-red roses in such profuse bloom that they approached decay. Elena's skin reminded him of spring and potent pink buds just beginning to open.

He'd grown up with the queen's motif, a claim and a poignant reminder, throughout the castle. But Elena had somehow taken it and changed it. There was beauty and hope in the buds and strength with resilience in the thorns when she touched them.

"You're trying to distract me," Elena protested. They'd parted only enough for air. Her words were a soft whisper of breath against his lips. He was already rampantly erect. He throbbed against the heat she'd settled firmly against him. He ran his hands from her hair, down the delicate curve of her back to cup the firm mounds of her bottom. He pressed and she hmmmed an approval. The sound vibrated against him.

"You need to forget what happened earlier tonight. We both do. What better way than this?" he asked. He lifted his hips to rub his shaft against the hot V between her legs, and she moaned in response. Her eyes rolled back and she slid her hands up from his shoulders to his face. She cupped his jaw and met his eyes. It was dark. There were shadows that hid thoughts of what might come between them. It was a stolen respite. A chance to focus on the intense physical connection they'd found without the battle of where it might lead them.

He would protect her. He would pleasure her. Until the Ether claimed him.

And he would gladly be swallowed by Ether for eternity to keep her safe.

* * *

When he gently flipped her off his hips and onto the quilts that padded the rock beneath them, Elena didn't have time to protest. When he stood to shrug out of his shirt and leather jerkin, she didn't want to protest. The view was too spectacular. Not only the broad expanse of his masculine chest, but the backdrop of a thousand stars behind him. The sapphire's glow caused the mica to sparkle. It also highlighted the dark waves of his wild hair and bathed every inch of him in pale blue light.

He was tall and broad and his erection swelled out his pants between his muscled thighs. He stood above her as if he appreciated the look of her spread beneath him. His attention tracked over her body from her head to her feet and back again. Her nipples hardened beneath his gaze. The heat of her flush was obvious against the cool air.

"I've never shared this cavern with anyone else before," he said quietly. He stepped closer and dropped to his knees between her slightly parted legs. She smiled and opened to make room for him. He accepted the unspoken invitation to settle warmly against her, and the heat of her flush was nothing compared to the heat they generated when his naked chest was so close to her.

Elena was suddenly very happy that he'd shared his refuge with her.

Ivan touched the soft corner of her smile as if he wanted to catch the elusive expression before it faded from her face. She wanted to tell him her smile wasn't going anywhere while they were together. Instead, she reached to twine one long silky lock of his hair around her finger, and then she caught hold and used it to pull his mouth to her lips. He pressed closer and more intimately between her legs as they kissed and his weight was glorious. He'd worried about her knee before and she'd enjoyed riding him, but the length and breadth of his large body on top of her was a different sort of thrill all together.

"It's cold here. You might want to stay dressed," Romanov said. His hand held behind her good knee as she'd lifted that leg to allow his hips better access to her heat.

"I'm not cold. I'm never cold with you. In the middle of a snowy courtyard, you make me steam," Elena said. It was true. He had. And not only from exertion. While they had trained, she'd been on fire in much more intimate ways. He chuckled low and deep. Then he grew suddenly still and serious. His hand on her leg tightened.

"You know I noticed. Every tremble. Every sigh," he said.

She claimed his confession by licking the edge of his slightly parted lips with a teasing tongue.

"As I noticed your response to our closeness. Your tension. Your heat," Elena replied. "There's no chance I'll be cold when we're lying together, skin on skin."

She helped him, then, to pull off her tunic and slide her leggings down her hips. Her underthings came away easily, as well. The air was cool. Her nipples pebbled and gooseflesh rose on her skin. He stood to pull off his boots and pants and he paused only a moment to throw all their clothes to the side, but that pause made her mindless of the chill.

Because he was beautiful in the soft blue light. He was as perfectly formed as a statue, except he was warm and real and hers…if only for a little while. His erection jutted from a nest of black curls and the sight of his eagerness caused her to flood with need.

He might be a tormented legend, but he was naked and hers to soothe for the rest of the night.

He came to her then and gifted her with the skin-to-skin she'd craved almost since they'd first met, and definitely since they'd practiced side by side in the courtyard. They had ostensibly been training and not engaged in foreplay with swords, but her body and his had known that every glance and every brush of their fingers was leading to this.

"I'm not cold at all," Elena said. She wrapped her arms around his back and placed her hands on the sensual curve above his bottom. She spread her fingers, but she thought it was the embrace of her open legs that made him moan. She pulled him close, and he rewarded her with the hot and heavy press of his erection against her moist, throbbing folds.

He undulated his hips to stroke his shaft teasingly against her, and she lifted her hips to meet his strokes in a rhythmic welcome. The slide and friction was almost more than she could bear. Her body was hungry for a complete connection. She murmured pleading suggestions of where she needed him, and he complied.

The sapphire's glow seemed to bless their union when he found her opening with the head of his shaft. He reached to position himself and she held on to his back as he worked his hips to fit fully inside of her. She was wet and ready. He'd melted her from the start, but his naked body on top of her caused an even slicker reaction. He was well-endowed, long and thick with excitement, but her body eagerly stretched to accept every inch. In fact, she was the one who increased the speed of their thrusting and only then did he throw caution aside to match her frenzied writhing.

"We've reclaimed this night," Elena promised into his hair as he buried his face into her neck. "All else is forgotten." His hands had come up to cup the heavy globes of her breasts and he held one to suckle as he thrust and thrust, completely lost to claiming what she offered. She cried out from the heat of his mouth and her body tightened around his shaft as she came. He might refuse to claim her with his words, and her heart may have been wounded, but her body knew his rejection was a lie. Her body knew the truth. They were a team.

He was her mate.

His body knew the truth, as well. He rose up, bracing himself with his hands on the floor on either side of her shoulders. His hair spilled down all around her, creating a wild tent that tickled as he moved. In the blue light, she could see the intensity tightening his face even before he opened his eyes. But when their gazes met and held, she saw the truth shining even in the shadows.

She looked into his eyes as his body jerked and tensed. He didn't close them against her as he buried himself all the way to her womb. He came with quaking spasms and a harsh cry that was nearly a howl. Only then did he close his eyes and throw back his head. The heat of his seed sent her over the edge again and her body quivered around him as her soft cries of pleasure joined his.

While Romanov slept, Elena walked around the edges of their sanctuary. She'd wrapped one of the quilts around her shoulders when she rose from the makeshift bed after she'd pulled on her discarded boots. The quilt trailed behind her as her fingers trailed along the walls. The mica seemed magical even though it was only caused by nature. She tried to memorize every silvery speck of dust.

She would never forget Romanov's touch or that he'd allowed her to come to this place that seemed a physical representation of the magic in his heart. He wouldn't allow himself to love her, but he had opened up and given her all he could while still trying to keep her safe.

She wished she could convince him that he needed her by his side. His safety was important too. Together, they could defeat Grigori and face the Ether.

Elena looked down at her hand. Some of the mica from the walls had transferred itself to her fingers. She closed them into a fist to hold the sparkle in her palm. She willed it to be actual power. The sword had dimmed. It glowed softly near Romanov's sleeping form, but with every second she stood apart, its glow faded. As Vasilisa had told them, making love didn't complete their connection.

Romanov had to accept her as his mate. If he didn't, he would fight Grigori alone. If he fought the witchblood prince and he didn't shift, he would lose. If he did shift, the entire assemblage of witches would be after his head. Never mind that he might lose himself to the beast. If she could wield the sword, it might make the difference between whether Ivan Romanov lived or died or faded away.

Elena opened her hand. She dusted the loose mica away from her fingers. Sparkling dust wouldn't save him. She had to work with what she had. If Romanov didn't choose to make her his mate so she could wield the powerful sapphire sword by his side, she would agree to leave with Grigori.

Her heartbeat slowed, thick and sluggish, in her chest, but the hollow she'd had since she'd lost the dance was gone. It had been filled with burning purpose. She was a warrior. She'd fight for Romanov.

She might not have the sword's power, but she had the power to become the swan.

It would be her choice, not Grigori's. She could endure the cage and the bloody feathers if Romanov lived on. The legend she loved couldn't be allowed to fall.

Chapter 17

There was no denying it. The girl had shaken her. Vasilisa the Luminous, the Light *Volkhvy* queen, wasn't used to surprises. The few she'd experienced in her extraordinarily long life had not been well-received. One of those, the betrayal of her champion and lover, Vladimir Romanov, had resulted in the longest and most enduring rage she'd ever experienced.

Her home was the royal seat of the Light *Volkhvy*. It was one of hundreds of islands that formed an archipelago that surrounded Scotland. To the outside world, it was stark and barren. Even the birds that made their home on most of the other islands shied away, repelled by a force they could neither see nor touch. Vasilisa's ability to manipulate the Ether kept the true enchanted nature of the island hidden from man and beast, as well as provided an artificial atmosphere protected from the extremes of climate that the other islands in the Outer Hebrides experienced. As she walked through the rose garden that formed the innermost sanctum of her private retreat, she tried to slow her heartbeat and ease her jangled nerves.

She'd been so angry she hadn't felt Elena Pavlova respond to the sword's call.

The petite dancer claimed to have been called from a young age. If that was so, Vasilisa had been blind for two decades while her enchantments ran on without oversight or tending. That wasn't the behavior of a queen. The wild tangle of her rose garden only served to illustrate the same irresponsibility. She'd been furious. And not only because she'd experienced real pain when Vladimir betrayed her.

She'd loved him.

He'd been her gray wolf for years, loyal and true. Or so she'd thought. She'd plucked him from the royal Romanov family. He'd been an obscure cousin who was eager to prove himself once he was given the chance. At first, he'd seemed the perfect choice. He'd taken to the shift amazingly well. He'd recruited and developed an army of followers to fight by his side. Then he'd sired three strong sons and pledged them to her service, as well.

She'd given him Bronwal as a reward. She'd given him the sapphire sword for his wife and then later the ruby sword for the wife chosen by one of his sons.

Madeline.

Poor Madeline and her tiny babe.

The women had been even more precious to her than the wolves because they had chosen to serve her and the Light *Volkhvy.* She honored their service. Which was why she'd never approached Vladimir until his wife and her prince consort had died. She hadn't loved her prince.

Their marriage had been one required by her followers to cement her rule. But she had been faithful to him until he was gone.

She should have stayed away. It was wrong even then to go to Vladimir. She'd dishonored the memory of her sapphire warrior and her prince consort with her lust, and she deserved the horrible price the universe had exacted from her.

She had only worn purple for centuries. No one had ever wondered why. Her grief was her own, abiding and deep.

In the center of the rose garden, on a rough marble dais, a glass enclosure seemed to rise up out of the stone itself. Its edges were obscured and crystallized where rock met glass, but in the center of the oblong container, the glass was clear enough to see the two sleeping forms held and protected inside.

Even in her rage, her love of the women who wielded her swords had won out. She couldn't abandon Madeline and her newborn son to the Ether. Instead, she'd allowed the Ether to put them into a deep sleep, nearly as deep as death, and she'd brought them here. She didn't visit the center of her garden often. She couldn't bear to see the peacefully sleeping baby. Not when her own baby had been murdered by Vladimir Romanov. Today, as she looked down on the innocent faces so soft in repose, she knew her pain didn't excuse what she'd done. Vladimir had been the one who killed her daughter, Anna.

Her revenge against the other Romanovs was wrong.

It had taken the ferocity of Ivan's swan to ease her rage and open her eyes.

Elena had claimed the sapphire sword. And she'd done it even knowing that Vasilisa was a flawed leader.

Her warrior women were more honorable than their queen.

The Gathering approached on swift, ruthless wings. She'd turned a rage-blinded eye toward the *Volkhvy* who attended every year to torment her wolves. She'd even participated, encouraging the decadent ball in order to hurt the last Romanov when she'd known the Romanov who'd actually hurt her had been taken by the Ether almost from the start.

Vladimir hadn't been strong. He'd been weak. If his betrayal hadn't proven that to her, his disappearance had. But the curse had also been the making of the new alpha. Ivan Romanov had become everything she'd hoped her champion would be. Her rage and grief over her daughter's death had blinded her to that.

It had taken Elena Pavlova to open her eyes.

The girl and her connection to the sapphire sword had been entirely unexpected. Vasilisa's wolves inherited their abilities. Her magic had manipulated their father's genes to create the powerfully enhanced champions she needed against the Dark. She had ordered the swords to be made so that the wolves would have companions in battle. Her magic had infused each gem with Light.

But the women who were called to the swords picked them up of their own accord. They, of all her followers, chose to fight for the Light. They hadn't been born to it. They hadn't been made. And yet they were the strongest of all. Mortal women who chose to take up the fight.

Vasilisa pressed a kiss against the glass and backed away. Neither of the container's occupants stirred. Madeline cradled the baby in her arms, but neither of them seemed to breathe and neither had aged or changed. Beside their bodies, the ruby sword lay, dark and dull.

Could she abandon her newest warrior to the Dark or to the Ether?

As always, the sleeping baby reminded her of her own lost child. Her rage hadn't faded. She hadn't loved her prince, but she *had* loved. As only a mother can love. It shook her now and caused her hand to close too tightly around a rose. Its ruthless barb pricked her finger. The blood welled blackish scarlet against her pale skin, but she didn't lift it to her lips. She stared, transfixed, as it swelled. The blood ran down her finger and fell to the ground, unstopped, where it disappeared into the soil.

Vladimir had betrayed her in a more horrific way than most people knew.

Her deepest pain had been a secret expressed only by the ruthlessness of the curse and her mourning garb. Anna was gone. She'd been dead for centuries. Vasilisa had hidden her child from Vladimir with innocent villagers. In his gray wolf form, Vladimir had attacked the village of Sovkra. And from the first she'd heard of Anna's murder Vasilisa held her name close to her heart unable to bear the sound of it on anyone else's lips.

But Vladimir was also gone. He'd been gone a long time and perhaps it was time to forgive his sons.

She was the Light *Volkhvy* queen and it might not be possible to stop what she'd set into motion. The witch-blood prince had laid a powerful mark on Elena. If the black wolf didn't accept her as his mate, the sapphire sword's power was nullified. She could try to stand in Grigori's way. She could buy Ivan Romanov time to claim the warrior's heart that Elena had offered him.

But her pain stood in her way. She couldn't forgive. She would never forget. The Romanovs suffered for what their father had done because she suffered. Her grief was as fresh today as it had been centuries ago.

Even if Romanov claimed Elena, Vasilisa could only lift the curse if she wholeheartedly blessed her wolves and their warriors once more.

Her blessing would have to be given freely and fully at the exact time when it was needed, but could she cleanse the taint in her heart left by Vladimir Romanov?

The prick on her finger tingled. She was the queen, but she was vulnerable. It had always been so. Power attracted those hungry to claim it and never more so than in the *Volkhvy* culture where power mattered most.

She closed her eyes against the sight of her blood seeping into the ground. Had Vladimir torn tiny innocent flesh with the vicious teeth she had given him? Tears flowed freely to join with her blood in the shadow of her roses.

Chapter 18

Only freeing the wolf had allowed him to deny her.

Ivan Romanov stood on the ramparts of the castle. The sun rose above the horizon to bathe the neighboring mountain peaks with golden light, and the wind whipped Ivan's hair wildly around his head. He played a dangerous balancing game. He was still in control. He still walked on two legs. But he'd allowed the wolf the greater part of his heart since last night. He'd discovered the ability when Vasilisa had asked him about Elena and the sword. The black wolf allowed him to deny his feelings for her because the wolf had been tamped down for so long that now all it wanted was the hunt and the feast, the run and the fight. He'd allowed those feelings to overwhelm his feelings for Elena during those moments with Vasilisa.

He'd immediately caged the wolf after that, but he'd had to loose it again last night. When he'd taken Elena into the hidden cavern to shield her from Grigori's touch, he'd opened himself too much to their connection. He'd shown her his secret sanctuary and she'd shown him her heart. She didn't simply offer to wield the sword or to fight by his side. She offered to care for him. The sapphire had lit the cave in a way he'd never seen. It had almost seemed as if his lover was responsible for the starlike glitter on the walls.

He closed his eyes against the strands of his hair that lashed against his face. But then he held them away with two hands fisted at his temples instead. When he closed his eyes, he saw Elena with her head thrown back and her hips thrusting up to meet him. She'd been bathed in the soft blue light of the sapphire blade and he'd known she was meant to bring it to life.

He'd allowed the wolf to rise because that knowledge almost led him to doom her with a pledge he could never allow himself to make.

Was this how his brother Lev had begun to degenerate? Had the white wolf claimed his brother's heart before it had completely claimed his form? The black wolf howled with his every heartbeat. He could hardly see the glow of the sun because what he wanted to see was the blood of his enemies. The alpha had been too long denied. It was thirsty for *Volkhvy* blood. Dark, Light, it made no difference. The wolf wanted them all to fall before him.

When the time came, it would be easy to shift and allow the black wolf to devour Grigori. He could almost anticipate the perfect vengeance of showing how he felt about Elena by destroying the creature that had tormented her mercilessly for years. It would be the only way he could express what he felt without exposing her to the Ether. The only thing that marred his anticipation was the knowledge that in saving her he would also lose her forever.

The black wolf howled inside the heart it controlled as it waited impatiently for the shift it knew was coming. It was only a matter of time before the wolf devoured him, heart and soul.

Choosing to fully loose the wolf would be his last conscious act as a man.

Elena wasn't sure what had gone wrong. Ivan had been opening to her. She'd sensed his emotion. He hadn't brought her to the cavern simply to hide her from Grigori. He'd wanted to show her the refuge he'd sought when he was younger. He'd shown her his secret place and he'd shared the vulnerabilities he'd felt as a child.

But as their connection had seemed to burgeon, he'd given himself completely over to passion. She hadn't complained. She'd joined him in physical release, again and again. Even when she'd lost all hope of him declaring his love.

It was enough for her that he declared it with his refusal to claim her as his mate. He was protecting her, and for a champion that was the greatest declaration of all. Unfortunately, it wasn't enough for the sword.

Her only pain came in wondering how he was able to keep silent about the feelings she couldn't deny. Just as the mica sparkled on the walls of his cavern, her love for him seemed to radiate from every cell in her body, as they lay naked together.

But, again, it wasn't enough.

The sword had gone dark.

She'd been awake when the stone dulled. By its dying light, she had traced the face of the man who refused to love her. With trembling fingers, she'd lightly brushed over his forehead, the full sweep of his dark lashes, the hollow of his cheek and his square jaw as if she could memorize his features. His lips had been soft and full in repose. The thick sweep of his hair, for once, had been swept back and out of his face by his position. She hadn't fallen in love with his appearance, but it was beloved to her all the same. The cavern's walls had retreated into shadows as all the artificial starlight had died. Tears had filled her eyes when she could no longer see his face. Romanov had slept through it while she cried. No one had seen her, but if they had she wouldn't have been able to stop. She was strong in all things but this.

He was determined to save her even if it meant losing himself.

She would try to stop him.

She would give herself to Grigori if she had to.

But she was afraid. Because if he loved her as she loved him, her sacrifice might make him seek out the oblivion of the wolf even if he didn't need to shift to fight Grigori.

Chapter 19

She and Romanov moved around the entire castle, each avoiding the other but fully aware of every step taken. It was an elaborate dance as the sun tracked across the sky. The sword had come between them even as it was supposed to bind them together. She saw the awakened sapphire as proof that she could stand against Grigori. Ivan saw its glow as proof that the Ether would take her and torment her the way it had all the loved ones he'd ever cared about. It was a standoff and a stalemate. One she didn't know how to break.

It wasn't until late in the afternoon that Elena realized her black wolf had disappeared.

Romanov was no longer in the castle. She didn't know how her body recognized that he was gone. There was only a vacuum she couldn't explain. She wasted no time going for her ski suit and snow boots, although she was terrified it would be too late to find him.

What if he had decided to end his fight and disappear into the Ether in order to be certain that their connection wouldn't overcome his "honorable" intentions?

What if she had ended his long-enforced isolation in a way she hadn't intended when she'd tried to claim the sword?

The snowstorm had ended days ago. The sky was clear and the sun beamed brightly in the sky, but it was still hard on her knee to trudge out beyond the castle walls into the deep snow. She did it anyway.

If she found the wolf or the man, it would be worth the hike to ease her mind.

Of course, Lev could also be outside the walls. It was a risk she had to take. She'd strapped the sapphire sword around her waist. It was still a sword even if it didn't glow. Romanov had taught her how to use it. Lev would be practically invisible against the blinding white of the sunlit snow. Unlike her. She wore the bright red cloak over her snowsuit to add another layer against the mountain cold. But if Lev attacked she would defend herself. Until then, she'd look for Ivan Romanov. Her cloak might make her more visible to Lev, but it would also help Romanov to see her. She'd bring him home. It had been wrong to avoid him all morning. She should have pushed her pain and pride aside to make sure he wasn't contemplating a desperate act to try to save her.

She followed a trail that had been broken in the deep snow. It led to a thick evergreen wood on the west side of the wall. *Evergreen.* Romanov's scent was her only clue besides the beaten pathway. Once she stepped into the forest's shadows, she was able to walk with less effort. The ground had been protected from most of the

snow. It was barely dusted with white. Frozen pine needles crunched under her boots, and above her a heavy,
frozen canopy of white blocked out the sun.

Would she find the wolf or the man or nothing at all?
Or would the white wolf find her first?

Elena heard something besides her own footsteps.
She paused and the forest fell quiet. She drew the sword
from the sheath at her side. The sound of metal rasping
against leather was loud in the silent wood. Had it been
her imagination or a breeze around the trees? No birds
sang. No rodents stirred. For long, breathless seconds it
seemed she was alone.

Wolves were predators and the shadows were deep.
Lev could very easily creep up behind her and she'd never
know until he pounced. Elena spun around, betraying
her fear with her sudden movement. But there was no
one there.

"Romanov," she shouted. It came out quieter than
she would have liked. Fear compressed her lungs. She
couldn't draw enough air to propel the call from her tight
chest. She wouldn't go back without him. If he hadn't disappeared into the Ether, she would find him. She would
face the black wolf or the man.

A sound much farther in the distance disturbed the silence. She barely heard it over the pounding of her heart,
but it sounded like animals fighting. She heard growls,
barks, then the sharp yelp of a canine in pain. The noise
was too far away to be the noise she'd heard moments
before, but that was explained as Soren melted into sight
from the evergreen shadows.

He came to her side showing no fear of her drawn
sword. Like her, his ears pricked at the sounds of fighting.
He looked up at her and then toward the distant melee.

"Did you follow me outside the walls or did you follow your brother?" Elena asked.

Soren simply blinked before he bolted deeper into the woods. Elena followed. She had told Romanov that she was a warrior. She had yet to prove it to him or to herself. Soren howled and picked up speed when more yelps rang out. Elena followed as fast as she could run on the uneven ground. She was glad that she didn't have to run through the snow. She would never have kept up. As it was, she relied on the sounds of the fight to guide her whenever Soren slipped out of sight. And yet he was always waiting for her when she came around a rise or a bend. He would take off again only when he was sure she saw and followed.

He was purposefully leading her to the fight.

They burst out of the woods into a sudden dazzling glare of sunlight. But Soren halted at the edge of the clearing they found, and her forward momentum was stopped by his giant body. He stood sideways, barring her passage. The pause gave her eyes time to adjust and her mind to comprehend what they'd found.

A huge pack of natural wolves had Lev surrounded. They'd bloodied him until his fur was splattered with scarlet. The snow was trampled and pink around him. He was an enchanted shifter, twice their size and preternaturally ferocious, but there were dozens of wolves trying to kill him. Elena's hands tightened on the hilt of her sword.

They would have succeeded already if Lev hadn't received reinforcement. Romanov was the cause of the yelps they'd heard. He hadn't shifted. He was still a man, but he wasn't an ordinary man. He wore his fur-capped cloak and brandished a sword. He cut down every wolf that leaped for his throat, one after another.

While he slashed, he yelled curses at the white wolf and the red. The white wolf for seeking annihilation. The red for endangering *her* life by leading her here.

Romanov was the one surrounded by a vicious pack of hungry wolves trying to kill him and his brother. But he worried about her joining the fray. Elena quietly spoke to the red wolf that stood in her way.

"I am his partner. Whether he has accepted that yet or not. The sword has chosen. And I have chosen. Now get out of my way," she said.

She didn't have magic to help her. She only had muscles and determination. They were all she'd ever needed. She ran into the clearing easily, glad that the fight had already flattened the snow. If she died, she would die by her lover's side, by her own choice and because of her own actions whether Romanov liked it or not.

Soren ran with her. He didn't try to stop her again. He outpaced her in a flash and leaped over the fallen wolf bodies to land beside Lev. There were fewer wolves than Lev had had to face alone. Soren made fewer wolves still with his wicked teeth and claws.

Elena went to Romanov. He was an incredible sight. All fury and fight and righteous anger over her and Soren's disobedience to his will. She ignored his rage and did what she had to do. Slashing and stabbing until the wolves in between her and Romanov began to give way.

Then she saw Romanov's eyes. They blazed nearly black even in the sun. His curses were more like howls and his fighting wasn't smooth. His wolf was close to the surface. As close as it could be without the shift. She was certain of it. In spite of her desperation to keep the wolves from her own throat, she spoke to Romanov.

"Shift if you must, but not because of me. I don't need the black wolf anymore. I need you."

Suddenly, more wolves came from the forest. One, two, a dozen more ran to join the fight. The movement called her attention to the edge of the wood. There were half a dozen men standing there. They stared at the clearing where the fight raged on. She'd been wrong. The wolves weren't behaving as natural wolves would behave. These were multiple packs joined together by enchantment.

"Is this Vasilisa's work? Are those her men?" Elena shouted. She had made it to Romanov's side, and now they turned to press their backs together as he'd taught her to do when they'd practiced in the courtyard together. She was small, but she used his size and strength to her advantage, bracing off him to shoulder the attacks against her.

"This is the work of the Dark *Volkhvy*. Several have banded together to attack us. They lured Lev into the woods. If I hadn't been keeping an eye on him, he would have gone down. He didn't even begin to fight until I arrived," Romanov shouted. His voice vibrated against her. "And you've brought them the sword they seek."

"They may pry it out of my cold, dead hands," Elena said. Adrenaline caused the words to come out as a laugh from deep in her frozen middle. The wolves had shredded the edges of her scarlet cape as they continued to attack, but so far she had managed to keep their teeth away from her skin. The edges of the cape fluttered in the winter wind.

"The shift isn't pretty to witness. Do not turn around," Romanov ordered. This time Elena obeyed. Not because she was squeamish about his abilities. She couldn't divide her attention from the wolves that attacked to see what he intended to do.

She already knew.

He'd risked the shift to try to frighten her away from the sword.

Now he would risk the shift to protect her and his brothers against the *Volkhvy*.

She'd been a fool to think he would escape into the Ether and leave them to face the Gathering alone. He would stand as long as he could. It would be the shift or the *Volkhvy* that would take him in the end. He would never give up.

She would bet her life that the black wolf would continue to stand as Bronwal's champion even when every ounce of his humanity was gone.

His shift happened behind her back. She could only feel the trembling earth beneath her feet, and then her body was shaken with the force of the black wolf's howl. The lesser *Volkhvy*'s enchantment of the pack couldn't stand against the alpha wolf's presence. Dozens of wolves had piled onto Romanov's form as he'd fallen to the ground during his transformation. Elena whirled in time to see the pile explode away from the black wolf in all directions as he rose to his feet.

The wolves and the *Volkhvy* who controlled them ran at the sudden appearance of the powerful black wolf. Elena couldn't blame them. Her knees went weak and she had to tighten her fingers around the hilt of her sword. She took in the aftermath as she ordered her own feet to stay planted right where they were, no running away allowed.

Lev was down. His white coat was covered in blood.

But Soren had protected him. The red wolf stood over the white wolf. Soren's sides heaved and he, too, was speckled with damp splotches of blood.

Elena could only spare the two wolves a glance before her gaze was drawn back to the black wolf. He approached her. She stood her ground. She lowered the sapphire sword. He was still Romanov and he wasn't her enemy. He stopped in front of her and without a pause she lifted one hand up to cup his mighty jaw. He blinked at her, but he didn't jerk away. He allowed her touch. He even briefly rested his muzzle in her palm.

And then he spun away and called to his brothers with an ear-splitting howl. Only Soren could obey. Lev wasn't able to get to his feet. The black wolf ran toward the spot where the Dark *Volkhvy* had thought to watch their bewitched pack kill the weakest of the Romanov brothers. They hadn't counted on Soren, Ivan and Elena showing up to defend Lev. The witches had disappeared into the trees, but Elena had no doubt the black wolf would hunt them down.

She turned to make her way over to Lev's side. He was alert and breathing. He whined as she approached, but he didn't get to his feet.

"Did you really take on that pack alone? Contemplating suicide, are you? As if Romanov would ever let you go. He's determined to save us all. Even if it kills him," Elena said. She stabbed her sword into the ground and began to rip the scarlet cloak into bandages to bind the worst of the white wolf's wounds. He was enchanted. Surely he would heal. He growled once or twice but she ignored it. Her heart was full of a warm sense of sisterhood. Lev had been the mate of the woman who had wielded the ruby sword. Helping him was the least she could do. Even if he threatened to bite off her hands.

Soren returned with a team of servants to carry Lev back into the castle. They came prepared with a wooden sled pulled by Soren himself. His power was evident in the way he effortlessly brought the heavy sled, even through the forest where the pine needles formed the only track for its curved treads.

Elena didn't ask about Romanov. She would find out soon enough if he was lost to the wolf. For now, she could only trudge back to the castle behind the sled. She refused to add to its weight. She had made it through the entire fight without a single injury. Her silk cloak was shredded and her snowsuit's downy insulation spilled from several tears that would have been gruesome if the thick material hadn't protected her skin.

But she was unscathed.

Except for the shaking. She allowed one of the servants who had returned with Soren and the sled to place a blanket around her shoulders. Shock was settling in as adrenaline faded away. She was shaken by the violence and Lev's injuries and by the evidence of Ivan Romanov's abilities. She'd seen him as the black wolf. She'd seen his intelligence shine from the black wolf's eyes. But this was the first time she'd seen the black wolf shine from his even before he shifted.

It was the first time she'd felt the power of his shift. It seemed as if the quaking of the earth was still with her.

And it was another first, as well. She loved him, wolf and all. Not in spite of his ferocity, but because of it. Perhaps she was still looking for the black wolf after all.

* * *

Ivan tended his wounds alone. The shift had taken care of many of his injuries, and he would heal quickly from those that didn't entirely disappear. Even though he had shifted back to his human form, he could still feel the tentative touch of Elena's hand. She hadn't cringed away from him. She had been afraid, but she'd still extended her fingers. He'd been eager to hunt down the Dark witches, but he'd paused for her touch. He'd taken that moment to make sure she wasn't hurt. Remarkably, she hadn't suffered a single bite. She faced down a pack of cursed wild wolves and she'd done it with the Romanov blade gripped perfectly in her hand.

It hadn't glowed. Even as they'd fought together, the stone had stayed cold and dark.

He should be happy about that. He'd succeeded. He'd rejected their connection even though it was the most powerful force he'd ever felt. Why did he feel as if it was a mistake? If Elena stayed free of the Ether, then he would have saved her from a torment he could barely withstand. Others were more easily consumed.

Yet he'd seen her face so much, time and time again, with incredible strength and fortitude. It would be a lie to say that he still believed the Ether would take her easily. She would stand. He was certain of it.

If he chose to continue to stand against the Ether alone, it wasn't to protect Elena from a trial she couldn't face, but, rather, a trial she shouldn't have to face.

This was a Romanov burden. One he would continue to shoulder alone. He would stay away from Elena. From a distance, he'd seen her follow the group of servants he'd sent to fetch Lev. She was fine. He didn't need to hold her to prove it. He didn't need to kiss her to celebrate their victory.

The black wolf had taken care of the Dark witches with Soren's help. That had been the only celebration he needed.

But the wolf in his heart disagreed. It urged him with a primal need to hold his mate close after battle.

Elena saw Lev settled with Bell and several others attending him. Soren was close by if his brother became unruly. For now, the white wolf accepted the ministrations of his people.

"His wounds will heal quickly. It takes a lot to bring him down, and he's never down for long," Bell said. She straightened from the bandages she had knotted carefully around one of Lev's hind legs. She met Elena's eyes. "This isn't the first time he's tried."

They both knew Bell was talking about Lev's flirtation with death. Apparently, losing himself to the wolf wasn't enough for him. Maybe even fading into the Ether wouldn't stop his deep-seated grief. He must have loved his family very much to feel the pain of their loss so keenly even when he was no longer the man he'd been. He'd risked a bloody, painful death to end it.

"Thank you for helping to save him," Bell said. She glanced from Elena to the red wolf who stood a silent vigil in the far corner of the great room. The fire blazed and a makeshift bed had been made for Lev near enough to the hearth for warmth and light, but not near enough to overheat him as he healed. The direction of her attention quickly shifted back to Lev, but Elena still understood. Bell was grateful that Elena had helped Soren in order to prevent his sacrificing himself for Lev.

"When I heeded the sapphire sword's call, I chose to defend Bronwal and everyone in it," Elena said. The sword was back in its sheath at her side. She'd cleansed its blade in the snow with an edge of her ruined cloak. Suddenly, she was very aware of her own aches and pains, as well as the wolf blood that had dried on her clothes.

Always observant, Bell noticed her discomfort.

"Go up to your room. I'll send up some hot water," she said.

Elena wanted to refuse the extra trouble, but she didn't have the will. Cleaning up would settle her shakes and get her away from the stares of the servants who had come to help with Lev. Besides, Romanov hadn't made an appearance yet, but he was bound to check on his brother. She couldn't face him yet. Not with trembling fingers and wobbly knees.

The tower was dark and quiet even though the sun was still high outside. The fight had been over much sooner than it had seemed. There were still many hours left in the day before she had to worry about the sun going down and the possibility that Grigori might return.

Elena unfastened the cloak and allowed the ruined red silk to fall to the ground. She kicked it to the side. She unbuckled her belt and laid the sword on the foot of her bed. She hadn't been injured, but it took a close look to see the blood on her clothes wasn't hers. Maybe that's why the servants stared when they carried several buckets of water to the tub that stood by the fireplace.

While Elena waited to remove the rest of her clothes, Patrice arrived with a small bar of soap and a large linen cloth. She placed them on the edge of the wooden tub and then she leaned over to stir and wake the coals in the fireplace. She added two oak logs to the embers.

Elena was surprised to see her. The older servant had seemed to be becoming more and more addled as the Cycle wore on. But Lev's injuries must have woken her from the walking dream she seemed to have retreated into.

"Bell said that you saved the boys. She said Romanov wouldn't have shifted except to protect you," Patrice said.

"Bell is wrong. Romanov will always protect his brothers and everyone in this castle. However he must," Elena said.

Patrice murmured in response, but Elena couldn't make out her words. After a moment of clarity, it seemed as if the older woman was back to her dream. She walked out of the tower room without saying goodbye.

And Elena was finally alone with a steaming tub.

She pulled off her ruined clothes and threw them on the pile with the scarlet cloak. The logs Patrice had placed on the fire had caught. They crackled and burned and the room's chill was softened, but not so much that the water didn't beckon. She stepped into the water and sank down into its welcoming heat.

The bar of soap Patrice had brought was lightly scented with evergreen. Elena breathed deeply as she lathered it up in her hands. It reminded her of the wintry wood, but also of Romanov's skin. Her after-battle shakes were fading away.

"I completely destroyed this door," Romanov said from the threshold. It was an understatement. The bars were twisted and the door sagged to the side. He'd practically ripped it from its hinges to help her the night before.

Elena had thought he would check on his brother. She should have known he would check on them all. He stood at the door and he held the edges of its frame with a white-knuckled grip as if he'd hoped to find it locked against him even though the lock was ruined.

Instead of a lock, he had to depend on his own strength to keep him outside.

She hoped his strength would fail.

"A lock wouldn't protect me from Grigori," Elena said.

She was covered in the frothy lather Patrice's soap had created in her hands. Her skin only showed in several wet flashes against the white bubbles, pink from the water's heat. But she noticed the direction of Romanov's eyes and how they widened when the lather began to slip away from her breasts. First the hardened nipple of one breast was revealed and then the other.

He didn't look away.

The last of Elena's shock was gone. She'd needed to see him on two legs. But there was also no room for shock when her body was reacting to his presence. Her stomach grew heavy and heated as her nipples peaked beneath his gaze. He still held the door's frame. He still refused to step inside. But one of his legs had bent at the knee as if it would carry him forward without his permission. And his knuckles were whiter as if he used every bit of his strength to keep himself from answering her body's silent invitation.

It was a sudden decision that caused her to stand. Water and bubbles sluiced off her body.

"Elena," Romanov said. Was it in protest or appreciation? She thought the latter. His color was high. His chest rose and fell as if he'd grown winded while merely standing at the door. He also leaned slightly inward and his bent knee extended to place one booted foot inside the door.

Another sudden decision had her reaching for one of

the small buckets that a servant had left by the tub. She dipped it in the water at her feet while Romanov stared, riveted by her actions and all the pink skin her movements revealed. She watched him as she lifted the bucket high. His chest was no longer rising and falling. He held his breath. When she upended the warm water over her shoulders and washed most of the lather away, he released a long exhalation.

In the firelight, her wet skin glistened.

And Romanov let go of the door.

It was her turn to hold her breath as he stepped inside. He came to the tub with no further hesitation. Her body shivered now from cold and anticipation. The battle was far from her mind. She trembled when he stopped at the edge of the tub. He towered over her. Would she ever grow accustomed to his size and strength? She was used to leaner, more graceful men. Romanov's muscles were intended for battles like the one they'd just fought. He needed to swing a sword and plant his feet. He was so solid, she couldn't imagine him ever giving way to an attacking foe. Not a pack of enchanted wolves or a troop of Dark *Volkhvy*.

The idea that something as amorphous as time and Ether might fell him caused her to reach out her hand and place it on his downturned face. He looked at her as if he would memorize her features in the firelight. She looked up at him to do the same. He'd received several deep scratches. They joined the white scars of previous battles on his handsome face.

"I watched you return to the castle from the ramparts, but that wasn't enough," Romanov said. He reached to touch a tendril of her hair that had escaped the messy bun at the top of her head. And then he moved more decisively to burrow into the mass of waves to remove the pins she'd used to hold it up and out of the way. The battle had already loosened it. His strong fingers quickly caused it to fall down around her shoulders as the pins flew.

Elena was fascinated by the play of emotions over his face—concern, frustration and desire. She gasped when he finished with her hair because he immediately pulled her to him with a warm calloused hand on the nape of her neck.

His lips descended to crush against hers. She wound her damp arms around his neck to hold on and to press her naked body against him. He was fully clothed. The contrast was thrilling. But it was also poignant. She laid everything bare while he remained a mystery.

She held nothing back. Her mouth opened eagerly for his plunging tongue. He held her head for his crushing kiss and she gloried in his complete loss of control. He wasn't holding back now. For the first time, he gave in to the connection between them. Even more so than he had the night before.

But the firelight was suddenly overwhelmed by the flash of blue light from the sapphire behind them. It blazed and the entire room was bathed in blue. Romanov ripped his lips from hers and jerked away. He whirled away from her arms. They fell at her side, but only for a moment before she wrapped them around her aching middle.

Now, she shivered from the cold. The water at her feet had chilled. The fire had already burned low. The sapphire faded as Romanov moved away.

"We killed them all. Every last one. The black wolf was eager to fight," he said. "You don't need the sword to fight Grigori. You have me."

He left the room before she could reply. She watched him leave and he didn't even glance back over his shoulder. The sapphire was cold and dull again before his footsteps had faded away.

"But I don't have you," Elena said. She stepped from the tub and wrapped a sheet around her cold skin.

Chapter 20

The black wolf had interfered. Grigori had been touching his swan for the first time. His hands still tingled from the forbidden contact with her skin. The protection her mother had bought from the universe with her blood was almost gone. She'd been softer than silk beneath his hand.

And she'd been so very afraid.

Her fear was an aphrodisiac because it fueled his power like a battery that he could constantly recharge with the mere application of his dark desires. The memory of her trembling and vulnerable beneath his touch was better than any trembling he'd inspired with dreams. Who knows what he might have been able to do to her if the Romanov wolves hadn't interrupted?

Her mother's knowledge of hearth magic had taken him by surprise, but it was Elena who had shocked him. He hadn't been prepared for his little swan to take flight.

He'd never imagined she would seek help from the one being who might be able to stand in his way. He'd been so certain she would be his when the power of the blood ran out. He'd never suspected that she might know *Volkhvy* secrets. The Light queen of the *Volkhvy* had been practically sleepwalking for centuries. Her anger at her Romanov champions had caused most of the old protections against the Dark to fade away. The old legends were dead. Or so he thought. No one spoke of them anymore. Cell phones and social media had taken the place of books and campfire stories that had armed generations against his kind.

Except one old woman who had taught her daughter and granddaughter the old tales and the old ways.

She'd been too canny and wise for him to kill. He'd had to wait for nature to take her in its own sweet time. But he'd never imagined she'd passed on the legend of the Romanovs to her granddaughter or that a woman born in this time of lattes and laptops would take the legends to heart.

It wasn't her belief that truly shocked him. It was her determination to travel a thousand miles and climb a mountain in the snow to find a cursed castle and a mythical champion to fight him.

That…and the sapphire sword.

The delicate swan he craved was not a warrior woman. He would put her back in her place…in his cage, under his power, forever at his mercy. The sword would be lost to the Ether and entirely out of her reach. She would be delicate and vulnerable once more. Even if he had to clip her wings and her uninjured leg to ensure that she accepted her true nature.

He preened as he thought, literally soothing his ruffled feathers. They were as black as obsidian, but they weren't a raven's wings. They were much larger and more powerful than that. When he shifted, he was larger than a natural bird, just as the Romanov wolves were larger than natural wolves. And just as Elena was a womanly swan with some of her human features intact. She would have feathers on her breast, but they would be full, lush womanly breasts. Her wings would stretch from her perfect, delicately boned shoulders.

His Ether-fueled powers gave him infinite possibilities for his pleasure. Currently, he was a large cob swan anticipating making Elena his mate. He was capable of being fully formed as a bird, but he could also keep his human arms…and other attributes…if he chose.

He would choose with Elena.

And they would mate for life…or as long as her life lasted.

His pets never lasted long once he had full power over them. His appetites always got the best of him once they had free rein.

In order for all of his plans to proceed to fruition, he would need to destroy the black wolf first. The creature had been created by the Light *Volkhvy* queen to fight his kind, but, in truth, the queen had never fully understood what his kind was capable of becoming. The Dark *Volkhvy* themselves didn't know of the power they could channel from the Ether if they were brave enough to seek it. No one had absorbed as much power as he had—not even his father, the king.

Elena hadn't been his only obsession for the last decade.

It was almost time to solidify the Dark *Volkhvy* behind a new leader, one who knew how dark they could be.

He would settle for no less than the black wolf's head, his vulnerable swan slave and the throne.

The servants who were left in the castle made no preparations for the Gathering. There was nothing like the usual hustle and bustle of a big event about to take place. If anything, the hallways were more deserted than ever as Elena sought out the one person who might be living in the present enough to help her.

There was very little time left to make Ivan see reason. She was down to hoping she could convince him on the night of the ball before Grigori arrived to make his claim. And if she weren't able to convince Romanov, then her last chance before she chose to leave with Grigori would be the Light *Volkhvy* queen.

Elena had been a performer her entire life. She knew one didn't inspire a queen's intervention in rags or jeans.

"I need help to get ready for the Gathering," she said when she finally found Bell. The young woman greeted her with a big grin. Her determined good humor was a welcome relief from the hopelessness Elena found in everyone else. "I need a dress fit for a warrior, a wife and a swan. My main accessory will be the sapphire sword."

Bell was wearing a maid's gown paired with more modern combat boots and her usual boy's hat. Her smile tilted slowly with a hint of mischievousness.

"Maybe you'll be worth all the water I've had to carry after all," she said. "I'd survive the Ether one more Cycle if it means you'll give those witches hell. This castle needs a new mistress."

"Romanov doesn't want me here. And I might not be able to stay. But I'm going to do all I can to change his mind *and* Vasilisa's before I go away," Elena promised.

At the mention of the Light queen's name, Bell stopped smiling. Her face tightened and her eyes grew grim. Under the shadow of her oversize cap, her big hazel eyes tracked over Elena's face as if to ascertain if she meant what she said. Elena thought Bell would warn against trying to influence the queen, but she should have known better. Once the young woman seemed to determine that Elena was earnest, a small smile returned to her lips.

"We've got our work cut out for us if that's what you're trying to accomplish," she said. "We'd better get going."

Bell was a survivor. You didn't survive by giving up without a fight.

Elena stopped her friend with a firm hand on her shoulder.

"Anywhere but the baby's room, you understand? I promised Lev I wouldn't disturb that room again," she said.

Bell nodded. Her eyes softened.

"Trevor was a fine lad. And he was loved by all. You're kind to care," she said. She continued pragmatically, "Madeline's dresses would never fit you. She was tall. Almost as tall as Lev. Well, as tall as he used to be, God rest his soul."

Bell's pragmatism warred with all the losses she'd suffered. Elena reminded her of all the people Bronwal had lost, but she also offered a course of action. Staying busy seemed to be something the young woman relied on.

"This place has been reduced to mourning for too long," Bell said. Elena squeezed the small shoulder beneath her hand. Bell was too young to have to shoulder all the work, responsibility and worry that she must have had to take on since Patrice lost her mind. And yet, more often than not, the young woman smiled.

"I came here for help, but I found a place that needed *my* help. But I can't do this alone," Elena said.

"I can find you a dress," Bell replied. "The castle is full of clothes that people have left behind." The other woman walked around Elena slowly. She narrowed her eyes and seemed to be gauging her shape and size. "I always forget how small you are. You seem bigger somehow when you leave a room than when you first come in."

"There's more to me than meets the eye," Elena said. "I've felt from the start that the same could be said about you."

Bell's eyes widened. Maybe the young orphan wasn't used to people noticing anything about her. She looked up to meet Elena's gaze, and her smile grew slightly bigger.

"The first night you arrived I recognized something in your eyes—a feeling I've often had. When times are dark, but you know you can put one foot in front of the other as long as it takes," Bell said. "I haven't had the easiest time of it since the curse. In the beginning, there were plenty of sane people to keep the first ones who fell apart from harming anyone in their madness. But with every Cycle, fewer and fewer returned. Until one day I was pretty much on my own. Since then, I've had to take care of myself."

"You couldn't ask Romanov for help?" Elena asked. Bell stood next to her, shoulder to shoulder. They seemed to be close to the same size with only slight differences in the width of their shoulders and hips. Bell was curvier with an hourglass figure. It had been some time since Elena could take to the stage, but her body had been honed by too many years of discipline to soften now.

"He's been busy the last few Cycles. He has to keep up with his brothers now that they're in their wolf forms full-time," Bell said softly. She bit her lip and Elena regretted delving into subjects that made her sad.

"Soren can still look out for himself," Elena said, trying to lighten the mood.

"The red wolf tries to look out for all of us. But he's kept busy with Lev," Bell said. She sounded wistful. Her eyes had gone glassy, as if she was no longer seeing Elena's measurements, but rather something that made her pensive.

"Lev is a challenge. He's very dangerous," Elena said.

"I'm afraid he won't last much longer. Once he disappears into the Ether for good, Soren… I'm not sure how he'll survive it. They were born only seconds apart. They've been inseparable ever since," Bell said. The young woman stilled, and suddenly Elena saw behind her smile and her busy behavior. She was a survivor, but how much longer could she survive once the red wolf was gone?

"I'm going to try to prevent that from happening," Elena promised.

Elena was glad to have Bell's help. The young girl knew the castle like the back of her hand. There was no corner she didn't know how to reach, and many could only be reached through back passages and secret doorways that Elena would never understand.

"The Ether changes everything. Including the layout of the castle. It never comes back the exact same way twice. But there are clues to watch for. Landmarks, if you will. A tip-tilted lantern or a mark I've left on the wall," Bell instructed. She pointed at a white mark painted on the wall ahead of them. It almost looked like a flower. "That's me. It's supposed to be a bellflower," Bell explained. Then she continued, "It must be hard for you to imagine what Bronwal was like before the curse. Before it deteriorated. It was enchanting, specially blessed by the Light *Volkhvy* queen herself. I was the little orphan child who had woken in a storybook."

"It's hard to grow up with legends," Elena said.

Bell had stopped in front of a door. To Elena it looked like every other door they'd passed, but Bell pointed to a swirl in the oak that looked like a leaping frog.

Elena hesitated on the threshold when Bell opened the door to step inside.

"Don't worry. You aren't disturbing anyone here. This room was the dressmaker's workplace. She had a team of seamstresses and they sewed night and day to keep us all clothed—from Soren's mother, Naomi, and Madeline, all the way down to me. And the men, as well," Bell said.

Elena followed her into the room. Bell ran her hand along a table and it came away covered in dust. But for the neglect, the room looked as if all the seamstresses had simply stood and walked away from their work for a coffee break. There were unfinished pieces on each station. Scissors and thread, needles and material left where they had fallen when the women faded away.

Bell dusted her hands together and smiled a rueful smile.

"Believe me, I regret not showing my appreciation more for them when they were here. I'm horrible with sewing. I can't manage one straight stitch," she said.

"I've never tried," Elena said. Her time had been all for the dance. There hadn't been any left over.

"The work they completed is stored in these wardrobes and trunks back here," Bell said. She turned and motioned toward a long line of mahogany wardrobes that lined one entire wall. Stacked around the wardrobes were trunks like the one Elena had helped Bell lug up to her aviary.

"Most of the dresses should have been protected from dust, and the wardrobes were lined with cedar to try to keep the moths away. Not so in most of the living quarters. We used up most of the more practical clothes long ago. That's why so many servants you see are in rags," Bell said. "It takes a lot of effort to maintain any semblance of normalcy, but it's also horrible to not even try."

She smoothed her skirts as she said it. Elena realized her unconventional appearance was as much necessity as personality. Bell made do with what she could gather and scrounge.

Elena reached to tip Bell's hat up. The crown often threatened to cover her pretty hazel eyes, although the shadows it caused on her features did tend to make her smile shine.

"I wondered what the hat was about. I guess it's what you could find," she said.

But the other woman grabbed for her hat as if Elena was trying to take it. She pulled the rim tight against her brown hair.

"I'm keeping this safe for someone else. When he comes back, I'm going to give it to him," Bell said.

"I'm sorry. I didn't know," Elena replied. She allowed her hand to drop to Bell's shoulder and she gave it a squeeze. The wide panicked eyes and somber mouth that had claimed Bell's face seemed like a glimpse into her true self, as if the forceful cheer she usually conveyed was a persona she used to survive.

"Most of us are waiting for someone or lots of someones. When you lose hope, the Ether takes you," Bell whispered. Elena understood. If she hadn't had hope, she thought Grigori might have been able to take her long before now.

"But, look, there'll be lots of formal dresses here to choose from. The practical things have been picked over, but the most elaborate gowns haven't been disturbed in ages. The *Volkhvy* are the only ones who dress for the Gathering. It's become the grandest occasion for them. They all try to outdo each other," Bell said.

"That's why this is important. I want to show the queen that the Romanovs haven't given up the fight. And I want to show Grigori that his swan is armed and not in a cage. Most important, I want Ivan to give me his heart and the sword. I want to finally claim it fully, empowered with our connection."

"I want to help you," Bell said. "The Romanovs have been too disconnected for too long."

She flung open one of the wardrobes, and a swarm of fluttering moths flew out surrounded by a cloud of fabric dust.

"Oh, well. I was wrong about that one. Let's try the next," Bell said sheepishly.

They went down the row of wardrobes checking one after another until they finally found several that hadn't been invaded by gnawing insects. And in the dresses they found, Elena finally got a glimpse of the scope of Bronwal's previous splendor.

"I told you…an orphan among legends," Bell said. But she said it with a smile because Elena's wonder was contagious.

She buried her hands in the textures of damask and brocade. She feasted her eyes on the sheen of silks and satins. She laughed out loud at the airy lightness of chiffon and organza.

"This reminds me of home. Although these kind of skirts would only get in the way," Elena said. She lifted one of the full ball gowns out for a closer inspection. It was far too heavy and cumbersome for her needs, but she twirled around in it anyway.

"You were a dancer before you came here," Bell said.

"I'm a dancer still. Once a dancer, always a dancer. Once you've been forged in the fire of the Saint Petersburg Ballet Company, it never goes away," Elena said. She placed the dress back in the wardrobe. She needed a dress that was light and airy around her legs, designed in such a way that it wouldn't impede her movements with the sword.

They rifled through trunks and drawers in companionable silence broken occasionally when a dress elicited appreciative or horrified sounds. Until Bell exclaimed, and Elena turned to see the other woman holding a green dress made of liquid silk. As Bell unfolded the dress from its tissue-lined drawer, its train spilled down and thousands of embroidered flowers showed on the backdrop of green.

"They're bellflowers," her friend said. There were tears in her voice, as if something poignant from the past had been taken from the drawer.

Elena went to her. Beside Bell's current patched and worn outfit—a pauper's clothes—the dress seemed meant for a princess. But, when Bell lifted her eyes up to meet Elena's, her eyes matched the green dress, not her servant's clothes. The sheen of the silk had turned her eyes from hazel to a forest green.

"That dress was made for you," Elena said.

"I never went to dances or parties. Some thought I

should," Bell said softly. Elena immediately supposed that by "some" Bell referred to Soren Romanov.

"Of course you should have," Elena said. "He was right. Did he have this dress made for you before the curse fell?" she asked.

"I don't know," Bell said. "I'll never know."

She folded the dress back into the drawer. She covered it carefully with the tissue paper. Maybe it would have been too painful for her to try it on.

"Besides, we're looking for something for you to wear to the Gathering," Bell reminded Elena.

There was nothing she could do for her friend except respect her wishes to forget about the green dress. Elena turned back to the project at hand, but her mood had been tainted by yet another reminder of how cruel the curse had been to the people of Bronwal. She was silent for a long time, until a brush of feathers against her hand caused her to cry out and pull away.

"What is it?" Bell asked. She'd been lost in thought in front of the drawer she'd closed on the green dress, but she rushed back to Elena's side. She reached for the hand Elena was cradling to see what had caused her to emit the cry of distress.

"It's nothing. I'm fine. The feathers startled me, that's all," Elena said. She forced herself to reach into the wardrobe and bring out the dress that had frightened her. It was weightless in her hand, crafted almost entirely of layers of chiffon. The feathers decorated the bodice and the shoulders, and they'd been expertly applied. They would lie crisscrossed over the breasts in a smooth pattern exactly as they would lie on a bird's chest. The feathers on the shoulders were looser and accompanied by down so that they conveyed the idea of wings when they fluttered with the slightest air currents.

"This one, you'll have to try on," Bell said. She touched the soft down on the shoulders with one finger.

There were several screens in the room decorated with enameled nature scenes. Elena would have been perfectly comfortable changing out in the open, but she didn't want to startle the young woman who came from another time. Maybe the Middle Ages had the equivalent of locker rooms or dressing rooms, but Elena couldn't be sure.

Besides, there was something of her nightmares and her shattered dreams in this dress, and she was too shy to face it in front of curious eyes. She'd worn feathers many times before. She'd been feathered in her nightmares many times before.

But she'd never donned them for a purpose that was completely her own.

The appropriate undergarments had also been in the wardrobe, but Elena chose to wear nothing with it but the panties she had on. She wasn't so curvy that she needed the support, and she wasn't inhibited enough to need the coverage. The dress would fit her perfectly with no help. It settled against her as if it had been made to ride her bare skin.

The feathers provided enough modesty so she didn't feel like an exhibitionist when she came from behind the screen. And her shyness had faded away. This wasn't a nightmare where she was trapped in a swan's body. This wasn't a reminder that she'd lost the dance of her dreams. If anything, it reminded her that she would always have the dance in her heart. Because she walked gracefully in the flowing layered skirts. They didn't impede her movements at all.

Bell sighed out loud when Elena came into view. She'd been looking at the other dresses, but she turned around and her eyes went wide again along with the sigh.

"You're no foundling," Bell said. "You would have fit in at Bronwal before the curse."

She slowly walked to Elena's side. In her hand, she carried a delicate cap of white. She set it on Elena's head and then placed her hands on Elena's upper arms to turn her around toward a large mirror. The cap was little more than a wisp of lace shaped like a tiara. It softly framed her forehead with delicate swirls of feathers on either side of her temples.

"This is it. There can be no better choice," she said.

It was true. Elena could face Grigori in this dress. She could make one last plea to Romanov about her place by his side. And she could face the Light *Volkhvy* queen.

Chapter 21

As night approached, Elena struggled. The sapphire in her sword didn't glow. Grigori would be able to find her. But the wolves had vanished and Romanov was nowhere to be seen. The windows in her tower were shut up tight, but they'd been tight the night before when Grigori had flown inside. Only the power of her mother's sacrifice had kept her inaccessible. With that protection almost completely faded, there wasn't a tower or a lock on earth that could keep her safe. She could feel her vulnerability all the way to her bones.

But Grigori wasn't her only concern.

If she went to the black wolf's lair for sanctuary, she would also be stepping into Romanov's arms. He had rejected her time and time again as the bearer of the sword. How could she indulge in his kisses and his touch when he was closed off to more?

She briefly considered Bell's aviary. In it, she wouldn't

be alone. She would have a friend by her side and one of the wolves at her feet. But, in spite of her fear, she couldn't bring herself to intrude. The orphan and the red wolf seemed to have some sort of special bond. It was obvious that Soren watched over the child his father had saved so long ago, even though she had become little more than a servant to the family. In turn, Bell seemed to watch over the red wolf. They were an odd pair but a pair nonetheless.

Besides, if Grigori followed her to the aviary, she would be placing Bell and Soren in grave danger. Neither of them could stand against the witchblood prince, and no matter her training or her determination, her sapphire sword might not be enough to stop him without its glow.

Frustration bubbled up in her chest and stole her breath. Romanov was too stubborn. He was so busy doing the right thing to protect her that he didn't stop to think how it placed everyone in greater danger. Herself included.

She had no choice but to seek refuge in the cavern. Grigori wouldn't dare penetrate the black wolf's lair. If he found her in her dreams, so be it. At least she wouldn't have to be helpless under his actual physical touch.

This time, Elena brought her flashlight and a handful of spare candles she'd found in a drawer in her room. Without the sapphire's glow, the cavern would be too dark.

She tucked them in her backpack, along with her book and her last energy bars and bottled water. She had no idea if Romanov would even be in the cavern when she got there, but, if he was, she had no intention of winding up in his arms.

She struggled for nothing.

The cavern was empty when she arrived except for the bedding Romanov had carried there the night before. When she sank down on the furs and blankets, she tensed because the scent of roses and winter came from the soft bed beneath her. Romanov's skin and hair always held the scent of evergreen and fresh snow. But he had another headier scent that was purely masculine—a combination of wood smoke, leather and heated muscle.

She couldn't avoid his scent on the bed they'd shared. She breathed it in and accepted that it was mingled with her scent because their bodies had mingled perfectly together.

Elena had told herself she would resist her desire to be with him tonight, but, now that he wasn't here, memories rose up swift and hot to claim her. She shifted, still tender between her legs where they had thrust so hungrily for connection. Her body had already responded to mere recall by becoming hot and wet. She gathered the quilts and furs and held them close beneath her in substitution for the hot thighs she'd prefer to straddle. The bulk of the blankets were nothing compared to the solidity of the man. She missed his hard muscles and the heat of his eager erection.

Elena moaned softly as she undulated against the bedding that smelled like the man she desired. She hadn't come to the cavern for refuge. She'd come for Romanov. She admitted it now that she'd found him gone.

"I tried to stay away." The voice was almost a growl from the mouth of the tunnel that led to the lair.

Elena stilled, and a hot flush washed over her skin in response to the grit of desire in his tones and to being found in the grips of the sensual memory of riding him.

She pushed herself up from the ground and waited on

her hands and knees as he approached. The fur beneath her knees protected them from the hard stone. Nothing protected her from the raw hunger her position inspired. She saw it in Romanov's eyes as he slowly stalked toward her. Their emerald depths reflected the candlelight, as did the mica all over the walls. The candle's glow was warmer than the sapphire's soft blue. Tonight, the mica looked like thousands of flecks of gold.

"I went to find you when night fell. I was going to send you down here alone, while I kept watch outside," Romanov said.

"I was going to keep my distance," Elena said. "If you don't want me to have the sword, then you don't want me."

A harsh, raw laugh erupted from Romanov's chest. It reminded her more of a rumbling growl than an expression of humor.

"I've never wanted anyone or anything more than I want you," he said. But it wasn't a proclamation of love. It was a tortured confession.

"You can't have me without the sword. We've become a package deal," Elena said. But she didn't rise. She stayed as she was, and her body tightened and moistened as he stepped closer and closer.

"You can't have me without the wolf," Romanov said. He was close enough to drop down on his knees on the bedding in front of her. He dropped, but he didn't relax. He towered over her, even on his knees. "I've tried to deny it, but the wolf is part of me. We've been a 'package deal' all along. And the Ether only makes us wilder."

She gasped when he reached for her hair. He plunged his hands into the silky waves on either side of her head, and he held her head in place when he swooped down to kiss her. She whimpered into his hungry mouth, but she didn't pull away. Even if he hadn't held her so tightly, she wouldn't have moved. She was held as much by anticipation and need as by his strong hands.

If wilder meant that Romanov would finally give in to their connection so that they could truly be together, in every sense of the word—physically, emotionally, partners against the Dark—then wilder was what she craved.

She sought the deep recesses of his mouth with her tongue and gloried in the heat and velvety friction she found. His tension softened. His elbows gave. She was able to press forward as they kissed and climb onto his bent legs. He took her slight weight easily—leaning back to give her a place to sit on his hard thighs. She wrapped her legs around his waist and buried her hands into the mane of hair that had always seemed to reveal the wildness he tried to suppress.

She had never been very attracted to soft, sophisticated gentlemen. Now she knew why. Her heart had held out for a legendary shifter as wild and fierce as the black wolf he could become. She was a warrior. A civilized and polished partner would never do.

His hands left her face and fell to cup the globes of her bottom and pull her even closer against him. He pressed her heat to his already swollen erection. She undulated against him.

"No chance I would stay away. None," he groaned against her lips. His face fell to her neck, and she threw back her head to give him access to the sensitive pulse point he sought. His lips were hot, even hotter than her flushed skin. He nipped and licked his way to her cleavage, and then he indulged in slower sucking kisses on the swell of her breasts that rose above the low V of her T-shirt.

Elena moaned as the different textures overwhelmed her with sensation—the tickling strands of his snow-scented hair, the rough stubble on his jaw and the soft but firm swell of his lips. The moist velvet sweep of his teasing tongue caused her nipples to peak into hardened nubs that pressed against the fabric of her T-shirt. She sought to satisfy their throbbing urgency by rubbing them against his hot, muscular chest as she continued to rock against his erection.

But it wasn't enough.

Her body knew what it was like to be filled by his heat and naked against his skin. It would never be satisfied fully clothed again.

She reached between them to undo the crisscrossed laced fastenings of his leather pants. Her fingers fumbled, and he pressed her away to make room for his own hands. She slid down his legs and waited with her knees on the fur and her hands on his thighs. His more practiced movements were able to undo his pants and press them open and slightly down. His underwear came slightly down with the pants and she could see the prize she'd sought. His erection was fully engorged.

Elena took over from there. She grabbed the edges of his fly and opened it farther so that his erection fell free. She looked from the shaft she craved up to his shadowy green eyes. The golden light brought out the flecks of gold in his irises. They matched the mica in the walls. His lips were swollen from her kisses. His hair was mussed. The color in his pale cheeks was high. His flush matched his passion-darkened mouth. But it was the intensity in his expression that seduced her the most. He didn't avoid her perusal. He met her eyes and allowed her to see all that he felt in that moment. His wild need was as obvious in his eyes as it was in his body.

He wanted her and he'd come here to be with her. Not to protect or reject her. He wasn't here as a champion or as a cursed man who had to refuse his needs. He was here to mate. She'd returned to the black wolf's lair to do the same. This was about the oldest enchantment that existed between a man and a woman. No *Volkhvy* magic required.

When she leaned down to slowly take him in her mouth without breaking the connection of their eyes, he cried out. He grabbed for her hair, but he didn't stop her or manipulate her movements. He simply held on softly, with trembling hands. He was salty, sweet and fiery hot against her tongue. His mouth fell open to allow heavier respiration to come and go between his swollen lips. His eyelids drooped to half mast, but he didn't close his eyes. Neither did she. She held her breath and took him deep with a harder suction and she watched his pleasure.

"Elena," he breathed. It sounded like a prayer.

She pulled back to the head of the shaft she suckled. She held its base with her hands and licked its swollen head.

"What, my wolf? Why do you call my name?" she teased.

"I let the wolf have my heart. I thought he would keep you out. But he is me, and we must have you," Romanov said.

"I'm here. I'll always be here. The Ether won't take me away. And neither will Grigori," Elena vowed.

She rose up to reach for his tunic and he reluctantly allowed it. His hands slid away pausing only briefly on her face. She pulled his shirt from his large frame, revealing his perfectly sculpted muscles, inch by impressive inch. He'd spent every waking moment over enumerable Cycles fighting Dark *Volkhvy* and training to keep himself sharp. He'd held the Ether madness at bay all alone for so long.

The candlelight and the reflection from the walls painted his skin with gold.

She leaned to press soft kisses over his hard flesh. On his shoulders. On his arms. On his chest. "I'm here," Elena repeated against his hot skin. "I'm here."

He trembled beneath her lips, especially when she kissed over the planes of his lean stomach. His erection wept and she throbbed with the desire to mount him. She stood to quickly pull off her clothes, but the intense gaze that followed her movements caused her to slow down. As she had taken her time with the revelation of his chest and arms, she slowly worked her own shirt off, exposing her stomach inch by inch and then her naked breasts. They were heavy with need, and her nipples were swollen into tight buds, pink with passion against her porcelain skin. She arched her back and stretched her arms over her head to remove the shirt. Then she met his eyes again. She dropped the shirt at her feet making no effort to be modest.

Still on his knees, he reached for her. His calloused hands wrapped around the two soft mounds she'd brazenly displayed for him. He cupped them and weighed them. He gently brushed over her nipples with his thumbs and forefingers, lightly pinching.

It was her turn to breathe out his name like a prayer.

He responded by tracing his hands down her sides until they got to her waist. He continued on the downward track only after he'd grabbed the waistband of her leggings. He pulled them down. Not suddenly. Not impatiently. But, following her lead, he inched them down. He exposed her skin a little at a time until she was trembling as he had done.

Only then did he use the material he gripped to pull her closer. He tugged her to his face. Her quivering intensified when his hot breath tickled over her stomach. Then she cried out because he followed his breath not with the kiss she expected, but with the fiery heat of his moist tongue. He licked her stomach as the jeans continued to come down. When his movements had revealed her hipbones, he licked those and suckled beneath them. Arcs of heat penetrated deep and rushed lower from his teasing tongue to her throbbing mound.

And still, slowly, slowly he worked her jeans down until he reached the top of her panties. His fingers softly gathered the edges so that his movements lowered her panties with the jeans until he revealed the curls they'd covered.

This time when his tongue teased the trembling flesh above those curls, she cried out. But seconds later, when his tongue delved into the curls to find the moist slit at the V of her legs, she silently grabbed the back of his head to keep herself from falling.

He teased in and out with his tongue, mimicking the thrusting she craved and her cries became cries of release. He held her hips and pressed her close to lap up her response with his hungry tongue.

She had to crumple then. He slowed her descent, but allowed her to fall. Once her body was on the bedding, Romanov pulled her leggings off her legs one by one. She thought he would settle between them once she was naked. She tried to reach for him, but he was still on his knees. He caressed her hips and thighs as she recovered from the climax he'd given her with his tongue. Softly, gently his fingers teased.

Elena's hands gripped the bedding beneath her as her body began to hunger again. She arched her back and closed her eyes. Her legs opened. He rewarded the silent request with a thick penetrating finger. Her eyelids flew open and she saw that he watched her heated reaction to his touch.

"I don't want to frighten you. But this is only making me wilder," Romanov said gruffly. She could feel the tension in his hand even though he kept his touch gentle. Too gentle. She wanted more.

"Don't mistake me for delicate, my wolf. I train to appear graceful, but there's strength behind the grace. You know that," Elena said.

She thrust her hips up to increase the penetration of his finger. And her sudden impatient movement was all the encouragement he needed. He withdrew his hand, but only to place it on her hips to roll her over. A thrill of surprise washed over her, but it quickly turned to a thrill of desire when he spread her legs and teased his finger back into her from behind. She undulated against the furs and came again. Her body pulsed around his finger.

"You're so beautiful when you become lost in your pleasure. I could spend eternity watching you come again and again," Romanov groaned. This time, he didn't wait patiently for her to recover. He lifted her hips and she found herself on her hands and knees, as she'd been when he'd first stalked into the cavern.

"I've never been so easy to please. You hardly have to touch me. I'm wet when you enter a room," Elena confessed.

"That you're always slick for me...it makes me ache,"

Romanov said. He illustrated his words by pressing behind her so she could feel the hot length of his erection against her.

"I like to make you ache," Elena said. "I like to drive you wild."

"Done," Romanov said.

And he claimed her with a single thrust from behind. Elena cried out his name and the cavern echoed around them. He held her hips so she didn't collapse as waves of pleasure shook her body. And then he used his hold to rock her forward and backward for his penetrating thrusts. She had to depend on her good knee to help him, but the soft furs cushioned the other so she felt no pain.

Even from this position, she wasn't a passive lover. She arched her back and pressed her bottom against his stomach, again and again. Even as he thrust with powerful, frenzied strokes, he matched the rhythm she set with her athletic, muscled movements. Only then did the sword awaken and join the golden glow on the walls with its sapphire blue.

But this time, Romanov didn't pull away.

And his acceptance of the sword's glow brought her to a shuddering release. Her body pulsed around his shaft and she cried out his name. He held her hips as her body tried to collapse. He buried himself deep and hard and came at the entrance of her womb.

When she woke in the wee hours of the morning, Romanov was gone. But the sword still glowed faintly. She used its light instead of her flashlight to walk quietly down the tunnel. The mica shimmered on the walls as she passed. Romanov must have known when she entered the main body of the cavern, but he didn't say a word.

The light from the sword didn't reach the high cathedral ceiling, but she saw a deeper shadow and recognized the broad shoulders of her lover.

He stood, a silent guard at the outside entrance to the cavern.

Elena went back to the empty bed.

He was still determined to protect her even though he knew she could protect herself. The curse would stand between them forever if she couldn't convince Vasilisa that it was time to forgive the Romanovs. What she must accomplish at the Gathering wasn't humanly possible, but she had to try.

For Lev, who was determined to die.

For Soren and the young woman he watched over every night.

For poor Patrice and all the other inhabitants of Bronwal.

But mostly because Ivan Romanov could not continue to stand alone. He was the last Romanov, but he couldn't continue to punish himself for what his father had done. He deserved peace and happiness. He deserved reprieve. Maybe she couldn't give him those, but she could give him a partner.

If only he would relent and accept it was her decision to brave the Ether.

The cool night air didn't soothe him. He wanted to go to Elena when she slipped from their bed to check on him, but he held himself back instead. She didn't speak. Once she saw him, she stood for only a moment, silently watching, before she went back to bed.

The Gathering was tomorrow night.

All the Dark and Light *Volkhvy* would come to dance

in the power of the Ether that Bronwal radiated and to bask in the humiliation and subjugation of Vasilisa's curse.

Ivan fisted his hands. They were still warm from the memory of touching Elena. If he closed his eyes, he could see her pleasure, but he could also sense the intensity of his feelings for her.

He'd denied the wolf for so long. He'd denied any and every emotion. He'd had to turn away from his heart to go on and on and on. Earlier, when he and Elena had made love, he'd let go of that control.

The resulting connection had shaken him to his core.

He had never been the stoic ruler of Bronwal. He'd been pretending all along. He'd always pined and longed and hungered for something more. Elena was the answer to his hunger. She fed his wolf and his human soul.

And he could never experience that connection again, not if he was going to succeed in letting her go.

She deserved to be free from Grigori and also free from him and the Romanov curse.

Chapter 22

She polished the sword until it gleamed. The stone had continued to glow, not as brightly as it had ever flared, but it was definitely not dead. Now, the scrolling silver on its hilt and the steel of its blade also shone.

Bell had sent servants up to the tower with a formal scabbard tooled of red leather and decorated with thorny vines and roses, along with her dress and shoes. It was as if her hooded cloak had been remade into a belt for her sword. The dress had been aired outside and its chiffon held the scent of winter snow. The shoes were white leather ankle boots with solid square heels and sharp pointed toes—artfully designed and also practical. She could appreciate both.

She'd carried her own bathwater this time. The effort dispelled her nerves and kept her busy during a day that might have dragged otherwise. She hadn't seen Romanov since the dawn. She washed her hair early and dried it by the fire, combing out the long thick strands of pale blond until they were smooth. Then she braided the thick mass into one long plait that began on the left side of her head, curved to the right and ended over her right shoulder midway down her chest. Ringlets of loose curls extended from the bottom of the plait, where she'd bound it with an elastic band. She wanted her hair to be as artful and practical as her shoes.

She belted on her sword and found that her hair was perfect. Her right hand was free to draw from the scabbard that hung on her left side. Only then did she open the wardrobe to use the full-length mirror in its door to check her appearance. She hadn't packed formal makeup. Bell had loaned her the bare minimum of old-fashioned rouges and kohl. She'd managed to line her eyes and darken her lashes and lips. She hadn't bothered to contour her cheeks. The last few weeks of power bars and stress had given them natural contours no powdery tricks could match.

Above the soft white feathers on her breast, her skin was porcelain pale. Her sword, lips and eyes stood out vividly against the white. She was surprised how closely her eyes matched the sapphire gem's glow. She did go back to the tiny glass pots Bell had loaned her then to add a touch of color to her cheeks. The woman reflected in the glass was too pale.

Even with the added rouge, she looked less a warrior than a waif. She was afraid she'd miscalculated. She'd wanted to reclaim the swan princess Grigori had stolen from her, but she was afraid she would only reinforce his desire.

But there was no time to choose another dress.

Besides, she might look graceful and delicate in the swan gown, but the truth could be seen in her eyes. They matched the sapphire in intent as well as color. She was no waif. She would enter the ballroom as a swan, but not as Grigori's swan. She'd make sure all who attended would see the difference.

The enchanted castle was sprawling. Since she'd arrived, she'd searched and explored through many rooms and levels. But she'd never been to the rooms that made up the grand ballroom and its adjacent withdrawal chambers. The doors had been locked. Bell had assured her there was nothing inside but dusty chandeliers and wide-open spaces.

Tonight, she wound down the tower staircase alone. She walked through dozens of deserted corridors until she arrived at the massive arched double doorways to the ballroom itself.

The sun had set. The Cycle was almost over. Tomorrow Bronwal would return to the Ether and Ivan Romanov and all of his people would disappear one more time.

Unless she could change something tonight.

This time, when Elena tried the doors they pressed open beneath her hands. They swung inward easier than she had expected on a whoosh of displaced air. The expansive space revealed to her eyes made her pause outside the door. Her stomach tightened and her breath caught in her throat. It seemed a million candles illuminated the room, suspended from the ceiling in dozens of elaborate crystal chandeliers. The candlelight bounced off the multifaceted crystal beads, causing the very air to glimmer with reflected light.

The whole room was empty.

Save for the shadowed silhouette of one man.

He turned toward the doors as they opened, and Elena was drawn toward him in spite of his silence. Even the giant, empty room didn't make him appear smaller. If anything, he seemed even taller and more intimidating as the focal point. The sheen of his tuxedo both absorbed and reflected all of the light until he seemed a living shadow come to life when he stepped to meet her. It was the first time she'd seen him in more modern clothes. The tuxedo was still vintage, only slightly less out of time than the man who wore it, but unlike his cloak, leather and furs, the suit rode his muscles in tailored perfection as he moved.

He hadn't tamed his hair.

It was a wild mass of black waves all around his face and shoulders. And she was glad. She was also glad when she was close enough to see the emerald of his eyes. He wasn't a living shadow. He was a living legend. Her legend, whether he was fully ready to accept it or not. It didn't matter what he wore. He wore it well. And he wore it with the same wild energy she'd been drawn to from the start.

"They'll arrive closer to midnight. It's always been so. Lev and Soren stay out of sight. They would be too tempting a trophy for the Darker *Volkhvy*. For many Cycles I've watched and waited alone," Romanov said.

"Not tonight," she said. Unspoken was the promise that he'd never have to wait alone again if he would relent. "I'll wait with you."

"Grigori will not stay away. He'll brave the black wolf to have you," Romanov warned. He reached to trace the side of her face. His touch was soft; barely the pads of his fingers skimmed her skin. And still she released a quavering sigh as gooseflesh rose and her nipples tightened. "Don't be emboldened by the sword's glow. Let me handle Grigori. That's why you came."

"I climbed the mountain for help, not for salvation. I didn't need to be rescued. I needed to be reinforced," Elena said. "The legend of the Romanov wolves brought me here, but I heard the sword, as well. I answered its call."

"The Ether can't have you," Romanov vowed. He lifted his other hand to join the first. He cupped her face and her chin lifted in response. She met his eyes. She hoped he would see what she'd seen in the mirror—determination and the power of the sword beaming from some place inside of her. "Even if it means I can't have you either."

"You will always have me, Ivan Romanov. Because you are mine and I am yours. We belong to each other. And nothing and no one will come between us once we've decided to stand together," Elena said.

He leaned to kiss her then. Not because he agreed. She could feel the tension in his shoulders when she moved to hold him. He kissed her because they didn't have much time. There was desperation in the flick of his tongue. She wished he believed her. There was so much to overcome—Vasilisa, Grigori, the curse and the Ether. But she believed they could do it because she'd always believed in the stories her grandmother had told her, and her grandmother's stories always ended well for the legendary wolves.

Music began somewhere in the distance.

Romanov pulled away from her lips and she allowed it, although her heart was breaking. He wouldn't kiss her again once the night progressed. He would be too preoccupied.

One thing was certain: he couldn't be allowed to shift to save her.

She had to stop Grigori before Romanov thought the black wolf was needed. He'd said Lev and Soren stayed away from the Gathering because they would be tempting trophies for the *Volkhvy* that came to the ball. There would be no greater trophy than the black wolf's head.

Luckily, tonight, the black wolf had a defender.

Romanov broke their kiss, but he didn't step away. He pulled her into his arms instead. Like his tuxedo, the waltz was after his natural time, but Ivan Romanov had lived through many different ages. Modern life had managed to touch Bronwal every time it appeared. It was only as the curse dragged on that Romanov had become more and more isolated. He hadn't been truly alone until she'd found him, this Cycle, after all of his loved ones had disappeared.

He waltzed as well as he fought. She wasn't surprised. He was large, but athletic. He could move with speed and grace. He easily whirled her around the large empty room beneath the chandeliers and she allowed it. The layers of her skirt floated away from her bare legs as she stepped quickly to follow his lead. The downy feathers on her shoulders fluttered as if she'd taken flight.

And that's how the Light *Volkhvy* queen found them when she entered the ballroom.

The music stopped.

Romanov continued to circulate around the room until they came to the entrance. He made the queen wait for their audience. He made her watch them fly. And then he effortlessly caught Elena's momentum and brought them both to a halt directly in front of the queen. Only a powerful partner could have executed such a complete stop without a stumble or stuttering step. Without thinking, completely directed by instinct, Elena dropped into a low curtsy. She balanced on her good leg, but her injured knee screamed. No one watching would have known it. After all, a prima ballerina danced through pain. It was her primary skill.

"Lovely. I've never been greeted by a swan princess and her cob," Vasilisa said drily. But a hint of a smile curved one corner of her perfect lips. She was in purple again. Like Romanov, the clothes she wore never seemed to be static to one time period. Elena had seen her in Victorian. Tonight, she wore a Tudor court gown with an elaborate brocade underdress crafted of silk. It was covered in a velvet gown that split down the front to show off the brocade, in contrasting shades of plum and violet. The violet brocade had a square neck, and the plum velvet had wide bell sleeves embroidered with the perpetual thorns and roses.

On Vasilisa's head was a Tudor cap with two horns crafted from quilted black satin. The horns rose up from her temples and curved back and around like a ram's horns until they ended facing forward beside both of her high cheekbones. From the back of the cap, steams of violet silk flowed behind her in a long train.

Elena's dress was simple and natural in comparison, and she was suddenly glad of it. The queen was charmed by her delicate grace, but when she rose from her curtsy she knew the savvy witch could see the glow in her eyes.

"A swan that wears the sapphire sword," the queen continued. Behind her, a crowd had formed. Elena was certain that they appeared one by one out of the Ether that couldn't be seen. It existed in and around Bronwal. The better to take the enclave when it was time.

"Will you dance, Your Highness?" Elena asked before Romanov could say that he still rejected her.

Vasilisa seemed taken aback for the first time.

"He's a graceful partner. And I've had plenty to compare," Elena said with a smile. She was terrified. The crowd behind the queen had swelled into a hundred witches or more. And the Dark *Volkhvy* hadn't even begun to arrive. If Grigori came and if she couldn't defeat him herself, Romanov would shift in a ballroom full of hundreds of witches who wanted him dead.

Was Vasilisa as vengeful as the curse made her seem? Was there any hope she would decide to fight on her black wolf's side?

Something about the purple garb the queen favored niggled at the edges of Elena's mind. Until she understood the queen, she couldn't truly understand where they stood against Grigori.

"And what does the cob say about this invitation?" Vasilisa asked. "He's never asked me to dance before."

Elena held her breath. Romanov might well stiffen and walk away. He had many reasons to hate the Light *Volkhvy* queen. Her curse had cost him everything and doomed him to centuries of struggle. She was the one who had used her enchantments to change the Romanov genes. She had created the wolves without once pausing to consider what the shift would mean to men.

Air released from Elena's lungs when Romanov extended his hand.

The queen stepped forward. The music began again as invisible musicians followed her unspoken cue. None of her entourage dared to question her decision, although many of them gasped, whispered and stared. They had come with the hopes of a wolf hunt after all. Time and time again they had arrived at the Gathering hoping for Romanov's fall, led by their queen's anger to hate the wolves they'd once depended on to keep their Dark brethren in check.

Elena gripped the hilt of her sword and stared them all down, one by one, while the queen and Romanov began to waltz around the empty ballroom floor. As each witch lowered his or her eyes, they melted away to pair up and join their queen in the dance. Soon, they had all flowed away like water released from a dam. Elena watched them dance. The other *Volkhvy* were also dressed eclectically. Every time period she could imagine was represented, from wide skirts to flapper fringe. The men wore everything from tights, to kilts, to tuxedos in every style, but one thing common in all the men and the women was extravagance.

As Bell had said, the witches tried to outdo each other. In her simple gown, Elena shone like the candlelight that illuminated the ballroom. In the middle of a shifting rainbow of brilliant fabrics, only Elena wore white.

And only she wore one of the queen's enchanted swords.

She turned to follow the queen and Romanov with her eyes as they whirled around the floor. She doubted if anyone else present would have been strong enough to handle the queen's heavy skirts, but it was obvious that Romanov's muscles propelled the witch with ease. Elena had experienced the swoop and swirl herself, moments before. She wasn't surprised to see the Mona Lisa smile tilt higher on the queen's face. Even in the midst of pain and loss, there was joy in the dance.

Pain and *loss*.

Purple, like black, was the color of mourning.

The Light *Volkhvy* queen was in mourning for someone she had lost.

Elena took two steps toward the dancing couple before she caught herself at the edge of the dance floor. Did
Vasilisa mourn Vladimir? That seemed unlikely. He had
betrayed her and her affections. Their relationship had
been a sham he'd used to try to steal her position.

But if not her Romanov lover, whom did she mourn
and why?

As Elena's mind struggled with this new piece of the
puzzle, the music stopped once more. Every couple on
the dance floor paused as if their moves had been cho-
reographed. Except Romanov and the queen. He ignored
everyone else to whirl the queen around to where they
had begun as he'd done with Elena. This was his castle.
He was the last Romanov. He ended the dance when he
was ready to end the dance and no sooner. Every eye in
the ballroom followed their graceful waltz.

Including every eye of the Dark *Volkhvy* horde that had
arrived. Elena had been watching the dance. Its graceful
circular motions had almost hypnotized her. When her
eyes focused on the horde, she was startled. They had arrived silently because they'd arrived from the Ether. One
minute the spot where they appeared was empty marble.
The next it was filled with Dark *Volkhvy*. Others, like
Elena, noticed the horde with sudden horror. Gasps and
murmurs of dismay rose up around the room, but then
hushed as if the guests were afraid vocalizing their fear
would only gain the attention of the Dark witches.

An unnatural hush fell. The atmosphere vibrated with
expectant tension.

Romanov and the queen seemed to have no care. Other
than the music ending, which must have been silently or-

dered by the queen, there was no other indication by the couple that they'd seen the Dark *Volkhvy* arrive.

When they stopped in front of the man leading the horde of Dark witches, Elena held her breath. Romanov was a man, not a wolf, but the black wolf gleamed darkly from his eyes.

"Well, this is a surprise. The doomed man dances with the one who has doomed him. Surely you would rather rip out her throat?" the man said. His voice was charming but oily. It seemed to ooze against Elena's skin in the same way that Grigori's oozed. His syllables seemed to reach out and touch the listener in intimate ways without permission.

She shuddered. Romanov and the queen simply stood. Romanov didn't drop the queen's hand. In fact, Elena thought he might have held on tighter to keep from attacking the man who spoke of their centuries-old conflict as if it had been staged for his entertainment.

"King Josef. We all come to dance while Bronwal stands. Each Cycle might be its last. There is no better waltz than a poignant one, I find. And there's never been a better partner for that than Ivan Romanov," the queen said.

Romanov stood proudly beside her. He hadn't dropped her hand. She was the one who let him go. He brought his released hand up to join his other behind his back. Only Elena saw the white-knuckled grip she knew so well as he held himself in check.

"Better than Vladimir?" The man laughed, and the horde laughed with him. It was an exaggerated show of deference that told her the man must be the Dark *Volkhvy* king.

Elena looked at the king who had fathered her darkest nightmare. He tormented a man quadruple his worth.

"Be careful, Josef. Don't test the limits of my hospitality," the queen replied.

Elena's hand had inadvertently pulled on the hilt of her sword. She'd partially brought it from its scarlet scabbard. The movement and noise in the silent room drew attention. Every eye, including the king's, moved her way.

And then the light in the sapphire died.

Her fingers went numb before she noticed the slight blue glow was gone. She froze. The Dark *Volkhvy* horde seemed to draw in a collective breath. Unlike the numbness in her hand, the numbness that claimed her body wasn't caused by the loss of magic. She looked down at the dull, dead stone and then she immediately sought Romanov's face.

He still stood tall and straight beside the queen.

He refused to meet her eyes.

Her stomach fell in one sudden swoop, but it found no bottom to the pit that sucked it down. Dizziness claimed her and she ground her teeth against it. She braced her legs even though the move pained her knee. She stiffened her spine.

This was the ultimate rejection in front of their worst enemies. He had severed their burgeoning connection with a force of will that staggered her with its finality. It didn't matter that he'd done it to protect her. The loss was sharp, then devastatingly hollow. She accepted that she was meant to be a warrior and now that choice was taken from her. By the man she loved. He'd also made a decision. The dead sapphire gave him away. He was going to shift if Grigori came to the Gathering. He was going to sacrifice everything to try to save her rather than allow her to risk the Ether to save herself.

"Queen Vasilisa, the Dark *Volkhvy* have never depended on the Light's invitation to this Gathering," the words came from a silky voice that caused Elena's numbness to jolt away. The witchblood prince stepped from behind his father's retinue. "We come to dance at our pleasure. And, you must know, we come to watch and wait for greater pleasures."

She'd dreaded the moment when Grigori would arrive, but he'd already been here all along.

Grigori met her horrified gaze. A smile like she'd never seen curved his lips. It was feral. At complete odds with his quiet, civilized appearance. He wore a tailored black suit that was ruthlessly cut to his lean masculine shape. His shirt and tie were also unrelieved black, as were the onyx gems in the lobes of his ears. His sleek black hair fell straight to his shoulders. Its oily sheen reflected the candlelight when he moved with liquid grace to his father's side. His obsidian eyes matched his smile. Those eyes took in her appearance with the ease of possession. He skimmed from her head to her toes, and his gaze seemed to leave a smudge on her skin that sank to her soul.

That's when she saw the feathers.

The queen had called Romanov her cob, but it was obvious that Grigori had stolen that designation without her permission. Black feathers protruded jaggedly from his neck in a shiny ruff. More feathers protruded from the back of each hand, making them look like wing tips when he gestured as he spoke.

His hungry black eyes echoed the hollow in her stomach. She was still falling. She would never stop. There was no sword to catch her. No partner in this fight. Romanov's sacrifice wasn't a salvation. It only dug the pit of her despair deeper than it had to be.

"My swan," Grigori purred. There was no softness in the endearment. It was as slickly used as a sharpened knife against her skin, and he intended it to cut. He wanted to draw blood.

Elena forced her hand to release the sword. She trembled. The numbness had fled. In its place was an adrenaline rush with no outlet. She stood, helpless, as Grigori smiled.

"You're mistaken if you think the curse is evidence of my weakness," Vasilisa replied. "You have no idea what I'm capable of doing for the ones I love."

"Be still. You distract me from my moment of triumph," Grigori said. It was a sharp shout that rang throughout the ballroom and echoed off the distant ceiling and walls. Elena jerked, startled.

But the rest of the room, including the flickering flames in the candles, went perfectly still. Only she moved when Grigori approached. She took one single step away only to come up against the Light *Volkhvy* dancers who had paused when the Dark horde had arrived, but now stood frozen midstep because of Grigori's shouted spell.

She'd known he was a powerful witch. But seeing his control of all other witches in the room caused her heart to race. She couldn't help it. She looked to the one man who might be able to save her. She didn't court his sacrifice, but instinctive terror caused her to seek him out.

Romanov was frozen too. He stood like a statue beside the queen. And for a split second she was struck again by his stature and his legend. Neither seemed to intimidate Grigori as he ignored everyone else in the room to zero his entire focus on her.

She pressed back against the dancers behind her, but

there was no escape from Grigori's advance. She'd meant to boldly reclaim the swan as her own. But Grigori's lascivious gaze negated her efforts. In his eyes, she was his, and her dress was only a preview of the dark pleasures that were to come. With his black feathers, he made them into partners. He stepped into the spot Romanov had vacated by her side.

In the same room was too close. By the time he'd slowly walked to face her, she could barely take in enough oxygen to survive. She risked hyperventilation because the quick intake and exhale of her panicked respiration didn't fuel her lungs. When he suddenly leaned to speak against the vulnerable pulse point behind her left ear, her breath held without her permission. "I've waited for this moment for too long. I hardly know where to begin," Grigori said. The rush of his whisper against her skin caused gooseflesh to rise. She swayed as her oxygen-deprived system caused her head to go light.

Grigori saw her distress. He straightened. His smile tilted higher. He liked her fear. He courted her pain. But he was a connoisseur. There was no rush in his movements as he reached to pull her into his arms. The music had stopped when the queen had stopped dancing. Grigori began to hum as he pulled her into mimicry of the waltz he had witnessed between Romanov and the queen. His moves were more savage. He jerked and pulled. She struggled to keep up. His fingers dug into her skin.

She still had the sword. It wasn't glowing with power, but it could still stab and slash. She wasn't sure what good it would do to try to attack him if he could simply freeze her as he'd frozen the whole room of witches, but she would try. She would never be too afraid to fight him.

But, as she decided to spill his black blood, their dance

became something more dizzying and horrible. A frigid atmosphere enveloped her with an unrelenting vacuum so that she was forced to hold on to the man she despised rather than be sucked away. Her vision faded to gray and her body seemed to disintegrate like a vapor into the freezing air.

And then she was back to herself once again as Grigori laughed maniacally.

He continued to spin her around the ballroom, weaving in and out of the other couples who were frozen in place.

"Others fear the Ether. I dance in its shadows. Come, dance with me, pet. Tread on forbidden pathways. Dwell with me on the edges of oblivion," Grigori taunted.

The Ether.

The cold vacuum claimed her again and again. Her tormentor forced her to desperately hang on to his arm and neck in order to survive. He played with the Ether that Romanov had rejected her to help her avoid. Only now did she begin to know what Romanov had done.

She hadn't understood.

The Ether was the absence of everything and it was always hungry for more.

Each time Grigori teased her into the nothingness, she cried out, but her screams were lost as the sound waves were eaten away. Each time they rematerialized, Grigori laughed at her frantic grip.

"Your tears are as delicious as I knew they would be." He suddenly stopped in the center of the room. Elena held on to keep from falling to the floor. Her knee throbbed. The very atoms of her body seemed disjointed and slightly loosened, as if she would never recover from the disembodiment he'd forced her to endure again and again. Grigori viciously pulled her against his chest and he leaned down. She recognized the blackness in his eyes now. *The Ether is inside of him.* He'd toyed with its power for too long. It had eaten his soul. The entire orb of his eye had gone black as he played. Elena shuddered in revulsion as he slowly extended his tongue and licked the salty moisture from her cheek.

But her revulsion wasn't his only reward.

He couldn't move. He couldn't breathe. He thought that even his heart had stopped midbeat. But his love for Elena couldn't be halted by Dark *Volkhvy* magic. He'd tried to deny it. He'd tried to protect her from the Romanov curse and from the savagery the black wolf brought to his nature.

To no avail.

The sapphire blade had known him better than he knew himself.

He'd been made into an enchanted champion by Vasilisa while he'd still been in his mother's womb, but it wasn't Vasilisa's enchantments that had caused him to fall in love with the woman Grigori currently tormented around and around the dance floor.

She'd fascinated him from the first moment he'd seen her determined limp up the icy mountain pass and his fascination had grown into something much more binding since then.

She didn't need protecting from a wolf who loved her. She didn't need shielding from a curse they could face together.

The sword simply recognized a soul-to-soul connection that would have been forged if she'd been a baker with a warrior's heart and he'd been a chimney sweep with a wolf's teeth.

It was that savage love that finally broke through his last reservations about claiming their connection. Not a timid one. Not a gentle one. But a love that accepted and freed the part of him he'd always thought he needed to deny.

As he stood frozen in place by Grigori's power, the alpha wolf inside of him no longer threatened to consume his humanity. When the witch held her close and licked the tears from her cheek, there was only one man the black wolf intended to consume.

The floor began to shake beneath their feet. It was Grigori's turn to hold on. He gripped her tightly and looked around to ascertain who had so rudely interrupted his gross celebration. Elena thought she knew. She wasn't distracted by the *Volkhvy* who had begun to move around them as if they slowly woke from a trance. Her eyes were drawn to only one place in the cavernous ballroom.

The last Romanov had been the first to break from Grigori's powerful spell.

He had somehow managed to begin the shift while she was flickering in and out of the Ether. The chandeliers swayed now. Wax rained down in hot, fragrant spatters and the candlelight jumped crazily all over the walls. Romanov had completed the shift while she endured the slick brush of Grigori's tongue.

She'd glimpsed the final moments of his transformation, but it wasn't horrible to her. The change from human to wolf was beautiful compared to the sucking emptiness of Ether in Grigori's eyes.

The black wolf was surrounded by hundreds of

Volkhvy who were eager to kill him. But the roar of his first howl violently shattered thousands of crystals above their heads. Broken glass tinkled down like a sudden ice storm. Elena shielded her eyes against the dangerous dust as others ran and screamed.

It was one thing to fantasize about killing a legend. It was another to suddenly face him.

"You're going to die," Elena said. She whispered the words. They weren't for the black wolf.

Because the sapphire stone had blazed into glorious life.

The candlelight had been mostly snuffed out by the chandeliers' destruction. A few flames still flickered here and there. The bright blue glow from the gem in her sword was vivid against the shadows. Even more so when she jerked away from her captor and freed the blade. The Romanov sword. Her sword. Because she was the black wolf's mate. The sword had called her and she'd been brave enough to claim it.

And now the legendary shifter claimed her in return.

Her sword had never blazed so brightly. Grigori backed away from her. His hands were held up defensively as she advanced. But she was momentarily distracted by the Light *Volkhvy* queen. Vasilisa stood behind the black wolf as he met attack after attack. Her back was to his tail, and Elena recognized the defensive strategy she'd been taught. The queen was helping Romanov against Dark *Volkhvy* as they came for his head. Energy shone from her hands and her lips moved with words Elena couldn't hear.

Grigori tried to take advantage of her distraction. He stepped forward as if he would grab her again. She knew it would be a mistake to allow his touch. He was too connected to the Ether. He'd learned to use it even as it ate away at him inside. He'd been too greedy for power and for the pain of others.

He'd danced at the edge of the Ether, but now it could have all of him, with her compliments.

Elena pressed the tip of her blade to Grigori's throat and he froze. She didn't need a magic spell to make him freeze. She had a warrior's heart. Another howl ripped through the air and Elena saw the Dark *Volkhvy* king go down under the black wolf's attack in a torrent of black blood. A few of the Light *Volkhvy* had fallen before they realized the intent of their queen. Now, they fought against the Dark witches rather than the black wolf. With the king's death and Grigori's capture, the Dark *Volkhvy* began to disband.

From outside the ballroom, Elena heard more screams and growls. Reinforcements had arrived. Her endless fall had stopped, but her insides were still hollow. Lev probably wasn't fit to fight and Soren wasn't as big and strong as his alpha brother. He was quick and clever. Much faster and brighter than the brightest natural wolf. But he risked his life to fight on her behalf.

"If Queen Vasilisa hadn't decided to stand with the black wolf, you wouldn't have stood a chance," Grigori hissed. As he spoke, his throat moved an infinitesimal amount, but ribbons of black blood trickled down his feathered neck as a result of the unrelenting pressure from her sword. She didn't waver. His eyes were still completely black. She was certain he couldn't change that. The Ether dance had taken him over an edge he'd skirted for too long.

"I don't stand with the black wolf. I stand with my warriors. I always have," the queen said as she approached.

She was covered in steaming blood too black to be her own. It sullied her perfect gown, but she was regal still.

"If you stand with me, then you stand with my mate. You can't separate us in your affections," Elena said.

The queen paused, brought up short by the intensity of Elena's declaration. Then she resumed her steps.

"It wasn't until the sword called you that I began to understand my mistake," Vasilisa said. "I'll never forgive Vladimir for his savagery, but he and I are the only ones to blame."

"Too late. Far too late. You hurt the ones who loved you the most," Elena said. "Madeline and the baby…"

"All is not as it seems," Vasilisa replied. "But there'll be time for explanations after we deal with this Dark prince."

Grigori had lowered his hands. He stood with them fisted at his sides as his blood continued to soak into his shirt and coat. He didn't cringe when the black wolf reappeared from the corridor where he had chased after the escaping horde. The arched double doors were barely big enough to allow him to enter without ducking his head. To Elena's relief, he was followed by a red shadow and then a white. His brothers flanked him on either side as he stalked into the room.

And a smaller figure in green.

"Bell," Elena breathed. She tightened her grip on the sword when Grigori attempted to turn.

The other woman was wearing the green gown. It fitted to her curves and revealed that her petite size was no indication of her age or maturity. Elena had been right. Bell had loved the dress that had been made for her long ago. She must have decided to wear it to the Gathering in hopes of waking the man in the red wolf she loved.

Elena's heart squeezed when she realized the dress was stained with black blood. Bell hadn't arrived in time to dance before the fight. Now, she would never have the chance.

"Oh, I see. The red wolf has also inspired someone to stand for him," Vasilisa said. She turned from the wolves to face Elena once more. "Vladimir was an aberration. He didn't deserve the powers he was given. He abused them. I allowed his actions to blind me to the truth. I must stand with my wolves and the women who love them. We all must continue to stand against the Dark."

"Together," Elena said. She said it to the approaching wolves and to Bell, who had paused halfway across the room as if she didn't deserve to approach the queen. There was no fear in her face. Only resignation. Elena didn't know what had become of the third sword, and it wasn't her place to determine which woman it would call to stand with Soren.

But she did know who had been standing with him for centuries. The resourceful orphan stood now as if at a loss on how to proceed. She was more used to devoted service than fighting witches, but she'd been fighting the Ether all along. Bell was a survivor and more importantly she helped others survive. There was no finer quality in a warrior than that.

"You'll forgive me if I don't linger," Grigori suddenly interrupted. "I have no interest in meeting your black wolf. Goodbye, my swan. I'll see you in your dreams." Elena thrust with her sword, but it was too late. The man with Ether in his eyes had slipped easily into the vacuum. His body disintegrated from the head down, and her move met nothing but particles of dried blood left to float away in the air.

But the black wolf was more practiced with the Ether than she was. He knew to pounce for the witchblood prince's feet. Elena shouted a warning, but it didn't stop Romanov from clamping his teeth down over Grigori's boots before they, too, began to disappear.

Elena's horrified gaze met a familiar pair of emerald eyes. Her lover, her Romanov, had leaped to grab the prince before he could escape into the Ether. Had he known he would be taken into the vacuum Grigori manipulated at will? As the mighty wolf's black body disintegrated into the air and disappeared, Elena screamed.

Chapter 23

The tip of her sword clanked onto the floor once it was no longer lodged in Grigori's skin. Soren and Lev had leaped too late. They both whined and snuffled the floor where Grigori and the black wolf had stood. Lev limped, but he wasn't slowed down by his injuries. He snuffled and whined as urgently as the red wolf. Maybe more.

"He warned me how bad the Ether was. I didn't understand why he was so determined to spare me from it even if it meant losing himself," Elena said.

"He's strong. He'll come back. He always does," Bell said. She had run forward to catch Elena before she crumpled to the ground. The small servant was much stronger than she seemed. But Elena had known almost from the start. Like calls to like, and they had been fast friends because they saw each other better and more clearly than others saw them.

"I'm sorry. The Ether is seductive. The Light *Volkhvy*

resist its allure. I used it to curse Bronwal. This is all my fault," Vasilisa said.

"You always wear purple. It's the color of mourning. Who do you mourn, my queen? You didn't do this because Vladimir betrayed you. There's a secret behind your greatest pain. One deeper than your love for Vladimir Romanov," Elena said. She leaned against Bell. Her friend took her weight without protest.

The queen looked from Elena to Bell and back again. But then her gaze was drawn to the petite servant in green silk. Her eyes traced the bellflowers embroidered onto the stained gown.

"Vladimir killed my daughter, Anna. I had placed her with a mortal family for her protection. I knew something was wrong. Vladimir had begun to act strangely. I was afraid he would betray me, and I wanted her well away from danger. But I never imagined my greatest champion would murder a Light *Volkhvy* princess in cold blood," Vasilisa said. "He destroyed the whole village of Sovkra. No one survived. It wasn't until then that I realized he might have killed my consort, as well. My prince died in the same battle as Vladimir's wife. The Dark *Volkhvy* had managed to surround them and the gray wolf never reinforced them." Tears streamed down her perfect pale cheeks. "I didn't know. I turned to him for comfort only to receive an even greater betrayal." And still she didn't blink or look away from the bellflowers on Bell's dress.

"He didn't kill your daughter," Elena said. Anna's story was too similar to Bell's to be a coincidence. Sovkra had been Bell's home. It was only the ending of the tale that Vasilisa had gotten wrong. She straightened. Bell's hands had fallen away from her shoulders.

"No," Bell said. "It isn't true."

The curse had traumatized Bell for centuries. The queen was the devil in her eyes. No better than Grigori was to Elena. A tormentor. A horror.

Her eyes tracked the movements of the red wolf as they always did. But, at her agonized denial, he stopped and stared. He whined. Elena reached out to Bell as her friend's face petrified into a look of disbelief.

"He didn't kill your Anna," Elena said. "He brought her to Bronwal. Maybe he thought her presence would shield them from your wrath once you knew he'd betrayed you. He didn't stop to think that you might not know she'd survived his attack on the village."

"Dark witches killed my family. The gray wolf saved me," Bell said.

Soren whined. He took one step toward the girl he'd protected for centuries.

"The gray wolf killed them all. He didn't save you. He kidnapped you," Elena said. The puzzle was finally complete. "Vladimir was darker than the darkest witch." She looked at Soren when she said it. "I'm sorry, but it's true. He risked you all for a power grab that failed. He killed his wife, Naomi, and the prince consort by delivering them to the Dark *Volkhvy* king and then refusing to come to their aid during the battle. He seduced Vasilisa. She was vulnerable. She had lost her warrior, her husband and the father of her child. But when she began to suspect Vladimir wasn't what he seemed, he kidnapped the baby she'd hidden. The only reason he didn't kill Anna was that he thought he could use her. When his whole plan failed, he gave himself to the Ether rather than face the consequences of what he'd done."

"My…daughter?" Queen Vasilisa said. "I remember

the fields of bellflowers. It seemed a safe place, a happy place to shelter her."

She reached for Bell, but the shocked girl jerked away. She stumbled back from Elena's supportive grasp and from her mother.

"I could never forgive Vladimir for murdering my daughter. Even when I realized I needed to free his sons from my wrath. Now, the curse is broken. I'm sorry. I'm so sorry," Vasilisa cried.

"I put on this dress because I wanted to claim a place in Bronwal. I've been an orphan and a servant most of my life. Scrambling to survive. But I was wrong about needing to claim a place. I had a place. And a wolf by my side," Bell said.

Soren had backed away from them. His legs were spread wide and, when Bell took several steps toward him, he growled deep and low. Lev limped to join him. His ferocity had always been tempered by Soren's civility. Now, his growl rumbled up from his chest to join with the red wolf's. Both of them looked fully capable of turning on the Light witches they'd been fighting for seconds ago.

"She can't help who her mother is any more than you can help who your father was," Elena said. But the red wolf didn't relent, and Bell lowered her hand.

"I didn't know," Vasilisa said.

"But you did know that abusing the Ether's power was wrong," Elena said. "And you sacrificed Madeline and Trevor because you thought Vladimir had killed your baby."

"No," the queen said. She blinked and pulled her attention from her daughter. "They have been protected from the Ether all this time. They sleep on my island home. I protected her and her baby even though I thought no one protected me and mine."

"Madeline isn't gone," Bell said. She spoke as if she begged the red wolf to hear her, but Soren and Lev had edged farther and farther away from the witches their animal instincts obviously warned them not to trust. They were almost out the door and Bell couldn't follow. Not when both wolves had their teeth bared against her. But she held back from her mother. She stood, all alone, deserted by her wolf and claimed by a Light *Volkhvy* queen. Elena wondered if Bell would ever feel at home at Bronwal again now that she knew the truth. Or if the others would welcome her, as a princess, or at all.

"Romanov should be back by now. Where is he?" Elena suddenly asked. Long minutes had passed since the black wolf had disappeared into the Ether. She couldn't follow him. She didn't know how. Like Lev, she was left to watch and wait for her love to return.

"Grigori was nearly consumed. I saw the Ether in his eyes. The only way he could have defeated Romanov was to devour him in the vacuum. He would have to sacrifice his life to kill the wolf," the queen said.

"He would do it to hurt me," Elena said. "If he can't have me, he would destroy me instead."

The sapphire in her sword still glowed. It was the only sign that she had any hope of seeing Romanov again. She refused to sheath it. The Light *Volkhvy* were tending to their injured and sending the dead into the Ether. Elena looked away from their rituals and their pain. The Dark *Volkhvy* had all vanished without ritual. They had fled, leaving their dead and injured behind. Those that had been left disintegrated. Either they traveled through the

Ether to the place they called home or they were consumed.

Elena didn't care.

She waited for the black wolf to return with her sword drawn and ready.

Romanov couldn't disappear. Not when their connection was finally causing the sapphire to shine, brilliant and strong.

Even though secrets, revelations and reunions took place all around her, her attention was riveted on the spot where the black wolf and Grigori had disappeared. No one tried to move her. They wouldn't have dared. She was finally the warrior who truly wielded the sapphire sword.

And she would watch and wait for her mate to return for an eternity if need be.

She willed him back to her with every beat of her heart and every breath that passed through her slightly parted lips.

When the air wavered in front of her eyes, she raised the sword. But instead of the black wolf she expected, it was Ivan Romanov who appeared. He held a struggling Grigori with his powerful hands clasped around the witch's chest from behind. The witchblood prince had a black viscous liquid running down his cheeks from his obsidian eyes. Elena didn't think it was blood. She thought the energy from the Ether had filled him to the brim and now it overflowed. He screamed and cursed incoherently as he fought the man who held him.

"I brought him back to you," Romanov said. His legs were widely braced and his muscles bulged, but it wasn't physical power that he fought against. Grigori was weaker in muscles and form. It was the Ether. Grigori caused them to flicker in and out of existence as he'd caused

Elena to do during their dance. It was the disintegration Romanov fought. Tendons strained in his neck and his jaw was clenched. He spoke through clenched teeth. "I was wrong. When I saw him torturing you with the Ether, I knew that standing between you and the sword's call was wrong. I will stand with you forever, as the black wolf and as a man, but you must fight this fight. He is your demon to slay."

As Romanov spoke, he and Grigori flickered in and out of existence again and again. Every time, Elena's heart seemed to follow Romanov into the cold. But it was the frigid memory of Ether in her chest that told her what to do. She lifted the sword and braced the back of the hilt against the palm of her free hand. She timed her thrust against the flicker of here and gone again to be sure she penetrated Grigori's heart while it was materialized. The sapphire blazed, and Romanov let go of the witchblood prince. Her legendary shifter remained solid in front of her as the evil *Volkhvy* who had stalked her since she was a young teen disintegrated in a sudden implosion. Every molecule of his body was sucked into the black hole of Ether her sword had unleashed from his corrupted heart.

The bright blue light of the sapphire's glow wrapped around her and Romanov. It held them tight in this world until the black hole that had been Grigori disappeared in on itself with a hissing pop.

And, after, the glow continued as her lover stepped toward her. She lowered the sword so he could take her into his arms. They were solid and real. She pressed into his chest to absorb his heat. She placed her cheek against him so she could hear the steady beat of his heart. He'd always been more than a story. The sword had called her to his side, but it had been the legend that had awakened her to the sword's call.

"I've loved you longer than I realized," Elena said. "I heard the sword's call because I loved you before we'd even met."

Romanov held her as if she anchored him in this world. He didn't yet know that the curse had been lifted. He would have to be told about Lev and about Bell. There was good news and bad to share. For now, she shared her embrace and her heat. She shared the modern world she'd brought to him and her dancer's strength.

"I think I knew when I first saw you climbing in the snow. I hadn't felt so alive in ages. I had to go to you. But I couldn't accept the evidence of my own eyes when the sword first glowed. It's too cruel. The Ether…you don't deserve that fate, Elena, my love," Romanov growled.

"No one does," Elena said. "Except maybe those like Grigori who court its darkness."

She pulled back to look up into Romanov's emerald eyes. They were haunted as they always were, but there was a new light in them too. Maybe it was the sapphire's glow influencing the gold flecks in his irises, but she decided to call it hope.

"Bronwal is free," she said softly. His eyes widened. Only then, did he look away from her to see what had been happening while he was fighting Grigori. His hands tightened on her back when he saw the queen and Bell standing side by side. His brothers were by the door, alive even if they weren't quite well.

"You came to us for help, but it's you who saved us all," Romanov said.

He looked back at her, and Elena wrapped her free arm around his neck. She pulled him down to her mouth and their lips met in a kiss that was long and leisurely. They'd fallen in love as a ticking clock counted down their last moments together, but every moment from now on was theirs to enjoy.

"I was afraid to call the wolf, but I didn't let that stop me," Elena said, when they finally came up for air.

"I was afraid when you picked up the sword, but that didn't stop me from loving you with all my heart, even when the black wolf ruled it," Romanov said. "He is me and I am him. Can you love an enchanted shapeshifter after all *Volkhvy* magic has forced you to endure?"

"My mother's sacrifice taught me that the greatest power is love. She bought me time to find my way to you. And now our love is more powerful than *Volkhvy* enchantments. We'll fight for the Light together with the sword and the wolf," Elena said. "There are still difficulties ahead. Bell is Vasilisa's daughter. Your father kidnapped her for leverage. The queen thought he'd killed her. That's why her rage was so long and deep."

Ivan Romanov stiffened at the news of his dead father's further treachery. He looked at the queen and her daughter. Elena followed his gaze. Their reunion wasn't warm. In fact, Bell looked as if she'd rather be swallowed up by the Ether.

Soren was gone. He and Lev had slipped away once Romanov was safe. The white wolf didn't know that his wife and baby had been found. He might be too far gone to ever know. Soren was his lost brother's only hope and yet the red wolf had his own heartbreak to face.

"Bronwal stands," Romanov said. His attention came back to Elena.

"And whatever comes as we recover from the curse, we will fill this castle with love," Elena replied.

Epilogue

Vasilisa left without a word. Her entire entourage disappeared. What could she say to the black wolf she'd almost killed? It wasn't until Elena went searching for Bell that she realized her friend had disappeared too. Her aviary was abandoned. All her magpie collection was gone.

Except for the trunk of male clothes that Elena had helped her drag up the stairs. It was open at the foot of Bell's bed. On top of the carefully folded and preserved garments was the boy's hat Bell had always worn.

Elena lifted it from the trunk and blinked against the moisture in her eyes. Soren had growled at Bell when he'd heard the truth about her parentage. He had lashed out at the girl who had kept a silent vigil for his return for centuries. The hat must have been Soren's. She was certain of it. And the trunk was probably full of his clothes, as well.

The dress Bell had worn to the Gathering was abandoned on the floor. She wouldn't be able to abandon her feelings for the red wolf as easily. Had she gone to live with her mother to escape the wolf who had always protected her? Elena already missed her determined smile, even though she realized now that it and the hat she'd always worn hid much of her true feelings. Bell… Anna… had persevered through it all. She'd shouldered much of the brunt of her mother's curse and she'd survived, in large part, because of the debt she thought she owed the Romanovs for saving her.

Only to find out it was all a lie…

There was nothing she and Ivan could do to repair the damage his father and the Light *Volkhvy* queen had done. They could only work toward a future where Bronwal thrived once more. Romanov was already consulting with the people who had reappeared when Vasilisa lifted the curse. There were more survivors than they'd known. Patrice was in the thick of things. By her side was a man who called her "my wife." It seemed her long-lost husband had been looking for her for many Cycles. She'd been looking for him too. Much of her distraction was caused by that search, not by being Ether-addled after all. Most of the survivors decided to stay and reclaim a life with others who were also like time travelers in a strange new world.

The Dark *Volkhvy* had lost their king, but they were still a threat that had to be controlled. All of Romanov's plans included empowering his people to continue to champion the Light. The training courtyard would be full once more. The halls would be lit and alive and full of people with purpose. Now that Bronwal wasn't coming and going from the Ether, he planned to update and modernize their home. For that, they would need to reach out to the queen for help. Their location was inaccessible without her abilities.

They had time.

Currently, her head was full of more sensual plans.

She'd brought her grandmother's book with her to the castle's roof. She lit several candles that had been left in the aviary, but she sat on one of the openings in the ramparts to open the book beneath the stars. The illustrations sprang to life in her hands, but they were nothing compared to the reality of Ivan Romanov when he came to her side. She looked from the book up to the man. He was larger than life as he always was—tall, broad and handsome. This time there was an added thrill though, because he was also hers.

Finally, she and Romanov were alone.

Her swan gown was rumpled and dirty, but she didn't care because the look in Romanov's eyes was one of desire and appreciation. She stood to meet him. As usual, her head came only to his chest. She had to lift her chin to watch his face. His eyes were highlighted in the soft glow of stars, candles and the sapphire's gleam. He reached for her belt and she placed the book on the wall in order to raise her arms out of the way. He unbuckled it slowly, never once breaking contact with her gaze.

The stars above his wild hair reminded her of the mica in the cavern, but the cold breeze and the distant expanse of snow-capped mountains reminded her that they were free. She didn't have to seek refuge in the black wolf's lair.

"Every time we've been together, I've resisted our connection," he said. The belt came free, and Romanov placed the sword in its scarlet scabbard carefully on the wall beside the book. "I'm not resisting anymore. And every second away from you tonight has been torture."

"We're free. I don't have to be afraid to sleep or to dream. I don't have to be afraid to show you how I feel," Elena said. "And you don't have to be afraid of our connection."

"You were always the braver of us. I was afraid to allow myself to love you. I didn't want to ensnare you in the curse," Romanov said.

"Your strength and control were a siren's call. I'd been relentlessly pursued. I'd never been given a key and told that I could say no," Elena said. "Of course, with you, I wanted to say yes. Again and again."

"You killed me when you refused to use the key. I thought I would die from wanting what I couldn't have," Romanov said. "But every kiss, every sweet sigh only brought me back to life."

As they'd spoken, he had found the fastenings beneath the feathers on her shoulders and he'd unhooked them. The top of her dress slid down her chest revealing her naked breasts to his intense perusal. Her nipples peaked in the chilly air, but the rush beneath her skin that caused gooseflesh to rise was all warm anticipation, not cold.

There was a fireplace in the aviary, but Elena didn't want to lose the stars or the wide-open sky above their heads. She wanted to see the mountains she'd braved to find her alpha wolf and the legend that called her home to his arms.

"You're shivering," Romanov said. He reached for her waist and pulled her against his chest. Her breasts were crushed against his loosened shirt. Sometime after the fight, he'd shed the jacket of his tuxedo and his white silk shirt had come untucked. His tie was long gone, and his buttons were unfastened all the way to his rippled abdomen. This was her lover, a man from a less-civilized age who had survived through the centuries to come to her.

"I hadn't even noticed," Elena said. Her attention was fully caught by the man who held her. She buried her face in his neck when he leaned down to scoop her up into his embrace. As always, he was careful with her injured knee when he arranged her in his arms. She held around his neck and breathed deeply of his wintry, evergreen hair. She wanted to go back into the woods with him soon. She wanted to see him, there, among the trees when nothing was trying to kill them. She knew from the worn trails and the scent on his hair and skin that he walked there often.

"I wanted to kiss you the first night you carried me to the tower," Elena confessed. "When you gave me the key. When you explained that you weren't locking me in. I began to desire you at that moment."

"I needed you to lock me out. I knew I wouldn't be able to stay away," Romanov said. He nuzzled the top of her head as he carried her into the aviary.

"I'm glad I didn't hide in the tower," Elena said.

He placed her on the bed and turned to start a fire. She watched him lay the logs and strike a match. There was no rush, but she thought she saw a tremble of anticipation in his hand. The flame on the match danced more than it should have before he tossed it on the logs.

"So am I," he said as he turned around.

He unfastened the rest of his buttons while she stared transfixed by the hardened body he revealed. He was so unlike the other men she'd known, but some part of her had always known she would need to leave the ballet and Saint Petersburg. The legend had called her long before she'd felt the sapphire's call. The fire caught behind him and its golden glow illuminated his muscular form. Elena rose to reach for his waistband. She helped him loosen his pants and, as they fell, her body tightened in response to what they'd revealed.

He was hard all over. From his head to his feet. But some parts of him were even harder.

Romanov reached for her skirts, but the bodice of her dress had fallen over the fastening at her waist. She gasped when he tore the chiffon rather than patiently burrow for the means to release it.

"I've been waiting too long to do that," he said.

Elena stood nearly naked in the firelight. Her silk underwear was translucent and so were the gossamer stockings on her legs. She kicked off her shoes, but that was all he allowed her to do before he pushed her back onto the bed. Her legs embraced him. She cradled his stiff erection at the moist juncture of her thighs. She wound her arms around his muscled back.

"Don't wait. Not any longer," Elena whispered urgently.

She moaned when he tore the fabric of her underwear to slide it out of the way. She raised her hips to meet his thrust when he joined his body to hers. She was slick with need and she only got slicker as his shaft filled her. She cried out when he began to rock. Their bodies moved together in perfect rhythm.

"I don't know how I didn't carry you to the lair and keep you there from the moment you arrived," Romanov growled against her ear. She gloried in his hunger. She undulated beneath the urgent movements of his hips. Her body tightened around him. The cold mountain breeze whistled around the shutters, but it didn't cool the perspiration that had risen on her skin.

"You were too used to being strong and alone. You

didn't know we could be stronger together," Elena said. She punctuated her words with a push, and Romanov allowed her to roll him over so that she could straddle his hips. Her knee protested, but not too much, because other parts of her body were too pleasured to be interrupted.

"You're so small and yet so fierce," Romanov groaned. His head arched back on the pillows as she braced her hands against his broad shoulders. The position gave him total access to her depths. She cried out as she was stretched wide and the head of his penis found the entrance to her womb.

"The better to take my black wolf to the stars," Elena said.

They didn't need the mica cavern or the sky. They didn't need the sapphire's glow. On the wall outside, it beamed its light alone. They only needed each other. When Romanov came, he cried out her name and it sounded very like a howl she'd once heard in a distant wood. His release caused hers, and she joined him in shouting her pleasure to the mountains.

Their pleasure rang out to echo down Bronwal's lonely halls. Their love dispelled the castle's curse as a lone red wolf tucked his tail and ran far away.

* * * * *

Jane Kindred is the author of the Demons of Elysium series of M/M erotic fantasy romance, the Looking Glass Gods dark fantasy tetralogy and the gothic paranormal romance *The Lost Coast*. Jane spent her formative years ruining her eyes reading romance novels in the Tucson sun and watching *Star Trek* marathons in the dark. She now writes to the sound of San Francisco foghorns while two cats slowly but surely edge her off the side of the bed.

Books by Jane Kindred

Harlequin Nocturne

Sisters in Sin

Waking the Serpent
Bewitching the Dragon
The Dragon's Hunt
Seducing the Dark Prince

SEDUCING THE DARK PRINCE

Jane Kindred

Chapter 1

Like the ethereal substance his last name evoked, Lucien Smok was breathtaking—literally. The moment Theia saw him across the temple reception hall, the air rushed from her lungs as though it had been sucked into a vacuum. Pale blue eyes like pieces of ice locked on hers from beneath long lashes, dark brows in an ivory face lifted in amusement above them as if he was well aware of the effect he was having on her.

She'd seen him before somewhere. In a dream or a dark premonition. Beneath the reception hall's Baroque quadratura-painted ceiling—invoking the blessing of the gods of Olympus—he reminded her of a painting by Waterhouse, Narcissus winking just for a moment at the viewer before returning to his reflection.

But beautiful or not, this wasn't some breathless lust at first sight. She really couldn't breathe.

Theia clutched at her throat and tried to make a sound, but nothing came out. Her lungs were locked in a spasm, convulsively trying to take in air against some obstruction.

Her dark-haired Narcissus crossed the reception hall in two swift strides and embraced her from behind, arms wrapped around her waist and hands clasped tight beneath her breasts, a gesture of intimacy. Vertigo swam over her, making her feel as though she were floating within herself, a lighter-than-air balloon encased in a human frame, bobbing against its edges.

He hugged her forcefully, jolting her against him, almost off the ground—once, twice, thrice.

Another spasm of her diaphragm forced what remained of the air in her lungs through her windpipe and dislodged the champagne grape she'd swallowed wrong. Such a small thing to cause so much trouble.

Air rushed in so quickly that she choked on it, gasping and coughing until tears ran down her cheeks.

"All right now?" The soft voice at her ear brought her fully back to herself. His hold around her hadn't loosened and was decidedly more intimate than it had been when he'd been performing the Heimlich on her.

Theia realized she'd relaxed into his embrace, her arms sliding around his, and she let go with a jolt and bolted from his grasp. Though the moment had seemed epic and prolonged, none of the other guests were paying any attention.

His smile was one-sided—a slight leftward lift that combined amusement, smugness and a hint of offense. "You're welcome."

"Sorry. I didn't mean to… I mean, thanks. I appreciate the—"

"Don't strain yourself, darling. It's okay. I'm used to this reaction."

Theia's embarrassment dissipated, and she narrowed her eyes, wrapping her arms around herself. "What reaction?"

"Women going weak in the knees and tongue-tied around me. I expect it's being this close to money." His voice had the lazy, sardonic drawl of James Spader's bad boy Steff in *Pretty in Pink*. "Does that to some women, I understand."

"Wow. I take it back. You're a complete ass."

"Not the first time I've heard that, either." He held out his hand. "Lucien Smok, heir to the Smok Biotech fortune and your hero today."

Theia kept her hands tucked under her arms. "Gosh, how fortunate for me. And I've heard of you."

"Of course you have. Hence the reaction." His hand dropped casually to his side. "Are you going to reciprocate?"

Theia blinked at him. "What?"

"Your name. Not going to give it to me? Then let me guess." Before she could react, Lucien had drawn her left arm from where she'd tucked it, his fingers stroking the crescent moon and descending cross tattooed on her inner forearm. The slow, sensual touch sent a shiver down her spine. "The mark of Lilith. You must be a Carlisle. I'm going to guess Theia." He let her go, and Theia wobbled a bit from having planted her feet so firmly to steel herself against him.

Heat bloomed in her cheeks. "How do you know that?"

"I cheated. I asked the groom."

"No, I mean Lilith. How do you know about Lilith?"

A fleeting look she couldn't interpret crossed his features. "I've studied astrology. I'm familiar with the symbol."

She was sure he'd meant something more than just the astrological symbol—a representation of the Black Moon Lilith, the elliptical focal point opposite the earth at lunar apogee. He'd associated it with the Carlisles. But Lucien didn't elaborate.

"Well, you're wrong," said Theia. "I'm not a Carlisle."

His brow furrowed, as though he didn't care much for being wrong. "Oh?"

"My name is Dawn. Theia Dawn. My sisters are Carlisles." She'd taken her middle name as her last after learning about the second family her father had kept hidden until his death. She didn't want the name that belonged to a cheater and a liar. But Theia didn't bother to explain any of this to Lucien Smok. Let him wonder. She turned on her heel and left him staring after her.

Gliding up beside her, her twin put her arm in Theia's. "Who was that?" Luckily, she'd taken Theia's right arm. Theia wasn't about to let Rhea anywhere near that Lilith tattoo, especially now that Lucien had touched it. Where Theia occasionally had prophetic dreams and visions, Rhea could cut right through the annoying interpretation of symbolism with her "pictomancy" readings to see the future in tattoo ink. And Theia absolutely did *not* want to know any specifics about her future.

"Lucien Smok. His family owns the biotech firm that recently partnered with Northern Arizona University. I think he's a friend of Rafe's."

Rhea wrinkled her nose. "I wouldn't say friend. Phoebe was telling me about the Smoks. Rafe's family knows them, but she doesn't remember sending them an invitation. Some uncle of Rafe's must have brought Lucien along."

Before Theia could speculate on what Lucien was doing there, a commotion broke out at the front of Covent Temple's reception hall. A tall, Nordic hunk of beefcake was literally thumping his chest at the best man, who stood coolly observing the former and looking perfectly at home in his Armani tux, graying temples adding to his sophistication against the rich hue of his skin.

"Looks like your man is fighting with Dev." Theia nudged her sister. "Go get him, sweetie. We don't want Kur getting out and eating the guests." Dev Gideon, their sister Ione's boyfriend, had an unfortunate tendency to transform into an ancient Sumerian dragon demon when provoked.

Rhea sighed. "Leo must have been celebrating a little too enthusiastically." Like the thousand-year-old Viking he was, Leo Ström was fond of a good, hearty drink.

Theia watched Rhea weave through the guests to get to Leo, the shin-length red chiffon of her bridesmaid's dress swinging and swishing gracefully. It was odd to see Rhea in anything but pants. Not that Theia was much for dresses, either.

She glanced down at her own, smoothing the fabric beneath the crisscross bodice. Only Phoebe could have gotten her and Rhea cleaned up this good. Well, Ione had, really. But Phoebe had chosen the fabric as part of her red rose-themed Beltane wedding—red, blush and white ribbon draped the room, woven around the support at the center of the hall like a Maypole and fanning out to form a latticed canopy.

Theia had to admit the dress looked fantastic with both her natural dark bob and Rhea's short, bleached-blond cut sculpted into points—the dead giveaway for those who had trouble telling them apart. Rhea had curled her points at the tips for the occasion, adding a dab of cherry-red dye. She'd added some of it to the points of Theia's bob, too. It was more difficult to see against the dark color, but Theia preferred subtlety.

With Ione officiating as high priestess in her longer, dusty-rose version of the dress, the twins' red had made Phoebe stand out. She'd been absolutely gorgeous in a fairy-tale bone-white off-the-shoulder sweetheart gown with beaded lace and a vintage mantilla from Rafe's own grandmother.

Theia glanced around, realizing she hadn't seen Phoebe in a while. Or Rafe. God, you'd think they could wait a few hours for the honeymoon.

Her glance fell once more on Lucien Smok, flirting with one of the younger members of Ione's coven. An unfamiliar irritation prickled along Theia's skin as his hand rested on Margot's shoulder while he leaned close, Margot laughing at something he'd said. Theia shook off the sensation. *No. Absolutely not.* This couldn't be jealousy, because she had absolutely zero interest in Lucien Smok. Or the heart-stopping contrast of his pale eyes with his nearly jet-black, effortlessly messy hair.

He caught her watching him and winked.

Theia looked away deliberately, her eyes on Rhea leading Leo away from the open bar. It was always amusing to see Rhea, her form slight beside him, managing the Chieftain of the Wild Hunt. Having spent the last thousand years under the control of a Valkyrie, he seemed perfectly content to let a woman take charge despite his outward bluster.

On the opposite end of the room, where the reception

hall connected to the temple nave by a breezeway, the Sedona winds had apparently kicked up, and the doors blew open with a bang. Ione moved to shut them, her long, ironed-straight hair whipping about her head in a halo of setting-sun ombré, but paused and stood deathly still, staring at something on the other side of the doorway. Theia moved around the support column that blocked her view.

With the wind had come an uninvited guest—the necromancer who'd made more than one attempt on the lives of both bride and groom in recent months. Theia's jaw dropped open, and she sensed Rhea's shock echoing hers from across the room. Carter Hamilton was supposed to be rotting in prison.

His overly whitened smile flashed in his overly bronzed face as he stood bracing his hands between the double doors like Maleficent making an appearance at Sleeping Beauty's first birthday. "Am I too late to toast the happy couple?"

"How the hell are you here?" Ione's voice seemed icy calm as she faced her psychotic ex, but Theia knew she was barely keeping it together.

Carter's gaze acknowledged Dev as he appeared at Ione's side. "And there he is, like a good little cur, looking for a pat on the head."

A low rumble came out of Dev's throat—too low to be human.

Ione took Dev's hand. "Don't trouble, love. He isn't worth it."

Their newly minted brother-in-law emerged from the stairwell to the bell tower that was doubling as a dressing room, moving toward Carter in a way that ought to unnerve the other man. Even without the Quetzalcoatl tattoo visible at his shoulders beneath the white linen wedding shirt, Rafe Diamante was imposing. And the knowledge that Rafe possessed the necromantic power Carter had killed to try to get should have had the slighter man quaking in his boots. But Carter's smile persisted.

"You have no right to set foot on Covent property," Rafe warned.

Carter's gaze flicked over him. "Nor have you, my friend. I understand you've been formally expelled from the Covent for oath breaking."

"I'm not your friend. No one here is your friend."

Phoebe, descending the staircase behind Rafe, paused on the bottom step with one slipper-clad foot wavering over the floor, her face a white mask of shock. She'd been the one to put Carter in prison while she was still practicing law.

Ione's hand tightened around Dev's. "What do you want, Carter?"

"Just to see your faces when I tell you my good news. The conviction for the crimes you framed me for has been overturned. I'm a free man."

Cake and champagne churned in Theia's stomach.

Phoebe voiced her shock. "How is that possible?"

Carter's eyes settled on her, bitter amusement dancing in them. "So you don't deny you framed me."

"No one framed you," Rafe growled. "You murdered four people."

"Well, the state doesn't seem to agree. Nor does the Covent."

Preceded by a flourish of his hand in the air, a champagne flute materialized in Carter's fingers. "To the bride." Carter raised the glass toward Phoebe. "Who looks almost as lovely in white as she does in nothing at all. And I have the pictures to prove it."

A collective gasp rustled through the hall.

As Carter drank, Rafe charged him, the snake tattoo twisting and roiling beneath his shirt, but Carter's physical matter seemed to dissolve into smoke at Rafe's contact with him, leaving Rafe's fingers to close around a nonexistent collar. The bright grin was the last thing to go, like an evil Cheshire Cat.

Chapter 2

Ione was livid. "That was an astral projection. He's out of prison and accessing powerful magic. What the devil is going on?" She was staring at Dev, as if he ought to know.

"I don't know a thing about it, love, I promise. I haven't been privy to Covent business since I resigned my commission as assayer."

Rafe closed the adjoining doors forcefully and turned back to face the hall. "I, for one, am not going to waste a moment of my wedding day thinking about that insignificant, third-rate sorcerer. He wasn't really here, and that's precisely the way he should be treated." He stepped toward Phoebe and took her hand. "Care to dance, Mrs. Carlisle-Diamante?"

Phoebe smiled gamely. "I'd love to, Mr. Diamante-Carlisle."

The mariachi band Rafe had hired—its members all

magical connections of the Diamante family—began to play, and Rafe led his wife out onto the floor.

Theia took a step toward Ione, intending to try to re-assure her, but a hand on her shoulder made her turn.

"May I have this dance, Ms. Dawn?" Lucien's smile was mischievous. How did he manage to make an offer to dance sound dirty?

Before she could decline, he'd tucked her hand into his and slipped his arm around her waist, turning her toward the dance floor.

He pulled her closer as she started to draw back. "You wouldn't embarrass me in front of all these people by turning me down, would you?"

"I might."

"I've never been turned down before. It might damage my confidence. Could set me back years emotionally."

"Then I definitely should."

Lucien grinned. "But you won't."

"Won't I?"

"I fascinate you."

"Oh, for heaven's sake." Theia shoved away from him and stalked to the bar.

Like a persistent mosquito, he was buzzing at her side as she ordered her drink. "What if I blackmailed you? Would you dance with me then?"

Theia whirled on him. "Excuse me?"

"That was an odd little display from the groom. And I swear I saw the best man's eyes glow with their own fire. Not to mention the fact that someone just demate-rialized right in front of us, and everyone is acting like nothing happened."

"Who the hell are you, anyway?" Theia narrowed her eyes. "Do you even know the Diamantes?"

"Of course I do. I'm exactly who I say I am. You can ask Rafael. Our families go back a long way. And there have been rumors about the Diamantes for just as long. Looks like today I've seen evidence that those rumors are true."

"Then maybe you should take up your concerns with *Rafe* himself, if you know him so well. I'm sure he'd find them very interesting."

"Ooh." Lucien gave a sexy little shiver that Theia tried not to physically respond to and failed. "It sounds like you're suggesting something untoward might befall me. Are you threatening me? I suppose you're one of them, too."

Theia's fists clenched at her sides. "One of what?"

Lucien leaned in intimately close. "Witches, of course."

Theia laughed. "That's what you're planning to blackmail me with? We're standing in the reception hall of the temple of the Sedona branch of the world's largest organized coven. It's not exactly a secret that there are witches here."

"But it is something of a secret that Rafe Diamante is a necromancer, isn't it? And that Dev Gideon is the host for a demon?"

It hardly seemed useful to argue the finer points of Rafe's incidental command of the dead or Dev's shared physicality with an enslaved dragon from the underworld. The fact was that Lucien's statement was irrefutable.

Theia hoped the look she was giving him was as murderous as she intended. "What do you want?"

Lucien's eyes widened and he let out a laugh of pure surprise. "Did you think I was seriously going to blackmail you? Sorry. I have a tendency to take a joke too far. I was just having a little fun with you."

"Oh, well, I'm *so* glad it was fun for you. Now you can fuck off."

"There *is* a little something I was hoping you could help me with, though."

Theia sighed, steeling herself for more innuendo.

"I understand you're working on your master's in molecular biology at NAU." That wasn't creepy-stalkery at all.

"So?"

"I'm sure you've heard that Smok Biotech is undertaking a joint venture with the university microbiology lab."

Theia acknowledged this with an uninterested lift of her eyebrows, even though the new lab actually interested her a great deal. Smok was just the sort of corporation she didn't want the university to be associated with, a for-profit pharmaceutical giant. At the same time, it offered unprecedented funding opportunities for expanded research.

"I need someone I can trust to provide some oversight on a special project—someone who won't be fazed by...odd goings-on." Lucien flashed his crooked smile again, trying to charm her, but seemed to realize the smile wasn't working on her and let it fade. "To put it bluntly, someone familiar with the supernatural who also understands the science."

Theia crossed her arms and studied him. "And are you? Familiar with it?"

Something dark seemed to cloud his vision for a moment, but he shook it off and smiled. "Not quite as familiar with it as you are, I'm sure. You might say my family is magical adjacent. Our business intersects with the magical community. It's sort of a quid pro quo."

"Unless you're implying that I owe you for saving me from choking on a grape, there's no quo I could possibly want from you or your organization. I'm sorry, Mr. Smok, but I'm not interested."

Lucien met her gaze with a reproachful look. "Mr. Smok? Really?"

"Pretty much." Theia caught Rhea's eye across the room and moved away from the bar, but Lucien stepped in front of her once more.

"Talk to Rafe. Before you write me off completely, ask him about the mutually beneficial relationship the Smok family has had with the Diamantes for ages." He took a card from his shirt pocket, crimson with black lettering, and handed it to her.

Theia thought about refusing it, but that would just prolong the "dance." She snatched it out of his hand and walked swiftly away before he could say anything else, meeting Rhea halfway as she came to her twin's rescue.

"I saw your signal." Rhea glanced at Lucien still standing by the bar. He raised a glass of champagne toward them. "I wasn't sure you really wanted rescuing, though. He looks tasty."

"He's a creep, and I'm not interested. I'm more concerned about Carter's little magic show."

Rhea glowered. "Yeah, what was that? How the hell did Malibu Ken get out of prison?"

"I'm guessing one of his dirty friends in high places fixed it for him."

Lucien's words about quid pro quo and his family's relationship with the magical community came back to her. Both Rafe and Dev had spoken of connections that helped keep Covent business—and other supernatural events—

from the public eye. Could that be the connection with the Smok family? Maybe she should talk to Rafe after all. Not because she had any intention of getting involved in Lucien's project, but because she and her sisters had a right to know who else knew about their business.

It wasn't until she was helping clean up after the reception ended that Theia found her opening. Phoebe and Rafe were about to leave for the Yucatán, and she wouldn't have another opportunity.

Theia stacked the folding chairs as Rafe collected them, his thick, dark waves tied back in a high, bobbed tail. "What do you know about Lucien Smok?"

Rafe paused in picking up a chair. "Was he bothering you? I saw him talking to you, but I figured you could handle him. I'd keep him at arm's length if I were you."

It wasn't quite the answer she'd expected. "So your family doesn't have some kind of simpatico relationship with the Smoks?"

Rafe's look was guarded. "I wouldn't call it simpatico, exactly, but there *is* a relationship. It goes back centuries. To the time of the founding of the Covent, in fact." The Diamantes had been founding members.

"You mean they're a Covent family?"

"No, not exactly." He handed her the folded chair. "There were no witches among the Smok family—that I know of. But I read a lot of Covent history in my father's records after his death. Information that isn't generally known."

It was unlike Rafe to be so cagey.

"What kind of information?"

Rhea's laugh rang out from the stairs as she came down with Phoebe after helping her change. Rafe set another chair on the stack and smiled at the sight of Phoebe in her usual bouncy ponytail, bangs across her forehead instead of swept back as they had been under the mantilla. "My father kept several volumes on Covent history and politics," he murmured, still smiling at Phoebe. "Ione has the keys to his house. Tell her I left some books for you in the library."

After seeing Phoebe and Rafe off with much ribbing and a fair amount of sisterly tears, Theia and Rhea flopped together onto the bench by the door, and Rhea kicked off her heels with a groan.

Theia removed hers more sedately. "Where's Leo?"

"I told him to go ride with the Hunt for a while and work off some of his buzz. It's weird. Alcohol doesn't usually affect him this much. He's got a pretty high tolerance."

"I thought the Wild Hunt only appeared between Halloween and Yule."

"It does, normally. But now that he's mortal, he's not bound by the Norns' rules and he can conjure the riders when he likes. There's always some sicko out there that needs a one-way ticket to Náströnd."

Theia poked at her décolletage. "It seems a little like playing God. How does he determine that someone is deserving of having their soul ripped out and escorted to hell?"

Rhea shrugged. "It's a scent or something. I don't ask too many questions. He gets all Gunnar the tenth-century Viking on me sometimes, like his soul is taking the reins even though he's no longer under the curse, and Gunnar can be a little...pompous."

"But you've ridden with him."

"Yeah."

"And you don't feel weird about it? About taking somebody out of the earthly plane?"

"And having one less pedophile or rapist walking the earth? Not so much."

Theia had to admit she didn't exactly hate the idea. As long as their guilt was certain.

When Ione and Dev came back from closing up the temple, Theia could see the tension on Ione's face. Carter had really gotten to her. She couldn't blame her. Carter Hamilton was like a nasty rash that just kept coming back. It hurt to see his manipulative bullshit affecting Ione like this.

As Ione picked up one of the plastic bins of supplies, Theia hopped up from the bench and grabbed another. "Do you need any help getting things back to the house?"

"No, I think we're good. Dev's already loaded up the car with the rest."

Theia followed her out with her bin. "By the way, Rafe mentioned something about getting the key to his dad's place from you. He wanted me to take a quick look in on it while I'm watching Phoebe's."

"His dad's place?" Ione set the bin on top of the others and loaded Theia's next to it. "I thought he was selling that."

"I assume he still is, but I guess nobody's been by regularly except the gardener, and he wanted me to take a look around."

Ione could always tell when one of them was bullshitting her, and the fact that she didn't push back on the request spoke volumes about her mental state.

She took a set of keys from her purse and handed them to Theia. "Just make sure you get them back to me."

As Ione got into the car, Dev took Theia aside. "She didn't want me to tell you this, but our unwanted guest pretty much ruined her plans for the reception." Dev glanced at Rhea leaning into the car to block Ione's view. "It was supposed to be ours as well."

Theia stared at him, confused. "Your what?"

"Reception. Don't react. She might snap if she realizes I'm telling you. But we drove up to Vegas a few weeks ago and tied the knot." He allowed himself a little grin while Theia suppressed the urge to squeal and jump up and down.

"You complete bastard. I can't believe you're telling me this now when I can't do anything."

"I suggested to Tweedledum that you and she could plan a little celebration for Ione later when she's cooled down."

"You're lucky you didn't say Tweedledee. Because Rhe is definitely Dum." Theia grinned but kept it subtle. "And you can count on us."

Rhea joined Theia as Dev and Ione drove away, waving like Stepford wives only to start jumping and squealing in unison the second the car was out of visual range.

"Can you believe the ovaries on that one?" Rhea laughed as they spun around. "Eloping and stealing Phoebe's thunder? Phoebe's going to be furious."

"I don't know how she kept it to herself all this time." Although Ione was certainly better equipped to keep a secret than the rest of them. Theia glanced at Rhea as the dance died down. "You'd better not tell me you and Leo are up to something similar."

"Me?" Rhea laughed. "Right. Like I'd get married." She winked, which wasn't reassuring. Everyone in the family was pairing off, and Theia was the odd one out.

Rhea, as usual, could see what she was thinking. "Why don't you just let me read you again?"

"*No.* There's no reason to rehash what I already know."

"Which is what? That your love life is cursed? I think you're being way too literal about it. Just let me ask a more specific question."

The night was getting chilly now that the sun was down. Theia pulled the shawl she'd borrowed from Ione around her shoulders, tucking her tattooed arm underneath it. "I'm good, thanks. So, takeout?"

Rhea sighed through her nose, her mouth in a thin line of annoyance, but shrugged her acquiescence. "Indian?"

Theia gave it a thumbs-up. "You order. I'll drive." She held out her hand for the keys.

"You're not driving Minnie Driver."

"Your car is not a person, and yes, I am. I saw how much champagne you had."

Rhea tossed her the keys and got in on the passenger side, patting the dash. "Don't listen to her, Minnie. You are too a person." She pulled up the delivery app on her phone and started making selections. "Whose house are we going to? Phoebe's or Rafe's?"

"Neither, actually." Theia ground the gears, and Rhea swore, gripping the seat. Theia ignored her, putting the car in gear properly. "Do you still have the address for Rafael Sr.'s place in your phone?"

Rhea glanced over at her. "The Ice Palace? Yeah, why?"

"There's something I need to pick up. We can pretend we're filthy rich, like Phoebe." She grinned without looking over.

"Ha. Phoebe, married to the richest man in town, and still keeping her little bungalow."

"I think she's still freaked out about those reporters outside Rafe's window filming him going spelunking in her *cave* that time."

"He *is* quite the cave diver. Oh, dammit."

"What?"

"We totally missed the opportunity for cave-diving puns. They're visiting cenotes on their honeymoon."

"Ah, damn. We're off our game."

Driving the labyrinthine route from Covent Temple back to the highway was much easier than driving in. A proximity glamour kept passersby from noticing the otherwise startling white byzantine spires against the sienna red hoodoos and hills of Sedona, and the disorientation spell on the road was an extra measure to confound those who might be purposefully looking for it.

Rhea's red and white Mini was a blast to drive up Highway 179 through the walls of rocks and around the curves threading through the pines on the way to the secluded community hidden in the hills. Theia drove an automatic hybrid, which didn't quite have the same kick.

"So what did you want to pick up, anyway?"

"Some papers Rafe's dad kept. He said there's some stuff about the original Covent and Madeleine Marchant I might want for my genealogy research." There was no point in giving Rhea ammo to tease her by letting know she was researching Lucien Smok.

"Don't we know all we need to about her?"

"Nothing is ever all you need to know about anything."

Rhea rolled her eyes. "Right. I forgot I was talking to Brainiac's daughter."

"So you're not at all curious about the origins of our Lilith blood."

"I just think you can overanalyze things. A little mystery in life is nice."

Mystery was exactly what Theia didn't want. She liked to know the whys and wherefores of things. Knowledge was power. And mystery… As far as Theia was concerned, mystery was danger.

Chapter 3

Lucien watched the revenant from the rooftop. Starlight lent a pale, unearthly glow to the proceedings as it swallowed up the dusk, leaving the red landscape sepia toned and casting flat, colorless shadows. The demon wore cowboy boots and a leather duster with a gambler-style cowboy hat, his horse tacked up in the Western style, but this was a Hunt wraith, an undead revenant of the Viking era who roamed the earth in search of dark souls. Less substantial wraiths rode beside him, their mounts, like themselves, phantoms. No one would notice them, even staring at them head-on. No one but a black-souled phantom like himself.

But the leader was different. He was no phantom but flesh and bone, unnaturally maintained, living tissue that ought to have perished centuries ago. And Lucien had seen him before. Just hours before—at the wedding of Rafael Diamante to Phoebe Carlisle.

Lucien followed the horse's trajectory, tracking the revenant with the scope on his crossbow. He'd slipped a little something into the Viking's drink to see if he could trigger him. The most it had done was to get him arguing with Dev Gideon, the eldest Carlisle sister's faithful companion. Rumor had it Dev was a shape-shifter, part man, part demon himself. The entire Carlisle family seemed to be magnets for unnatural beings. Not surprising, given their bloodline.

He wasn't sure what he'd expected when he'd decided to check out the Carlisle sisters for himself, but Theia's large, passionate eyes challenging him with far more moxie than her slight frame warranted was certainly not it. He hadn't expected someone witty and intelligent who took no shit. She hadn't fallen for his player persona. And she hadn't been impressed by his name—if anything, there'd been a little sneer on her face when she'd heard it—or acted impressed by his family's money. But maybe it was a different kind of power that impressed the Carlisle women. The kind that was infernal in origin. If only she knew.

Lucien turned in a slow arc to follow the horseman with his scope. Leo Ström's origins were what concerned him right now. How had he come to be the leader of the Wild Hunt? And what was the Hunt doing appearing on a lovely spring evening in Sedona, Arizona? Traditionally, it was said to appear around the winter solstice and was better suited to snowier climes.

They'd scented someone now, it seemed, and even from this distance, Lucien thought he heard their victory hoots as the phantom storm that followed them swallowed up their victim and they disappeared into the night, leaving it calm and warm.

He'd have to find out more about this Leo Ström. The man was involved with Theia's twin, Rhea, which could mean anything in terms of unnatural origin. It might even be Rhea's own magic animating him. It was unlikely she'd created the revenant herself, since the long dead were nearly impossible to give a convincing living appearance to, no matter how much magic the practitioner had. So perhaps she'd taken possession of a revenant created by some other unnatural power. And Lucien just happened to have access to information on any of a number of unnatural powers.

He stashed his gear and changed into something more appropriate. People might talk if he showed up at Polly's dressed like a cat burglar.

Polly was entertaining in her booth when Lucien walked in. Aware of her out of the corner of his eye, he made a point of not glancing in her direction, knowing it would drive her crazy. His ploy worked, and in less than five minutes, she'd ditched her patrons and sauntered over to the bar where he stood waiting for his drink.

"Well, look what the cat dragged in." She lifted her drawn-on nearly crimson brows with a little smirk as she leaned back against the bar beside him and raised her voice for the bartender's benefit. "Whatever he's having, it's on the house."

Lucien put down a twenty as the craft beer arrived. "That's sweet, but I've got it covered."

Polly pushed the bill across the slick wood toward the bartender. "That's a tip."

Lucien sipped his beer. "You're such a control freak."

"I like to treat my friends well."

"Oh, we're friends now?" Lucien turned to mimic her stance, elbows back against the bar.

Polly flipped her cherry-red hair over her shoulder, nails painted a dazzling sapphire blue. "Well, maybe frenemies."

"Seems fair."

"So what brings you back to my neck of the woods?"

"Edgar does." He always used his father's first name, never calling him Dad or Pop. "Smok Biotech is partnering with Northern Arizona University on a new venture. He sent me to supervise."

"That doesn't explain what you're doing in Sedona. NAU is in Flagstaff."

"I know where it is." Lucien took a swig of his beer. "Went to a wedding."

Polly's eyes sparkled with interest. "The Diamante wedding? Lucky you. Those invitations were highly coveted."

Lucien shrugged. "I didn't say I was invited."

Polly laughed. "Of course you weren't. So you crashed the quetzal's wedding and now you're slumming at my joint. Who are you after?"

"Who says I'm after anyone?"

Crimson waves swayed as she shook her head. "Darling, don't grift a grifter."

He finished his beer and set the bottle on the bar. "What do you know about the Wild Hunt?"

Polly pushed away from the bar and grabbed his hand, drawing him with her through the jostling patrons trying to get the bartender's attention. The joint was hopping tonight.

She led him to her booth, where the patrons she'd

ditched were still waiting. "Meeting's over, boys. I'll get back to you when I hear anything."

The two pale twentysomething men with slicked-back blond hair shrugged and scooted out of the booth.

One of them frowned and hung back as she slid onto the seat. "Don't make us wait too long. The consequences may be dire."

"Stop being so dramatic, Kip."

Lucien sat on the bench. "*Kip?*"

Polly grinned. "Preppy vampires turned in the '80s. Eternally embarrassing." She gestured to one of her staff, presumably ordering a bottle of something. "So why do you want to know about the Hunt?

"Because I saw it tonight. And unless I've been doing way too much molly, it's May, not December."

"You saw it?"

"Why does that surprise you?"

The woman she'd signaled arrived with a bottle of wine and poured them each a glass, despite Lucien shaking his head.

"Generally, only someone who's a target of the Hunt is treated to that sight." Polly sipped her wine with a curious lift of her brow. "Have you been very naughty, Lucien?"

"No naughtier than usual. Why is the Hunt still in town at this time of year?"

"What makes you think I'd know?"

Lucien played with the rim of his glass. "Pols. You make it your business to know everything of interest— everything paranormal—that happens in the entire Southwest. Information *is* your business. Are you really going to make me pay for it? After what we've meant to each other?"

Polly laughed, her eyes twinkling in the wavering light of the candle on the table. "Don't push it, Hellboy."

"Ouch. Below the belt."

Beneath the table, the pointed toe of her shoe stroked the side of his leg. "Best location."

He moved his leg, and she uncrossed hers and crossed them the other way.

"But in the interest of our continued frenmity, I'll tell you what I've heard." She paused to top off her glass. "Last winter, the Hunt blew into town to deal with some riffraff, and the leader of the Hunt struck some kind of a deal that let him remain in the mortal realm indefinitely. Word is, it's because of—"

"Rhea Carlisle."

Polly tipped her glass toward him. "The quetzal's sister-in-law, yes. And today you crashed the quetzal's wedding. I take it Leo Ström is the reason."

"One of a couple of reasons." Lucien swirled the wine in his glass, thinking about Theia's large eyes. And the way she'd held on to his arms after he'd saved her from choking.

"And would another of those reasons be Rhea Carlisle's identical twin?"

Lucien glanced up, caught off guard. "Why in the world would you say that? I just met her today."

Polly shook her head knowingly. "Those Carlisle women have a way of getting under a man's skin. I'd be careful of that one if I were you. She's deceptively humdrum."

"What's that supposed to mean?"

"She's very *normal.*" Polly said the word as though it were a terrible insult. "Very sweet. People think of her as the least talented of the bunch, but I wouldn't want to be anywhere near her with a secret I didn't want found out."

It was a warning he'd be wise to pay heed to.

"As for Ström, he used to come in here with a redhead years ago. A real redhead." She grinned and flipped her hair. "Not like me."

"And?"

"And apparently she's a rogue Valkyrie. A couple of regulars knew her—also Valkyries—and didn't care much for her."

That was the missing piece. The Valkyrie must have been the one to create the revenant. And somehow she'd made a deal with Rhea Carlisle.

Full of mango lassi and sweet Kashmiri naan, Rhea wasn't interested in reading an old man's treatises about the history of the Covent written in longhand. Which suited Theia just fine. Alone, she wouldn't have to hide what she was looking for. She drove Rhea back to her car before heading to Phoebe's place with Rafael Diamante Sr.'s archives.

Puddleglum, Phoebe's Siamese tabby, curled up with her in the guest bed while she pored over the materials, looking for anything about the Smok family. As she turned the pages, she noticed a peculiar effect when she lingered on an entry: the text on the page began to shift beneath her touch. Rafe hadn't mentioned anything about magically enhanced pages, but here it was. Like clicking a magical hyperlink to load a page of related content, touching a reference in the text made the copy on the page transform into the detailed document to which Diamante referred. When she lifted her finger off the page, it returned to the original journal entry.

Fascinated, Theia thumbed through an entry on the Smok family's history. But it wasn't about the Diamantes at all. It was an accounting of Madeleine Marchant's belongings, given to the nobleman who had been her benefactor—none other than one Philippe Smok, Vicomte de Briançon. And among those "belongings" were Madeleine's children: seven daughters, in fact. *Seven sisters.*

The Lilith blood allele—a hypothesis Theia had formulated when she and Rhea had first traced their genealogy—was passed down through recessive genes, only resulting in the Lilith phenotype when daughters were born to two carriers of the gene in Madeleine's direct line. And this always seemed to result in the birth of seven sisters with the gifts. But she hadn't realized that the first set of sisters were Madeleine's own daughters.

Puddleglum plopped down in the middle of the journal to announce that Theia was done reading. She hadn't realized how late it had gotten. Lying back on the bed and staring at the ceiling, she tried to work out what Lucien Smok's game might be. There was no way his appearance at Phoebe's wedding was a coincidence. Rafe was right. She should keep her distance. But if his family had a connection not just to the Covent but to Madeleine herself, then Lucien surely knew it and had sought them out deliberately. Theia had to find out what he was up to. Particularly with regard to Smok Biotech.

The arrival of the vision was the first indication that she'd actually fallen asleep.

It flew out of the night like a carrion bird, circling overhead, waiting for death, casting a heavy shadow on the creatures below: the crow. The wolf. The dragon. The flying thing drew closer, and now she was looking up at it, standing with her sisters. It was both a vulture and a reptile, a prehistoric lizard with wings—a pterodactyl, perhaps—its head birdlike, with glowing red eyes, bat-like wings stretching out from the lizard body.

In the distance, a rooster crowed, and the sound became a screech in the thing's beak, a scream of laughter as it dived, talons outstretched.

The rooster crowed again. Light blazed through a crack in the blinds. Dawn light. The rooster was somewhere outside. Nice. Phoebe hadn't mentioned the built-in neighborhood alarm clock. Theia pulled the pillow over her head and rolled onto her side.

Before the cock crows twice. What was that from? Something in the Bible, she thought. New Testament. She hadn't been to church in years, but she remembered it now: Peter's denial of Christ. The cock outside had crowed twice. Not that unusual, probably. But why was that sticking in her head? Cock, not rooster. Theia giggled, knowing what Rhea would have to say about it.

Cock crows twice. The vision came back to her in a rush. It wasn't the Bible phrase she was thinking of, after all. The flying thing—it hadn't been a pterodactyl like she'd speculated in the dream. It was a cockatrice. And it was coming for them.

In middle school, she'd once gone with a friend to her church, an evangelical one. The preacher had spoken of some mad theory about human-animal hybrids and the evil plot of godless scientists who wanted to bring back such things as griffins, harpies and cockatrices. His theory claimed such creatures had roamed the earth before the Great Flood because of the sins of unnatural men who'd bred them, and God had wiped them out.

Theia had barely been able to contain her laughter, and her friend had been furious. Even at twelve, Theia understood enough science to know how idiotic such a theory was. Nobody was trying to splice genes across species to create monster hybrids, and even if they did try, it wouldn't work.

Except... Lucien Smok had said Smok Biotech's research at NAU was both scientific and supernatural. And what was more supernatural than mythical creatures that turned out to be real?

She certainly hadn't believed dragons were real until recently, when she'd seen two of them with her own eyes. Dev Gideon shared his form with the dragon Kur, and Rafe was a scion of Quetzalcoatl who sprouted iridescent feathered wings and snake flesh and commanded the dead. And she hadn't seen Leo shift, but according to Rhea's account of their time battling another ancient dragon in the Viking underworld, he could transform into a serpentine creature with the destructive energy of the mythological Jörmungandr—who maybe wasn't so mythological after all.

What if the Smok family's "magical-adjacent" connection was that they were bioengineering other such creatures?

Theia unhooked her arms from the pillow, and her eyes focused on the crimson business card on the nightstand. If she wanted to get to the bottom of this, she was going to have to take Lucien up on his offer.

Chapter 4

Lucien's phone vibrated in his jacket pocket. He'd been out on a job all day and had turned his ringer off. He took it out and glanced at it, surprised to see a voice mail notification from Theia Dawn. And annoyed that it seemed to make his heart beat faster.

Theia's message was brief: "We should talk."

Somebody else had talked, obviously. From the tone of her voice, he could tell she was better informed about the Smoks than she'd been yesterday. Lucien lay on his back on the Berber rug on the floor of his penthouse suite while he returned her call.

He grinned when she answered. "I knew you couldn't resist me."

"I can resist you just fine. It's your company I find intriguing." There was a pause as she apparently realized how her word choice sounded. "Your firm," she said quickly, followed by an adorable, mortified gasp.

He put her on speaker and crossed his arms behind his head. "So what can my...*firm*...do for you, Ms. Dawn?"

"I thought we were going to talk about what I can do for your..." She swore softly at herself in the background. It sent a little shiver down his spine to know how flustered she was when he wasn't even standing in front of her. "About the job. With Smok Biotech," she hastened to add. He wondered how flushed her skin was right now. With the chocolate-brown hair bobbed sharply at her chin and those little points of cherry red at the ends, it would make her eyes seem even larger.

"You want the job at the lab." He spoke lazily, imagining her large gray eyes blinking at him.

"If the offer's still open. And it depends on exactly what the job is."

"The offer is most definitely still open. Why don't we meet for dinner tonight to talk over the specifics?"

"Tonight?" Her voice went up slightly at the end, a little squeak of surprise.

Lucien smiled. "Is that a problem?"

"It's almost eight o'clock."

"Too close to your bedtime? I'm sure I can accommodate that."

"*No*, it's just—it's short notice. I wasn't planning on going out tonight. It would take me a little while to get ready."

"It's just a business dinner. You don't need to impress me."

"That's not what I meant." Her tone was clipped.

He loved getting under her skin. Lucien grinned at the thought. He'd like to get deep under it. Or inside it. In a manner of speaking. Lucien shook himself out of his little daydream. That wasn't going to do him any good.

"Why don't we meet at Cress at L'Auberge in an hour? Is that enough time?"

"Are they open that late?"

"They will be for me."

The last time he'd seen her, she'd been dressed as a bridesmaid in a bloodred chiffon dress that swung around her hips when she walked. Undeniably flattering, but he'd suspected it wasn't the sort of thing she normally wore. Neither was what she had on tonight—a conservative navy blue pencil skirt with a cream-colored blouse buttoned up far too high. It was an interesting look, perhaps something she thought a scientist would wear to a business dinner. The one departure from the conservative style was the pair of red crushed-velvet heels that drew attention to her fantastic legs.

"You really didn't have to dress up for me," he said as he pulled out her chair at their al fresco table above the babbling Oak Creek.

Theia sat almost suspiciously, like she wasn't sure what he was doing. "I didn't. I mean, this isn't for you. It just didn't seem like Cress was really a jeans and Tinker Bell T-shirt kind of place."

He smiled, picturing her in a Tinker Bell T-shirt. That seemed a lot more her style.

"It's whatever kind of place you want it to be, darling. Seriously. They know me here, and you may have noticed the place is empty."

Theia's eyes narrowed. "This doesn't impress me, you know."

"Of that I have absolutely no doubt." Lucien laid his napkin in his lap. "I hope you don't mind that I've ordered ahead. I should have asked if you had any food allergies, though. Is filet mignon all right?"

"No. I mean, yes, filet mignon is fine. No, I don't have any food allergies." She was gripping her water glass tightly.

"You don't have to be impressed, but there's no need to be so tense, either. Would it help if we dive straight into business?"

"*Yes.*" She'd answered almost before the words left his mouth. He was really enjoying how flustered he seemed to make her.

"Okay, so to start, I take it you spoke to your brother-in-law about us."

Theia took a sip of her water as if trying to buy time. "I got some information from him, yes."

"So you know what it is we do. Outside the lab, that is."

A questioning look appeared on her face for a moment before she masked it. "I do." She didn't. But she knew something. Something that was making her very nervous.

"As you know, there are two main divisions of Smok International: Smok Consulting and Smok Biotech. Let me explain how the consulting side of things intersects with the biotech business. Part of cleaning up other people's messes is dealing with what triggers those incidents in the first place."

Theia nodded, pretending to follow. The first course had arrived, and Lucien paused to try the bacon-wrapped lapin.

Theia's face lit up as she took a bite of hers. "Wow. This is fantastic."

"It doesn't suck," he agreed with a wink. "There are *some* perks to having too much money."

"Do you?" Theia took another bite, visibly relaxing. "Have too much?"

"Me personally?" Lucien shrugged. "I don't have any, as a matter of fact. This is all being expensed." He smiled at her dubious expression. "Still unimpressed? My inheritance is all held in trust, and it's dependent upon a few conditions I haven't met yet, so I get to represent my father's business, but everything I have belongs to him. Or to the company." He indicated the suit he was wearing. "This thing? Expensed." He flicked some mustard from his fork onto the jacket.

Theia laughed, the laughter obviously surprised out of her as she tried to cover her mouth, still full of rabbit. He liked seeing her laugh. It changed her whole face, like she'd let him in for a moment and let down her guard—something that was in place not just because she didn't trust him but a guardedness that seemed ingrained in her.

"You said something about triggers." Theia tried to go back to her frosty demeanor, moving beet curls around her plate. "What kind of triggers were you referring to?" She was obviously trying to get him to explain more about what she was pretending she already knew. He figured he'd oblige.

"Your brother-in-law, for instance—Rafe Diamante. I noticed that the uninvited guest at his wedding reception—the *other* uninvited guest—triggered a partial transformation. Strong emotion is often a trigger for such things. Most shape-shifters learn to control when they shift. Or to adapt, if the trigger happens to be out of their control, such as a full moon."

"You seem to know an awful lot about Rafe."

"I know an awful lot about everybody, darling." He noticed her visible flinch at the familiarity, and he tried not to react. Part of being able to indulge in his extracurricular activities depended on making sure people saw him as a spoiled brat who'd never grown up. And part of him *was* a spoiled brat who'd never grown up, so it wasn't all that hard to pull off. "I know a lot about a lot of influential people with unusual problems, I should say."

The waiter arrived to take their starter plates and replaced them with calamari salad. Theia picked up a set of little tentacles, holding them up in the light.

"Not a fan of squid?"

"Hmm?" Theia had popped the calamari into her mouth, and she chewed for a moment before responding. "No, I love squid. I was just admiring it. I love it when they include the tentacles instead of just the rings. They're the best part." She took another bite, this time with her fork. "So these unusual problems." She paused to chew and swallow. "Shape-shifting." She'd lowered her voice on the word. "It's actually fairly new to me, so I'm not used to people talking about it so openly. Are there really a lot of them?"

"More than you'd suspect. The job of Smok's consulting arm is making sure no one does suspect. Sometimes it's literally cleanup—which I don't do." He showed her his hands—no calluses, manicured nails. "We have crews for that. People who don't mind getting their hands dirty and who can be counted on to be discreet. We had a crew out to your sister Dione's house a few months—"

"Ione," Theia interrupted him with her mouth still partially full.

"Sorry?"

She swallowed and wiped her lips with her napkin. "She goes by Ione. It drives her crazy when people pronounce her name wrong, like you just did, so she dropped the *D*." Theia paused, apparently only just registering what he'd said. "You were at her house?"

"Not me personally. Like I said, I'm not big on cleaning things. But we sent a crew at Rafe's request to do some repairs after a certain dragon demon stomped around in her living room. And I understand *his* trigger was, well, fairly intimate."

Theia reddened slightly. Dev's transformation was reportedly triggered by sex and blood.

"My point is that responding to unwanted supernatural activity, whatever the trigger, by cleaning up after the fact may be lucrative, but it's inefficient. At Smok Biotech, we develop technologies to suppress unwanted transformations. Among other things." He figured any more information would just overload her if she'd only recently learned that shifters were real. "And people will pay a lot of money for that kind of control. Particularly people in the public eye. Entrepreneurs. Actors. Politicians. Imagine how the public would react if the president turned into a poison-spitting were-newt in the middle of a White House press conference?" Lucien glanced up with a smirk. "Bad example. He's clearly not bothering to use our tech."

Theia laughed again, her nose wrinkling. He definitely liked making her do that.

The main course arrived, and they were distracted for a bit by both the presentation and the flavor, truffle and fungus in wine sauce drizzled over the top of the perfectly grilled steak and an artful swirl of béarnaise surrounding mashed root vegetables with edible flowers on top. Lucien found he liked watching Theia eat food that delighted her almost as much as he liked making her laugh. But not quite as much as he was sure he'd like tasting her mouth the way she was tasting that filet mignon.

Lucien focused on his own food for a moment, trying to think more appropriate thoughts.

"So what is it you'd want me to do?"

He glanced up sharply, nearly choking on a mouthful of mashed turnip as he inhaled at the wrong moment. It would really be something if she had to return the favor from the wedding reception by performing the Heimlich maneuver on him.

"At the lab," Theia clarified, eyeing him suspiciously. "Why do you need me?"

Managing not to choke, Lucien set down his fork to take a drink of mineral water. "We have an excellent staff of researchers but only a handful of lab techs who know the full extent of what we do. I thought it would be good to have someone on staff that I don't have to hide things from." Not those things, anyway. He'd gotten used to hiding everything else. "And you'd be well compensated," he added. "In case that wasn't clear."

"You want me to be a lab technician?"

"More than just a lab technician. I mean, that, too. But…" He hadn't really thought about how he was going to broach the subject of her gift. They'd talked around the reputation of the Carlisle sisters, but he hadn't actually mentioned clairvoyance outright. "Someone with both technical and esoteric knowledge would be invaluable. Someone who could make…educated predictions of the likely outcomes."

Theia's body language had loosened up significantly over the course of the meal, but in an instant she was back to being stiff and tight and on guard.

"Sorry, did I say something wrong?"

"What exactly is it that you think I can do, Mr. Smok?"

Oh, crap. He was Mr. Smok again.

"I…understood you had oracular powers."

"Oracular." Her forehead creased with irritation. "You think I can see the future. That I can just look into my little crystal ball and tell you how Smok stock is going to do tomorrow."

"Well, not exactly—"

"Who told you I had these oracular powers?"

Lucien was beginning to feel uncomfortable under her gaze. She might not have oracular powers, but he was starting to think she could burn a hole in his family jewels with those eyes.

"It's common knowledge in the community. The magical community."

"And the magical adjacent, of course."

Lucien shrugged helplessly. "Sorry. I've obviously stepped in it here, and I'm not really sure how."

"Let me ask you something, Mr. Smok."

"Fire away."

"Do you and your kind think my sisters and I are some kind of magical Pez dispensers? Is there a creep board out there on the internet somewhere, some ugly little masculinist corner of the deep web where you guys swap stories about how to hit on magically gifted women?"

Lucien nearly choked again at the word *masculinist*.

"I'm not sure what you think my kind is, but I think you're taking my interest the wrong way."

"So you don't want to sleep with me to get your magical rocks off."

Something in her words made him snap, like a percussion grenade had gone off inside him. "Listen, sweetheart, if all I wanted to do was sleep with you, I wouldn't have wasted the company money on a fancy dinner. I would have just done it, and right about now is when you'd be gathering your clothes and making your exit so I could roll over and go to sleep."

Theia pushed back her chair and stood, her napkin falling to the floor. "Thank you for the dinner, Mr. Smok. Enjoy rolling over and sleeping next to your hand."

Still suffering the effects of the mental percussion grenade, he wasn't entirely sure what had just happened, but it was both delightful and painful to watch her walk away in those heels and that skirt.

Chapter 5

Theia ordered a car on her way outside, and in fifteen minutes she was back at Phoebe's ranch house yanking off the skirt and kicking off her shoes and grabbing a startled Puddleglum for a forcible cuddle in the papasan chair by the picture window.

Who the hell did that asshole Lucien Smok think he was, anyway? God's gift to women, obviously. Showing up at Phoebe's wedding trolling for Lilith blood was bad enough, but making up a job offer to get into her pants was pathetic.

Her phone rang underneath Puddleglum, and she ended up accidentally answering as she wrested it from under him before she saw who was calling.

Lucien's voice carried from the speaker as she stared at it. "I didn't think you'd answer."

"I didn't. It was my sister's cat."

"Her…cat?"

"His butt. Some people butt dial. He butt answers. Goodbye." Her finger was poised over the button.

"Wait. Please hear me out."

For some reason, she did.

"I'm calling to apologize. I screwed up."

"Ya think?"

"I really did ask you to dinner to talk about the job. There was no ulterior motive. I'm sorry I handled the topic of your gift badly. I didn't realize it was a touchy subject and maybe not for public consumption. And I'm sorry I snapped at you. I'm not sure why I overreacted. But what I said was inexcusable."

Well, damn. That was an unexpectedly sincere apology. But maybe this was part of his game. She wasn't going to be stupid enough to fall for it twice.

"Okay, well, thanks for calling. Have a nice evening."

"Theia?"

Something about the way he said her name, almost a plea, made her hesitate.

"Are you still there?"

Theia's thumb hovered over the button. "Sort of."

He laughed softly. "Sort of? Listen, the job offer was genuine. I realize I made assumptions, but I think you'd be an asset to the enterprise, gift or no gift. Is there any way we can start over and discuss it?"

She did need to learn more about the Smoks, and the whole trigger-suppression concept was intriguing.

Theia sighed. "I'm not a psychic, I don't read people's fortunes and I don't perform on command."

"Of course. That's perfectly understandable. Can I ask…" There was a rustling sound as he changed position. "Can you tell me how it does work? If it's none of my business, that's perfectly cool."

Theia hesitated, and Puddleglum jumped down to wander to the kitchen, offended at no longer being the center of attention. "I've been known to have dreams. Visions. But honestly? I don't even know if they're anything."

"I think you underestimate yourself."

"How would you know?"

"Just a feeling."

Theia smiled despite herself. "That's usually my line."

"Why don't we put the feelings and intuitions aside then? I'll be at the lab tomorrow around two o'clock. Just come by and take a look around, see what we do. If it doesn't interest you, no harm done. You can walk away. And if you do get any impressions of a possible prophetic nature, I'd be happy to hear those, too. But no pressure."

"No pressure."

"Cross my heart and hope to die."

"Let's not go that far."

Lucien gave her that soft laugh again. "I get the feeling you doubt my sincerity. Suppose I can't blame you. So will I see you tomorrow?"

The word *tomorrow* seemed to float before her in brilliant blue letters. Synesthesia wasn't unusual for her, but it was often a precursor to a waking vision. Either way, it seemed to indicate that tomorrow was significant. A sign she should heed. Interpretation, of course, was always the tough part. Was her gift telling her she should go tomorrow? Or stay away?

"Theia? You still there?"

"Yeah, sorry. Tomorrow it is."

The same brilliant blue haunted her sleep. Not letters or words this time, but blue in the form of a small dragon. Like the cockatrice she'd dreamed of before, it had webbed, bat-like wings, the joints ending in sharp claws, and stood on two legs, the head and barbed tail the classic shape of a dragon from fantasy—the sort Rhea had collected as figurines when they were kids. But there was something wrong with this dragon. It dragged itself along the desert floor the way a wounded bat might, using its winged forelimbs to "walk." And above it, the shadow of the carrion-eating cockatrice circled as before. And it was growing closer.

She forgot about the dream images by the time she'd finished grading papers from her Friday morning class and headed over to the lab.

Smok was using the university biotech labs while a larger, permanent facility was being built off campus. Theia already had an access card for her own research, though she'd never been in the biotech section.

Lucien greeted her in the atrium, looking almost surprised that she'd actually shown up. "Theia. Welcome." He squeezed her hand like they were old friends. "It's nice to see you in something more comfortable."

She'd worn ruby plaid skinny jeans and a black fitted T-shirt—not exactly something she'd just thrown on, but she wasn't trying to look good for him. The words of Violet Bick from *It's a Wonderful Life* popped into her head: *"This old thing? Why, I only wear it when I don't care how I look."* Theia, of course, couldn't pull off the sassy hair flip.

She just wanted to feel confident, and looking exceptionally cute made her feel confident. So did the approving look he gave her as his eyes lingered over her curves for just the briefest moment. Not so long that it was obtrusive and objectifying, but long enough that she knew she'd chosen well. And as much as she hated to admit it, that little feeling of breathlessness was back.

She'd tried to ignore it at dinner the night before, tried not to think about how his arms had felt around her, like he was protecting her from the world—or like there was no one else in it but her. But every time she'd looked up from her food into those depthless ice-blue eyes, her lungs had tightened like when she was a kid and had felt an asthma attack coming on. She'd had to chew very carefully to make sure not to end up in a repeat performance of the moment they met.

Today, of course, she'd gone with comfortable black cotton Mary Janes instead of the velvet heels, which made Lucien seem exceptionally tall, though he was probably just under six feet. She'd been wearing heels both times they'd met before, but now she was at her full height of a whopping five foot two.

Beside Lucien, an older woman in a lab coat held out a clipboard. "Before you go in, we'll need you to sign a standard confidentiality agreement."

Lucien gave her an apologetic smile and a little shrug.

Once Theia had signed it and returned the clipboard, Lucien led her into the Smok wing of the lab, which required a special passkey. "I can have them add the access code to your existing card right now if you like." He held out his hand as if expecting her to put her card in it.

Theia kept her arms crossed. "I haven't agreed to your offer yet."

Lucien smiled. "You will."

Researchers were hard at work despite the lab only having been in operation for a few days. The equipment—and presumably the technology behind it—was cutting-edge. Theia had microscope envy.

Lucien seemed pleased by her reaction. "This is our pharmacogenomics division."

"Pharmacogenomics?" Theia wondered if she'd heard wrong. "Not pharmacogenetics?"

"Nope. Genomics. That special project I told you about is particularly dependent on genome-wide study. Smok is currently trying to pinpoint variations in a single nucleotide within the genome to understand the pharmacokinetic and pharmacodynamic effects for our newest drugs in development."

Theia's heart skipped a beat at the way the words rolled off his tongue. Most people's eyes glazed over when she talked genetics. She was starting to see Lucien in a new light.

Encouraged by her interest, he gave her a little smile and went on. "The market for this drug is unique, as you know, and every patient responds differently. Understanding the epigenetics involved is crucial."

Epigenetics. Now *there* was a term that was near and dear to Theia's heart. The Lilith blood phenotype she'd postulated was epigenetic in nature, not caused by changes in the DNA itself, but by changes in gene expression.

"Have you been able to isolate the autosomal mutations responsible for the…condition?"

"We have, indeed. We're well past that stage." Lucien looked thoughtful before moving toward an isolated room at the rear of the lab. "Let me show you something." He used his key card once more on the door. "Another access code I'll provide you with. This one's highly classified, since it has to do with our special research."

He held the door for Theia and she stepped in, not realizing at first the significance of what she was looking at. Cages lined the walls of the small room, containing what seemed to be perfectly ordinary specimens—mice, rats, a snake.

Lucien closed the door behind him. "These are all animals in which we've been able to induce lycanthropy through gene manipulation."

"Lycanthropy?"

"As a generic term, it doesn't refer strictly to wolf-human forms but to any kind of trans-species shift."

Theia moved closer to the snake—a juvenile albino ball python—to get a better look. "You mean...they all shift?"

"It makes it easier to study the triggers and suppression mechanisms when we know exactly what genes we're dealing with." Lucien pushed a button next to the glass of the python's cage.

"What does that do?"

"Triggers the shift by introducing a mild toxin into the sealed environment."

Theia bristled. "A toxin?"

"It won't harm it. It's more of an irritant. We'll remove it and rebalance the environment in a moment."

Theia was about to give him a piece of her mind about humane lab practices, but the snake had begun to uncoil, raising its head as if sensing them or perhaps just sensing the change in its air. And as it lifted its snout, the yellow and white pattern of the scales began to ripple and grow, becoming feathery, while the snout elongated into a beak. The reptile shuddered as it morphed, although she'd seen much more violent transformations. This, at least, didn't appear to be painful.

The body shortened. Limbs grew—a pair of legs with talons. Soon it was covered in feathers, wings bursting from the flesh at its sides and a comb and wattles elongating out of the remaining scales on the head. A rooster…a cock. Theia shivered.

"Amazing, isn't it? And just as we've triggered the metamorphosis, we can trigger the reverse." Lucien pressed the button again, and in moments the creature was shuddering back into its original python form and curling up into its previous coil. "The gene manipulation is a shortcut, of course. We can't exactly experiment with genetic modification on human subjects. Although human trials for the serum are the next phase. We're not quite there yet, but we're actively recruiting volunteers who already have the shifter gene."

Theia turned to stare at him, thinking he might be pulling her leg, but his expression was serious.

"You see why we have a need for ethical oversight from someone familiar with the sensitive nature of the work."

"You expect me to help you experiment on human volunteers?"

"Like I said, the actual clinical trial comes later. Probably at least a year away. What you would be doing is helping us map triggers based on genome. And making sure confidentiality is maintained as well as helping to establish a sensitivity protocol for screening volunteers. Which is where your special skills would come in."

There was something unsettling about the idea of people volunteering such information to a large, profit-driven corporation, but she supposed someone with lycanthropy who was desperate to control it might be willing to sacrifice some privacy for the promise of a cure. Or at least the promise of a regimen for managing it.

The idea of mapping triggers, however—mapping them to *genes*—it almost made her toes tingle with giddy excitement.

Lucien smiled knowingly. "It's a lot to take in all at once. I don't expect you to answer right away. Take your time and think about it."

Once he'd started talking pharmacogenomics, there wasn't really any question of what her answer was going to be, and she suspected he knew that. But it wouldn't hurt to sleep on it and think it over rationally. Or pretend to.

Theia held out her hand and gave him what she hoped was a businesslike handshake. Her palm felt small in his. Despite his claim that he didn't do physical labor, his hands were surprisingly muscular. Not in an unpleasant way, but like he was used to using them for more than just writing checks from his trust. Maybe he worked out a lot and it was from gripping weights or something. As with his earlier greeting, his grasp was warm and familiar. Not businesslike at all.

Theia tried to keep from blushing at the contact. "I'll definitely think it over. Thanks for taking the time to show me around."

After holding her hand a moment longer, Lucien winked as he let it go. "Anytime, darling." There was something in the way he said *darling* combined with the wink that seemed deliberately alienating, as though he'd realized he'd been behaving much too civilly. Like he was reminding her that he was a jackass. *Well, it worked, buddy.* She didn't feel flushed or breathless anymore, just annoyed

Chapter 6

For some reason, the meeting with Theia had agitated him. Lucien took the company Maserati and drove south from Flagstaff with the top down, deliberately speeding, taking the switchbacks and hairpin turns down Highway 89A without slowing, just to hear his tires squeal.

He liked her more than he wanted to. He didn't really want to like anyone. Wanting something—wanting *someone*—made you vulnerable, and that was something Lucien didn't intend to be. He needed to be vigilant. The family curse might be nothing more than a legend, but he wasn't about to be caught with his metaphysical pants down. The last time a firstborn son of the Smok family had been required to pay the price demanded by the witch in Briançon before she burned, the Smoks had only just immigrated to the New World. Every seven generations, so the legend went. The last Smok to pay it had fought against the British in the American Revolution.

Lucien wasn't going to be the next.

At the same time, he kind of hated himself for turning on his manufactured "Lucien Smok, spoiled brat" persona just as he'd parted ways with Theia. He could see the disappointment in her face. She'd been warming up to him, and he'd yanked the rug out from under her on purpose.

When he got back to his rented suite, he found an envelope had been slipped under his door. It was a little unsettling not knowing who this "helpful citizen" was, but the source had been right on the money every time. It was better intel than he could get at Polly's—at least not without her expecting something in return. Then again, everything had a price. He just didn't know what it was yet. It ought to worry him more, but right now he needed to send something to hell.

He opened the manila envelope, expecting another name, maybe an active vamp who preyed on the living—unlike the pasty poseurs at Polly's—or an animated corpse. Instead, it was a URL. Lucien was surprised to find it took him to a genealogy website. The page was for the Carlisle family. What was the point of this? He already knew their history. They were descendants of the witch, and they'd inherited her gifts. Witches might have the potential to create supernatural havoc, but they weren't supernatural themselves. It wasn't like *they* were demons.

Lucien closed the browser just as a message appeared on his phone from Polly.

Got something juicy for you, hon. Come by tonight.

He headed to Polly's after dark, trying for low-key in a tan Versace suit.

Polly laughed when she saw him. "What is this, the Obama surprise?"

"Hey, that was a damn fine suit. So's this. Just because some people have no appreciation for style…"

"Whatever you say." She was at her usual booth, surrounded by pretty-boy vegan bloodsuckers and assorted half-shifted weres, and she gave no indication that she intended to dismiss them.

"So what is it you wanted to tell me that you couldn't just text me?"

Polly pretended to pout. "Now you're just being mean. Is it so terrible to have to see me in person?"

Lucien sighed. "That's not what I meant, and you know it. It's just that you look awfully busy, and I wasn't really planning on hanging out and drinking tonight. I felt like shit the next morning after the last time we chatted."

"It's not my fault you can't handle your liquor. Anyway, I thought you might want to be here tonight, because there's someone special visiting."

"Who?"

She nodded toward a table near the stage, partially lit by the spillover of the spotlight on the singer. "Check out the Amazon with the short bald guy."

Lucien noted the tall, leggy blonde and her considerably less impressive companion. "So? Who are they?"

"Who cares who he is? Probably a snack. *She's* Brünnhilde."

Lucien's brows drew together. "Who the hell is Brünnhilde?"

Polly gave him a smug grin. "She's a Valkyrie, baby. I found you a Valkyrie."

The bloodsucker beside her frowned. "Who's this asshole? Why does he get a Valkyrie?"

Polly slapped his hand. "I'm not giving her to him,

you idiot. She's a freaking *Valkyrie*. And have some respect. This is Lucien. He's the—"

"Thanks, Polly. You can quit there. A little discretion?" He turned toward the table where the Valkyrie
sat, but Polly put her foot in his path.

"Hey. No thank-you? Not even a little kiss?" She tilted
her head and pointed to her cheek.

Lucien smiled, remembering his manners. He'd be
wise to keep Polly on his good side. And she *had* done
him a favor. He leaned in, but instead of kissing her
cheek, he lifted her hand from around the vamp's shoulder and kissed the back of it, to the annoyance of both
parties.

Polly flipped her hair, black this evening, over her
shoulder. "Come by tomorrow at two. You can thank
me properly."

Lucien approached the Valkyrie's table, realizing halfway there that he didn't know what to offer for information from a Valkyrie. What did Valkyries want? Souls?
They didn't need him for that. And he wasn't likely to
be able to give them any valiant, heroic ones. He lucked
out, though, as she seemed thoroughly bored with her
companion.

He smiled winningly at her as she glanced up. "Pardon the intrusion, but would you care to dance?" No one
else was dancing, but Brünnhilde rose and accepted as
if eager to escape.

The song that had been playing was more on the swing
spectrum, but the band switched to something slow and
melodic. Lucien put his arm around her waist and took
her hand, feeling like an adolescent next to her. It was
like dancing with a tree.

"I'm Lucien," he offered.

"Brünnhilde."

"That's a lovely name."

Brünnhilde's brow arched. "Is it? In 2017 in the South-western United States?"

Lucien laughed. "Well, Lucien isn't exactly in fashion, either. Your name stands out. And it suits you."

"I get the impression you want something from me, Lucien."

"Can't a guy ask a beautiful woman to dance?"

She gave him another brow arch, this time without amusement, and he laughed.

"All right. I'll cut to the chase, since you've been gracious enough to indulge me. I understand you're a Valkyrie. I hope that's not out of line to say."

Brünnhilde shrugged noncommittally. "Perhaps."

He wasn't sure if she was half-heartedly confirming her identity or agreeing that he was out of line, but he forged ahead. "I wondered if you might have heard anything about the Wild Hunt."

"You speak of Odin's Hunt."

"I believe so, yes. But one that's out of season."

Brünnhilde's green eyes flickered with annoyance. "Indeed it is. The Chieftain of the Hunt defies propriety. No surprise, given his protector."

"His protector?"

"A mortal who wields peculiar magic. She somehow bested one of my sisters to win him."

"That's surprising. Why does he need protection? And from a mortal, no less?"

"Because his body is meant to sleep while he rides. But when Kára removed her own protection from him, she also gave him the power to ride while in his skin.

It's a disgrace. Of course, Kára was a disgrace long before this latest stunt."

"Kára? She's your sister?"

Brünnhilde nodded tersely. "She calls herself Faye these days. She was once a great warrior, but she defied the Norns to coddle this man, fallen in battle. Instead of taking him to his reward in Valhalla, she kept him as a pet. In exchange, he was cursed to lead Odin's Hunt."

"This man, the chieftain—you say he was fallen. You mean he died?"

"Precisely. Died in battle, but Kára broke the laws of the Valkyries, the laws of Odin himself."

"So he shouldn't be here. His life is unnatural."

Brünnhilde shrugged. "Well. None of the wraiths of the Hunt *should* be here. And yet they are. They are all unnatural. That's what makes them wraiths, does it not? How else would we have the Hunt?"

The music ended, and Lucien thanked her for the dance.

Brünnhilde glanced back at the table where her inexplicably dull companion was waiting for her. "I suppose I'll have to take him now. Warriors aren't what they used to be. She sighed and headed back to her table.

Lucien had the answer he needed. Leo Ström was as unnatural as a man could get. His soul might once have been destined for Valhalla, but now it belonged in hell.

He donned his hunting attire and made sure the arrows in his quiver were all equipped with his specially designed arrowheads. Having Smok labs at his disposal had come in handy In his quest to rid the world of revenants and demons. The exploding tips were filled with a serum known at the lab as the Soul Reaper. Developed for those dangerous and recalcitrant creatures they occasionally came across on their consults, it was deadly to the inhuman. And if the inhuman creature it struck happened to have a human soul remaining in it, the remnant was dissolved and relegated, presumably, to hell.

In all honesty, Lucien wasn't sure he believed in an afterlife of reward or punishment, but he'd seen plenty of evidence of an underworld—or perhaps underworlds—a plane where the supernatural elements of living things, whether spirit or soul or something else, could travel. Virtually every religious tradition had its own version of this soul realm—and a ruler of it.

He took a more discreet car this time and drove to the home where Rhea Carlisle and Leo Ström were staying. No point waiting to see if the Hunt would ride tonight. He knew what Leo was. And if the revenant was already out for the evening, Lucien would wait. He'd brought a ski mask to avoid revealing his identity to Theia's twin.

A little twinge of conscience tugged at him, reminding him that an insult or injury to one twin was likely to be felt by the other. Not physically, necessarily, but in terms of emotional harm, regardless of how close they were. And these two had seemed particularly close when he'd seen them together. He and his sister Lucy didn't see eye to eye—after years of sibling rivalry fueled by their father's vagaries, sometimes they downright hated each other—but he knew that if anything happened to Lucy, if anyone dared to hurt her, he'd be furious. He'd want retribution.

But he couldn't allow his feelings to get in the way of his mission. This wasn't about him, in any event. It was about the kind of people the Smoks had cozied up to for hundreds of years. No, not people, but *things*. Lucien felt it was his duty to make up for the evil his family enabled.

Helping a foolish family that had invited a demon into their home was one thing, and the routine cleansing of unwanted spiritual activity was a necessary service, but Smok Consulting had covered up depravities—cleaning up blood-spattered rooms after a nest of bloodsuckers had engaged in a Caligula-style orgy and fed on their half-dead victims for days; disposing of bodies when a shape-shifter lost control and slaughtered its own family, and then allowing that shape-shifting abomination to start a new life somewhere else with no consequences. The thought of how many lives his own family had allowed to be destroyed, looking the other way in the name of professional reputation and profit, sickened him.

One of the key sources of tension between Lucy and him was her blasé attitude toward all of it, her seeming acceptance of the status quo. She was ambitious and had made it her life's goal to show Lucien up and prove to their father that he'd made a mistake in choosing his heir. It was never going to do any good. Edgar was immovable, but Lucien was happy to let Lucy take the lead and the credit, to let himself seem lazy and spoiled. The longer his father was motivated to keep putting off retirement, the better. And Lucy was just better at business, which didn't interest Lucien in the least.

Rhea and Leo were staying at one of Rafe Diamante's properties in his absence—Lucien had been tracking them since the reception—a gated community in northeast Sedona. Luckily, the Smok family connections gave him access to any of a number of exclusive communities here and around he world. He had no problem getting in. Rhea's car, a red Mini, wasn't parked in the drive at Diamante's house, which could mean they were both out. But the lights were on inside.

He pulled his ski mask over his face as he got out of the car, loaded an arrow in the crossbow and lined up the sight on the scope.

Luck was on his side tonight. The revenant walked in front of the large picture window, looking down at something on the coffee table in the great room. Sheer curtains were drawn across the window, giving Lucien the advantage. He could see Leo perfectly through them but wouldn't be visible from within.

The image of Theia's face popped into his head, making him hesitate just for a moment. But Lucien wasn't responsible for the fact that the Valkyrie had created an abomination Theia's sister happened to be dating. This creature had stalked the earth long enough. It needed to be put down. *Forget about Theia.* Easier said than done, but anger at himself propelled Lucien forward, and he took his shot straight through the glass, not wanting to waste the opportunity.

The split second between the penetration of the glass and the arrow's impact in his target wasn't long enough for a normal person to react, but the revenant turned, causing the arrow to hit him in the shoulder. It had missed bone and gone straight through. Lucien grabbed another arrow, but Leo moved faster, charging through the broken window, and the arrow wasn't fully loaded as he came at Lucien.

Lucien dropped the bow, ready to defend himself in hand-to-hand combat. He only had to hold the revenant off for a little while. Despite the miss, the arrow tip would have delivered its poison, and it should be taking effect any minute.

But Leo didn't even seem impaired. Lucien bobbed and wove as Leo grabbed for him, throwing a right hook. Leo was faster, his fist catching Lucien on the jaw. The revenant barreled into him as he tried to take another swing, flattening him on the ground. Gravel and cactus tines from a decorative cholla ground into Lucien's shoulder as the revenant pummeled him. The Soul Reaper wasn't slowing this guy down a bit.

A knee to Lucien's groin ended any chance of regaining the upper hand.

Leo climbed on top of him, hands around Lucien's throat, the shaft of the damn arrow still skewering his left shoulder. "Who are you? Who sent you? Was it that necrophiliac?"

The lack of oxygen to his brain as the large hands constricted his airway must be impairing his understanding. That couldn't have been what the revenant said.

Lucien's vision was going gray.

"Leo! What the hell are you doing?" Theia's voice rang out as a car door slammed, and she was running toward them. "What's going on?"

But it was Theia's twin, not Theia herself—which made a lot more sense, Lucien realized before he lost consciousness.

Chapter 7

Rhea's message was baffling.

That guy you pretend you don't want just went rogue.
Get over here. NOW.

Theia tried calling, but it went straight to voice mail, and her texts weren't being read. That was unnerving. What was going on? She hopped into her car and drove straight to Rafe's place, rattled enough to speed. Normally, according to Rhea, she drove like a granny.

A car Theia didn't recognize was parked out front, so she had to park farther down the drive. As she approached the house, she tripped over what looked like a quiver of high-tech arrows among scattered gravel and broken cactus littering the normally immaculate walkway. Theia dashed to the door and burst in without knocking after seeing shattered glass around the front windowpane.

"Rhea? Are you okay? Are you here?" She hadn't had any visions about Rhea being in danger, but her Spidey-sense was triggered like crazy.

"In here."

Theia breathed a bit easier at the sound of Rhea's voice. She hurried toward it and found her sister and Leo in the kitchen—with Lucien Smok tied to a chair. He looked like an angry bull had trampled him. Lucien glanced up at Theia out of one eye, the other swollen shut, and quickly looked down.

Leaning against the counter with his arms folded, Leo had a bandage around his shoulder and blood soaking his white T-shirt. And there were bruises on his knuckles.

Theia found her voice after a moment of what was becoming a familiar sense of breathlessness, except this was breathlessness of disbelief. "Lucien? What in the world is going on? What happened to you? What are you doing here?"

"That's what we've been asking him, but he won't talk." Rhea kicked at the leg of Lucien's chair. "He shot Leo with a goddamn arrow." She indicated Rafe's large oak table with her gaze. A crossbow with a high-powered scope attachment lay on it.

Theia rubbed her forehead. "Lucien?"

He didn't glance up, but he finally spoke. "I'll talk to Theia. But not with *him* in the room."

Leo made an angry noise that sounded like a wolf growling, but Rhea took his hand. "Come on. Maybe she can get something out of him." Reluctantly, he went with her, and Theia closed the kitchen door.

She took a breath and turned around to find Lucien

staring at her, his one open eye bloodshot and defiant. "Are you going to tell me what's going on? Did you really attack Leo with a…" She glanced at the table. "A *crossbow*?"

Lucien's voice was calm and measured. "Your sister is living with a man who ought to have died a millennium ago."

Theia crossed her arms. "I'm aware of that."

"You're aware."

"How is this any of your business?"

"Because *that's* my business. My real work. Putting unnatural creatures down. Demons. Revenants."

"Revenants?"

"That's what the reanimated dead are called."

Theia laughed, but Lucien wasn't kidding. "Leo is *not* a revenant. You can see that, can't you? I mean, I know your vision is a little limited right now, but, seriously, Lucien."

"He died over a thousand years ago."

"He was *supposed* to die over a thousand years ago. I take it you're aware of the Valkyrie's bargain?"

"Dead is dead. The Valkyrie created a revenant in defiance of the Fates."

"Even if she did, what does that have to do with you? Why do you care?"

"I told you—"

"Yeah, yeah. You said. It's your job. Is this why you showed up at Phoebe's wedding?"

Lucien inclined his head. "One of the reasons. The other reasons were a demon and a necromancer."

Theia's temper flared in the face of his calm composure. "So your bullshit job offer was just that. Something you made up on the spot as an excuse to get close to my family so you could go on some purity crusade against them. Are you working with Carter Hamilton?"

Lucien opened his mouth but paused as her words registered before he spoke. "Hamilton?"

"The *actual* necromancer who crashed the reception. The man who murdered Rafe's father and apprentice along with at least two innocent women."

"I'm aware of who he is. Why would I be working with him?"

"Because he's made it his life's work to destroy my family, and you seem to be very conveniently helping his cause."

"I'm not trying to destroy your family. This isn't about your family at all."

"Could have fooled me."

Lucien sighed, glancing down at the floor, where droplets of blood had dried around him. "First of all, my interest in having you join the genome project at Smok Biotech was genuine. *Is* genuine. That has nothing to do with any of this."

"Any of this? You mean the trying-to-kill-members-of-my-family this? Did you think I'd just be like, 'Oh, that's okay, Mr. Smok, let me map these triggers for you. I don't need time off for the funerals. Can I get you a coffee?'"

"I didn't think you'd find out," Lucien burst out.

Theia unfolded her arms and clenched her fists, tempted to add to his bruises.

He had the sense to look embarrassed. "I mean, this is what I *do*. It has nothing to do with anything else. I compartmentalize the Lucien I have to be for the company so I can do this. You have no idea how dangerous these inhuman abominations are. Revenants rip people limb from limb. They're unstoppable. They're not human, and they do not experience empathy or remorse. My work with Smok Consulting means letting creatures like these walk free, and I was tired of being the cause of it, so I decided to take matters into my own hands—unofficially. I'm sorry it happens to affect you personally, but I can't let my feelings for you get in the way of what has to be done."

Through the haze of anger, Theia's airway did that funny tightening thing again. "Feelings for me?"

"I didn't mean *feelings*, I just meant—I mean, of course I'm attracted to you, that's not... Fuck." Lucien threw back his head in frustration but clearly regretted the movement as soon as he'd made it, judging by the sharp cry.

"What was that? What's wrong?"

Lucien looked a little green. "Nothing. I think I might have... I just have a little..." His eyes fluttered shut, and his head slumped forward.

"Lucien?" Theia tried to rouse him with a gentle shake, to no effect. She raised her voice as she turned her head toward the door. "You guys? I think I need some help in here."

The door opened abruptly, Rhea's palm flat against it as though she'd been standing just on the other side with her ear pressed against the wood. "What did he do now?"

"I think he passed out. He moved his head sharply and it jarred some injury."

Leo grunted from the doorway. "Probably his broken arm."

Theia whirled on him. "You broke his arm?"

"*Arrow*," Rhea reminded her. She pointed at the table with a glare. "Crossbow."

"I'm not saying it wasn't warranted, but you don't tie

up a guy with a broken arm and torture him for information."

Rhea snorted. "Nobody tortured him. He's a big goddamn baby."

"You have to take him to the hospital."

Lucien stirred and groaned. "'M fine. No hospital."

Theia rolled her eyes. "You're not fine. You got the shit beaten out of you by a Viking. Deservedly, it sounds like."

Lucien gritted his teeth like he was struggling to stay conscious. "Call Lucy."

Theia looked at Rhea, who shook her head and shrugged, then glanced back at Lucien. "Khaleesi?"

Lucien groaned, this time a sound of frustration rather than pain. "Call. *Lucy*. My sister. Number's in my phone." He paused for a breath. "Under 'Bitch.'"

"Um…" Theia raised an eyebrow.

Rhea picked up the cell phone lying next to the crossbow. It was a bit dented, and the glass cracked, but apparently it still functioned.

"Password?" Lucien gave it to her and Rhea typed it in. "Yep. Here it is—Bitch."

"She's my twin," said Lucien.

Rhea shared a look with Theia. "Seems about right," they said together.

Lucy Smok was at the door twenty minutes later. She had the same ice-blue eyes and long lashes as her brother. The same dark brows and darker hair—though Lucy's was considerably longer and hung in a loose braid—contrasted starkly with the porcelain-fair skin in a slightly more feminine frame.

Lucien's twin leaned casually against the entryway,

a black leather attaché case in her hand, glancing from Rhea to Theia as they opened the door. "Which one of you is the biologist?"

"I'm Theia." She stepped forward and shook Lucy's hand as though they were meeting in a normal social situation. "This is Rhea. Please come in. He's in the kitchen, through here."

Rhea had agreed to let Theia untie Lucien, but he still sat in the chair, guarded by a scowling Leo.

Lucy took in Leo's size with a glance and burst out laughing at her brother. "God, you're an idiot."

Lucien glared, holding his right arm awkwardly in his lap. "Thanks." His voice was tight and clipped. "Knew I could count on you."

"You'll have to forgive my brother." Lucy smirked at him from the doorway. "He thinks he's some kind of vigilante superhero." She stepped into the kitchen and set down the bag to look him over, clucking her tongue at his bruises.

He swore loudly when she touched his arm. "I think it's broken," he said through gritted teeth.

"That's what they told me."

"Did you bring it?"

"I did. You sure you want it?"

Lucien nodded curtly.

Lucy straightened. "We're going to need to get that shirt off." She looked around. "Got any scissors?"

Rhea rummaged through the kitchen drawers and dug up a pair. "Looks like you've got this covered." She handed them to Lucy. "I think Leo and I should leave you to it." She nodded at Leo, who pushed away from the counter with a sigh and followed her to the door. Before she left, Rhea turned back to Lucien. "And by the way? He's not a revenant, you jackass. He's mortal."

Lucien hissed in pain as Lucy cut the black sweater up the side, muttering something under his breath.

Lucy shook her head, continuing to cut without pausing. "You shot a mortal with that thing, idiot. You're lucky he didn't kill you."

The sleeve came away, revealing an odd twist to Lucien's elbow that made Theia's stomach churn.

From the black case, Lucy retrieved a small glass vial and a disposable syringe and ripped open a sterile wipe, which she used on his elbow. "This is going to hurt."

Theia peered over Lucy's shoulder as she opened the vial and filled the syringe. "What is that?"

"It's like Fix-a-Flat for bones." Without a warning, Lucy jabbed the needle directly into the joint, and Lucien let out a barrage of obscenities.

Theia had to turn away to keep the sudden lurch of her stomach from becoming something more. When she turned back, the twist in Lucien's arm seemed to have magically straightened.

"It's a little something we make at Smok Biotech." Lucy nodded to her brother as he cautiously flexed the joint. "You'll need to have it set properly before it starts to mend wrong. But for now, you should be able to use it."

As Lucien pulled off what remained of the sweater, Theia caught a flash of blue ink on his back just below the right shoulder. Brilliant blue, like the color she kept seeing everywhere—in her dreams, evoked in sounds and words.

Lucien glanced at Lucy. "Did you bring me—"

"Of course." She handed him the sweater she'd taken from the case, the same as the one he'd been wearing

He turned as he stood to pull it on, giving Theia a good look at his ink.

It was a tattoo of a small web-winged dragon in flight.

Chapter 8

As Lucien struggled to pull on the sweater without showing that it was a struggle, Lucy stopped him.

"You've got something sticking out of your back."

"Cactus." He'd rolled in plenty of it. The minor irritant had paled against the other aches and pains he was beginning to feel now that his arm wasn't killing him. He couldn't remember ever taking such a beating, even from a raging wendigo. He'd been overconfident and unprepared.

Lucy sighed and got a pair of tweezers from her case. "Sit down. Let me get them." She went to work pulling out the tiny spines as he eased back into the chair. "So I understand you're going to be working at Smok's new lab," she said to Theia.

Lucien snorted. Like that was happening now.

Theia stayed behind him, watching Lucy from a few feet away. "I hadn't made up my mind."

"Well, if you don't mind a little unsolicited advice, I suggest you don't."

Lucien tried to turn, but Lucy held his shoulder—the one that was still sending out flares of pain.

"Oh?" Theia's voice was cool. "And why not?"

"I think it's a little beyond your abilities."

Lucien wanted to slug her, but her grip on his shoulder was firm.

"I mean, I'm sure you'll be a fine scientist someday, but this is serious work. It's not a graduate project."

"Give it a rest," Lucien growled under his breath.

"On the other hand, I hear you've already been in the White Room."

"The White Room?"

"Our special project. *Lucien*'s special project, really." She was yanking out cactus spines roughly to let him know she thought he'd overstepped his authority. "It's highly classified. Even the government doesn't know about it. But you...you know about it."

Theia stepped closer. "Is that some kind of threat?"

"Threat?" Lucy stopped plucking and turned to look up at Theia. "No, of course not. That's a little paranoid." She went back to her work. "It *is* a warning, however. I know you've signed our nondisclosure agreement. Not sure if you read the fine print."

Theia's voice hardened. "What fine print?"

"*Lucy,*" Lucien warned, but she ignored him.

"The fine print that says you've agreed to return any intellectual property you may have removed from the lab."

"I didn't take anything. What are you talking about?"

"Your memories." Lucy stood and dropped the tweezers into the case, turning to face Theia as Lucien rose, wanting to shut her up but not knowing how—and realizing as he stood that the room was spinning.

"And how exactly am I supposed to give back my memory of the visit?" Theia scoffed.

"We've developed a special technique."

Lucy had a syringe in her hand, and Lucien grabbed for it, but the floor seemed to tilt under him, and he grabbed her arm instead as he pitched toward the table.

Theia stepped in to steady him while Lucy regarded him with cold eyes, as if she would have let him fall. He'd fucked up, and he was on his own.

She stood back while Theia helped him into the chair. "I suppose you got your head knocked around by that delicious Viking."

"I may have hit my head on the concrete once or twice," he acknowledged.

"Are you having trouble seeing?"

"Not much." Things *had* been a little blurry.

"Not *much*?" Lucy shook her head. "Looks like you've earned yourself a pretty good concussion there, little brother. Someone's going to have to keep an eye on you overnight. And it's not going to be me. I have a date."

"Well, he's not staying *here*," Theia's sister objected from the doorway.

"I'm fine," Lucien insisted. "It's just a little vertigo and blurred vision." He stood again but couldn't seem to find the room's level.

Theia grabbed his arm once more. "I'll give you a ride home. I'd like to discuss this intellectual property issue a bit more, if you don't mind."

With both Rhea and the Viking now standing in the doorway, Lucy was reluctant to make a scene. Lips pressed together, she discreetly dropped the syringe back into her attaché case as she picked it up. "Suit yourself. But I warn you, he's a pain in the ass when he's convalescing."

"Thanks for all your help," Lucien said to her sweetly. "I think we can take it from here."

Lucy shrugged. "Get that bone checked tomorrow. And don't come crying to me if you slip into a coma."

"If I slip into a coma," said Lucien, "I promise you will be the last person to whom I come crying."

Lucy gave him a saccharine smile and headed for the door.

Theia's sister frowned at the two of them. "You sure about this, Thei?"

"No. But I'm doing it anyway." Theia picked up the crossbow and gave Lucien a stern look. "I'm going to hold on to this for you. If you can convince me you're not a danger to my family, maybe I'll give it back."

Leo stepped in the way as Theia led Lucien toward the door. "Don't come at me or mine again. Next time you won't be walking away, with or without assistance."

Lucien was too tired to argue with any of them. All he wanted to do was lie down and go to sleep. He let Theia walk him to her car without comment or protest, leaning back in the seat and closing his eyes once he was inside.

"I'm going to talk to Rhe for a minute," Theia said. "Don't fall asleep."

"That's not actually a thing," he murmured. "It's a myth that you shouldn't fall asleep after a concussion."

"I meant because we're going to have words. A lot of them." She slammed the car door, and Lucien wanted to grab his head to stop it from ringing, but his arms were too tired.

* * *

Theia glanced back at the car as she gathered the scattered arrows. Lucien might be dangerous, but his sister was definitely more so. She hadn't exactly been subtle in her threats. Smok Biotech might not literally have a way to wipe Theia's memory, but she wasn't about to give Lucy the chance.

The rhythmic snap of a pair of flip-flops announced Rhea's approach on the stone path. "You're not really going to give those weapons back to him?"

Theia straightened and put the last one in its quiver. "Not if he doesn't give me some satisfactory answers. But I'm sure he's got plenty more where these came from."

"He just tried to *kill* Leo."

"I know. I'm going to try to talk some sense into him about this obsession he has with Leo being a revenant."

"You realize there's a good chance that he's actually unhinged."

"Yeah."

"Want me to read that tattoo of his? I caught a peek from the doorway. Maybe we can verify his motives, see if any of this stuff about hunting down 'unnatural creatures' is true. And maybe find out a little more about him, if you know what I mean." Rhea raised an eyebrow suggestively.

Theia was 99 percent certain that whatever Rhea might read in Lucien's ink was the last thing she wanted her to see.

"Maybe some other time. I'm not sure how his mental state right now would affect it. And I'd prefer if we had his consent." Which Theia was going to make damn sure they never got.

Rhea studied her for a moment, her expression suspicious. "You call me when you get home. I want to know you're all right before I go to bed."

Theia booped Rhea's nose, guaranteed to distract her with aggravation. "You got it, Moonpie."

Rhea rubbed her nose with the back of her hand. "Gross. Weirdo. And stop calling me Moonpie."

Theia headed for her car. "But you look like a Moonpie."

"What does that even mean? I look like *you*."

"Go play with your Viking."

Theia tossed the quiver onto the back seat and climbed in. Lucien's eyes were closed, his head lolling against the headrest. Theia reached over to draw the shoulder belt across him and fasten it before starting the car. With a wave at Rhea, she headed out, only to realize once she'd exited the gates that she had no idea where Lucien lived.

"Lucien?" She nudged him gently. Nothing. God, he wasn't slipping into a coma already, was he?

His phone was propped in the cup holder under the dash. Maybe his address was in it. Theia pulled over and entered the password on the cracked screen and found the address in his contacts, committing it to memory. Before she set the phone down, a message notification appeared from Lucy. Theia couldn't resist taking a peek.

This one's for the little pixie girl.

Pixie girl? Theia glared at the screen and continued to read.

No doubt he's sitting next to you in the car snoring right now.

He was, a little bit, now that she listened for it.

Make sure you wake him up every two hours to check his responses. I don't like the blurred vision. If you can't wake him, call me. I'll send one of our doctors. Lovely to meet you. Finish our talk later.

Every two hours? She tried to respond, but the keyboard wasn't letting her press most of the keys. Theia sighed. She was going to have to take him to Phoebe's place. She'd left the house without feeding Puddleglum.

Someone was shaking him.

"We're here. Come on."

After a more vigorous shake, Lucien opened his eyes and focused on Theia's face. Still a little blurry. But eminently kissable. Shit. He was really out of it.

"Hey." She peered at him. "You awake? It's Theia Dawn. We're here. Time to get out."

Lucien looked around at the shrubbery laced with fairy lights in front of the cozy ranch-style bungalow. The night was silent except for the pleasant rhythm of chirping crickets, and the air was heavy with the perfume of jasmine blossoms. He was completely lost.

"Where's here?"

"My sister Phoebe's place. I'm cat sitting. And now apparently I'm babysitting. You," she clarified when he squinted at her in confusion. "Lucy told me to wake you up every two hours and check on you, so you're staying with me tonight."

"I thought Lucy left before we did. How long was I asleep?"

"About an hour. I let you sleep a little longer while I was feeding the cat. And she did leave before us."

"The cat?"

"*Lucy.*" Theia narrowed her eyes at him. "Are you sure I shouldn't take you to a hospital?"

Lucien rubbed his eyes. "No, I'm fine. I'm awake now." He tried to get out of the car, impeded by the seat belt, and finally managed to fumble in the dark and find the release. As he got to his feet, he groaned and clutched the door.

"Lucien?"

He stared at the ground for a moment, suddenly flushed, his forehead breaking out in a sweat. "I'm possibly going to throw up in your sister's front yard."

"Oh God. Please don't."

"I'd prefer not to." He stood still for several seconds, willing it down, and finally straightened. "Lead the way."

"To the bathroom?" she suggested as she took his arm.

"Sounds wise."

The ground tilted and swayed beneath him, echoing the motion of his stomach, as if he were navigating the deck of a ship on a choppy sea. He managed to make it to the little powder-blue room and close the door before pitching toward the floor once more. Lucien sank to his knees and grabbed the edge of the toilet, literally hugging the bowl as he dredged up what he was certain was every last thing he'd ever eaten.

By the time he was able to get to his feet and clean himself up, his head felt like someone had shaken his brain and bashed it against the inside of his skull—which he supposed was pretty accurate—but at least the dizziness and nausea had subsided.

Theia sat waiting for him in the living room when he

made his way gingerly down the hallway. "So where do you want to start?"

"Start?"

"Explaining yourself."

Lucien stepped down into the living room with a sigh and grabbed for the couch. "I already told you that Leo Ström is a revenant, and—"

"Except he's not. He was immortal. He was never a revenant. In Leo's tradition, I believe, revenants are known as *draugr*. Rhea dealt with one once when she was fighting to save his life. It was what you said—an abomination. A shuffling, inhuman monster that tried to suck out her soul before Leo's warden spirit destroyed it. Leo isn't a monster. He's a good man."

Lucien studied her for a moment. He'd put down a *draugr* or two. They were just about the most unpleasant creatures he'd ever encountered. But that didn't mean that every revenant raised from the corpse of a Norseman had to be a *draugr*. Valkyries had great power over the dead.

"Your sister said he was mortal."

Theia nodded. "He is. It was part of the Valkyrie's bargain with the Norns when she released him."

"But he leads a hunting party of wraiths."

"Yeah, you'll have to ask Rhea how that one works, because I haven't quite wrapped my head around it. But it doesn't make him a revenant. I'm sure Leo would be happy to explain it to you himself after you've apologized for trying to kill him."

Lucien leaned forward and rested his arms on his knees, looking down at the wood floor as he contemplated the facts. He couldn't let guilt or desire sway him. Cold, hard, rational facts were the enemy of the esoteric. The stupid. Of supernatural shit. And feelings.

He lifted his head sharply and regretted it. "Where's my gear? My crossbow?"

"I've put it away for safekeeping."

The tip of the arrow that had hit Leo Ström should have exploded on impact with flesh, leaving behind its poison. A revenant would have gone down within seconds, the unnatural blood in its veins turning to acid and eating it from the inside until there was nothing left of it. But Leo hadn't. The serum hadn't affected him at all. The arrow had only wounded him. Those were the cold, hard facts.

"I may have made an error."

Theia laughed, and he smiled without meaning to.

She shook her head, the red tips of her hair swinging. "Jesus, you're a stubborn son of a bitch." She leaned back against the cushion of the round rattan chair, looking like Venus in her scallop shell. Perhaps he'd hit his head harder than he thought. Theia's velvety gray eyes fixed on his, her gaze piercing. "So about that nondisclosure agreement."

Lucien rubbed his eyes. "Lucy didn't have any business bringing that up. She tends to get a bit aggressive when it comes to the company."

"Is that really what I signed? An agreement to have my memory wiped? Can she do that?"

"Yes." He shrugged. "No. And yes. The NDA does include a clause about not removing any intellectual property, but, legally, I think we'd be hard-pressed to make the case that you were agreeing not to leave with your memories intact if you chose to reject the offer. As for Lucy, well… I wouldn't turn my back on her if I were you."

"So there *is* a drug that can erase my memories of what I saw."

"And any memory that we've had this conversation about it, yes. But it's not my intention to implement that protocol."

Theia lifted an eyebrow. "You say the darnedest things."

"None of that's relevant, though, if you choose to accept the offer."

"Oh, I see. So *if* I agree to keep my mouth shut and help you with your little genome-mapping database, you won't physically assault me and tamper with my mind."

Lucien closed his eyes against the increasing intensity of his headache. "Can we... Do you mind if we continue this in the morning?" He could feel her gaze intent on him, studying him, perhaps to see if he was bullshitting her.

"Of course." Theia slipped from the shell-like chair and held out her hand to help him up as he opened his eyes. "Or in two hours. Whichever comes first."

"You're really going to wake me up every two hours?"

"Still have the blurred vision and vertigo?"

"No." Lucien reached for her hand and missed. "Yes."

"Then, yes, I am." Her hand closed around his. "I've made up the guest bed for you. Actually, I was sleeping in the guest bed, so I didn't really do anything but straighten it— Are you allergic to cats?"

He tried to follow her train of thought as he rose and went with her. "Allergic? No."

"Good, because Puddleglum pretty much thinks that room is his, and there's no way to get all the fur off the bedspread."

"I don't want to displace... Puddleglum? Or you, for that matter. I could sleep on the couch."

"That would be stupid. It's a two-bedroom house," She opened the guest room door. A well-fed tiger-stripe

Siamese regarded him from the center of the largest pillow with unblinking aquamarine eyes.

"That's his pillow," she said unnecessarily. "If you need anything, just let me know."

"Theia?"

She paused as she turned to go. "Hmm?"

"I'm not sure why you're being so nice to me after I…well, anyway. You don't have to be, and I appreciate that you are."

Theia wondered the same thing as she set the alarm in Phoebe's room. She could have ignored Lucy's instructions and driven him home. Yet here she was, preparing to interrupt her sleep every two hours to make sure Lucien's own arrogance didn't kill him.

But despite his misguided attack on Leo, she couldn't help being secretly pleased to learn there was more to Lucien than just a privileged rich boy for whom everything was a game—including seduction. If what he'd said was true, he'd taken a principled stand against his own family legacy. If Smok Consulting was in the business of covering up paranormal crimes for the wealthy, Lucien's clandestine efforts minimized the harm they caused in doing it. And Theia wanted to find out more about both.

Chapter 9

The alarm went off what seemed like minutes later. Theia rose bleary-eyed and shuffled down the hall to the guest room, where Puddleglum opened one suspicious eye from his perch on the pillow.

Lucien was hard to rouse, but he jolted awake when she put her hands on both shoulders to shake him. His hands closed around her upper arms, and he flipped her across his body onto her back on the bed and leaped over her on all fours, eyes looking slightly wild. Puddleglum disappeared under the bed.

It took Theia a moment to catch her breath and speak. "Lucien, it's me."

He blinked down at her, his feral stance slowly relaxing. "Sorry. I was deep in a dream. I was fighting off—"

"A thousand-year-old Viking who was kicking your ass?"

Lucien grinned sheepishly. "Something like that." He sat back on his heels, and she was intensely aware of his thighs—muscular and firm—on either side of hers. He might not be able to compete with Leo in size, but he was obviously extremely athletic. "So this is my two-hour wake-up, I take it."

"And I take it you're not in a coma."

"Not at the moment."

"And you know your own name."

"Of course. Anakin Skywalker."

"Interesting choice. Who's the president of the United States?"

Lucien scowled for a moment, pondering the answer. "Alec Baldwin?"

"Close enough. You're cleared for another two-hour nap." Theia waited for him to move, raising an eyebrow when he continued to stare down at her. "Are you going to get off me?"

Lucien seemed to color as he rolled onto his hip, but it was hard to be sure in the monochrome tones of the dark bedroom. Maybe it was just her imagination.

Theia turned to face him, head propped on her hand. "How long have you been…"

"Hunting unnatural creatures?" He considered for a moment. "It started by accident, I guess. High school. Junior year, on a job cleaning up a vamp den."

"As in *vampires*?"

"Yeah."

"They're real?"

"Everything's real."

A little shiver ran up her spine, and he must have noticed it.

"There's nothing sexy about them, I can assure you.

Every one I've ever met was as dumb as a post. They exist on instinct, feeding their hunger. If they're part of an organized brood, they're fairly harmless, only clever enough to follow orders. The master negotiates with sources and puts them to work delivering shipments, doing busywork, so they don't wander off and try to hunt on their own."

"Sources?"

"Blood sources. There are black-market blood banks… and voluntary donors."

Theia shuddered, this time with revulsion. She could just imagine how the "voluntary" donor system worked. Probably a lot like Carter Hamilton's afterlife sex ring, where the shades of dead sex workers were coerced into servicing clients who paid to have sex with someone being controlled by a "step-in."

"The business runs pretty smoothly," Lucien confirmed. "The syndicates keep everything relatively clean. But every so often, a bloodsucker goes rogue. Sometimes a handful of them will splinter off the brood and try to go it alone. That's when it gets messy. Which is when they call in Smok Consulting."

"Your father's company."

Lucien nodded. "Edgar didn't trust me to handle the consulting work. Probably rightly so."

"Edgar?"

"My father." He shrugged. "It turned out a rogue brood had been keeping a…" Lucien swallowed, his expression no longer neutral. "An illegal blood farm. Kids they'd taken off the street—junkies, runaways. There's a strict set of rules for voluntary donors—consent forms, maximum donations, minimum nondonation periods to make sure the donors remain healthy, a mental-health screening process—these kids bypassed all that. Probably traded sex—or even a willing donation if they were savvy enough about who they were dealing with—for a place to sleep for a night. And then found themselves being harvested...indefinitely."

Theia's gut twisted. "Jesus."

"Yeah. Some of them lasted..." Lucien's voice trailed off, and he swallowed again before going on. "A long time. I was supposed to be cleaning up corpses, and there was this kid, this little girl, maybe twelve years old, chained to a radiator. Vamp tracks up and down her arms...everywhere. She was supposed to be dead, but she moved."

Lucien's face had gone white. "God, she *moved*." He sat up and drew his knees to his chest, and Theia stared, transfixed, not wanting to hear any more but unable to stop him. "I called in the crew foreman to get her help. I stayed with her, told her it was going to be okay, she was safe now. And when the foreman showed up, he... put a bullet in her head."

"Oh my God. Lucien..."

He dropped his forehead to his knees and shuddered, and Theia sat up and put her arm around him, rubbing his shoulder, not sure what to do.

"I don't know why I told you that. I've never told anyone that. Not even Lucy."

"It wasn't your fault."

Lucien straightened and jerked away from her. "Of course it was my fault. I'm a Smok. That's what we do."

"You tried to help her."

Lucien laughed bitterly. "Yeah, and you see how that turned out."

"You were a kid yourself." Theia was pissed on his

behalf. "It's outrageous that your father would have put you in that situation. You were what, seventeen?"

"Sixteen. It doesn't matter."

"Of course it matters." She wasn't sure how to get him out of the dark place he'd descended to, and it seemed suddenly urgent and imperative that she did. "And that was when you got started with your own hunting? At sixteen?" The calm questioning seemed to work. The shadow in Lucien's eyes faded.

"Not right away. It was just the catalyst. I asked what was going to happen to the bloodsuckers who were responsible, and my father said their sire would deal with them. It's not good for business to have rogues on the loose, so they'd likely be put down." His affect had changed, his words now emotionless, as though he'd dissociated. "I couldn't stop thinking about it, so I decided to look for them and find out for sure. I used a fake ID and signed up as a donor."

Theia gaped at him. "But you didn't actually…"

"Of course I did. The ID said I was eighteen, the minimum age allowed. They paid by the hour. You could do a private donation with a single patron for fifty dollars an hour, or you could go to a party and be available on tap. Five hundred a night."

"On tap? Not a literal…"

"No, though that's not unheard of. Mostly with fetishists. Groupies. But this was purely a financial transaction. I signed up for a party. There were two other donors, both girls who looked like minors. I thought it would be like the movies, with everybody at a cocktail party, lots of velvet, vamps biting us on the neck." A slight, embarrassed smile animated his face for an instant and was gone. "But it was way less glamorous. Apparently the telltale wound draws too much attention for donors, and it's dangerous anyway. Too easy—and too tempting—to drain the donor dry. They needed access to less visible veins. We stripped down to our underwear. The girls were topless."

Lucien's expression had gone flat. "The party was in a hotel suite. We were told to circulate—that got some big laughs—and the vamps started feeding on us as we moved around the sitting room. We all tried to make small talk at first, but they weren't interested in us as people. We were food. The girls were more popular, and one of them ended up passing out because they drained her too quickly. They carried the other one off to the bedroom, and three of the vamps stayed in the outer room with me and pulled out the sofa bed. Apparently, they prefer to feed lying down."

Theia rested her hand on his wrist, wanting to stop him, but he seemed determined now to get it out.

"When they'd had their fill, they got a little more talkative, and I managed to turn the conversation to the rogues, pretending I was a groupie and I wanted to be owned. I said it was a shame they were gone, but one of the bloodsuckers told me they'd just relocated. He gave me an address, a ranch. I was taking archery at school, and I showed up at the ranch the next morning with my bow loaded with Soul Reaper arrows—the kind I had tonight, to split the demon from the undead frame and send the soul to hell. And I staked every last one of them while they were sleeping." Lucien shrugged, as if the last part had been incidental. "Didn't do anything like that again until I was in college."

Theia was at a total loss for words.

"I've talked your ear off." Lucien had been staring at

the wall, and he turned his head to look at her with an apologetic smile, but the smile faltered. "You're crying."

Theia put her fingers to her cheek. "I am?" She was. She hadn't even noticed. "I'm sorry." She wasn't sure exactly what she was apologizing for. The tears were coming faster.

"Theia. Don't." He reached out to her, taking the hand she was still holding in front of her, tears on her fingertips. "I didn't tell you that to play on your emotions."

"I know you didn't. It's just...my gift."

"Your gift?"

"It comes with the visions. Sometimes instead of images, I pick up on other people's emotions." She shrugged, again apologetic. It always seemed like a bit of an intrusion, and one she usually kept to herself. "These aren't my tears."

She could feel it now, like a physical blow to her soul. Lucien was in pain. Torn up inside as much as he was bruised and battered outside from his fight with Leo. More so, probably.

He squeezed her hand, wordless, shocked, and didn't deny it.

Theia started crying in earnest. "Okay, maybe they're a little bit mine, too." She grabbed for the tissues on the nightstand, but Lucien reached for her, stopping her. His hands went to either side of her face, thumbs brushing away the tears, and he lowered his mouth to hers and kissed her.

Every dark warning she'd ever dreamed was rising to the surface, threatening to engulf her. He was mystery. He was danger. There would be no turning back if she dived into these waters. There was no telling how deep they were or what was hiding in them. But she didn't care. She wanted to drown in him. His kiss was like air beneath the dark waves. As long as she breathed through him, she would survive. Theia threaded her arms through his, hooked them around his neck and let go, giving herself to the deep. The relief at no longer fighting was immediate and intense. She was immersed.

Lucien made a soft sound of pain, and it took her a moment to realize it was physical.

Theia drew back. "Your shoulder?"

"I think I may have sprained it a bit."

"Maybe next time be more aware of who you're going after."

Lucien nodded and lay back on the bed, pulling Theia with him. "I solemnly swear only to hunt actual revenants and demons from now on." He wrapped her in his arms and started to kiss her again, but Theia hesitated. Lucien frowned. "What's the matter?"

"About the demons…"

He stroked his hand down Theia's side. "What about demons?"

Theia grabbed his wrist and pulled his hand away with a scowl. "You've threatened certain members of my family. I need to know if you're still planning to harm them."

"You consider them your family."

"Absolutely. They're both my brothers-in-law, but they were family long before that."

Lucien cocked his head. "I thought Phoebe was the only one who was married."

"Apparently Dev and Ione eloped. No one is supposed to know. But that's beside the point."

She'd gestured with her hand, and Lucien took hold of it and kissed it. "Tell me about Dev, then. Is he possessed or isn't he?"

Theia sighed. "He's not. Technically. He was bound to a demon by a sorcerer he was apprenticed to. The demon was tortured and forced to occupy Dev's physical form as though it were a cage. Dev nearly died. He didn't even know what his mentor had done to him until after he woke up in the hospital and something triggered the demon's release for the first time. Dev has it under control now. They've come to an understanding, and the demon is contained by a magical sigil tattooed on his body."

"An understanding." Lucien scowled. "How do you come to an understanding with a demon? It's a monster. A killer."

"Kur is actually very sweet once you get to know him."

"*Kur?* The demon has a name? And you've met this abomination?"

"I have. And please stop using the word *abomination*. It makes you sound like a hellfire-and-brimstone preacher."

Lucien laughed. "My great-grandfather was a hellfire-and-brimstone preacher, as a matter of fact."

"Well, that's delightful." The touch of his skin, his hand holding hers, was distracting, but she didn't want to let go. "Listen, why don't you just meet with Dev? Let him tell you about Kur. Maybe he'll even let you meet Kur so you can see for yourself. He's not an abomination, I promise you."

Lucien seemed to consider it seriously. "If you want to arrange a meeting," he said at last, "I promise to hear Dev out—but I'll make up my own mind about the demon."

It was a start. "Now, about Rafe."

Lucien groaned and rested his forehead against hers. "Can we talk about him in the morning? I've only had two hours' sleep, and there's a beautiful woman in my bed, and everything hurts."

She smiled reluctantly, her cheeks warm. "I would, except…" She glanced at the window behind him. Pale streaks of gold and pink were visible on the horizon, peeking between the tips of the spires of Cathedral Rock in the distance.

"Except what?"

"It's already morning."

Lucien turned and followed her gaze. "Well, damn." He rolled onto his back with a slight wince. "Can I have my two hours anyway? Or do I get kicked out at dawn?"

Theia curled against his side with her head on his chest. "I'll tell you when I wake up."

Lucien tightened his arm around her and closed his eyes. "Tell me I'm not still lying in the gravel getting my head kicked in and you're not some fevered hallucination that will disappear when I open my eyes."

Theia yawned. "I'm pretty sure I'm not a hallucination. But you did hit your head pretty hard."

Chapter 10

When Lucien woke again, a cat was in Theia's place. It figured. Even though he knew this was the infamous Puddleglum, it would be just his luck if Theia were a shape-shifter. Puddleglum sat staring at him like some infernal imp, blinking knowingly as if to say, "Takes one to know one, buddy."

Theia saved Lucien from imminent hypnotism and enslavement by returning with coffee and a box of doughnuts.

"Thank God." Lucien sat up and took the cup she handed him. "I think your cat was plotting the trajectory to my jugular. I was playing dead, but I think he was onto me."

Theia grinned. "He's way too lazy to bother with live prey. He'd just sit there and wait you out until you died of starvation and then eat your corpse. And probably stalk off in a huff because you weren't the right texture."

Lucien took a powdered doughnut from the box with a little offended sniff as Theia climbed into bed and displaced the cat. "I assure you, my texture is everything it ought to be."

"I take it you're feeling better." She examined the eye that had been nearly swollen shut the night before. "I thought I'd let you sleep. I figured it would do you some good."

"Let me sleep?" Lucien took a bite of his doughnut. "What time is it?"

"One o'clock."

Lucien inhaled powdered sugar and nearly choked. "In the afternoon? Damn. I have to go." He kissed her and stuffed the rest of the doughnut in his mouth as he rolled out of bed as gingerly as possible while still maintaining a modicum of masculine dignity. The sharp sting from the cuts and scrapes and cactus spines had given way to an all-over throbbing ache and muscle stiffness.

"Go where? It's Saturday."

He couldn't exactly tell her he had a date with his ex-girlfriend to express his "gratitude" for the information she'd given him about Leo. "I have to meet with a client at two." He kept his head down over his coffee cup, hating that he was already lying to her. This was the other problem with having feelings for someone.

Theia set down her cup and got up. "Your car's at Rafe's. I'll have to drive you. I don't think you should be driving with your vision messed up, anyway."

He'd forgotten he'd left his car. There was no time to go across town to get it and still meet Polly by two. And she was very unforgiving of people who made her wait.

"I can have a car pick me up."

"Lucien, I'm right here with a car right now. What's

the big deal? I can wait in the parking lot while you meet your client."

If he made this an even bigger deal, she was going to get suspicious. "You promise you'll stay in the car? It shouldn't take long." He crossed his fingers behind his back, praying to whatever forces controlled the universe that Polly wasn't going to want something he couldn't give her with Theia waiting outside.

Lucien was moving like an old man, and the broken bone in his arm was starting to feel stiff and cold as the ectoplasmic gel Lucy had injected began to solidify. It wasn't intended as a long-term fix.

Theia pulled into the parking lot at Polly's, obviously curious but not asking any questions, and Lucien drew himself up straight to walk in with his usual casual aplomb. It took every ounce of control he had.

Polly's hair was blue today, clipped up in a loose fall of sapphire curls. Seated at the bar reviewing the books, she glanced up at his entrance and let her gaze wander over him with amusement.

"Just coming from goth yoga, are we? Where's your mat?"

"Very funny."

"Oh, wait, I know...you left her in the car." She glanced up at the television over the bar, tuned to a closed-circuit security camera on the parking lot.

Lucien slid onto the stool beside her with manufactured grace. "Jealousy, Pols? Aren't you above that?"

"I wouldn't call it jealousy. I'm just looking out for you, sweetie. I warn you about her, and the next thing I know, she's chauffeuring you around town. In the clothes you obviously slept in. And apparently were mauled by a bear in." Polly scrutinized him more closely, touching his puffy eye with a metallic-teal fingertip. "Took him a while to go down, did it?"

Lucien picked up the highball she was drinking and tossed it back. "He didn't go down."

"You're kidding. Your fancy arrows didn't work?"

"He was human, as it turns out."

Polly covered her mouth, trying not to giggle—and not trying very hard. "Oh, no. Oh, Lucien."

"Did you know?"

Polly didn't answer right away, reaching over the bar with her ass in the air to get the bottle of bourbon and refill the glass. "How would I know? He hasn't been in here in years. He certainly wasn't a human then. At least not a mortal one. I guess he broke the curse." She took a sip and smiled, savoring it in her mouth. "You asked for information on the Valkyrie. I got you a Valkyrie so you could get it straight from the horse's mouth. I can't help it if you didn't ask her the right questions."

"I'm so glad this is amusing for you."

"Oh, come on, sweetie. I'm sorry." Polly kissed his cheek, her lips damp with bourbon. "You really took a beating, didn't you? And the girl? The psychic sidekick? Does she know how you got hurt?"

Lucien turned the bottle on the bar, feigning interest in the label. "Theia isn't psychic, as it turns out. She's an empath."

"Lucien." Polly moved the bottle out of his grasp, all teasing gone. "You're playing with fire. I'm the one who picked you up out of your own vomit when you couldn't stand to stay sober long enough to have an emotion. She'll end up knowing everything about you. Things you don't even know. That self-loathing that eats away at you that you manage to project as cockiness and arrogance, the fear that made you run away from Edgar and his ice-in-his-veins ideas about family and duty straight into my bed." Polly smiled sadly and lifted his chin. "Your Maggie May. All of that is going to be laid bare to her. You might as well be walking around without skin, waiting for her throw salt on your raw flesh."

"I don't need you to tell me that."

"Don't you?" Polly turned his chin toward her and shook her head. "Poor baby. I wish I could give you immortality, make you immune to human weaknesses like love."

"You know I don't want to be inhuman."

"Oh, I know that, sweetie. Which is what makes your path so much harder. Be careful, sweet boy. She'll break your heart."

"I didn't come here for a lecture. I came to thank you for the information you facilitated—as unfortunately inaccurate as it turned out to be. You wanted me to meet you here, and I'm here. So what do you want?"

Polly turned her wrist, the jewels in her charm bracelet catching the light. "I was going to ask for a drop of blood." She fingered a garnet teardrop. "But just look at you." She shook her head and sighed. "Considering what's waiting for you outside, I suppose I'd better have what you gave her."

Lucien's brows drew together. "What I gave her?"

"A tear, sweetie. Before she drains you of all of them." Polly held her finger to the corner of his eye and a tear fell onto her fingertip as if commanded, solidifying into something that strongly resembled a diamond. "Lovely, isn't it? The devil's tears. It'll be worth a pretty penny one day."

Chapter 11

Lucien was quiet. Theia didn't ask what the meeting was about. After what he'd told her last night, she wasn't sure she wanted to know. She drove him to his car, which he insisted he was okay to drive home. He needed a shower, he said, and some more rest, but he'd see her later.

Theia wasn't sure what later meant, precisely, but he kissed her goodbye, and the kiss was promising. In the meantime, she was going to burst if she didn't talk to someone about what had happened between her and Lucien. She needed sisterly advice, but there was no way she could talk to Rhea about him after what he'd done. Ione had raised them after their parents were killed in a car accident, and Theia wasn't in the mood for her disapproval. Phoebe would have been perfect—she was always easiest to talk to—but Phoebe was somewhere in the Yucatán climbing pyramids and getting laid by a demigod.

But Theia hadn't talked to Laurel in a while.

Laurel Carpenter was their half sister, one of three born to their father's secret second wife.

Rhea wouldn't be happy about it, but despite Laurel's past sins against them as Carter Hamilton's apprentice, Theia considered her a friend. Laurel had grown up in foster care, unaware of her own magic and resenting the half sisters who'd gotten all her father's attention. She'd been ripe for Carter's head games. Theia couldn't hold that against her.

She needed to pop into her apartment in Flagstaff anyway to get some materials for the final exams for a class she was teaching, and Laurel, it turned out, was more than ready to take a break from studying for her own.

As they set out the tea things on Theia's balcony, Laurel watched her, cautious as always. "I guess you've heard about Carter's conviction being overturned. In case you're wondering, no, he hasn't contacted me, and no, I have no interest in ever speaking to him again."

"I did hear, actually." Theia grimaced. "When he magically crashed Phoebe's wedding reception."

"Oh, shit. He didn't."

"Sadly, he did. But don't worry. That's not why I called you. Although I do have a bit of an ulterior motive." Theia grinned as she poured the tea. "To be honest, there are some things I can't talk to anybody else about, and I really need some advice."

"From me?" Laurel set out the plate of homemade lemon bars she'd brought. "I'm not sure what advice I could possibly give you."

"I've had these visions lately—one in particular that I've had since I was little." Theia sat and took a lemon bar. "I think it started when I heard a story in church about being the bride of Christ. The priest said if we weren't Christ's, we would be the devil's. I dreamed I was wearing a red wedding gown and veil and running from someone hiding in the shadows. The faster I ran, the closer the figure got, until I realized I was running straight to hell. At the end of the path was a throne. And the dark figure that had been chasing me was sitting on it and holding out his hand."

"And now you think you've met the dark figure."

Theia shivered despite the balmy weather. "Bingo. You're good."

Laurel smiled as she stirred sugar into her cup. "You know I see things, too." Laurel's gift was a true ability to see the future without all the interpretation Theia's visions required.

"So…what exactly have you seen?"

"It's not always perfectly clear, you understand. I see future events like they're on a layer of film laid over the top of what's in front of me, and right now… I see some kind of contract in your hand."

"And?"

Laurel set down the spoon and smoothed her fingers over her closely cropped hair. "And I think it says you've promised the devil your soul."

"Ah."

"I take it you were hoping for something a little less literal."

"Well, it is very specific. The thing is, this man I met…there's more to him than this 'dark prince' persona he shows the world. I guess I was hoping I was imagining things. It wouldn't be the first time I've avoided getting close to someone because of my dreams. But I…"

The look on Laurel's face when she glanced up made her pause. "What?"

Laurel colored. "It's not important. Sometimes I get flashes of events that aren't any of my business."

It was Theia's turn to blush. "I'm going to sleep with him, aren't I?" She groaned into her hands for a moment before looking up again. "See, this is another thing I can't talk to Rhea about. As close as we are, I've never told her that… I've never actually…done it."

Laurel's eyes widened over her cup.

"Yeah." Theia lifted her shoulders helplessly. "I've been having visions all my life, and every time I got involved with a guy, I'd see something about him that just, I don't know, made me think the devil was around every corner. And I don't even believe in a literal devil. Of course, with the things we've seen lately, I don't even know what to believe. And Lucien—that's the guy—has been telling me about a whole underground society of 'unnatural creatures,' things I had no idea were real."

"I see it," said Laurel. "That underbelly. Things no one else sees. Until I met Carter, I thought I must be schizophrenic or something when I'd see shades and ghosts. I was afraid to tell anyone when I was in the foster system, so I just kept it to myself."

Theia glanced at her, impressed. "I didn't know you could see ghosts. It's good to know I have another sister I can turn to for supernatural help."

Laurel paused with her cup halfway to her mouth. "You think of me as a sister?"

Theia couldn't help but laugh. "Well, not to state the obvious, but we *are* sisters. Just because we didn't grow up together doesn't mean we aren't."

Laurel set down her cup, visibly moved. "I've never

really had a sister before. I know that sounds funny, but Rowan and Rosemary always seemed so much older than me. When our mom died, we went to separate foster homes, and we lost touch." Laurel shrugged. "Nobody's ever needed my advice. About anything."

Theia smiled. "Well, I do. Do you have any?"

"I don't exactly have the greatest track record. I mean, the last guy I was into was, you know. Ugh."

Theia poked at the crumbs of her lemon bar. "That's kind of the advice I want. How do you know when you're into someone who's not good for you? Should I run away from this? Or toward it?"

"I guess you have to trust your instincts. I didn't trust mine. I was looking for external validation because I didn't believe in myself. And now—I mean, I'm still struggling with that, but I'd never fall for someone like Carter today. He only told me what I wanted to hear."

The question was, what was it Theia wanted to hear? That Lucien wasn't dangerous? That he wasn't the Prince of Darkness after all? Or was she looking for someone to tell her it was okay if she sold her soul to the devil?

Lucien stood in the shower with his head bowed under the water, letting it pour over him. Every muscle in his body ached, and the broken bone felt like it had been replaced with solidified latex polymer, like rubber cement that had been left out with the cap off. Using it was going to become more difficult if he didn't see the company doctor soon.

When he emerged at last, the corner of an envelope poked out from under his door. After towel-drying his hair and wrapping the towel around his waist, Lucien bent to pick up the envelope. His body protested. Inside was the same URL his source had sent before. Had he missed something last time? Lucien looked at the Carlisle family tree once more, still baffled by what this had to do with hunting rogues. He already had the information the source had provided on Rafael Diamante and Dharamdev Gideon.

But there was something here he hadn't seen before. A document had been added to the family records, some kind of research paper on recessive genes.

As he examined it, he realized it was Theia's research on her own family, documenting her discovery of her father's polygamy—a second wife he'd taken in secret without divorcing the first. Lucien started to feel uncomfortable. How was this a public document? Maybe he should just close it and forget about it.

But something farther down the page caught his eye. Theia had discovered a genetic mutation. *Lilith blood*, she called it.

Lucien's own blood ran cold. According to Madeleine Marchant's claim, she'd been descended from the first demoness. Lucien had never believed it. But Theia had written this history as though it was fact. If her research was accurate, the demon blood was real, and all the Carlisle sisters possessed it. Their magical abilities, their gifts of vision and prognostication and communicating with spirits—they were all aspects of the demoness. The Carlisle sisters weren't just the gifted descendants of a powerful witch, they were literally part demon. *Theia* was part demon.

Chapter 12

Lucien stared at the laptop, trying to get a grip on the sudden rage filling him. He'd given her the benefit of the doubt despite her sisters' penchants for unnatural men—and now here it was, a confession in her own words that she herself was unnatural, that she was the worst kind of unnatural. Theia was what he'd been trying to escape his entire life. In fleeing Edgar and his stupid rules, Lucien had been fleeing the stain of the demonic—the Smok legacy: that he was doomed to serve in hell. Though the story had seemed allegorical when he was younger, it had become more theoretically probable once he'd been initiated into the family business.

The family made its money fulfilling the needs of demons and unnatural beings, hobnobbed with them, protected them. It had begun to seem unlikely that the legend was only that. By the time Lucien had started college, he'd been bitterly determined not to become what his father wanted him to be, what he was trying to make him into. He'd tried to drown his fears with drink—and then he'd met Polly. He'd followed the song of the siren, jumping headfirst into the world he'd been resisting.

It was a double standard, but becoming a slacker who hung out almost exclusively with inhuman and unnatural beings had been another kind of rebellion. Doing business with such creatures was one thing. One did not *party* with them, as Edgar had once told him in disgust. And they sure as hell didn't sleep with them.

Lucien had lost himself in that world for a time, not caring what fate meant him to be and not caring if he became it. If his father found it distasteful, then Lucien would wallow in it. And Polly had been more than happy to help him in that endeavor. Though she'd been less enthusiastic when he'd decided to hunt rogue unnaturals. Polly brooked no nonsense in her club. Any unnatural creature that tried to do business there involving humans without their consent was summarily tossed out on its ass. But hunting them down was something else altogether.

Avenging the little girl he'd found at the blood farm had been an act of grief and rage. But the first time he'd taken out a rogue in cold blood had been intensely clarifying. He'd found his calling. Eventually, it replaced his need to wallow in vice, and he'd moved on, parting ways with Polly amicably enough. He'd told himself then he was through being ruled by his fate, and he intended to dedicate his life to resisting it. And that meant staying clean in terms of unnatural contact—which included anyone not fully human. His vow had hurt Polly, though she would not admit it.

And until now, Theia hadn't threatened that. He'd resisted his feelings for her because of the inadvisability of entanglements, but this morning he'd allowed himself the luxury of ignoring his own rules. And despite his doubts about her family—and about himself—kissing Theia had felt very right. He'd never felt so instantly at home with anyone. From the moment his lips had met hers, he'd felt as though he'd been broken, missing something, and now he was whole. He hadn't wanted to talk; he'd wanted to touch her mouth, taste her skin, run his fingers over every inch of her and explore this wondrous thing that had happened.

But now…now she was the goddamn enemy. This was fate's cruel trick, getting him to let down his guard and share himself with someone—when fate had been steering him toward that someone all along. More than just Madeleine Marchant's descendant, she was the embodiment of Madeleine's curse. "Blood for blood," the witch's last words had been before the pyre was lit. She seemed to be mocking him from the grave. He couldn't escape.

Lucien slammed his fist into the laptop screen and shattered the LCD. Stupid, but momentarily satisfying. He'd once surrendered fully to the darkness and the deep to spite his father, willfully drowning himself in the seamy underbelly of the world Edgar inhabited only on the periphery. And now he was drowning again—only this time it was an unwitting submersion.

The question was: Who wanted him to know? Polly? Was this her way of trying to warn him away from Theia? But she'd done so directly earlier today. Why bother with cryptic game playing? And if she'd known this detail about Theia's blood, why not just mention it outright when they spoke? No, this wasn't Polly's style. Someone else was apparently as interested in his fate as he was.

His phone buzzed, and he remembered the screen was shattered on that as well. But at least it was still readable. It was Theia, wanting to know what his plans were for the rest of the day. Their conversation was still unfinished. She'd wanted a chance to persuade him of Rafe's "worthiness."

Lucien realized he couldn't respond. The screen was readable, and a few of the apps were responsive if he pressed hard enough, but he couldn't get the keyboard or the number pad to work. He supposed it was just as well. Let her think what she wanted about why he didn't text back. It was a coward's resolution to the situation, but Lucien was tired, in his head and in his bones, the aches and pains from last night's disaster demanding his attention. The decision was out of his hands. Fate had once again intervened.

Mindful of the bruises on his backside, Lucien flopped onto his stomach on the bed and fell asleep.

He wasn't expecting to find Theia standing on his doorstep when he awoke from his nap.

He'd answered the door half-asleep, the towel he'd wrapped around his waist barely tucked in, not quite registering that he was answering a door and not a telephone.

There was Theia. He'd been dreaming about her. What was the dream about?

Lucien rubbed his eyes. "Theia?"

"You weren't answering my texts, and then I remembered your phone was broken so I thought I'd stop by on my way back from Flagstaff."

"Flagstaff?" He was drawing a blank on what she was talking about. Or what day it was. "What time is it?" It was dark out but not fully.

Theia laughed, and the sound tugged at his heart even as something else about her was filling him with anxiety. "It's 7:30. I drove to my place in Flagstaff to get some things and I was heading back to feed Puddleglum. I told you in my text…which of course you didn't get."

"No, I got…something." He was starting to remember.

Theia gave him an amused smile. "Are you going to invite me in?"

An invitation. It was how one let in vampires. And the devil. Lucien shrugged and held the door wide. His towel slipped off, and he managed to catch it and tie it back on as she entered.

Theia's cheeks went charmingly pink, but she frowned at his reticence. "Did I do something wrong? You seem upset."

"I'm not upset." Of course he was upset. He wanted to scream at the universe and punch the Fates in the face. Theia had demon blood. And she smelled like sunshine and citrus, and he just wanted to kiss her and shut his brain up.

On the coffee table, the laptop displayed its spiderweb of bleeding crystal behind the cracked screen.

Theia glanced at it and back at him. "Lucien? Is everything okay?"

"Yeah. No." He closed the door and sighed. "You didn't tell me about your history."

"My history?" Theia stared at the broken screen once more. Enough was visible through the bleeding colors to know what he'd been looking at when he smashed it. She looked up, her smile gone. "Is that my research? How did you get that? That's private."

"It's not important how I got it."

"The hell it isn't. Have you been investigating me?"

Lucien folded his arms. "No. But I should have. You're not human."

Theia's face blazed with anger. "Of course I'm goddamn human. Who the hell do you think you are, anyway?"

"I don't know, Theia. I honestly don't. But I know I'm not a demon." No matter what the family legend said. "And after last night, I'm sure you know how I feel about demons."

"I'm not a demon, either. I'm the distant relative of Madeleine Marchant. Maybe you've heard of her. It seems your family and mine go back a long way."

"So *you've* been investigating *me*."

"Damn right I have been. When you showed up at Phoebe's wedding acting completely full of yourself and trying to tempt me with the position at Smok Biotech, you may recall you told me to ask Rafe about your family. What information did you expect him to give me?"

Lucien faltered. He'd forgotten he'd encouraged her to talk to Rafe. God, what had Rafe told her? What did Rafe even know?

"I expected him to tell you about what Smok Consulting does, how he and his family have contracted us a number of times. It was a reference."

"Well, he didn't have time to give me a reference. He was leaving on his honeymoon. So he gave me his father's papers. And Rafael Sr. apparently collected old Covent records. *Very* old ones."

"So you know." The realization tied his stomach in knots. She had utterly turned the tables on him, and he had no defense. "You know what my family did."

"You mean that they essentially owned mine."

Lucien blinked at her in confusion. "Owned? They

were Madeleine Marchant's patrons, if that's what you mean."

"So they received her *property* when she was burned at the stake. Including her daughters. They became the wards of the Vicomte de Briançon, who sold them off to his cronies."

This was something Lucien had never heard. There was only one daughter he knew about. The one who'd married the vicomte's youngest son.

"You didn't know about that." Theia studied him. "So what were *you* talking about? What did your family do?"

Lucien rubbed his hand over his mouth, smoothing his fingers over his stubble. Hell. Might as well just tell her. Everything was fucked anyway.

"The vicomte's family—his wife—denounced Madeleine Marchant."

After a stunned silence, Theia lowered herself to the couch. "Wow."

"It was apparently a not-uncommon practice. A way for noblemen to steal what little their vassals had. Unless their families could prove to have had no knowledge of the witchcraft, the belongings of the accused went to their patrons by default to pay for the execution." Lucien shrugged helplessly. "I'm sorry."

Unexpectedly, Theia began to laugh.

"What in the world is funny about that?"

"Everything. This entire fight. I'm supposed to be mad at you because of something some people who were distantly related to us did over five hundred years ago? I mean, it's ridiculous. You're apologizing for the Vicomte de Briançon."

Her laugh was infectious, and Lucien had to lower his eyes to keep from smiling. It *was* ridiculous, but she was still a demon. And she was still part of the curse Madeleine had put on his family.

Theia's laughter subsided. "But you're still mad at me."

Lucien looked up. "I'm not mad at you. I'm mad at the universe. I mean, yes, I'm angry that you kept the fact that you have demon blood from me—"

"I thought you knew. You're the one who brought up my tattoo at the wedding and kept talking about blackmail and witches."

"Your tattoo…"

Theia held out her arm. "You called it the mark of Lilith. You obviously knew about Madeleine's claim."

"Her claim, yes, but not what it meant for her descendants. Not about the Lilith blood and the generations of seven sisters."

"And now that you do, I suppose I'm on your list." Theia rose, her gray eyes darkening. "Should I watch my back, Lucien? What would one of those arrows do to me?"

"I would never come after you."

"Oh, well, that's a relief. You know what? You can take the job at Smok Biotech and shove it up your ass." She brushed past him, reaching for the door, but Lucien grabbed her arm, and tears spilled over her cheeks.

"Don't go."

Theia looked up at him, miserable. "Why?"

He was too close to her. His skin touching hers. It would enhance any empathic vibrations she was picking up. Polly had warned him to stay away. His own instincts had warned him. She could read him now. He was an open book.

"Because I need you," he said simply and drew her into his arms. "I don't want to, but I do."

Theia's tears were still falling. "Then I guess I'm insulted and flattered."

Lucien laughed, the release of tension he needed, and kissed her.

It was a mistake. All of it was a mistake. But right now it felt like the most delicious mistake he'd ever made. Screw the Fates and his own infernal blood.

Theia tasted like lemon drops, and her hair smelled like violets, and nothing mattered. Lucien had been with his share of women—he hadn't been kidding when he'd bragged to her at the reception about the effect the Smok name seemed to have on some—but he'd never felt anything like the jumbled-up confection of desire and nervous excitement and worry and affection and, yes, *need* that was threading through his veins as he drank her in. He gathered her to him like she was a figurine made of glass, delicate and hard at once. He couldn't stop touching her, stroking her arms and her hair, holding her face between his hands as he kissed her deeper and with greater desperation until he finally had to let her go to breathe.

Theia's skin was flushed and her pupils dilated, her eyes shining as liquid danced in them in the dim light of the one lamp he'd fumbled on as he'd made his way to the door.

Lucien stroked his thumb across her still-damp cheek. "These are yours, right?"

Theia laughed weakly. "I think so. Unless kissing me makes you sad."

Lucien smiled. "It does not." He kissed her again to prove it, this time less desperately, lingering over the texture and taste of her lips. "You taste like lemon candy," he murmured against them, and Theia laughed again.

"Laurel made lemon bars. I had them with tea."

"Laurel?"

"My sister. My *half* sister."

"You have a half sister?"

"Three of them."

"Three…"

Theia nodded. "And four makes seven."

That little feeling of alarm was back, rattling against the walls of his skull, but Lucien wasn't about to give it free rein. Not now.

"I guess you didn't read through all of my research." Her body had gone tense.

Lucien was determined to drive the tension out. He let his hand slip down her arm and wordlessly led her to the bedroom. Sitting on the edge of the bed, he drew her onto his lap and kissed the back of her neck beneath the little point of hair at the center of her bob.

"What are you doing?" she murmured, softer already.

"Tasting you."

Theia shivered delightfully.

Lucien was only wearing a towel, and there was no way of hiding what that shiver did to him. The little moan she followed it up with only made things worse.

He wrapped his arms around her, stroking hers once more. "I like touching you."

"I can see that." Theia's arms crossed over his.

Lucien chuckled. "Well, I don't think you can see it, exactly. Not yet." He pressed his lips to her nape once more and began working his way toward the front, lingering in that spot just beneath the hollow of her jaw.

"Lucien." Theia's voice was a soft gasp.

He tucked her hair behind her ear and licked her earlobe. "Hmm?"

"I should probably…tell you something."

Lucien shook his head, planting more kisses along her collarbone as he peeled back the edge of her shirt. "You don't have to tell me anything."

"I think you might want to know…this thing." Theia gasped again and grabbed his hand as it slid downward between her legs, not pulling it back but not letting him move it any farther. "I think you might *need* to know it."

"What is it? Is something wrong?"

"Not wrong, exactly. It's just that, well…" Theia cleared her throat. "I'm a virgin."

Chapter 13

She waited for Lucien to laugh or for things to get awkward. Guys generally had one of two reactions to this announcement: pulling away or pressuring her. But Lucien did neither.

He kissed her neck again. "So?"

"That's...not a problem for you?"

"I guess it depends on what you want to do about it."

"Well, I... I'm not sure." Theia turned to look at him, and he caught her mouth in a kiss that made her forget what they were talking about.

After a moment, Lucien moved his mouth to her neck once more, nuzzling beneath her ear. "You don't have to decide right now, if that's what you're worried about. I just want you near me. We can just cuddle. Or I could..."

"Could...what?"

Lucien smiled, a devious little upturn to one corner of his mouth. "I could keep tasting you."

"Oh." Theia felt her whole body blush, heat rising in her skin for a multitude of reasons. She could also feel his heat beneath the towel. It wasn't that she hadn't gone that far before—she had, once or twice—it was how much she suddenly wanted him to that was making her flushed.

Lucien slid her off his lap onto the bed and ran his fingers along the hem of her T-shirt. "Can I take this off?"

Theia nodded and let Lucien draw the fabric up, lifting her arms so he could pull it over her head. He tossed the shirt on the floor, tracing her curves through the thin barrier of her bra. Fortunately, she'd worn a nice one, black mesh lace with a halter closure. Theia closed her eyes, clutching the edge of the bed, as Lucien lowered his head and closed his mouth over the fabric, the heat and damp of his tongue making a mess of it.

She opened her eyes with a whimper of disappointment when he let go, but he'd dropped to his knees and was staring up at her with his hands at the button of her jeans. "These, too?"

Theia nodded again, not trusting her voice, raising herself off the bed as he unbuttoned them and worked them off and down, pausing to take off her canvas flats. He positioned himself between her legs with his hands against her thighs, looking like a Roman centurion in his towel, and without removing her panties he parted her with the flat of his tongue.

Theia bit her lip, fingers curled around the bedspread, as Lucien's tongue prodded and teased against the cotton. If the bra was a mess, the panties were going to be wrecked, wet from without and within. Lucien's teeth nipped at the fabric, tugging the damp cotton and shaking it with a little growl like a puppy playing tug-of-war as he grinned up at her. At the same time, he'd moved his hands along her thighs, his thumbs slipping inside the legs of the garment, and Theia gasped as he pulled the panties away with a swift motion of thumbs and teeth.

As they fell to the floor, Lucien gently loosened her grip on the bedspread. "Let go. Hold on to me instead." He threaded his fingers through hers and locked them tight, as though to keep her grounded in case she floated away.

Theia let out a moan as he buried his head in her lap, tongue persistently and enthusiastically opening her until she was writhing and rocking into him and forgot to care about how much sound she was making. And Lucien seemed to revel in it, rewarding her with faster, deeper strokes of his tongue and answering moans of his own the more noise she made, until she arched back, hips raised, and crooned as the waves of her climax rolled through her. Her vision had gone blue.

Completely spent and utterly relaxed, Theia flopped back onto the bed, and Lucien persisted until she had to stop him, overstimulated. He responded to the little twist of her hips without her having to say a word, raising his head and resting his cheek on her thigh.

Lucien softened his fingers in hers and stroked his thumb along the heel of her palm. "You okay, beautiful?"

Theia giggled, not sure if it was more at the question or the endearment. "I am very okay."

He lifted his head from her thigh and climbed onto the bed, the towel catching and sliding off, revealing his still very enthusiastic erection.

Theia rolled onto her stomach beside him. "Do you want me to…?"

Lucien leaned back against the pillows, stroking himself idly. "Take this off," he murmured, tugging on the band of her bra.

Theia sat up and loosened the halter at her nape to let the bra drop open, cheeks warming at the little sound he made as she unhooked the back.

He shook his head. "Damn, girl. Just stay there, just like that." His fist around his cock was sliding up and down in more deliberate strokes.

Theia sat back on her heels, watching with fascination. She'd never actually seen a guy jerk off before. Lucien's hand picked up pace, and his breathing matched it as he watched her back, the soft sighs and grunts of his exhalations punctuating the sounds of skin against skin. After a moment, he screwed his eyes shut and let out a whispered string of obscenities and went off like a geyser, pearly white drops spattering the tight washboard of his abs as he choked the blushing head.

With his eyes still closed, the long, dark lashes stood out against the flush in his cheeks. "Come here," he whispered, holding out his hand.

She crawled toward him and curled beneath his arm, and Lucien kissed her, his lips still sticky with her and her taste still on his tongue, unexpectedly pleasant.

Theia cuddled against his side. "Why didn't you want me to…return the favor?"

"It wasn't a quid pro quo, darling."

She flinched at the sardonic tone in his voice. She hadn't heard it since he'd given her the tour of the lab.

Lucien opened his eyes. "Sorry. Reflex." He rolled toward her, tucking her hair behind her ear. "I'm not used to not behaving like a prick just because I can." He kissed her again, the honesty in his touch reassuring. "When someone asks, 'Do you want me to?' it's generally not because *they* want to but because they think they ought to."

"It's not that I didn't want to—"

"Theia, it's okay. I would never want you to do something you weren't ready to do just to appease my arousal. I'm not one of those men who thinks he's owed something just because he's given something. The pleasure was in the gift." Lucien grinned. "Believe me."

Theia smiled. "Well, I'll keep that in mind. In case it…comes up again."

Lucien laughed. "And I have no doubt that it will." He snuggled closer to her. "Possibly after a short nap."

Theia closed her eyes for a moment, but they opened in a flash. "Oh, shit."

"What's the matter?"

"I was supposed to feed Puddleglum."

"Can't he wait until morning?"

"Seriously?"

"I don't know. I've never had a cat."

"Well, you have a stomach, don't you?" Theia sat up, scrambling for her clothes. Her panties lay in a soggy heap at the foot of the bed.

Lucien laughed as she held them up and scowled at them. "Just toss them in my hamper. The cleaning lady is coming in the morning."

"I can do laundry at Phoebe's."

Lucien took them out of her hand and tossed them into the hamper across the room. "I'm sure you can, but that's what I pay the cleaning lady for."

Theia wasn't a fan of going commando, but she'd have to grin and bear it. She pulled on her jeans, zipping them carefully, and wriggled into her top while stuffing her feet into her shoes. The bra she tucked into her back pocket.

Lucien's phone buzzed, and he picked it up from the nightstand, studying the message with a frown.

"Bad news?"

"No, just a client. I have to go to Tucson."

"Tonight?"

"Yeah, somebody's got a poltergeist problem at the university. Lucy's on her way over to pick me—"

The bell chimed on the door.

Lucien inclined his head toward the sound. "—Up."

But Lucy hadn't waited for an answer. The front door opened, and Theia stood frozen in her tracks as Lucien's sister came down the hall, while Lucien remained where he was—nudity, sticky abs and all.

Lucy paused in the doorway, staring at Theia a moment before glancing at Lucien and rolling her eyes. "I see you found your way home just fine, Lulu."

"Don't call me Lulu."

"I should go." Theia scooted past Lucy through the door.

"Hang on." Lucien followed her to the front door as if his nudity were incidental and gave her a kiss. "I'll call you tomorrow."

"With what?"

Lucien shrugged in acknowledgment. "I'll get another phone in the morning."

Theia lowered her voice. "Aren't you a little uncomfortable...like this...with Lucy being here?"

"Why?" Lucien shrugged. "She's seen me naked. Don't worry about it." He kissed her again and opened the door. As it closed behind her, Theia realized her bra was dangling out of her back pocket.

* * *

"Give me five minutes," Lucien called over his shoulder as he went into the bathroom.

Lucy appeared in the doorway as he stood over the toilet. "You really think this is smart?"

"What, taking a piss?"

"Fucking that witch."

"She's not a witch. She has visions. She's an empath."

"Oh, well, that's fine, then. Nothing could go wrong there."

"Why does it matter to you?"

"You just seem a little bent on giving away all your secrets to someone you barely know. And some of those secrets belong to me."

Lucien flushed the toilet. "It may surprise you to know, but we didn't actually spend any time talking about you and your secrets when we were in bed. We were occupied with more interesting things."

"Just clean yourself up and let's go. Our ride is waiting for us at the airport."

The ride turned out to be a helicopter. At least he could avoid small talk with Lucy on the flight.

Rhea called just after Theia got out of a long, luxurious soak in the tub and started getting ready for bed. She thought about not answering, but that would only make Rhea suspicious.

She hit the speaker and tossed the phone on the bed. "What's up, buttercup?"

"You sound cheery."

"No, I don't. I'm just getting ready for bed. I do have a big bowl of ice cream waiting for me, though. I'm pretty pleased about that."

"I told you to call me when you got home last night, and you didn't."

"Oh." *Shit.* "Sorry. You're right. I forgot."

"Did you have any trouble getting Oliver Queen home?"

Theia laughed at the Green Arrow reference—probably a little too enthusiastically. "No, he was pretty subdued. I straightened him out about Leo. He shouldn't give you guys any more trouble."

"Thei…is there anything you want to tell me?"

"Tell you? What would I want to tell you?"

"Is he there with you right now?"

Theia felt her face blaze scarlet. "What? Why would he be here?"

Rhea sighed into the phone. "You really think I'm dumb, don't you?"

"What in the world are you talking about?"

"I may not be the one getting a master's degree in molecular biology, missy, but I know when something's going on with you. We shared a womb. And Rafe's alarm has been set to record and report entries at the security gate ever since the paparazzi incident. I saw your key code on the security log from this morning when you came to get Lucien's car."

"Oh. Fudge."

"You slept with him."

"In the sense that we spent the night together in the same bed? Yes. His sister told me I had to wake him up every two hours to check his responses, so I brought him back to Phoebe's place, and we ended up talking after I woke him up. That's when I straightened him out about Leo. And Dev. We didn't quite get to Rafe because the sun came up, but I'm pretty sure he's not going after any of our family members again." Theia was talking fast, trying to avoid a lull in the conversation that would let Rhea pin her down on what had happened today. Which was of course a dead giveaway that something had.

"You talked."

"*Most*ly."

"*Theia.* I can't believe you're holding out on me. I could hear it in your voice the minute you answered the phone. You just got back from his place, didn't you? You've been there all day, and he screwed your brains out. The lunatic who tried to kill my boyfriend screwed your fancy little molecular-biologist brains out. And you *loved* it."

"I was not there all day."

"Ha!"

"And there was *no* screwing."

"Theia."

"I…there might have been…licking."

"Oh my God. Who licked whom? I want details. Juicy, disgusting details. It's my birthright."

"That is not even a thing."

"It is so a thing. Leo is out hunting, and you're hoarding ice cream, Puddleglum and juicy licking details. I'm coming over there."

"Don't you dare. There is *not* enough ice cream for you. It's Häagen-Dazs Deep Chocolate Peanut Butter, and it's all mine." Theia realized the phone had gone dead. "Goddammit, Rhe." There was no way her story would hold up under Rhea's in-person scrutiny.

Chapter 14

Luckily, Rhea brought her own ice cream—a pint of Ben & Jerry's Chocolate Fudge Brownie.

Theia opened the door in her PJs and looked down at a pair of fluffy slippers that matched her own. "I compliment you on your excellent taste in footwear."

Rhea pushed her way in. "They're yours. I stole them the last time I visited you in Flag."

"I thought I'd left them at the Laundromat."

"You did. That's where I stole them."

"Dammit, Rhe." Theia had spent hours online finding a replacement pair.

While Theia took her ice cream from the freezer and grabbed some spoons, Rhea commandeered the papasan chair.

"So spill," said Rhea after Theia tossed her a spoon. "How exactly did you get from wounded commando recovery to licking? And who licked whom?"

Theia sat at the breakfast bar separating the living room from the kitchen, swiveling on her stool so she could see Rhea without facing her. "He told me what Smok Consulting does—they clean up paranormal situations that get out of hand. It complements the biotech business, where they're working on developing pharmaceuticals to suppress the effects of certain switched-on genes—"

"Blah, blah, sciencey words, blah, blah, and?"

"And Lucien needed an outlet that would let him balance the harm he felt Smok was doing, so he started going after what he considered to be dangerous elements. The serum-tipped arrows are specially designed to destroy unnatural creatures."

"And he shot one into my very human boyfriend, got his ass handed to him and you nursed him back to health with erotic licking."

"That is *not* what happened."

"Was it like this?" Rhea licked a ribbon of fudge off the back of her spoon.

"Oh my God. I did *not* lick him."

"Aha. So he licked you. Did you pass out after? No? Didn't think so. My man can lick your man under the table any day." Rhea paused. "Which does not sound quite like I meant it to."

"He's not my man." Theia kept her head over her pint to keep the heat in her cheeks from showing, but Rhea never missed anything.

"You are such a terrible liar."

Considering everything she'd been keeping from Rhea for years, Theia might not be the greatest at verbal dissembling, but she seemed to be doing a bang-up job at sins of omission.

"So where is he now?"

"He got called away to a job with Lucy."

"Ah, Lucy. The bitchy twin."

"Yeah, you two have a lot in common."

"Yeah, we're both the hot one. Kind of gives you fuel for a twin fantasy, though."

Theia nearly choked on her ice cream. "I beg your pardon?"

"Not us, you dork. Ew. I meant him and her. You ever think about…?"

Theia gaped at her. "She's female, in case you didn't notice."

"What, you've never hung out at Muffy's Dive Bar? I thought that was what college was for."

Apparently Theia wasn't the only one who was good at keeping secrets. "You are totally blowing my mind right now."

Rhea winked, digging into her pint. "That's what she said."

"Speaking of dive bars…" Theia cleared her throat. "Do you know anything about a place called Polly's Grotto in West Sedona?"

"Polly's Grotto?" Rhea sucked on her spoon. "Sounds vaguely familiar, but I don't think I've ever been there. Why?"

"Not sure." Theia dug for a vein of peanut butter. "Lucien had to meet a client there earlier today, and it just seemed like an odd place for a meeting. Even for a paranormal cleaner." She pondered her scoop. "I don't think the place was even open yet, so whom was he meeting?"

"I can ask Leo about it. He knows a lot of sketchy characters from his years as an immortal." Rhea studied her for a moment. "So it sounds like you're kind of all in with this guy, huh?"

"I don't know about…" Theia felt her cheeks warming again. "Yeah. I guess maybe I am."

Rhea smiled. "It's about time. You've been weird about dating ever since that reading I gave you. I was beginning to think you were going to die an old maid." She ducked as Theia flicked peanut butter off her spoon. It landed on Puddleglum, who was hovering at the top of the papasan chair in hopes of sneaking a bite of Rhea's ice cream. The cat gave Theia an offended look but began studiously grooming the peanut butter glob from his fur.

"Just promise me you'll be careful," Rhea added after a moment. "This quest of his to hunt down 'dangerous elements' could be a hard habit to break." She smiled ruefully. "Take it from a hunting widow. And if he's still harboring doubts about any 'unnatural' members of our family, he could be trouble for all of us. I'd hate for him to end up being that dark prince you worry about."

Theia put the lid on her ice cream with a thoughtful nod and gave Rhea a sly look from under her lashes. "Guess you're not quite as dumb as you look."

"Yeah, well, joke's on you, genius, 'cause you look exactly like me."

Theia got up to put her pint in the freezer. "No, I don't. Moonpie."

Lucy eyed Lucien as their escort at University Medical Center led them off the helipad. "You didn't see the doctor like I told you to."

"I was busy."

"You know that's going to hurt like hell when the doc has to break up all that ecto gel. Especially if it completely solidifies and the bone has to be rebroken to set right."

"Yeah, I know."

"Hope her pussy was worth it."

"Shut up, Lu." Lucien held the door to the stairs for her. "And you bet your ass it was."

Their client, a frazzled-looking but distinguished older gentleman, was waiting in the hallway outside the closed-off wing. "Thank you for coming so quickly, Mr. Smok. I'm Roger Fitzhugh, the hospital administrator." He shook Lucien's hand, looking past Lucy like she was Lucien's assistant. "It's here in the NICU." He indicated the double doors beside them but seemed reluctant to open them.

"The NICU?" Lucy frowned. "You're sure you're dealing with a poltergeist? They generally attach themselves to adolescents. Sometimes prepubescent children, but I can't imagine what would prompt such activity around newborns."

"I suppose the diagnosis is up to your team. I'm no expert. But…*something* is in there, and it isn't happy."

"Is the ward clear?"

"Yes, we moved all the patients down to another level and sealed off the area."

"All right. We'll handle it from here, Mr. Fitzhugh. Thank you." Lucy opened the door, and Fitzhugh stepped back.

The air was thick with charged particles as the doors swung shut behind them, making the hairs on Lucien's arms stand on end.

"This feels like a haunting, not a poltergeist."

Lucy nodded. "That's what I was thinking."

"Are we even equipped to open a gate?"

Lucy reached into her bag and pulled out her kit. "We

should probably draw some blood now and be ready to use it. I've got the catalyst."

Lucien took off his coat and rolled up his sleeve.

She watched him with a frown. "Are you sure you're up to it? I could do this one."

"You know Edgar wouldn't like it."

"Since when do you care what Edgar wants?"

"I care when he gets mad at you and treats you like shit for something I did."

"Aw. I had no idea you cared, baby brother."

"Shut up and take the blood before it gets any freakier in here."

While Lucy took the needle out of its packaging, Lucien swabbed his arm and placed it on the nurse's station for her to tap a vein and draw. The same kit was useful for attracting revenant bloodsuckers. The only difference in dealing with apparitions was the catalyst, a compound developed by Smok Biotech that reacted with the supposedly infernal component in the Smok blood to create a thinning of the spectral veil that could open a gate to the other side. Useful for sending the already dead and disembodied packing.

Lucy filled the vial and transferred the needle to the glass tube containing the catalyst, red blood swirling into the clear liquid. "Ready to go."

"All right, let's do this."

As they moved down the corridor toward the nursery, the resistance from the malevolent spirit was palpable. Something definitely didn't want them here. To prove the point, a gurney came flying at them from a side corridor, and they jumped out of the way. It slammed into the wall hard enough to crumple the frame.

"There." Lucy pointed toward the window of the nurs-

ery as they straightened. A shadow figure stood on the
other side, the darkness of its misty form pulsing with
rage. She raised her voice and spoke to it. "You don't belong here. It's time for you to go."

A vibration of sound, almost subsonic, rose from a
deep rumble to an ear-piercing shriek, and the glass of
the observation window shattered outward.

Lucien instinctively turned and covered Lucy, flinch-
ing as a few shards struck his back.

Lucy shoved him off. "Dammit, Lucien. I can take
care of myself."

"I was making sure the vial wasn't hit."

"You were being a misogynist ass."

Supplies started hurtling toward them, and Lucien
ducked a tray of surgical tools. "We'd better get this done
before that thing takes an eye out. You want to approach
it? Be my guest."

Lucy covered her head with her jacket and darted forward, the vial in her fist. The shadow charged her, and
Lucy stiffened with a jolt as it went through her, now
swirling between them.

"Hit the juice." Lucy whirled toward him. "Now!"

Armed with the violet wand from Lucy's bag—designed to generate electric shocks for sex play, though Lucien really didn't want to know if Lucy ever used it for that
purpose—Lucien hit the button as the spirit flung itself
in his direction. The spark flared in the darkness, illu-
minating the human shape within. A teenage girl stood
petrified in the violet glow, and for a moment he could
see her face, twisted with grief and anger.

Lucy smashed the vial on the floor in the center of
the spirit's form, and the ghost began to scream. The
spattered liquid spread, thinning the veil where Lucien

had her trapped, kept in place with repeated jolts from the wand, while the air filled with violet sparks and the smell of ozone.

The wailing sound, Lucien realized, wasn't a wordless cry. She was screaming, "No!" and holding out her arms toward him. Lucien felt sick. There was nothing he could do to stop it now. The void swallowed her up, and only a soft weeping lingered as the thickness in the air dissipated. He heard a single word in it, a name: "Emma."

Lucy pushed her hair back from her forehead, holding her hand to the top of her head for a moment. "Jesus. That was brutal. Do you think that was her name? Emma?"

Lucien shut off the wand and dropped it into the bag. "No. I think it was her baby's."

Lucy's hand dropped to her side. "Damn. That's why the NICU."

"I hate this job."

"Yeah." Lucy straightened her coat and picked up the bag. The dimly lit ward looked ordinary now.

In the waiting area, Roger Fitzhugh got to his feet as they emerged through the double doors. "Did you find it?"

Lucy nodded. "All clear."

"And…the price?"

Lucy handled the financial arrangements. Lucien had done it a few times, and it always left a bad taste in his mouth. His sister was only too happy to step in and demonstrate her superior skills—a performance for the benefit of a man who wasn't even here to appreciate it.

She considered for a moment, looking tired. "It was a garden-variety haunting, Mr. Fitzhugh. It's on the house."

Lucien studied her as they headed back out to the helipad. The fee for any consulting job was the same. The price was a soul. Lucien had always assumed it meant nothing more than a life—as if a life weren't everything—but it was the Smok reputation that mattered. Clients believed the souls were collected for hell.

Lucy noticed him watching her. "What?"

"That was uncharacteristically nice of you."

"I wasn't being nice. We got our soul. No need for another."

"Yeah, well." Lucien shrugged. "I suspect you may have one yourself. But don't worry, Lu. Your secret's safe with me."

It was just after two in the morning when Lucy dropped him off. In addition to the aches and pains, he was really feeling the drain of the night's work. It was only a few milliliters of blood, but the opening of a gate always took something out of him. And it was just another reminder that he was running out of time. If the Smok legacy was true, he would become something inhuman before he took his place in hell—what form that would take, the legend didn't say. But Lucien wasn't taking any chances. He had to finish developing the antitransformative.

Lucien peeled out of his suit and lay on top of the covers, too tired to turn down the bed. It still smelled of Theia.

She was still part demon. That hadn't changed. But he didn't give a damn. Lucien laughed at the inadvertent pun. Whatever she was—whatever *he* was—Theia made him feel there was a reason to get up in the morning. And that, he realized, was something he hadn't felt in a very long time.

Chapter 15

After receiving a call from Leo at the crack of dawn to let her know he was back from the Hunt, Rhea went home from their impromptu pajama party. With a parting shot at Rhea about being penis whipped, Theia went back to bed and had vague dreams about Rhea's Náströnd, the Shore of Corpses in the Norse underworld where Rhea and Leo's astral projection in dragon form had rescued Leo's disembodied soul. Images of rotting corpses, reanimated and climbing from a foul primordial soup, were enough to shake her out of sleep, glad of the daylight. At the periphery of the dream's fading memory was the wounded blue wyvern diving into the hell lake pursued by the cockatrice.

Theia stood in the shower, goose bumps on her flesh despite the hot water, trying to wash away the image of those sloughing, scrabbling corpses—revenants for certain, if anything was. Revenants and cockatrices and wyverns, oh my.

"Wyverns?" Theia opened her eyes as she spoke the word aloud, the brilliant blue letters floating in the air as though the word was significant. Where had that come from? She'd thought of the creature as a dragon when she'd dreamed of it before but not a specific breed. Maybe it was something she'd seen in a video game. Or one of Rhea's books.

The doorbell was ringing when she turned off the water. Theia jumped out of the tub and grabbed her robe from the back of the door, throwing it on over wet skin as she ran to answer the bell.

Lucien stood on the stoop holding his phone. "I got the replacement but I still couldn't call you because I don't have your number. So I thought I'd drive across town and tell you that." He grinned then cocked his head as he took in her appearance with a sideways smile. "Funny...that's just how I fantasize you."

"You fantasize about me?"

"Constantly." Lucien beamed. "Can I come in?"

"Watch out for darting cats. I'm not supposed to let Puddleglum out." She unlocked the screen door, and Lucien stepped in and closed it behind him just as the cat skulked around the corner and tried to make a break for it.

"Curses. Foiled again," Lucien said in a cartoon villain voice, grinning at the cat. He glanced up at Theia, looking slightly chagrined. "I have no idea where that came from. I think I was channeling him. Is he a warlock?"

Theia laughed. "I wouldn't be a bit surprised."

Lucien kissed her, silencing her laugh, and pulled her close. "I missed you in my bed. I think I may have to keep you there." He stepped back after a moment and glanced down at the damp marks her robe had left on his khakis. "You're all wet." He untied the belt at the front of the robe, sliding his hands inside and around her ass. "Can I dry you with my tongue?"

Now she was definitely wet. But she hadn't thought about where this might go. As fantastic as yesterday had been, she couldn't just expect him to continue his one-sided pleasuring. But she wasn't sure if she was ready to take the plunge into post-virginity immediately.

Lucien's lascivious grin turned questioning. "No pressure, of course."

"Sorry. I just…hadn't thought about what might happen next."

"Theia." He played with a strand of her hair, a wistful smile on his face. "There's no timeline. I can dial it back a bit. I know I can be a little intense." He retied her belt, making a prim little bow. "For now, how about breakfast? If you haven't already eaten, that is. There's this cute little place on Cedar Street that makes fantastic lavender scones."

Theia grinned up at him. "Now I'm starting to think *you're* some kind of warlock." She turned toward the bedroom. "Just let me get dressed. You had me at scones."

"That was kind of the last word I said, actually, but at least I managed to reel you in while I was still speaking."

They had just ordered when Lucien received a text. He frowned as he read it.

Theia watched him over her coffee cup. "Anything wrong?"

"No." Lucien looked up. "I mean, yes. Another job. Lucy's unavailable, so I have to leave now to handle it."

Theia's mouth curved into a pout. "No fantastic lavender scones?"

"Not for me, I'm afraid. I'm really sorry about this. We're not usually this busy. But you should stay—I'll settle the bill."

"Why don't I just go with you?"

"You want to come with?" Lucien glanced at the message again with a dubious look. "It's a botched resurrection."

"Botched…resurrection?" Theia blinked, not sure she was hearing right.

"Someone paid a reanimator to bring a loved one back from the dead. It literally never works. It's the monkey's paw of spells, and yet people try it all the time. Like teenagers calling up vengeful spirits in the mirror as a drunken party game, trying to resurrect the dead never goes out of style, no matter how disastrous. Of course, Smok is very good at making sure those disasters never get publicized."

The idea of witnessing the results of a botched resurrection was both horrifying and compelling. She'd seen Phoebe and Rafe deal with the spirits of the dead before, but never the reanimated dead.

"I'm up for it, if it's not against the rules."

"There aren't really any rules—or if there are, I make them." Lucien grinned. "If you really want to come, I can tell them you're just observing as a new apprentice so they won't expect you to step in. And you have to promise to follow my directions. I'm not being an ass—I just have to be able to ensure your safety."

Theia smiled. "I do want to come. And I give you my word. I promise I have absolutely zero interest in getting in the way of a revenant. Because, you know—*actual* revenant."

Lucien grimaced. "Touché." He paid for the uneaten scones, and they hit the road.

"The client is in Oak Creek," Lucien told her as they drove through Uptown Sedona. "Nice to have something close by for a change."

"Aren't all of your clients local?"

"No, we're worldwide. I spent a lot of time on the West Coast and in Europe after college, working with our agencies there. Edgar wanted me home for the lab opening. Lucy's been handling things for him locally, but he's been trying to encourage me to take a more active role in the company."

"What about your mother? Is she not involved in the company?"

Lucien's expression was guarded. "They're divorced. The business was never her thing anyway. She kind of loathes the entire Smok enterprise. Can't say that I blame her."

"But you still do it." Theia realized it was a shitty thing to say. "I mean—"

"No, you're right. I take part in aspects of the business that I find morally and ethically...uncomfortable. I can't really justify it other than to say I feel a sense of familial obligation." Lucien was quiet, and Theia thought it better not to intrude on his silence.

He turned onto Jack's Canyon in the Village of Oak Creek and headed west.

"Ione lives a few blocks from here." Theia glanced at Lucien. "Which maybe I shouldn't have told you. You've abandoned the idea of going after Dev, I hope?"

"I already know where your sister lives. But unless Dev's demon goes on a rampage, yes, I've given up on that plan. I'm rethinking my sources."

"Your sources?"

"For information on rogue creatures. I have a few insiders who alert me to candidates in the area. And some anonymous sources." Lucien glanced at her. "That's what put me on your family's trail, actually. An anonymous 'concerned individual' tipped me off." He paused. "The same person that sent me the link to your personal genealogy research."

"Someone sent you that?" Theia frowned. Who could have been able to link to the file? It was a private upload to the genealogy site, which only immediate relatives could access without expressly having the link.

They pulled into the driveway of a modest-looking duplex. Theia wondered how the occupants were able to afford Smok Consulting's services.

"Keep behind me when we approach the subject," Lucien advised. "Sometimes they can move surprisingly fast."

"How do you…get rid of it?" Theia asked as he rang the doorbell. "Do you have to kill the revenant?"

"No, it's already dead. All I have to do is release the shade from the body." He shook his head. "It's really a cruel thing to tie a shade to a rotting corpse. It's unconscionable that anyone would do it."

A middle-aged woman opened the door. Dark circles under bloodshot eyes made her look somewhat manic, as if she hadn't slept in days.

"Mrs. Castillo. I'm Lucien Smok, and this is my colleague, Theia Dawn. She'll be observing—"

"Thank God you're here." The woman grabbed Lucien's hand and held it in both of hers. "*Es mi abuela.* She passed on a month ago, but my mother was distraught, and she couldn't get over the loss. I didn't know she had called a *brujo* until I came home from work on Friday, and I found her sitting with Abuelita. I didn't know what to do. My husband's cousin told me about your services."

Lucien patted her hand and gently drew his other out of her grip. "You did the right thing, Mrs. Castillo. Just let us take it from here."

As soon as they stepped inside, the smell nearly bowled Theia over. Her eyes watered, and she covered her mouth as Lucien's client led them to a bedroom in the back.

"Mamá? The doctor's here." Mrs. Castillo turned to Lucien and lowered her voice. "I had to tell her you were a doctor coming to help my grandmother. She has Alzheimer's. My mother, I mean. Not my grandmother." Tears sprang to her eyes as she opened the door.

The curtains were drawn, and it took a moment for Theia's eyes to adjust to the light. On a little day bed in the shadows, two elderly women sat holding hands. But one of them had a swollen face with a grayish-blue discoloration. The swollen one began to curse in Spanish. Theia understood just enough to know that the words were shocking.

Mrs. Castillo crossed herself.

Lucien touched her arm. "What's your mother's name?"

"Rosa Campos."

"And your grandmother?"

"Lupe Ramirez. Lupita."

"I'll need Rosa to move away from the—" Lucien caught himself. "From your grandmother." He held out his hand. "Mrs. Campos, I'm Dr. Smok. Can I speak with you?"

Rosa looked confused. "The doctor was here. Mamá was sick but the doctor made her better."

Obscenities continued to fly from the older woman's mouth—along with a terrible stench that Theia was surprised she could even distinguish next to the pervasive smell of rotting flesh.

"I just need to give her a checkup. And I have some vitamins for you." He took a bottle from his bag and emptied two pills into his hand. He turned to Mrs. Castillo. "Can you get a glass of water?"

The woman eyed the pills with mistrust. "What are those for?"

"I think it's best if she's sedated," he murmured, "before I take care of the—your *abuela.*"

Hands trembling as she stepped into the room to pour a glass of water from the pitcher beside the bed, Mrs. Castillo took the pills. "Come on, Mami. Take your vitamins and let the doctor look at Abuela."

The old woman reached obediently for the pills, but the revenant knocked them from her hand with a snarl, and Rosa began to cry.

"That's okay. I have more." Lucien shook out another two pills. "Can you come here to me?"

"You're not my doctor." Rosa began to speak rapidly in Spanish.

"She wants her granddaughter." Mrs. Castillo looked at Theia. "She thinks you're my daughter. She wants you to give her the pills."

"Me?" Theia glanced at Lucien. The smell of the decaying flesh was making it difficult not to gag.

Lucien shook his head. "You don't have to."

But Rosa had gotten up, reaching for Theia. "Conchita, be a good girl. *Dame las vitaminas.*" The revenant tugged at her hand, and Rosa tugged back. Theia swallowed bile as a layer of the revenant's skin sloughed away.

She took the pills and the water and stepped closer. "Here you go, Abuela."

The old woman took them, and Theia held the water for her, trying to ignore the rage—and stench—emanating from the revenant.

"*Puta!*" The undead woman spat the word at Theia, along with a viscous gray substance that struck her cheek.

Theia covered her mouth and stumbled back. For a moment, she was sure she was going to lose the battle and vomit.

Stepping to her side, Lucien wiped the trail of slime from her cheek with a handkerchief. "You're doing amazing," he murmured.

Rosa's eyelids began to flutter, and she leaned her head on her mother's shoulder.

"Mamá, why don't you lie down and take a little nap?" As Mrs. Castillo moved toward her mother, the revenant lunged for her, letting Rosa tumble onto the bed.

Mrs. Castillo screamed and threw her arms over her face reflexively, and the revenant sank her teeth into one of the upraised arms. Watching in horror, Theia thought incongruously how impressive it was that a woman in her nineties had died with all her teeth.

Lucien darted forward, taking a vial of clear liquid from his pocket. He opened it and flung the contents at the revenant, shouting in what sounded like Latin.

The revenant shrieked and let go, cringing and backing toward the daybed at the touch of the liquid as if it were acid.

"Lupita Ramirez." Lucien's voice projected with a deep, authoritative tenor. "You don't belong here. I command you to come out. Be free." He repeated the words in Spanish, and the revenant made an agonizing sound, a wail that seemed to encompass both misery and relief. The haunted, rage-filled eyes emptied, turning glassy and dull, and the body crumpled lifeless to the floor.

Mrs. Castillo began to sob. Mercifully, Rosa's eyes had remained closed, unconscious to the loss of her mother for the second time.

"A crew will be here shortly to take care of the remains." Lucien spoke soothingly, patting the woman's shoulder. "They should be done before your mother wakes up. It's entirely possible she won't remember any of this." He cleared his throat. "And while I hate to speak of business at a time like this, there is the matter of payment. I assume our policy regarding the timing in the case of a reanimation reversal has been explained to you?"

She nodded, wiping her eyes.

Lucien glanced at the sleeping woman on the bed. "If I can make a suggestion…it might be a mercy to let your mother make the payment."

"No, no." Mrs. Castillo shook her head vehemently. "It will be me. I've already made arrangements. My daughter will take care of my mother."

Lucien nodded and took a small vial from his pocket. "This will complete the transaction. I recommend that you take it at bedtime and go to sleep as usual."

As Mrs. Castillo took the vial, she grabbed Lucien's hands once more. "*Gracias*, Mr. Smok. You don't know what this means to my family. I haven't slept since Abuelita…" She glanced at the corpse and squeezed her eyes shut. "And now it's over. It's over."

Lucien pressed her hands and extracted himself from her grip. "You should see to that arm." He nodded to the bite mark.

Mrs. Castillo's eyes flew open, wide with terror. "It won't make me like her, will it?"

"No, no. Of course not. It's just that it looks painful."

On the drive back to Sedona, Theia was quiet, trying—and failing—to reconcile the events she'd witnessed.

Lucien glanced at her after a few minutes. "Are you okay? That was a rough one."

"What was that vial you gave her?"

"Holy water. Well, really, just plain water. Its power is in the belief of the shade. She actually left on her own, believing she'd been exorcised."

"No, I mean the other vial. The one you gave Mrs. Castillo."

"Oh." Lucien stared ahead. "I probably should have done that in private."

"*Lucien.* What was it?"

"A lethal dose of pentobarbital. It's painless."

Theia leaned back against the headrest, letting her breath out slowly. She'd wanted to be wrong. Wanted him, at least, to express some shock at the statement.

"So that's the payment. She's going to kill herself."

"Well, no. Not exactly. The payment for any of our services of this nature is a soul."

Theia's head throbbed as she turned to look at him. "What the hell do you mean, a *soul*?"

"It's my family's legacy. We…" He glanced at her for an instant before looking back at the road. "Legend says we collect souls for the devil."

"The devil. There's an actual devil."

Lucien shrugged. "I don't know. Maybe there's not even any such thing as a soul. But those are the bargains we make at Smok. And people enter into them willingly.

In most cases, the designated payer lives out his or her normal life. But to reverse a resurrection, payment is due in full when services are rendered."

Sweat beaded her forehead, and Theia gripped her door handle. "Pull over."

"What?"

"Pull over! Right now."

Lucien pulled onto the shoulder of the highway, and Theia threw open the door and vomited into the dirt. Her stomach lurched so violently she expected to see it in the gravel turned inside out.

Lucien held out his handkerchief when she straightened and sat back against the seat, and Theia yanked it from his hand, careful not to wipe her mouth with the bilious substance he'd cleaned off her cheek from the revenant.

"I'm sorry. I shouldn't have brought you."

"You shouldn't have brought me? That's what you're sorry about? You just told a woman to kill herself and go to hell—and handed her the poison to do it."

"It's the job. It's why I hate it so much."

"Oh! Well!" Theia threw her hands in the air. "As long as you *hate* it."

"Theia—"

"Just take me home. I need to be alone."

Lucien pulled back onto the highway without a word.

When they arrived at Phoebe's place, he looked over at her at last, obviously wanting to say something. Whatever it was, Theia didn't want to hear it. She got out and slammed the door and went inside without a backward look.

Chapter 16

Lucien drove home, the usual dark funk that hung over him after a job magnified by a thousand. Why had he taken Theia with him? In one afternoon, he'd revealed to her every repugnant thing about himself and the Smok legacy. He was so used to letting Lucy handle the negotiations that he'd forgotten just how personal and ugly it felt—especially this one. And yet he'd done it in front of Theia without even preparing her beforehand.

Yesterday, he'd been devastated by the news of Theia's heritage, ready to renounce her. Twenty-four hours later, he'd pushed her away with the ugly truth of his own, and all he wanted to do was get down on his knees and beg her not to leave him. As if she was even *with* him in the first place.

His smashed laptop screen greeted him when he got home, and Lucien punched it again for good measure.

And then punched it a third time and a fourth, imagining it was his face. The ecto gel in his arm reverberated with a sickening thud. Lucien kicked the laptop onto the floor and stomped on it. After a moment, he started to laugh at his own stupidity, dropping onto his knees on the Berber carpet and laughing until he was crying and could barely breathe. He tipped over sideways and rolled onto his back, wheezing and gasping, tears pouring down his temples into his ears.

"God, you stupid bastard." He sucked in air, holding his stomach. Honestly, he should just get himself one of those little vials of pentobarbital and put an end to it. Put himself and the rest of the world out of his misery. One fresh soul, coming right up.

It wasn't like anyone had a gun to his head forcing him to carry out his repugnant duties. What would have happened, after all, if he'd just neglected to give Mrs. Castillo the vial and let her live out her life? Was someone going to reprimand him? Maybe Edgar would have him fired.

The idea made him laugh again, but after a moment, his laughter subsided. What *would* happen if he didn't do it? Absolutely nothing, that's what.

Lucien got up and grabbed his keys and headed back down to his car. Screw his duties. He drove back to Mrs. Castillo's house and pounded on the door.

She looked shocked to see him. His was probably the last face she wanted to see. Behind her, visible through the open bedroom door, the cleanup crew moved about, calmly carrying out their work.

"Mr. Smok? Did you forget something?"

"I did," he said. "Myself."

Mrs. Castillo squinted at him. "I don't understand."

"I made a mistake, Mrs. Castillo."

Anxiety clouded her features, and her hand flew to her uncombed hair, a gauze bandage visible on her arm where the revenant had bitten her. "Is she going to come back? I don't think my mother can handle it."

And how would her mother handle the loss of her daughter so soon after?

"No, there was no problem with the service. It was a billing error. Usually, my sister handles these details, and I didn't realize we were waiving the usual pay-on-receipt-of-services clause. I'm so embarrassed, Mrs. Castillo, but if you wouldn't mind, could I get that medicine back from you?"

"The medicine? I don't understand. Is there something wrong with it?"

"It's just that there's no need for you to use it. The bill won't come due until your natural expiration."

"My...expiration?" She was sleep deprived, and it took a moment for the words to sink in, but when they did, her face lit up like beam of pure light. "I don't have to take it?"

Lucien smiled. "You don't have to take it."

Mrs. Castillo burst into tears and flung her arms around his neck, taking him by surprise. He indulged her, letting her weep until the cleaners emerged from the hallway behind her with the body bag to transport Mrs. Ramirez to the cemetery for reinterment.

Gently tugging Mrs. Castillo's arms from around his neck, Lucien moved her aside so they could get by. She stood watching them with her hand over her mouth, weeping quietly.

"The medicine?" Lucien prompted after the body had been loaded into the truck.

"Oh, yes." Mrs. Castillo grinned. "Of course, yes! Let

me get it for you." She hurried to her bedroom across the hall from the room where the revenant had been earlier but paused in the doorway, looking perplexed. "I had it right here. Did the other gentlemen take it already?"

Lucien followed her to help her find it. "I doubt they would have even known about it. They don't deal with this end of the operation. You've probably just forgotten where you set it down."

"No, it was right here by the bed. I had everything set up for when I was going to go to sleep tonight. I didn't want my daughter to have to worry about anything." Mrs. Castillo turned and went across the hall to check on her mother and let out a sharp cry. "Mamá! Mamá, no!"

From behind her, Lucien could see the old woman lying on the daybed on her back, staring up at the ceiling with eyes that had as much life in them as a Lucite marble. Next to her on the end table was the empty bottle.

Mrs. Castillo ran to her, shaking the limp body. With a sob, she dropped to her knees and embraced her mother. The devil, it seemed, had gotten his due.

Lucien meant to drive home again, but he found himself in Phoebe Carlisle's driveway. As he sat in the car trying to get his head right, he saw Theia's face appear at the window and disappear again. After a moment, the door opened, and Theia held the screen door for him, waiting.

He stepped out of the car and moved toward her, feeling like he was drowning in quicksand. If he could just get to her, he could keep his head above the mire. There was no welcoming smile, no forgiveness when he reached her, but she let him in, and Lucien clung to her, unable to move. His body began to shake, he realized with some horror, with silent sobs.

"Lucien?" Theia's hand hovered on his hair. "What is it? What's happened?"

He shook his head, not trusting himself to speak. He felt so raw right now that if he dared open his mouth, every cry he'd kept inside since childhood would come pouring out.

"Come inside." Theia drew his arms down to his sides and led him in, steering him to the little pleather-and-wood love seat. Lucien stroked the artificial texture of the vinyl, trying to stop thinking about Mrs. Castillo's sobs. He wasn't crying tears. Not yet. Maybe he could still get himself together and start acting like a man.

He heard his father's voice saying it: *Stop crying like a girl and start acting like a man.* He'd been eight years old. He'd forgotten that day. It was like it had never happened. Until now.

"I went back. I went back to the house, and it didn't matter. Nothing matters."

"What do you mean? To Mrs. Castillo's house?"

Lucien closed his eyes and nodded. "I went to get the vial back. I thought I could make a difference and change something. I thought I could do the right thing for once. She was so happy when I told her she didn't have to take it." His voice broke, and he dug his nails into his palms. "But it was too late. Somehow, they knew what I was going to do. Someone knew. The cleaning crew. I don't know…"

He was quiet again for so long that Theia must have thought he was sleeping, and she shook his shoulder gently.

"Lucien?"

He exhaled slowly. "It was Rosa. The old woman. Someone gave it to her. They collected the old woman's soul while she was sleeping. My act of rebellion, my grand gesture…it was just a joke."

"Oh, Lucien."

"You were right about me."

"Right? About what?"

"Whatever it was you thought when you first met me. Whatever you thought about me today after what you witnessed. I'm garbage."

"You are not garbage, and that isn't what I thought." Theia held his gaze, and Lucien looked away, but she turned his face toward her with both hands. "You're a human being. You're allowed to make mistakes."

Lucien laughed and then couldn't be sure whether he was laughing at "human being" or "mistakes," which gave his laughter a slightly hysterical edge.

Theia drew him into her arms, resting his head on her shoulder, and he remembered belatedly that she was an empath. She'd known he was going to break before he did. And when he broke, it was like a crack in a dam bursting under the pressure of a lifetime of unshed tears.

He wept for his grandmother— the only connection he'd had to his mother, who'd never come back—at whose death his father had told him to "act like a man." He wept for the souls he'd collected and the lives he'd seen ruined. And he wept for himself, knowing it was puerile and self-indulgent but unable to stop now that he'd started. Every loss, every wound came back to him, multiplying the ache in his chest, until he had nothing left.

"Lucien, it's all right. You'll be all right." Soothing, meaningless platitudes, but from Theia's lips, they were life preservers tossed into a turbulent sea. She might have said anything; it didn't matter. The sound of her voice was his lifeline.

He raised his head, afraid to see in her face that she thought less of him now, but when he met her gaze, she seemed to truly see him as no one had before.

Theia brushed a tear from his cheek and leaned toward him, reaching for his mouth with hers. Their lips came together, and Lucien surrendered to that drowning feeling he'd experienced the first time they'd kissed. It was as if they'd both gone under but shared oxygen with their breath. As long as they stayed together, as long as Theia was close to him, he'd survive.

It didn't even occur to him to want more. Kissing Theia was more satisfying than most sexual encounters he'd had. Maybe satisfying wasn't exactly the word— more of a physical communion, perhaps. He wanted to keep doing it, to keep tasting the salt of his own tears on her mouth, to keep feeling the silk of her lips and the velvety texture of her tongue with his.

They ended up curled together on the love seat, Lucien resting his head on her breast. So maybe he wanted a *little* more. He grinned to himself against the soft curve beneath her cotton shirt. But he wasn't going to push it right now. He liked where they were, comfortable, not needing words. No pressure. He'd said it more than once, but it was true. He felt none when he was with her—no pressure to put on an act. Not the confident arrogance of the playboy or even the everyday simple, stupid stoicism of being a man. With Theia, he was just himself. And for the first time, that felt okay. Maybe she was right. Maybe he wasn't entirely garbage.

"So what do I do now?" He hadn't meant to say it aloud.

"Now?"

"How do I go on being Lucien Smok, heir to the Smok fortune and all that comes with it?" He shook his head. "Don't worry. Rhetorical question."

"You've already made a start. Going after rogue creatures isn't exactly playing by Smok rules."

"I collect those souls, too, though. So maybe it's just me indulging my own need to feel self-righteous. Going after people like Leo."

"You said an anonymous source gave you his name. I think I have an idea who that might be."

Lucien propped his elbow on the couch cushion. "Who?"

"Carter Hamilton. It can't be a coincidence that he crashed Phoebe's wedding at the same time you did. It would be in his interest to have someone else do his dirty work and take down my family and the people close to us."

"Hamilton." Lucien nodded slowly. "That would make sense. We've done a lot of cleanup for him over the years. He knows my father fairly well. I've never met him, but if he was looking for a way to wreak some havoc, he'd only have to go to Polly's to get information about what I do."

"What is that place, exactly? Did you really meet a client there?"

Lucien sighed and straightened. He wasn't sure why he'd lied to her before.

"Polly…is my ex-girlfriend. She owns the club. It's a hangout for unnatural people. Enhanced people. And people pay her for information. She's one of my key sources."

Theia sat up beside him. "What kind of enhanced people?"

Lucien met her gaze. "Vampires. Werewolves. Valkyries."

"Valkyries?"

"Leo used to spend time there some years ago, according to Polly. With a rogue Valkyrie."

Recognition dawned in Theia's eyes. "Faye." She paused, brow wrinkling. "Wait...she and Leo were here in Sedona years ago?"

"The club can be entered from anywhere in the world. It's sort of...timeless. Not exactly fixed in time and space."

"Not *exactly*? How does that work?"

Lucien shrugged. "You'd have to ask Polly. But I doubt she'd tell you."

"And what about Polly? Is she...timeless?"

Lucien gave her a sidelong glance with a tentative smile. "Are you jealous of Polly?"

"Should I be?"

She was. The realization made his heart do a little flip. Jealousy meant she was invested in him. In this. It meant there *was* a "this." He'd never imagined a relationship was something he wanted. The warm glow at the idea that he had one surprised him.

"There's nothing between me and Polly anymore. She's just a friend. And I suppose, in answer to your question, she is a bit timeless. The club is a sort of extension of her, a web or a net she sends out to draw in people who interest her."

"A web? What is she, a were-spider?"

Lucien laughed at the idea. "No. Polly...is a siren."

Chapter 17

It took Theia a moment, her mind stuck on the image of a spinning light on top of a police car, before her eyes widened with understanding. "An actual siren? As in *The Odyssey*? As in luring men to their deaths?"

Lucien's smile was wry. "I doubt she's ever lured any man to his death—unless he went willingly—but, yes, those sirens."

Theia wasn't sure she wanted to know what he meant by that middle bit. She was going to have to compare notes with Rhea. Which was worse as an intimidating ex, a siren or a Valkyrie? She imagined a siren's experience would be impossible to compete with—even if Theia *had* any experience.

Lucien started to say something, but his phone interrupted. "Damn. Another haunting. I'm starting to feel like Bill Murray."

Theia rose as he did. "Do you usually have this much business?"

"No. Not at all." Lucien frowned. "It's starting to seem a little weird. Like something's stirred up the dead around here."

The last time something had stirred up the dead in Sedona, it had been Carter Hamilton.

"Lucy's already on it, so hopefully this will be an easy one. As soon as we finish up, I'll give you a call. Speaking of which, I'd better get your number in here." He glanced up with a sly half smile once he'd entered the number she gave him. "So you were just kidding about me shoving the job up my ass, right? I'm going to see you there tomorrow?"

Theia laughed. "I have a final in the morning, but I'll be there in the afternoon. You can consider your ass safe."

As he pulled out onto the drive and Theia closed the door, he texted her with an emoji: a smooching heart.

An irritated meow came from the guest room, accompanied by a perturbed doorknob rattle. She'd forgotten to let Glum out after stashing him to open the front door.

Theia stepped aside for his flounce after releasing him. "Sorry, buddy. Sucks to be thumbless."

He gave her a condescending stare before trotting to his window spot and peering out belatedly after the "intruder."

As she started to text Rhea about her bizarre afternoon, her phone rang, Rhea's photo popping up on the screen. "Speak of the devil," she answered.

"And how did you know I was going to do that?"

Theia took the phone to the papasan. "Do what?"

"Speak of the devil. I found out something interesting from Ione."

"You've lost me."

"She called to check on me. I don't think she trusts me with a millionaire's house. And I happened to mention the incident with Lucien the other night—"

"Rhe."

"I had to. I need to get some of the lamps on the walkway fixed and replace a windowpane, thanks to Oliver Queen. And she gave me an earful about the family Smok. Apparently, they go back to the time of Madeleine Marchant, and they're into some very sketchy things."

"I know that. That's the research I was doing at Rafe's dad's place."

"You know? Why didn't you tell me?"

"I don't know." And, honestly, she didn't, now that she thought about it. It was like she'd gotten so used to keeping things from Rhea that it was becoming a habit.

"Did you also know that Lucien has a nickname among the magical community?"

"No. What?"

"Little Lucifer."

Theia snorted. He was hardly little.

"It seems the Smok family has a reputation for making *infernal deals*. Like crossroads kinds of deals." She paused. "Theia Dawn. Are you going to tell me you knew about that, too?"

"I only found out this afternoon. I went with Lucien on a consulting job and witnessed a deal in action. It wasn't pretty."

"And that's okay with you?"

"No, of course it isn't. And I told him that and made him take me home. But then he went back to the client and tried to nullify the deal and found out it was too late.

You should have seen him when he showed up here. He was absolutely wrecked."

Rhea was quiet for a moment. "You're starting to worry me."

"There's nothing to worry about."

"You're working for Smok Biotech, and you're going with Lucien on his creepy crossroads client calls."

"I haven't actually started working for Smok."

"Because it's the weekend. Are you taking the job or aren't you?"

"Maybe. Yes. So?"

"Theia, your boyfriend collects *souls*."

"So does yours."

"That's not the same thing."

"Isn't it?"

Rhea sighed. "We're not talking about Leo Ström. We're talking about Lucien Smo— Oh, wow. *LS?* You couldn't even get your own initials. You always have to copy me."

Theia couldn't resist needling her. "Actually, you're the one who copied me. I dated Leo first, if you recall."

"Ouch. I can't believe you went there. Seriously, though, infernal deals aside, Lucien doesn't exactly have a sterling reputation. I talked to Leo about that place you mentioned. Polly's Grotto? He's heard of it, all right."

"From when he used to go there with Faye."

She could almost hear Rhea's mouth drop open in indignation. "What the hell, Theia? Have your visions gotten spooky accurate lately, or are you becoming a pathological liar?"

There was a distinct chance the answer to that entire question was "Yes."

"Lucien told me about it this afternoon. Apparently,

he used to be involved with Polly, the owner. He wanted me to know because he's not the creep you're trying to make him out to be."

"He dated her?"

"And she's a siren. So stick that in your Valkyrie pipe and smoke it."

"I don't even know what that means."

"Neither do I. It just came out."

"Go back to the part where Polly is a siren."

"Yes, he dated a siren. They're real. Apparently, everything is real. That shouldn't really surprise you. You're hooking up with the Chieftain of the Wild Hunt."

"Aren't you a little concerned that Lucien is popping off to visit his ex-girlfriend the siren on a Saturday afternoon?"

"She gives him information. That's how he confirmed his erroneous intel on Leo. Which he originally got from some anonymous source who's been tipping him off about our family."

There was a brief pause before they said the name together. "Carter Hanson Hamilton."

Rhea growled. "That absolute dirtball. It wasn't enough that he sent an actual Nazi after Leo to steal his soul, now he's setting up Lucien to send Leo to hell?"

"I don't have any proof that it's him."

"It's totally him. You know you're going to have to tell Ione about this."

As much as Theia hated the idea, Rhea was right. Which meant she was going to have to tell Ione everything about Lucien.

The haunting ought to have been routine. No over-the-top *Ghostbusters*-style vanquishing, no silly beeping

REM pod tech and primitive blinking flashlight communications. A haunting usually consisted of a simple soul collection. Easiest job on the books. Ordinarily, opening a portal wasn't even required. The haunting in the NICU last night had been an exception. As with Lupe Ramirez, often all that needed to happen was to convince the spirit or shade that it was in the wrong place, and it would go on its own. A forcible crossing, whether done with electrical current or by a practicing witch through spell casting, was generally considered undesirable and could be dangerous if not done right.

Lucien arrived in Litchfield Park west of Phoenix at ten after five, expecting to meet up with Lucy, who'd been in Phoenix already when the call came in. Her car was parked in front of the client's property. She'd gone in without him. Lucien swore to himself as he got out and approached the door. If she was going to handle it herself, why had she bothered to call him in on the job? He could be spending the evening with Theia.

The client, a young black man about Lucien's age, opened the door to his knock, looking frightened and harried. "You Lucien?"

Lucien paused. Something wasn't right. "Where's Lucy Smok?"

A hand reached from around the door and opened it wide. "Hi, sweetie! I'm right here." It was Lucy's voice and Lucy's body, but it was the most un-Lucy-like greeting he'd ever heard.

Lucien narrowed his eyes. "You're not Lucy. Don't bullshit me. Who am I speaking to?"

Her face broke into a grin. "And Lucy thinks you aren't the brainy one. Daisy Fox, at your service." She looked him up and down as she stepped around the client. "And you are absolutely dreamy." She stroked Lucien's cheek, and he stepped back with a shudder. "Guess you're not those kind of twins, huh?"

"What do you want, Daisy? My organization can help you without you having to resort to body theft."

"I doubt that. Besides, this is infinitely more fun." Daisy stroked Lucy's hands over her body before turning around to go back into the living room and flopping into an armchair like she owned the place.

Lucien addressed the client as he closed the door. "What happened?"

"My fiancée was acting weird—like your sister is now—and I worked out that she was possessed. So I called you people on the advice of a lawyer friend. Your sister showed up and tried to reason with the spirit. Next thing I knew, Sherrell—that's my girl—had collapsed, and the ghost was in your sister."

Across the room, Daisy beamed at Lucien out of Lucy's face.

This wasn't a simple haunting. It was a step-in, a forcible takeover of a living person by the deceased, unwilling to give up a life on the physical plane. And the shade had apparently hopped into Lucy when she'd attempted to compel it to release the body it occupied. As with a demon possession, this shade seemed to have the ability to move through the ether—and through hosts—at will. It was a rare shade that had such control, and Daisy's didn't fit the profile. Someone else was controlling it. They had a necromancer on their hands.

"Where's Sherrell now?"

"She's upstairs resting. She doesn't remember any of it. But I can't get this lady to leave. I mean, your sister. Or *not* her. Whatever it is."

"So Daisy Fox isn't someone you know?"

"Never heard of her."

"And when did this start, Mister…" He'd forgotten the client's name. Bad form.

"Mitchell. Jesse Mitchell." He held out his hand, and Lucien shook it. "Sherrell came home from work early yesterday acting funny. I thought she was sick. She didn't let on she wasn't Sherrell until this morning. That's when I called my friend. He represents some unusual clients, and I figured he might know what to do. He gave me your number."

That wasn't the usual method of client referral. Neither was the referral for the reanimation of Lupe Ramirez.

"Did your friend happen to explain how we work? I mean, he told you about the cost?"

Jesse stuck his hands in his pockets and swallowed before he nodded. "Your office explained it to me. I agreed to the terms. Your sister gave me a finger prick to sign the agreement." Traditionally, contracts for souls were signed in blood, but that was really just for show. They only needed a drop of blood, impressed with the signatory's thumbprint, to seal the deal.

Lucy-Daisy sighed loudly from the living room. "You boys are boring me to death." She laughed at the pun.

Lucien ignored her for the moment. "Thank you, Mr. Mitchell. I'll take care of the rest. It may take me a little while to get her to leave, but we'll get rid of her."

"Stop talking about me in the third person. It's very rude."

Lucien walked into the living room. "You're lecturing me about manners? You've violated at least two people intimately in the last forty-eight hours. That, Ms. Fox, is exceedingly rude."

"*Violated.* That's a very strong word. Ask our Jesse here. His girl is none the worse for wear."

"Just because someone can't remember what happened to them doesn't mean doing whatever you like with their body is okay. That's what violation is."

"You think I don't know what violation is? You think I don't know what it's like to wake up somewhere and not know what happened?"

"I don't know anything about you, Daisy. Why don't you tell me why you're doing this?"

"Why don't you go fuck yourself? I don't need you to condescend to me."

"Mr. Smok?" Jesse held out his phone with the browser open. "I found out who she is."

Lucien took the phone. A picture of a smiling young Navajo woman appeared. Lucien read the headline aloud. "Body Found in Phoenix Dumpster Identified as Daisy Fox, Missing From Window Rock Since April."

"Congratulations." Daisy gave them a slow clap. "You know how to use the internet."

Lucien handed back the phone. "I'm sorry that happened to you, Daisy."

"I don't need your pity, either."

"What do you need?"

"I've pretty much got what I need. Maybe some less stuffy clothes would be nice." Daisy rose, glancing out the window. "That my car? The black convertible?"

"You're not going anywhere with Lucy's car or Lucy's body." Lucien blocked her path to the door. "Why don't you tell me how you were able to step into her? She's not exactly inexperienced with people in your state."

Daisy laughed, an unnerving sound coming from Lucy's mouth. Not that Lucy didn't laugh, but it was usually a very dry laugh, indicating how deeply unamused she was by something.

"Did you have help?"

The laughter stopped. "What do you mean by help?"

"Is someone controlling you, Daisy?" If a necromancer was responsible, it was probably her killer—or at least someone with access to Daisy's bones. "Is it the person who hurt you?"

A flash of rage distorted Lucy's features. "He's not going to get me to give up this body, and neither are you."

"He will, Daisy. If he induced you to enter Sherrell, and he helped you hop from Sherrell to Lucy, he can make you do anything. But I can help you. I can make him stop."

"How can you help?" Lucy's face crumpled, another expression he'd never seen on his sister. "He took my body. I tried to get back in. I couldn't get back in."

A disturbing idea occurred to him. "Are you saying your body was still alive when you left it?"

Tears were streaming down Lucy's face. "He gave me a drug. Said it was just going to make me feel good. And then suddenly I was outside and I couldn't get back. He'd put something around my neck. Like a collar."

The necromancer had used a blocking object, something the shade couldn't cross to reenter her unconscious body.

"He said he wouldn't do anything to me—to my body—as long as I did what he asked. And I did. I went where he said. And now you're telling me my fucking body is a corpse!"

"You didn't know." Lucien touched Lucy's arm, and Daisy flinched. "I'm so sorry, Daisy."

Daisy jerked away from him. "So now he doesn't have anything on me and I don't have to give this one back."

"I'm afraid that's not how it works. He probably kept… a souvenir. A small bone is all he would need. That's how he could continue to dictate your actions. When you jumped into Lucy, was it a conscious thought? Or did you just find yourself here?"

Daisy shook her head, turning and looking around as if trying to find a way out. "I don't remember." She turned back to Lucien, her expression pleading. "Can't I just keep it? Can't I stay? I don't want to go."

Before he could answer, before he could even tell her it would be okay if he released her, that she could go where she pleased, Lucy's body collapsed.

Lucien caught her before she hit the ground. "Daisy?"

Her eyes fluttered erratically. "Fuck. *Me.* Goddammit."

Lucy was back.

She opened her eyes in a squint and glanced around. "Little bitch jumped me without warning. Did you vanquish her?"

"No."

"No?" Lucy pushed away from him, getting to her feet. "Then where the hell did she go?"

Lucien straightened. "Someone else appears to have forced her out. She was pleading to stay."

"Well, isn't that special?" Lucy gripped her head. "Ow. She gave me a damn migraine."

"I've got some ibuprofen." Jesse hurried upstairs to get it.

Lucy watched him go. "We should probably check on his girlfriend. Make sure the shade didn't just get pulled back into the original host."

"I doubt that's the case. Looks like you were the target. Daisy knew who you were. I think this whole thing was staged for our benefit. Whoever's controlling the shade was obviously trying to get our attention, letting us know we're vulnerable to their magic."

"Speak for yourself. She just caught me off guard."

Lucien folded his arms. "Lu. You've never been caught off guard in your entire life."

Jesse reappeared with the pills and a glass of water.

"Thanks." Lucy downed the pills. "If you don't mind, Mr. Mitchell, I need to look in on Sherrell. Just to make sure the problem is fully resolved."

Jesse nodded. "She's upstairs in the first bedroom."

Lucien nodded to Lucy. "I'll handle it. You take care of the business arrangements." He was being a coward, passing the responsibility of soul collecting back to Lucy after one attempt to do the right thing. But this wasn't a pay-on-receipt situation. There was time to remedy things if he found a way to later.

Lucien paused at the top of the stairs. Was that what he wanted to do? Was he going turn everything on its head and refuse to collect souls? The idea made him slightly heady. But the anxiety that followed immediately overshadowed the feeling. If he refused to fulfill the earthly duties of the Smok heir—what would it mean for the infernal ones?

Chapter 18

Lucy's post-step-in headache was still severe, so Lucien left his car and drove her back to Sedona in hers.

After several minutes, he glanced over at her, eyes closed as she leaned back against the seat. "You awake?"

Lucy scrunched her eyes together. "Unfortunately."

"I wanted to talk to you about something that happened at the job I went on earlier today. The reanimation reversal."

"Yeah, that sounded like a fun one."

"I gave the client the requisite dose for the payment, and she was prepared to pay in full that evening, but something happened to it. She found it in her mother's room. The old woman had taken it."

"Wasn't the old woman the one who was reanimated?"

"That was *her* mother. Rosa was the one who hired the reanimator. She has Alzheimer's, so someone must have taken advantage of her. She couldn't have had the presence of mind to think about how to bring her mother back from the grave. And now she's dead, too. I think the cleaning crew gave the meds to her."

Lucy opened her eyes in a squint. "The cleaning crew? They wouldn't even know what it was."

"Normally, I'd agree, but the client swore she'd put it in her own room in preparation for taking it that evening, and the old woman was still knocked out from the sedative I had to give her in order to vanquish the revenant." Lucien had meant to tell her about driving back with the intent of giving Mrs. Castillo her reprieve, but the story worked without the extra detail. Lucy would just assume the client had called him later. God, he really was a coward.

"Maybe the client's lying. Maybe she chickened out and didn't want to pay. It wouldn't have been the worst decision to give it to an old woman with Alzheimer's, after all."

"That's what I told her when I was there, but Mrs. Castillo was insistent that the payment was hers to make."

"I can't imagine why anyone from the cleaning crew would interfere in that. I suppose we can call the contractor tomorrow and ask." She closed her eyes again, and Lucien drove the rest of the way in silence, but his conscience was still nagging him as he dropped her off at her villa.

"Hey, Lu?"

She was already out the door, but she turned and leaned into the passenger window. "Yeah?"

"Have you ever…let a client off the hook on a deal like that?"

"Off the hook? You mean like the ghost girl the other night? Pro bono?"

"Sort of. I mean for the pay-on-receipts. Have you ever told them they didn't have to pay until the normal expiration of the contract?"

"Why would I do that?" Lucy peered at him with a suspicious expression. "Lucien. Did you tell that woman she didn't have to pay?"

"It didn't seem right. I drove back after I got home, and I asked for the pentobarbital back. I told her there had been a clerical error. You should have seen the joy in her face."

"We don't do this for joy."

"Why the hell *do* we do it?"

"You know why."

"Because of the curse."

"The curse?" Lucy laughed—the unlaugh he was used to hearing. "We do it because it's business. We offer a very important, needed service for a fee. Everyone goes into the agreement knowing full well what they're agreeing to. No one forces them to sign." She straightened and frowned. "This is that little empath's influence, isn't it? She told you it wasn't fair and said you were a bad man, so you defied centuries of protocol, jeopardizing our entire operation for some pussy."

"Don't talk about her like that."

"I notice you're not denying it. You'd better straighten up, Lucien. Edgar indulged your rebellious phase, and he turns a blind eye to the mystery archer who just happens to have all the same client information we do. But you start messing around with the business and he's going to rain down hell on your head."

Lucien laughed, copying Lucy's sharp sound of disdain. "What's he going to do, put me over his knee?"

"I'm not kidding, Lucien. Do *not* fuck with the business." Lucy slapped the hood of the car as she went around it. "And get your own damn ride home. This one's mine, and it's staying right here."

It was after ten by the time he got a car. He really wanted to see Theia, but he was bone tired. He'd have to call her and tell her he'd see her tomorrow at the lab. He had the driver take him home.

Lucien undressed on the way to the bedroom, looking forward to at least sexting with Theia for a few minutes before he passed out. She'd left him a message with pretty much the same conclusion he'd come to about the late hour and asking him to call when he got in. With his phone in his hand, he climbed into bed—and nearly sat on a brand-new laptop someone had placed there.

He smiled tentatively. Had Theia gotten him a gift? He opened the cover, which triggered some kind of automatic video messaging system, and found himself staring at his father, seated at his desk.

"Lucien."

"Edgar. I'm not really dressed for face time."

"Are you entertaining?"

"Not at the moment."

"Then put something on and sit down."

Lucien grabbed his robe from the bathroom and returned, trying not to let on that his stomach was in knots. For Edgar to want to talk to him in real time, face-to-face, he had to be in deep shit. Lucy had ratted him out.

Edgar was dressed in a conservative suit, as if he'd been conducting business at this hour, his steel-gray hair meticulously styled. "As you know, Lucien, being born a Smok comes with great responsibility."

"I know that—"

"Don't interrupt." Edgar's expression didn't change, but his voice dropped instantly into a deeper register. That tone had instilled fear in Lucien as a boy. It wasn't doing a half-bad job of it now. "I've been giving you space to grow up, to grow into these responsibilities. My father was so much harder on me. There was no sowing wild oats or running around like a spoiled adolescent doing as I pleased. I had to grow up fast. But I've never wanted to be hard and inflexible like my father. I've striven to give you and Lucy a better upbringing."

It was all Lucien could do to keep a straight face at the idea of Edgar as warm, loving patriarch.

"But there comes a time when a man has to take responsibility for his actions and to earn his keep. I'm not going to be around forever, and you're nearly twenty-five."

"Edgar—"

"I've spoken with the bank about your trust, which is slated to be fully under your control on your birthday." Which it almost certainly wasn't going to be now. "I hadn't planned to do this quite so soon, but a business opportunity has presented itself that makes the timing ideal. I'm prepared to start turning the business over to you." Edgar's mouth curved upward into what Lucien supposed was his idea of a warm, fatherly smile. "Think of it as an early birthday present."

Lucien had been concentrating so intently on Edgar's tone and facial expressions that he hadn't really been listening—because he'd thought he knew what was coming. But this was definitely not it.

"You… I'm sorry. What?"

"I've made arrangements for the day-to-day operations to fall to your sister. She really is the brain of the organization, and she's been handling much of it already. That will free you up to be the public face of Smok International and all our subsidiaries, which of course includes any and all business of a sensitive nature. I'd like you to meet with some of my colleagues tomorrow afternoon to get the ball rolling."

"I don't understand." Lucien struggled to follow. "You're turning the company over to me? Now?"

Edgar gave him that bizarre smile again. "Don't mention anything to Lucy until I have a chance to talk to her in the morning. I want to make sure she doesn't see this as some kind of a step down. The arrangement actually is quite favorable for her, but she's liable to overreact. She's very much like your mother in that regard."

"So... I'll be..."

"The chief executive officer of Smok International, with primary responsibility for the Smok Biotech division. Congratulations."

The knots in Lucien's stomach turned into a confusing mix of elation and anxiety. The company was his. He'd never dreamed Edgar would give up control of even the slightest bit of it so long as he was healthy and his wits were still sharp. The business opportunity he was willing to relinquish it for must be something astounding.

A million thoughts whirled through his head. He could change things now from the top down. If the company was really his to control, he could put a stop to the questionable practices that had bothered him all his life. He could actually help people, make their lives better. And he could make Smok's mission one that permanently removed the predatory elements they dealt with instead of rewarding them. No more turning a blind eye to abuse and mayhem. No more little girls trapped in blood slavery, considered expendable.

Edgar was still smiling. "I thought you'd be pleased. We'll go over all the details tomorrow, but there is one small condition I'd like to discuss with you before I make it official."

Lucien's mind was still lost in grand daydreams. "Condition?"

"I understand you've been keeping inappropriate company. Now, what you do for *recreation* isn't my concern. If you want to keep that what's her face, Polly, on the side, it's none of my business. Keep a dozen Pollys."

"I'm not seeing Polly anymore. You don't have to worry about me embarrassing you or the company."

"As I said, you can do what you like on your own time, in private. But I want you to stop seeing Theia Carlisle."

"Theia Dawn," he said automatically, before the meaning of his father's words struck him in the gut. "Wait. What are you saying?"

"You know perfectly well that the Carlisle sisters are the direct descendants of Madeleine Marchant. I don't have to tell you what harm that unsavory witch has done to this family. We've managed to turn the situation to our advantage over the centuries, but we do not forget where we come from, Lucien. And that will become even more apparent to you once I begin to show you the inner workings of the company. But I will not do so unless I have your solemn oath that you will sever ties with the girl completely. This is nonnegotiable."

Chapter 19

Lucien was dumbstruck. There was no way he was going to give Theia up. He needed her. More than he wanted to. But it was equally clear that Edgar wouldn't be swayed by any argument Lucien could make. When Edgar made up his mind about something, it was made up for everyone around him.

"Do I have your word, Lucien?"

"I… Can I think about this?"

"There is nothing to think about. If you refuse this one condition of mine, the company and all its holdings will go to Lucy. Your trust fund will be cut off. You will never see a penny of it. And Lucy will be under a legally binding oath not to turn around and give you a pity allowance after my death."

A moment ago, Lucien hadn't given a damn about the company other than the thorn it had always been in his side. Then he'd had an instant to reimagine it as his own before Edgar had taken it away again. But he'd never imagined being cut off completely. He wouldn't even begin to know how to survive by himself. For all his talk of wanting Lucien to become a man, Edgar had made him dependent on the company and his money, making sure he knew nothing about the details of living an independent life. Lucien felt like a fool.

"Edgar, I think if you met Theia—"

"I said this is nonnegotiable, Lucien. But if money alone doesn't sway you, perhaps you need a little bit of incentive to come to your senses and make a rational decision. I've sent you something via email. Look it over and get back to me tomorrow. I'll set up the meeting and send you the invite. If you don't show up on time, I'll assume you've made your decision, and I'll send someone to collect my property and revoke your access to Smok Biotech and any of our holdings. Good night, Lucien."

Edgar's parting shot had been straight to the heart. Lucien couldn't lose access to Smok Biotech's labs. He needed the research data on the anti-lycanthropy project. He needed the cure. Maybe if he went to the lab right now and downloaded everything he could onto an external drive… But Edgar would have thought of that. Lucien wouldn't be surprised if his access was temporarily suspended.

He pulled back his fist reflexively, preparing to punch the screen of the new laptop, but managed to draw his arm up short. This might be the only thing he had to his name by tomorrow. He couldn't afford to have a temper tantrum.

His phone buzzed, and Lucien picked it up, forgotten

on the pillow after finding Edgar's face staring at him. Theia wanted to know where he was.

Theia.

He could have everything he'd ever wanted—financial security, respect, power and the real possibility of effecting change in the world. Or he could have Theia—and lose everything he'd ever known. It shouldn't even be a contest. He should have been able to give Edgar his answer without hesitation: Theia was enough, she was everything, and Edgar could go fuck himself.

An email notification popped up on the laptop with a message from Edgar. He'd promised Lucien some additional incentive. What the hell could he possibly say in an email that would make a difference? But maybe Lucien shouldn't be hasty to make a decision. Maybe for once in his life he should weigh the evidence and come to a reasoned conclusion before making up his mind. It couldn't hurt to sleep on it.

The message notification on his phone chimed again. Everything okay?

Lucien typed in a response, his thumbs shaking.

Sorry. Took me forever to get home. Had to drive Lucy back from the job site. Long story. She wouldn't let me keep her car and I had to wait for a pickup.

He sent the message and watched Theia's typing bubble before writing another.

I really wanted to see you tonight, or even just talk for a bit, but I'm about to drop. Do you mind if we talk in the morning?

Her response came quickly enough, no sign that she was suspicious.

I totally understand. We'll see plenty of each other tomorrow. But I miss you already.

God, he missed her—like an essential amputated limb he hadn't even known he had until it was cut off. Talk about maudlin.

Miss you, too. Good night.

Theia sent a little heart emoji that made his actual heart twist.

Lucien turned off the phone, not wanting to allow himself to be distracted in case Theia texted again. He was going to read Edgar's email and give it due consideration, whatever it was. And then he was going to get some sleep. He'd find a way to make the right decision tomorrow. He just needed fortitude.

He opened the email and found that Edgar had sent him an attachment that looked remarkably similar to the one his anonymous source had directed him to containing Theia's genealogy research. If that's all it was, it wasn't incentive at all. He already knew about Theia's bloodline.

He breathed a sigh of relief. The scale had tipped toward Theia, and just that realization made it possible. He could do this. He could walk away from Smok's hold over him entirely. He could learn how to do something respectable for a living. He had some biotech knowledge, after all.

But that reminded him of the reason he'd painstakingly educated himself about the lycanthropy research.

If the legend turned out to be not just a legend, he might become what he'd always despised. And he wasn't sure how much time he had left. Without Smok, Lucien might become a monster.

He'd been scanning the document idly while his mind raced, when something caught his eye. This wasn't Theia's research after all. At least, not solely. Someone had made annotations.

The Lilith blood phenotype isn't simply a magical strain giving those with the dominant gene special abilities. Lilith blood is specifically designed to trigger paranormal abilities in those the Marchant-descended women choose to mate with. More than that, it seeks out such dormant abilities and acts as a pheromone, drawing in the unsuspecting mate. It is how Rafael Diamante Jr. became an avatar of Quetzalcoatl. It is how Dione "Ione" Carlisle controls her familiar, the demon within Dharamdev Gideon. And it is what led the immortal Leo Ström to Rhea Carlisle, one of the twin pair, released from the bond with the Valkyrie only to become bound to a descendant of Madeleine Marchant. It is the Lilith blood that makes these men surrender their human selves to these innocent-seeming women. And every one of the men ensnared becomes the embodiment of the beast: the serpent, the dragon, the snake—Lilith's companion. Together, the Carlisle sisters are the Whore of Babylon, riding on the back of the seven-headed dragon of the apocalypse.

Chapter 20

There was a problem with Theia's new access card when she arrived at the lab. When she came back down, the security guard at the front desk confirmed that it wasn't authorized for access to the floor where the Smok lab was situated.

"I guess something must have gotten mixed up in the system. Can you call Lucien Smok for me and tell him Theia Dawn is here?"

The guard dialed upstairs. "There's a Theia Dawn here to see Mr. Smok." After listening for a moment, she hung up, regarding Theia without expression. "Mr. Smok has left orders to revoke your access."

Theia wasn't sure she'd heard right. "My access… What?"

Someone spoke from behind her. "The job offer has been rescinded."

Theia turned to see Lucy, sharply dressed as always, giving her a cool, smug smile. "I suppose this is your doing."

"Not at all. Can't say I'm displeased about it, though."

"Why would Lucien rescind the offer? That doesn't make any sense. I just saw him yesterday. I talked to him last night."

"I'm well aware of the time you spend together. And I'm also aware that you got him to make a stupid mistake yesterday that resulted in an innocent woman's death. If you want to know why he's rescinded the offer, you can probably start there."

"That's ridiculous. I didn't make him do anything." Theia took her phone out of her bag. "I'm calling him right now to find out what's going on."

Lucy shrugged, arms folded. "Be my guest."

The phone rang once before rolling over to voice mail. Which meant he'd declined the call when he saw her name. What the hell was going on?

Lucy was smug. "Looks like he's busy."

Theia's hand curled around the phone at her side. "I want to know what this is about. Did something happen on the job you two were on yesterday evening?"

"Something always happens on a job. It's an unpredictable business. But we left a satisfied customer, as always."

"Oh, really?" Theia lowered her voice. "Someone was satisfied to sign away their soul?"

Lucy frowned, uncrossing her arms. "This is why it's a bad idea to bring outsiders in. You don't understand the nuances of these issues, and you aren't meant to. But this is not something you can just stand here in the middle of our lobby and talk about as you please."

"It's not exactly your lobby. This is a university building, and I happen to be a student here as well as faculty."

"That can change."

"Excuse me?"

Lucy turned and walked toward the exit. "If you want to have a candid discussion about the change of plan, follow me."

Theia paused, glancing back down at her phone. She could send Lucien a text and just wait here. He couldn't be completely cutting her off. Something had happened, and if she could just talk to him, they could work it out.

Lucy turned back at the door. "This is the only offer you're going to get. If you don't leave voluntarily, security is instructed to send for the campus police to escort you out."

Theia's mouth dropped open. They couldn't just kick her out of a university building. Could they? What if she'd been expelled from the graduate program? She could at least get some answers from Lucy—whatever grain of truth there might be to them—and try to reach Lucien again later. Dropping the phone back into her purse, Theia pressed her lips together and followed Lucy through the door.

Lucy walked her out to the parking lot. Maybe Theia was being a sucker, and Lucy wasn't going to tell her anything after all. She hesitated at the edge of the lot as Lucy pressed the button on her key fob and the convertible beside them beeped in response.

Lucy nodded toward the car. "Get in."

"Where are we going?"

"We're not going anywhere. It's the only secure place to talk."

Theia opened the passenger door reluctantly and slipped inside, leaving it open a crack.

Lucy got in beside her and reached across to close it. "I'm not kidnapping you, for God's sake. I'm trying to avoid being overheard."

"Overheard saying what?"

She fixed her gaze on Theia, the same startling pale eyes as Lucien's, her expression grim. "The reason Lucien isn't responding is that our father made him an offer last night that he couldn't refuse."

"What kind of offer?"

Lucy's mouth twitched. "He's turning over the entire enterprise to Lucien immediately, something we didn't expect for years to come."

Theia knitted her brow. "What does that have to do with my working for Smok Biotech?"

"It's not about you working for Smok Biotech—though I can't stress enough what a really stupid idea that was. It was a condition of the offer. Edgar insisted that Lucien stop seeing you."

Theia's eyes smarted as if there were smoke in the air. "He offered Lucien control of the company if he stopped seeing me?"

"Not just the company." There was that twitch again. "Everything. He either stops seeing you or he loses it all, cut off without ceremony."

Theia raked her hands through her hair, trying to process this. "I have to talk to him. He doesn't have to do this. And he doesn't want to. I'm sure of that."

Lucy's expression was cold. "I'm not here to help you jeopardize Lucien's livelihood. I just wanted you to know so you'd stop trying to contact him. You can't change his mind—Lucien needs Smok Biotech more than you can possibly understand—and you won't change Edgar's."

Theia frowned. "I don't believe you."

"That's your problem."

"I mean about why you're telling me this. Why not just wipe my memory like you threatened to? You could probably wipe Lucien clean out of my brain, couldn't you?"

"Do you want me to?"

"*No*, I don't want you to. I want to know why you chose to tell me the truth about what's going on with Lucien—if it's the whole truth—instead of just taking the easy way out. Making sure I'd never bother you again. There has to be a reason you're telling me this."

Lucy looked out through the windshield. "Lucien said you were intuitive."

"Sometimes."

She was quiet a moment before taking a preparatory breath. "There's something wrong with all this. Edgar retiring without warning, giving Lucien sole control of the company. I didn't see it coming. The way he's always talked about Lucien, I half expected him to eventually give the company to me after he got tired of waiting for Lucien to grow up. He's given me all the financial responsibilities—I've already been handling them, but he's officially making me the CFO—but the company will be Lucien's." Lucy paused. "And there's a silent partner."

"Meaning what?"

"Meaning my father has signed over a percentage of the company to an investor who doesn't want to be publicly connected to it. I suppose a secret partner is a better word for it. He wants to benefit from our success and meddle in the business without anyone holding him responsible."

A chill ran up Theia's spine as Lucy spoke. "Who is this secret partner?"

Lucy gave her a sidelong eye roll. "It wouldn't really be a secret if I shared it with you, now would it?"

"What if I guessed?"

Noncommittal, Lucy waited with an expression of mild interest.

"Would it happen to be Carter Hanson Hamilton?"

Lucy's dark brows lifted. "I guess you really *are* psychic."

"Not exactly. It's just what I'd expect of him. I suppose you know our history?"

"Who doesn't? The murder trial was highly publicized."

"He also tried to steal my sister Phoebe's soul and have her killed while he was in prison last year, and he sent a Nazi who was obsessed with Norse mythology after Leo Ström. The creep kidnapped me and unleashed a *draugr* on Rhea."

Lucy's eyes registered sudden understanding. "So that's what was up with that. We got an alert from one of our staff psychics that someone was using one of the holy relics from the Third Reich to raise the dead, but it was handled before we had a chance to investigate." She studied Theia. "So Ström sent the Nazi's soul to Náströnd, I take it?"

"And destroyed the *draugr*, yes."

Lucy laughed. "My baby brother has more in common with that Viking than he thinks."

"Baby brother?"

"Technically, I was born the day before he was—11:58 p.m. I ought to be the heir, but our father is a traditionalist. Which is why I can't imagine him agreeing to a partnership with Hamilton. We've consulted for him in the past, but Edgar could never stand him. Said Hamilton was an opportunistic amateur who didn't respect the limits of power. This whole thing came completely out of the blue, and it has me worried. And Hamilton has already sent me inappropriate emails. I don't know what he thinks is going to happen, but if he imagines for one minute that I'm one of the perks of his partnership, he's going to be sorely disappointed. If he so much as looks at me, he's going to lose his balls."

Lucy seemed to realize she wasn't alone in the car, and she drew herself upright. "At any rate, he's a problem, and I don't like problems. Whatever he has planned for Smok International, I intend to be a thorn in his side. But don't think I'm not pleased as punch about Lucien dumping you. I'd hate for you to make the mistake of thinking that this cozy little conversation means we're friends. And Lucien has nothing to do with this. I'm not going to mention to him that I've had any contact with you, and I'm not going to try to persuade him that he's making a mistake."

"Fair enough." Theia would find a way to get Lucien to talk to her. She opened the door, since it looked like the conversation was over. "Thank you for telling me. You didn't have to."

"I didn't do it for you. Lucien has enough on his plate to deal with. He doesn't need you complicating things."

Theia paused with her hand on the door. "Has it occurred to you that Carter might be using necromancy on your father?"

"You mean with a step-in?" Lucy shook her head. "No. He's definitely himself, even if his actions are unusual. A step-in wouldn't be able to fool anyone for a prolonged period of time. And I've talked to him at length."

Theia nodded and got out but turned back once more before closing the door. "Don't underestimate Carter Hamilton. One thing you can be certain of is that he has a plan. And he's obsessed with other people's power."

Chapter 21

Theia had left him another message. He ought to block her number if he was serious about this. And he *had* to be serious about this. She was dangerous to him. Even without the role her blood might play in the fulfillment of the Smok curse, being with Theia meant losing access to Smok's labs. And even if Lucy was willing to defy Edgar's wishes and allow Lucien access to the research, it was useless without access to the scientists working on his cure.

Until now, developing the anti-transformative had been a fail-safe, something to fall back on in case the legend turned out to be true. If, at some distant point in the future, his father's death triggered what lay dormant in Lucien's blood, Lucien would simply be able to take a pill and suppress the infernal transformation. But the warning his father had sent him about Rafe, Dev and Leo rang true. Which meant Theia's interest him—his very attraction to her—was fated. It was the Lilith blood that wanted to bring forth the devil in him.

Lucien turned off his phone, unwilling to sever the ties completely. Which was a bad sign, and he knew it. But he wasn't ready. Not yet. What he needed now was a distraction.

Polly had brought in a good crowd this evening. As Lucien threaded his way through it, he discovered why. Polly had booked a performer. To anyone unfamiliar with the clientele that frequented Polly's, it looked like an erotic dance performance. But the anemic-looking blonde was obviously a bloodsucker groupie, and it became apparent as she worked the pole and stripped down to her G-string that she had tracks in the less visible places that vampires with discretion preferred for feeding. The purpose of the striptease wasn't to titillate sexually, it was to arouse the vamps. And once she had, they came to the stage—not to put dollar bills in her G-string but to taste.

She clearly got a sexual charge of her own out of it. Lucien looked away in disgust as the bloodsuckers crowded around, dipping their fangs into the marks at the undersides of her arms, beneath her breasts, inside her thighs, and sucking greedily. The donor moaned and crooned with pleasure and finally climaxed loudly, and the crowd cheered.

"Not your thing, baby?" Polly smiled down at him, dressed tonight in poison-green silk with long aquamarine locks to match. She could easily have swum out of a pre-Raphaelite painting.

"Blood porn? No. Never. But then you know that."

Polly slipped into the seat opposite him, managing

to give him a sympathetic look. "I haven't forgotten. If I'd known you were planning on making an appearance here again so soon, I'd have moved the performance to another night."

"No, you wouldn't, but it's sweet of you to say so." Lucien downed his third bourbon.

Polly raised an eyebrow at his empty glass and signaled one of her staff to bring him another. "Anything bothering you? You usually don't drink alone these days."

"I'm celebrating." Lucien tried to smile and felt like he couldn't remember how. He was an alien pretending to be human. He gave it up and raised his glass after the waiter refilled it. "You're looking at the new CEO of Smok International."

Polly took the bottle from the waiter and picked up the glass he'd set in front of her. "Congratulations." She watched Lucien over the rim as she sipped. "Do I detect a note of dissatisfaction with your good fortune?"

"You haven't asked if Edgar's kicked the bucket." Lucien took another drink, and Polly refilled it. "He hasn't, by the way. He just decided out of the blue to retire and turn the whole thing over to me."

"And there's a catch, of course."

With a nod, he drank again. "No dirty Marchant blood allowed."

One green eyebrow twitched. "You mean Carlisle blood, I take it."

"Same thing."

"You like this Carlisle girl. A great deal."

Lucien shrugged and emptied his glass.

"Sorry, sweetie. I told you no good would come of that association, but I hate to see you like this."

The suckfest on stage was getting louder. They were

practically having a vampire orgy right in the middle of Polly's Grotto. The donor had been lifted into the air on her back—crowd surfing—so they didn't have to crouch to feed. Lucien was starting to wish he'd brought his crossbow.

He glared at Polly. "How far are you planning to let them go? They're going to bleed her dry."

Polly waived her hand dismissively. "They know the rules. She knows her limits. This isn't her first performance."

"No doubt. She's reaching another one of her limits right now, from the sound of it."

Polly reached across the table to take Lucien's hand even as she refilled his drink. "This thing is really eating you up. I wish I could do something to help."

Lucien laughed. "Is that an offer?"

Polly smiled knowingly. "There's always a standing offer for you, baby." Her thumb rubbed against his palm, a suggestive stroke and press.

"You're doing the silent song tonight, I see."

Polly's smile didn't waver. "We've always been so very much in tune."

He could take solace in her as he had before, both of them knowing it was only solace. Knowing she had any number of lovers and didn't need him one bit. Instead, she wanted him. He couldn't help being flattered. Lucien let his thumb move along the webbing between her thumb and forefinger.

The sweet scent of violets wafted toward him through the smoky air. The same scent Theia's skin had as he'd pressed his lips to it.

"Lucien?"

He jumped at the sound of Theia's voice.

Lucien pulled his hand out of Polly's—a bit force-fully, because she resisted—and turned to look up, mortified. But it wasn't Theia. It was her more colorful twin. Rhea stared ice daggers into him with Theia's gray eyes. And the Viking stood behind her, arms folded and fists clenched like he was resisting punching Lucien in the face.

Rhea turned her ice daggers on Polly. "Who the hell is this?"

"This is Polly. She owns the—"

"Oh, I've heard of Polly. Polly the siren. Nice. Jerk." Rhea turned back to Lucien as Polly raised her eyebrows with amusement. "Theia's sobbing her eyes out trying to figure out what she did wrong, and it turns out it's because she's not some tarted-up sex siren."

Polly's eyes narrowed.

"Theia didn't do anything wrong."

Rhea's gaze shifted, fixed over his head at the stage. "Holy shit." She looked to Lucien once more, her gaze now more fire than ice. "Is this what you're into? Live sex shows? Theia totally dodged a bullet with you, asshole. Come on, Leo. Let's go."

"It's not a sex show," said Lucien. "They're…" What was the point in finishing that thought, though, really? He took a drink of his topped-off bourbon.

"They're drinking her blood," Polly offered helpfully. "I believe your erstwhile immortal friend here has seen a similar performance a time or two." Polly smiled at Leo. "Isn't that right?"

Leo's face turned bright red, and he ran his fingers through his untidy reddish-blond hair in a nervous gesture that was amusing given his usual demeanor.

Rhea glowered, looking up at him. "Leo?"

"A long time ago," he muttered. "With Faye."

Lucien snorted. He'd drunk just enough to be extremely incautious. "I've heard a few things about you and Faye." He could feel Leo's eyes on him without looking up.

Leo took a step closer to the table, the awkward moment having apparently passed. "Care to elaborate?"

"Talked to a few Valkyries," said Lucien. "To hear them tell it, you were something of a kept man." He picked up his drink again. He'd lost count of which number this was. "Kept on a leash."

The glass spun out of his hand so fast, it took Lucien a moment to realize Leo had knocked it from his grasp.

While Lucien was still contemplating the unexpected speed, Leo grabbed his collar in both fists and hauled him from his seat. "Why don't you say that to my face?"

Rhea shifted her feet, boots crossed at the ankle as she bit her lip. "Leo, let's just go. He's not worth it."

Lucien met Leo's eyes and smiled. "Kept. On. A. Leash."

"Oh, shit." He heard the words from Rhea before he found himself flat on his back on the table with Leo's fist in his face. He wasn't really feeling it. Which meant he'd had way more to drink than he wanted to admit.

He slithered out of Leo's grasp and hit the back of his head on the table as he dropped to the ground. That smarted a little. It would smart more tomorrow. Lucien scrambled up and dashed past Leo, heading for the door, but Leo caught him by the arm—the arm Lucien had forgotten to see the doctor about. He heard the snap before he felt the thick pop of the solidified ecto gel stretching and bending.

Leo let go of him, looking slightly nauseous. Rhea's

eyes were wide, and even Polly looked a little green—notwithstanding the evening's wardrobe choice.

"What?" Lucien stared at them, swaying slightly. He wasn't sure if it was the blow to his head or the booze. And then he glanced down and saw his arm pointing the wrong way at the elbow. And a bone sticking out of it. And chartreuse gel oozing from it like an ectoplasmic emanation. Or putrefaction. He wasn't sure which one of those things made the blood rush out of his head before he dropped.

Head swimming, he was dimly aware of being carried off the floor to a back room while Polly spoke.

"I'd happily let him stay here for the night, but I have a business to run at the moment, and I think he needs medical attention." She seemed weirdly far away.

"Yeah, I'm sure you would be *thrilled* to." Rhea's voice, dripping with sarcasm. "Which is precisely why he's going with us."

"He's not our problem," Leo muttered under his breath.

"You *are* the one who knocked…*that*…out of his arm." Polly again. "Violence is strictly forbidden in the Grotto, as I'm sure you're aware. But I'm willing to overlook the infraction if you'll see that Lucien's taken care of. I suggest you call Lucy. No doubt she'll have experience with…whatever that is."

"I think she gave him some kind of shot the other night when it was broken," said Rhea. "Let's just call her, Leo. We can hand him over to her and be done with it. Her number's in his phone under Bitch."

Lucien giggled.

Someone was digging in his pockets. He'd left his phone at home so he wouldn't be tempted to check Thela's texts.

"It's not here," the Viking growled.

Lucien made a dismissive motion with his arm, trying to indicate that he didn't have the phone, but his arm evidently didn't quite do what it was supposed to, and everyone groaned.

He opened his eyes, focusing on Polly frowning down at him. "I'll get an Uber," he tried to say, but it didn't sound like that, either.

"Get Anubis?" Rhea glanced at Leo. "What is he talking about?"

Leo looked baffled. Lucien started to laugh. That's when he realized he was insanely drunk and that he was going to regret all of this, and he didn't care.

Rhea's disapproving expression made him laugh harder. "Okay, let's just get him outside. I'll call Theia. Maybe she has Lucy's number." For some reason, this made Lucien laugh even harder.

With a growl of disgust, Leo hauled Lucien off the couch he was lying on, one arm braced under Lucien's unbroken one. Polly showed them the back way out of her private suite into the alley, and Lucien stumbled along with Leo, giggling like an idiot.

Rhea walked ahead of them to the parking lot, her phone in her hand. "Thei? We have a bit of a situation here. Lucien's been injured. Again. Do you have Lucy's number? He doesn't have his phone on him." There was a brief pause. "Okay, well, you don't have to yell. And Leo didn't do it. I mean, he did, kind of, but it wasn't his fault."

A cheerful chirp and flash of taillights announced that they'd reached Rhea's little red car, and Leo opened the door and shoved Lucien into the back.

Rhea glanced inside dubiously while Lucien tried to

fold his legs into it, half reclining. "He'd better not puke in Minnie Driver." She spoke into the phone again as she got behind the wheel. "Just give us his address, then. We'll drive him home and he can call Lucy himself." Rhea listened for a moment. "Oh, for God's sake. Fine. Then we're coming to you."

Someone was operating a jackhammer in the next room. Lucien groaned and tried to cover his ears, only to find his right arm screaming with pain like someone had stuck a knife through it.

"What. The. Fuck."

"Lucien?" The jackhammering came again. Except it probably wasn't a jackhammer but someone knocking on his door. "Are you awake?"

He rolled onto his side so he could cover one ear and press the other to the pillow. "No."

The door opened, and light flooded the room. Lucien moaned in protest.

"I brought you some extra-strength aspirin." It was Theia. He could smell violets. Though he supposed it could be Rhea. Except she wasn't swearing at him. It was Theia. "Figured you might want it. For a number of reasons."

Without opening his eyes, Lucien held out his hand, and Theia placed the pills in his palm. He swallowed them dry before realizing she was holding a glass of water. She set it beside him on the nightstand. His mouth felt like he'd been sucking on gauze. He was probably going to need to sit up and drink that. Eventually. Maybe when he was dead.

Theia was still hovering. "I didn't know if I should

take you to the emergency room. I figured they wouldn't know what to make of that…stuff."

Lucien grunted, hoping it was an acceptable answer.

"Lucien, can you just talk to me for a minute? Like you give a damn that I'm here?"

Reluctantly, he opened one eye. And felt like the biggest asshole alive. Theia's eyes were red and puffy, like she'd been crying for hours. Probably all night and then some.

"I'm sorry." It was the only thing he could think of to say. Because he was. Sorry to his bones. Sorry he wasn't strong enough to stand up to his father. Sorry that he knew what he knew about her—and that he'd let it define his actions. Sorry that he'd ever met her, because how was he ever going to be normal again without her?

"I tried to call you. I texted you a dozen times."

"I know."

"Acting like I don't exist so you don't have to deal with your decision to choose money over me is a shitty thing to do. Can you just tell me to my face that you don't want to see me?"

Lucien sat up, clutching the bed to try to keep it from spinning. "No, I can't."

"You can't tell me to my face."

"I don't want to." The look on her face made Lucien's heart hurt. Dammit, hearts were stupid. Even stupider than heads, which in his case was pretty damn stupid. *Shut up, heart. Shut up.* "I don't want to because I don't want it to be true. But it is."

The pained look in Theia's eyes turned hard. "Okay. Well, I'm glad we cleared that up. I'll call you a cab." She slammed the door before he could say anything else, and the reverberating echo, like rocks smashing together in his head, made it impossible.

After a moment, Lucien realized he was in the master bedroom, which had a bathroom attached. He rolled out of the bed and made his way to the toilet, bracing his left hand on the bed for balance. He had to use the left hand to aim, too, which was awkward.

As he made his way back through the bedroom, he paused with his hand on the doorknob. What was he going to say to her? What the hell was he going to do?

Reflected in the full-length mirror in front of him was a painting hanging over the bed: John Collier's *Lilith*—the redheaded nude with the secretive smile—in the embrace of the snake. Maybe it *was* his fate. Maybe he should stop running from it. Leo and Rafe Diamante and Dev Gideon seemed perfectly happy with their lot. Maybe he could embrace the devil inside him and everything would be okay.

And maybe hell was real, and he would find himself dragged down into it, unable to escape Madeleine Marchant's curse.

His arm throbbed, and his head was pounding. And his goddamn heart hurt. He opened the door, ready to tell Theia that he was an idiot, that he was prepared to defy his father's wishes, and he didn't care if he was penniless and hell-bound so long as he was with her.

Theia stood by the open front door at the end of the hallway. "Your cab is here. Hurry up. I don't want Puddleglum to get out."

Chapter 22

The cab pulled out onto the drive, and Theia let the edge of the curtain fall. She was done crying over Lucien. He could go to hell for all she cared.

Rhea had told her about Polly and how Lucien had been having no trouble at all getting over Theia. It hardened her resolve. Let the siren have him. Theia had been ignoring all the omens, all the warnings, all the dreams. Now she didn't have to, because fate had decided for her.

With Carter's help.

Theia frowned. It was past time to talk to Ione. There was something happening here that was bigger than having her heart stomped on. Might as well bite the bullet and do it face-to-face. She still had Ione's shawl from the reception to return.

Theia texted her sister to tell her she was coming by with the shawl and headed out.

Ione was in a considerably better mood than she'd been after the wedding. Which of course Theia was going to ruin by bringing up Carter again. After dropping off the shawl, she lingered in Ione's garden, trying to figure out how to broach the subject while Ione trimmed her roses, but, as usual, her big sister managed to be one step ahead of her.

"Rhea says you have a new job. When does it start?"

Theia sniffed a cluster of tea roses. "It fell through, actually."

"That's too bad." Ione deadheaded a limp rose with her pruning shears. "You and that Smok boy looked pretty good together."

Theia groaned into the rose petals. "Why do you always know everything before I tell you about it?"

Ione gave her a cryptic smile. "I have my witchy ways."

"Nice. You're doing magic divination about my love life. Who isn't?"

"Rhea, for one. She says you won't let her read your tattoos."

Theia stepped back from the rosebush with a glare. "She told you about Lucien."

"She was a little worried about you. I'm sorry it didn't work out."

"That's kind of what I came to talk to you about."

"Oh? I thought you came to bring back my shawl." Ione gave her that look again that said Theia was fighting a losing battle if she thought she could ever put one over on her big sister.

"I don't suppose Rhea mentioned anything about Lucien's hobby."

"She did say something about an archery incident."

"Did she happen to tell you that someone's been feeding Lucien information about us to get him to target Leo and Rafe and Dev?"

Ione scowled. "It's *him*, isn't it? That's what he was doing at the wedding. Letting us know he had us in his sights."

Theia inspected another rose before broaching the rest of it. "I talked to Lucien's sister yesterday and found out Carter has signed on as a silent partner with Smok International. Lucy says he has some kind of influence over her father—I'm betting you and I can guess how—and the whole thing has her worried."

"Lucy?"

"Lucien's sister. They're twins. She kind of hates me. But I think she hates Carter more."

With a sharp snip of her shears, Ione managed to deadhead a happily blooming rose. "What does he want with a pharmaceutical company?"

"It's more like parapharmacology. I can't really get into the specifics. I signed a nondisclosure agreement. But suffice it to say, there are…magical applications. The company also has a consulting arm that cleans up after magical accidents. They cleaned up your place."

"*My* place?"

"After you, uh, let Kur out that first time."

Ione blushed but shook her head. "That was Rafe's crew."

"The construction crew was Rafe's. The cleaners were contractors. From Smok."

Ione's eyes darkened. "Which Carter now owns part of."

"Which means he has a potential foot in the door of every magical household in the world."

"Lovely."

Theia stepped away from the roses. "I have to drive to Flagstaff, so I'd better get going. I just thought you should know."

Ione walked her to the garden gate, frown lines etched into her forehead.

Theia turned back after opening it. "By the way, congratulations, Mrs. Gideon." She winked and gave Ione a kiss on the cheek.

Ione's eyes widened before narrowing into a glare. "I told him not to tell you. And it's Ms. Carlisle, thank you very much. I'm not changing my name."

Theia grinned. "Of course you're not."

Lucien gritted his teeth as the doctor extracted the last of the gel.

Fran gave him a disapproving look from behind her rimless glasses. She'd been treating Lucien's mishaps for most of his life.

"You know this wouldn't be this painful if you'd just called me the day after it happened."

"Yes, I know. Yes, I'm an idiot. Yes, I deserve every ounce of pain I've got coming."

Fran glanced over the top of her lenses. "I wouldn't go quite that far. But it is going to be painful, unfortunately. And not just right now. It's not possible to restore the bone fully since you've let this gel degrade. I'm removing as much as I can, but you're likely to retain some residual gel in the joint, which will probably cause some chronic stiffness and inflammation."

"You mean I've managed to give myself arthritis before I even hit my midtwenties."

Fran shrugged apologetically. "That's about the size of it."

"Fantastic."

The doctor straightened, holding up the large syringe full of fluorescent gray-green sludge. "That should do it. As for the break, I think we can avoid a full cast and keep it immobilized with a splint. As long as you promise not to get into any more fights until it heals."

"Yeah, I think my fighting days may be over."

"I heard you're taking the helm at Smok. Congratulations. I never thought Edgar would retire. Certainly not this early." Fran glanced up as she adjusted the straps of the splint. "How does Lucy feel about all this?"

"I don't know. I haven't spoken to her."

"Do you think that's wise? I mean, she is still the CFO. Not to mention your sister."

"She'll get over it." Lucien's response was a bit terse, but it seemed a little inappropriate for Fran to comment on family business. He supposed she saw the two of them as almost like family of her own, having treated them since they were kids. And she was also his shrink.

Fran was quiet as she finished and packed up her bag, and Lucien felt like a jerk. It was becoming a familiar feeling.

"Thanks for making the house call." He lifted his arm gingerly. "It still hurts like hell, but honestly, it feels at least fifty percent better."

Fran's warm smile was back. "That's what Edgar pays me for." She studied him for a moment. "Have you been sleeping well? You look a little wan."

Lucien laughed. He was born wan.

"There's been a lot to get used to. And I drank more than I should have last night."

"If you need a prescription for a sleep aid, I can write one up." She took out a pen. "Or a refill on your antidepressants or antianxiety meds."

"Thanks, but I think I'm good."

After she'd gone, Lucien discovered a message waiting for him from Edgar. He was being summoned: a command performance with the board of directors to meet the new financial partner—none other than Carter Hamilton. Nothing like being thrown into the deep end with the sharks. The informal meeting with Edgar's inner circle the day before had been tedious enough. This was the part of the business he'd never wanted to inherit. Lucien was beginning to think he'd made a very bad bargain.

His first official appearance as CEO would be with his arm in a sling. Not exactly the picture of confidence he wanted to project. He was the last to arrive. Lucy sat at what was usually Edgar's right hand, but Edgar stood behind the chair at the head of the table, waiting to turn it over to Lucien. Lucy's expression was stoic. Not that stoicism was anything new for her. Edgar gave Lucien a big, pretentious smile. It was all for the benefit of the board. Lucien was sure Edgar had never smiled at him genuinely in his life.

After Edgar introduced him and the board politely applauded, Lucien took the CEO's seat while Edgar moved to a seat among the other members. To Lucien's left sat Carter Hamilton in the flesh, polished and overeager, like a slick, blond, high-end car salesman. He seemed innocuous enough, but something about him raised the hairs on the back of Lucien's neck. Maybe it was the overdone tan that put Lucien in mind of a grifter politician.

After the preliminary business was out of the way and niceties had been exchanged about Lucien's place in the firm, Edgar turned to Hamilton. "As you know, Carter Hanson Hamilton has thrown in his lot with the Smok enterprise. He'll be working closely with Lucy in restructuring our executive operations." Edgar paused and laughed. "I should say *your* executive operations. As of today, I'm officially stepping down from active participation in the company." Surprised glances were exchanged around the table. "Carter, would you like to say a few words?"

Unnecessarily, Carter pushed back his chair and got to his feet. "Thank you, Edgar. I'm thrilled to be a part of the Smok family. I see a new, even more prosperous tomorrow for Smok International, and I'm delighted to be able to work with the lovely Lucy Smok on making our plans come to fruition."

Lucy's mouth curved into a smile, but her eyes weren't participating.

As Carter spouted a few more lines of inane corporate babble and the board began to discuss the day's business, Lucien's mind wandered. What was he even doing here? He could be with Theia, curled up in bed and nursing his hangover. Instead, he was becoming his father, the last person he'd ever wanted to be.

The meeting was over before Lucien expected it, and he started guiltily, wondering if he'd actually fallen asleep with his eyes open. The board members were approaching him to shake his hand and apparently to try to cozy up to him with more corporate babble and flattery.

Carter was the last to greet him personally. Though the other members had casually taken Lucien's left hand without comment, Carter made a point of reaching for the right and stopping short.

"My apologies." He offered his own left hand instead. "Tennis accident?"

Lucien shook his hand, annoyed by the unnecessary firmness of Carter's grip and the way he pulled Lucien in toward him like an insecure ape trying to assert dominance. "Archery. It's a hobby." For some reason he felt the need to add, "Crossbow."

Carter was still gripping his hand. "Ah, are you a hunter, Mr. Smok?"

"Like I said, it's a hobby." Lucien pulled back on his arm, and Carter finally released him. Lucien resisted the urge to wipe his hand on his slacks.

"I'm more of a racquetball man myself. I have a court reserved every Wednesday at 10:00 a.m. on campus. Perhaps we could meet tomorrow and…" Carter glanced at Lucien's sling. "Oh, right. Sorry. Maybe another time when you're feeling up to it." Carter turned to Lucy, who was packing up her briefcase. "Lucy, why don't you meet me there tomorrow? It will give us a chance to discuss strategy."

Lucy paused and glanced up at Carter as if he'd just suggested joining him in a naked mud bath. "I have some other commitments, so I afraid I can't…" Her words trailed off, and she stared openmouthed as Carter turned and started talking to one of the other members of the board without listening to her response.

As the board members filtered out, Lucien turned to go, but Edgar tapped him on the shoulder.

"If you don't mind, Lucien, I have some details to go over with you. Can you stay a few minutes?"

Lucien glanced at Lucy, who was heading out the door. He couldn't remember the last time he'd been alone in a room with Edgar. He was a grown man, and the idea actually made his stomach churn with anxiety.

"Can it wait?"

Edgar's dark brows drew together in disapproval. "No, Lucien. It cannot wait. Have a seat."

Lucien returned to the table reluctantly, hesitating at the chair he'd been sitting in before. Deciding it would be a gesture of respect to leave it for Edgar, he took one on the side, leaving a gap between them.

But Edgar remained on his feet. "You may have some questions about the timing of my announcement. I've already spoken to Lucy about it, but I thought you should know." He clasped his hands behind his back and paced around the table.

"Know?"

"I'm sure you're aware that I've used Smok's patented medication for some years to supplement my youthfulness. It turns out that prolonged use has some rather unfortunate side effects. Not surprising ones, really, when it comes right down to it." Edgar stopped pacing and turned to face Lucien. "Quite simply, things are falling apart. Rapidly. Both body and mind. I was very lucky to run into Carter Hamilton recently. He's in remarkable health for his age, as it happens, and has never used a drug." He crossed to the window and looked out at the mountains, perfectly framed. "I'm not well, Lucien. But Carter is extraordinarily well. He's agreed to share the secret of his good health with me in exchange for majority interest in Smok's holdings."

Lucien had known Edgar was older than he looked. Even as a small child, he'd been aware that his father was quite a bit older than the parents of his peers, but it was never spoken of. Lucien and Lucy's mother hadn't been his father's first wife, but they were the only children Edgar had fathered. Lucien had always suspected it was why his mother had left after performing the job she'd presumably been recruited for—producing an heir. For all he knew, she'd been paid for it.

"Why step down as CEO?"

Edgar turned, his brow creased with annoyance. "What?"

"I understand making a bargain with Carter Hamilton for whatever his secret is, but once you've done that, why not continue to run the company?"

Edgar's expression was stiff. "That wasn't the bargain. The company is yours. Stop whining about it."

"I'm not whining. I'm just curious."

"You're trying to squirm out of your responsibilities as always. Don't think I didn't notice your lack of interest and participation in the meeting today. And I wasn't the only one who noticed. You can't rely on Lucy to do everything for you your entire life, Lucien. You're a man. Act like one."

Lucien's face burned. There was no retort he could make to any of that, because it was true.

"If there's nothing else…" He got to his feet, eager to be anywhere but here.

"There is, in fact, something else." Edgar's expression was grim. "We need to discuss the legacy bequeathed by Madeleine Marchant."

The name, as always, sent a chill down Lucien's spine. "So there is one, then."

"Of course there is one. Why on earth do you think I've been prolonging my life?"

Lucien had assumed it was the reason anyone would: fear of dying. "I hate to state the obvious."

"You think it's vanity? That I'm afraid of looking old?" Edgar shrugged. "I suppose there's some truth to that. Age means frailty, and I cannot afford frailty. But more than that, my continued longevity means that Madeleine's payment can be deferred. As Smoks, we deal in souls. Not the least of which are our own."

Lucien had a sinking feeling he understood. "You've bargained your soul."

"Not mine, Lucien. Yours."

Chapter 23

The pain in Lucien's arm intensified. "What do you mean, mine?"

"You know the story. Every seventh generation is required to serve in hell. I found a way to skip a generation—staying alive."

Lucien wasn't following. "But according to the family tree, yours is the sixth generation of Smoks since the last to serve."

Edgar shook his head. "I've let you believe I was far older than I am so that you could get used to the idea of being the one to bear the curse. I'm not the first Edgar Smok. That was my father. Nevertheless, my lifespan was extended well beyond the time that my service was to come due, so the duty passed to my offspring. I know it seems callous of me, but you must understand that it was a decision I made many years ago, long before you were born."

Lucien was the eighth generation. Edgar had cheated, selling Lucien out—selling Lucien's *soul*—to avoid the Smok fate.

Everything made sense now. His father's distance and coldness. Even the way Edgar had let Lucien get away with everything short of murder despite the gulf between them. It hadn't made sense that Edgar wouldn't be harder on him given the lack of warmth in their relationship. Lucien had pushed every boundary, trying to find out just how far he could go before Edgar would step in. But he'd only done so when Lucien had started seeing a Marchant descendant.

"You realize my staying alive also benefits you, Lucien."

Lucien let out a choked laugh. "How the hell does it benefit me?"

"Because this isn't a 'pay on receipt of services rendered' transaction. The bill only becomes payable upon my death. So the longer I live, the longer you can go on about your life. In that respect, we're both very lucky that Carter Hamilton came along. The Smok family may lose a little power, but a Smok will remain the public face of this company. You're free to enjoy a long, full life." Edgar inclined his head. "But only the span of an ordinary human life. That was the deal. So you see, I can't prolong the inevitable indefinitely. My time runs out when yours does. And vice versa."

Lucien swiveled away from him. "And what happens, exactly, when the bill comes due? Say I die an old man, seventy years from now. Are you saying there won't be any consequences until then? No physical effects from the curse in our blood?"

"Do you see any in me?"

Lucien swiveled back reflexively at the question.

"For all intents and purposes, you are fully human, just like the rest of the Smok family. The change comes, as I understand it, once the soul is delivered—which occurs without it having to leave the body. A sort of transmogrification."

"You're saying I'm going to turn into some sort of monster on my deathbed and get sucked down into hell."

Edgar frowned. "You always see the worst in everything. I hardly think *monster* is the preferred term. As far as I know, you won't look any different. You'll simply *be* different. Most likely, youthfully restored. I expect you'll look much as you do now."

"Only I'll be a demon reigning in hell."

Edgar had on one of those smiles again. "Better than serving in heaven, as the saying goes."

"And yet you've spent decades making sure you never had to."

"Naturally, you make *me* out to be the monster. I've been the villain of your entire life. You have no idea of the sacrifices I've made for you. Am *still* making for you." Edgar waved his hand in the air in irritation, as if he couldn't articulate what he wanted to say. Perhaps his mind really was going. "That's enough. Go home."

Lucien had plenty to think about as he left the building. If Edgar was right about the terms of the Smok legacy, it could change everything. If shifting into something inhuman no longer loomed on the horizon, the threat of the loss of Smok Biotech was meaningless. What he had to consider was whether he could survive without the rest of what the Smok empire offered: power, money, a good life—everything he had access to now. He still had hopes of doing some good with that power, of changing how

Smok operated and putting a stop to its complicity in allowing evil to prosper and proliferate. He was doubtful that anything would change with Lucy at the helm. She was too pragmatic.

There was also the fact that his fate, like Edgar's, was only postponed. But it was hard to see something that was so many years away as the looming threat he'd always feared. Would defying Edgar affect that eventuality in any way? Could he even trust anything his father said? After all, Edgar had sold Lucien's soul to the devil.

Having left the boardroom with an increasing feeling of hope, he was already cycling back toward pessimism and mistrust. Maybe he *should* have Fran give him some meds.

He was so deep in the vicious circle in his head when he reached the parking lot that he stepped off the curb without looking. A horn blared, wheels screeching, and Lucien found himself just centimeters away from the hood of a silver hybrid. Angry at himself, he directed the anger at the car and slammed his palm on the hood, ready to cuss out the driver.

Through the windshield, Theia's wide gray eyes stared at him in disbelief. Both of them froze for a moment before Theia's shocked expression turned dark.

She lowered the window and leaned out. "Why don't you look where you're going?"

Lucien took his hand off the hood and stood in front of the car, realizing how much better he felt just being yelled at by Theia—having any interaction with Theia. "I don't know. I think I'm probably an idiot."

"You got that right."

The driver of the car behind Theia honked aggressively.

Theia glared. "Are you going to move or just stand there being an idiot?"

"Can I get in the car and be an idiot?"

Her mouth twitched, resisting a smile. "Depends on how idiotic you plan to be."

Lucien smiled. "I never plan. That's the genius of my idiocy."

The horn honked again, longer this time, to let them know the irked driver meant business and would honk again, by golly.

Theia's expression didn't change, but the lock on the passenger door of her car clicked open. Lucien wasted no time in taking her up on the tacit invitation.

He slipped in and closed the door. "Thanks for not running me down."

"It was touch-and-go there for a minute." Theia pulled out onto the main drive. "It's going to be awkward running into each other on campus like this. Although Lucy said she might fix that for me by making sure I got kicked out of my graduate program if I didn't leave you alone."

"She what? When did she say that?"

"Yesterday, when I tried to report for my first day of work."

Lucien ran his hand through his hair. "Dammit. I'm so sorry. I mean, not about Lucy—although that, too— but about me. About all of this. It just happened so suddenly, and I didn't know what to do."

Theia glanced at him. "And do you know what to do now?"

"Honestly?" Lucien sighed, wishing he could give her the answer she deserved, but he hadn't yet worked it all out in his head. There was still the issue of the Lilith blood. He wasn't sure if that was separate from the legacy. He shook his head. "No. But I know that I hate not being with you."

Theia kept her eyes on the road. "Well, that's something, I guess. So where am I driving you? I assume you had a car in the parking lot."

Lucien shrugged. "I can get another one."

Theia laughed, though not humorously. "Wow. Your life is something else."

"It is, isn't it? Where were you heading?"

"Me? I just finished my last final and was on my way home. To my place, I mean. My apartment here in Flagstaff."

"I haven't seen your place."

Theia threw him an annoyed look, the point of her bob swinging against her cheek with the quick movement of her head. "Well, yeah. Shortest relationship ever. Even for me." The word *relationship* made the little blip of hope attempt a comeback.

"There are some things I'd like to talk to you about."

"Things like Susie the siren?"

"Polly the—" Lucien stopped himself, reddening. "I'm not seeing Polly. She's not a factor in this."

"And what would 'this' be?"

"This would be me trying to figure out some very complicated things about who I am. And who you are."

Theia glanced over again and nearly rammed the car in front of her as it stopped when the light changed. She hit the brakes forcefully. "Who *I* am?"

"The Lilith blood."

"I thought we'd already discussed that. I thought you were okay with it."

"That was based on the information I had at the time. I have more now."

"So you want me to drive you to my *home* so you can tell me what else you don't like about me in my own personal space. I don't think so."

Lucien reached for her hand on the steering wheel, and she flinched but didn't pull it away. He felt a million times stronger, a million times surer of himself, at the touch of her skin.

"I want to figure us out. If you'll give me a chance. I can't promise where the conversation will end up, but I think we deserve to have it. We don't have to go to your place, if it makes you uncomfortable, but I'd like to talk to you somewhere private. We could just sit in the car, I guess."

Theia went through the intersection. "I have gourmet doughnuts at home. I think we might need them."

What she'd dreamed about and feared, her worries about the dark prince—everything Lucien told her about the Smok legacy while she nervous-ate three artisanal doughnuts confirmed her suspicions that it was all coming to pass. He was the one. And fate had brought them together, as surely as it had Phoebe and Rafe, Ione and Dev, Rhea and Leo. She'd just kind of hoped her fate wasn't really going to be this dark.

Theia leaned her head against her fist with her elbow propped on the back of the couch, trying to digest Lucien's words along with the doughnuts. "So according to your father, you won't descend to hell for sixty or seventy years."

"Barring some kind of accident or disease. It was the first time he spoke to me about any of this, and given his ulterior motive in staying alive as long as he can, I have no reason to disbelieve him."

"And Carter is going to help him do that."

"Apparently, he has some secret to the fountain of youth."

"Yeah, it's called feeding on the life energy of other people. How do you know he isn't planning to feed on yours?"

"That would be detrimental to Edgar's agenda. He's not going to do anything that would shorten my life." Lucien smiled ruefully. "For the first time, my father is actually rooting for me to succeed at something."

Theia returned the smile, but Carter's involvement was worrisome. He certainly wasn't doing anything out of the goodness of his heart. She was pretty sure he didn't have one. Maybe the secret to his longevity was that he'd had his heart removed and kept in a crypt somewhere, magically preserved—and magically preserving *him*.

"So what happens if you don't honor your father's wishes? Does that change things?"

Lucien breathed in deeply and exhaled. "I'm not sure. Given everything he told me, I don't see how it could. Except for one possible unintended consequence."

There was always an unintended consequence. "Which is?"

"It's the possibility that completely aside from Edgar's manipulation of the legacy, some other factor would trigger it." Lucien looked at her pointedly. "You."

"Me?" Before the protest was even out of her mouth, the connection became obvious. "You mean my blood."

"The theory is that it's what drew us together. That's why I tried to break it off with you so completely and so suddenly, without having the decency to tell you what was happening. I'm not proud to admit this, but I was scared. I was afraid that if I saw you again to tell you about Edgar's ultimatum, to try to explain to you that he'd forced my hand because of the anti-lycanthropy research, that you'd seduce me."

Theia couldn't help the surprised titter of laughter. "Seduce you? I've never seduced anyone in my life."

Lucien smiled. "But you have." He reached for her hand and wove their fingers together. "Everything about you seduces me every time I see you. You seduced me from all the way across the room that first moment at the reception."

"By choking on a grape."

Lucien shook his head, still smiling. "My God, woman. I've never seen anyone choke on a grape so seductively in my life."

Now she was laughing out loud. He stopped her with a kiss that, once again, took her breath away. Theia melted into him, moaning softly at the connection she'd somehow managed to convince herself wasn't real. It lent credence to the idea that it could be the influence of the demon strain in her blood, called home by Madeleine's curse—but if it was, more power to it. Something that felt this right couldn't be bad. Except...

Theia let out another moan, this time in frustration, and pushed herself away from the firm plane of his chest.

Lucien's strikingly pale eyes searched hers. "What's wrong?"

"I want this—you have no idea how much—"

"I think I have some idea." He dipped his head toward her.

She put her fingers against his lips as he tried to move in close again. "But I don't want to turn you into something you don't want to become." She shrugged helplessly and let her fingers fall.

Lucien's brow furrowed. "So now the thing we're afraid is drawing us together is going to be the thing that keeps us apart?"

"We have to think this through. We have to be sure about what we want."

"I don't want to think anymore. I'm tired of thinking. I want *you*."

"But doesn't that back up your theory? You came over here conflicted, depressed, wanting to tell me why this wasn't going to work—" She stopped midsentence and glared at the insistent shake of his head. "I could tell that was what you were thinking, Lucien. Don't deny it. I could feel it."

Lucien let go of her hand and launched himself off the couch with a one-armed shove. "So now I'm just some stupid pawn who doesn't know his own mind. Is that what you're saying?"

"That's not what I'm saying at all. I just want us both to be clear about what we're doing, why we're doing it and whether we're prepared to accept what might happen." She fixed him with an unflinching gaze. "Are you?"

Lucien clenched his fist in the hair at his forehead. "How can I know that, Theia? How can anyone know they're not going to die tomorrow? What I know is that I feel like my guts have been ripped out when I'm not with you." He gave her a helpless little attempt at a smile. "I'm not prepared to go through life without my guts. Don't make me."

Theia rose and wrapped her arms around his neck, and Lucien unclenched his fist and slid his good arm around her waist. Their bodies fit together like a set. His feelings for her were powerful and real—so strong that she had to make a conscious effort to separate them from her own. This wasn't about blood for either of them.

"If it's what you want, Lucien…" She took a breath of certainty. "It's what I want."

He bent to kiss her again, but something vibrated between them.

Lucien laughed. "That's not a phone in my pocket, I'm just happy to see you." He retrieved the offending device. "Let me just turn off…"

Watching the swiftness with which Lucien's smile dropped away felt like stepping off the sea floor in the shallows into a bottomless drop.

She withdrew her arms. "What's wrong?"

"My father… Lucy found him unresponsive on the floor of the boardroom. He's in the hospital."

Chapter 24

Lucien was quiet as they drove to the hospital. Lucy was already there, hovering in the waiting room as they stepped off the elevator.

She threw Theia the side eye as she hugged her brother. "What's she doing here?"

"I was with her when you called."

"Well, that didn't take long. Did you walk straight out of the boardroom into her car?"

"Pretty much, yeah."

"Convenient, then, that Edgar's unconscious and can't disown you."

Lucien stepped back and held her at arm's length. "Watch yourself, Lucy. This has nothing to do with Theia."

"Then I repeat, *what* is she doing here?" Lucy jerked her arm out of Lucien's grasp as he started to answer. "It was a rhetorical question, asshole." She paced away from them, facing the doors to the ICU.

Theia spoke quietly to Lucien. "Do you want me to go?"

"No. No, please stay. I need you here." He took Theia's hand, and Lucy made a derisive noise as she glanced over. "How did this happen?" he asked her. "Do the doctors know anything?"

Lucy sighed and folded her arms but didn't turn. "They think he's had a stroke. They said he has an unusual amount of plaque buildup in his arteries for his age." She glanced at Lucien. "Of course, I didn't tell them…" Her voice trailed off as she eyed Theia once more.

"You can say whatever you want in front of Theia. She knows about everything."

Heat flashed in the pale blue of Lucy's eyes. "Oh, well, isn't that just *swell*, Lucien."

"Edgar said he talked to you about his health problems. All he told me was that his health was deteriorating rapidly, and the partnership with Carter Hamilton was going to give him the opportunity to remedy that. Do you know anything more?"

Lucy turned toward them, regarding Theia icily. "You really want to talk about this in front of her?"

"Yes. She has experience with Hamilton."

Lucy's expression was slightly less hostile as she acknowledged it. "I suppose that's true." She dropped onto one of the awkwardly upholstered hospital waiting room chairs. "He was supposed to give Edgar an amulet. I assumed he already had and that everything was settled."

"Was there an amulet on him?"

"No."

Lucien considered. "Edgar seemed a little off when I left him, like he was exhausted by talking to me. I had the impression that whatever Hamilton was going to do for him, he hadn't done it yet."

Lucy pinched the bridge of her nose. "Do you think we should contact him? I hate the idea. He gives me the creeps. But maybe he can still reverse whatever's happening."

Theia was tempted to answer, to tell them that where Carter was concerned, they should run—fast—in the opposite direction. But this was their father, not hers.

"The deal's already been struck," said Lucien. "He'd just be fulfilling his end of the bargain."

"That's kind of what I'm worried about." Lucy sighed, staring up at the ceiling. "I'm not positive, but I have a sneaking suspicion that Edgar offered Hamilton more than just a controlling interest in the company." She leveled her eyes on Lucien. "I think he promised him me."

"*What?*" Lucien dropped onto the chair next to her, letting go of Theia's hand. "What are you talking about?"

"I don't know that Edgar meant it in quite the mercenary way it sounds. But I believe he thought Hamilton and I would be an obvious match and that promising me to him was merely a formality, because I would see the wisdom in such a 'merger' myself." She rolled her eyes. "And would apparently find Hamilton irresistible."

Theia had to swallow hard against the urge to retch. Not an uncommon reaction around the subject of Carter Hamilton, but this time it seemed clear it was Lucy's reaction she was picking up on. She certainly couldn't blame her.

Lucien put his hand on his sister's shoulder. "Hamilton's not coming anywhere near you as long as I'm around."

Lucy let out a sort of wheezing sound that seemed to be a laugh. "That's really sweet of you, Lulu, but I'm a big girl. I think I can take care of myself." She gave him a wry smirk. "I know the Russian martial art of Systema."

"I'm serious. If this was part of the deal Edgar made, I'm not standing for it."

Lucy's smirk turned into a glare. "Lucien, take the out when it's offered to you. If you don't stop patronizing me, I'm going to punch you in the throat and they're going to have to check you into your own room."

Theia had to look away to hide a smile. She could imagine Rhea saying the same.

"The point is," said Lucy, "I don't think we have a choice. We're going to have to call Hamilton eventually. He owes Edgar, and if he's withholding what he owes, he may find himself on the receiving end of one of my throat punches himself."

The elevator opened behind Theia. As she turned to move out of the way, she found herself face-to-face with none other than Carter himself.

He smiled, showing his overly white, perfect teeth. "Ms. Dawn. What a pleasant surprise. Though not an entirely unexpected one."

Theia sneered. "It's not mutual."

Lucien rose and came to stand between them. "Hamilton."

Carter offered his hand, but Lucien put his in his pocket. "Terrible news about Edgar. How are you holding up?"

"We're just waiting to hear from the doctor."

Lucy rose behind them. "We've already had some interesting news. My father's health is exceptionally deteriorated. I believe you and he had an arrangement for you to share the secret of your good health with him. Why wasn't that done?"

Carter moved past Lucien to take Lucy's hand in both of his. "I can only imagine how hard this must be for you. I did offer to share my health regimen with Edgar, but I fear he may be beyond a few protein shakes and a low-fat diet at this point."

Lucy yanked her hand from his grasp. "Cut the crap, Hamilton. You were supposed to give him an amulet to safeguard him against something like this. Where is it?"

Carter frowned, casting a glance at Theia. "Are we divulging the Smok secrets in front of outsiders now? Has she signed an NDA?"

"As a matter of fact, she has," said Lucy. "So you can answer any and all questions related to the business in front of her. I'll take full responsibility."

"Will you? What an interesting development." He reached into his inside suit pocket and pulled out a small square box. "As it happens, I do have the amulet. It isn't a magical cure, however. It would have been better for Edgar to have had it on him before this ischemic event befell him, but it may prolong his life. As to the quality of that life, I can't make any guarantees. There was a ritual involved that would have imbued Edgar with the strength of the magic behind the amulet. We were supposed to meet this evening, but life happens swiftly, doesn't it?"

He opened the box and lifted out a length of gold chain with what looked like a gemstone charm dangling from it—black sapphire—set in ivory. Only Theia was pretty damn sure it wasn't ivory. Carter had used the bones of his victims to make his charms when he'd attempted to steal Rafe's power. She shivered and hugged her elbows.

Lucy held out her hand, but Carter didn't offer the amulet. "I think we need to come to some kind of an understanding about what this is worth."

Lucy frowned. "What do you mean, what it's worth? You own a controlling interest in Smok International. That was the deal. That's what it's worth."

"This deal took several months of negotiation, and it involves a number of complex elements. If you haven't already reviewed your father's copy of the contract, I suggest you do so in short order." Several months. So he'd been wheeling and dealing from behind bars, knowing he had someone in the DA's office to make his entire conviction go away—and knowing when. "The upshot is that, as the controlling interest in the company, I do have certain rights. And certain privileges." He dangled the amulet in the light, admiring it. "And this particular bit of magic wasn't easy to come by. But you are correct in saying that it was a large part of the deal."

"Then give it to me, or I'm going to have to contact our lawyers. And trust me when I say they will be going over every line of that contract with a fine-tooth comb."

Carter gave Lucy a look of admiration. "I've heard you like to play hardball. I like that in a woman."

"I don't really care what you like in a woman."

After setting the amulet back inside the box and closing it, Carter held it out to her. "I look forward to sparring with you. Consider this a gesture of good faith."

Lucy took the box, but Lucien stepped in and put his hand over hers. "Are you sure you want to do this, Lu?"

"I told you, I can handle myself."

Lucien gave Carter a dismissive look. "Can I speak with my sister in private a moment, Mr. Hamilton?"

"Certainly. I'm sure Ms. Dawn and I have some catching up to do."

Theia stared him down. "No, I'm sure we don't."

Carter grinned, like some spray-tanned ghoul, and strolled away from them down the hall.

Lucien ignored him, intent on Lucy. "You can't give this to Edgar without reading the fine print in that contract."

"He needs it, Lucien. And, frankly, *you* need it. I'm not going to have Edgar dying on me and you following him." Her voice wavered, just the slightest bit, in what Theia was sure was a rare display of emotion toward her brother.

"But you heard him. The required ceremony hasn't been done. It's not going to restore him to health."

"But it will keep him alive. And right now, that's the best we can do."

That much turned out to be true. After Lucy found a nurse who promised to put it on Edgar when Lucy managed to work up some impressive tears, telling the nurse it was a religious symbol that she didn't want her father to die without, the doctor emerged with good news. Edgar had stabilized.

Lucy and Lucien were allowed to see him briefly, but only one visitor at a time. While Lucien went in, Theia sat awkwardly beside Lucy in the waiting area, keeping a wary eye on Carter, who, for the moment, was maintaining a respectful distance.

"So." Theia cleared her throat. "Are you planning to wipe my memory or have me kicked out of the university after this? Or both?"

Lucy exhaled, her head against the seatback and her eyes closed. "I reserve the right to do either at a later date if you intend to interfere in any way with how Lucien runs the business."

"I have no intention of interfering."

"You've already interfered, Theia. Your entire existence is an interference." She opened her eyes. "Lucien said he told you everything. Does that include the things he's done in the name of business over the years? Neither of us are innocents."

"I have some idea."

"You have no idea. And I suppose he told you about his suicide attempts and the fact that he's on antidepressants."

"No, he didn't. But it's not like I've never taken antidepressants before. Who hasn't?"

"You're almost adorably naive." Lucy wasn't smiling. "Almost. The only thing Lucien has ever done with any enthusiasm—besides drink and screw an endless parade of women—is his special project at Smok Biotech. He may not need it now. Maybe Edgar will hang on, and everything will be hunky-dory. But ask yourself what he's going to do without his research to keep him focused. And without his outlet of hunting rogue creatures. It's not an inexpensive hobby. How long will it be before he begins to resent you for taking everything away from him?"

Theia smoothed her hand along the seat's upholstery, studying the seams. "Are you saying that even with your father incapacitated, Lucien will be cut off if he continues to see me?" Lucy's momentary silence made her glance up.

"You are really something. I'm sitting here in the hospital with my father's life hanging by a thread, and you're conniving how to benefit from his misfortune."

Theia blushed, realizing that was exactly how it sounded. "I'm sorry. That's not what I meant. Of course I hope he recovers fully." She would have said more, but Lucien returned, looking grim.

He bent to give Lucy a kiss on the cheek, which seemed to alarm her.

"What's wrong?"

"He's stable, but he's barely there. He can't communicate. He doesn't respond when I speak to him—he just stares vacantly. If he survives, he's going to need around-the-clock home care."

Lucy's expression matched his. "And the amulet will keep him like that."

"Until I die, presumably."

She swore and shoved herself out of her chair, heading straight for Carter at the other end of the waiting area. "This is exactly how you planned it, isn't it?"

Carter remained seated, smiling up at her calmly. "How's that?"

"You never intended to keep up your end of the deal. You held on to that amulet until Edgar's body gave out on him, until all it would do was keep him alive as a living poppet."

"I think you're letting your emotions get the best of you, my dear. Totally understandable under the circumstances. But it might do you some good to go home and get some rest."

The tension in Lucy's body was clear even from where Theia was sitting. Lucy was holding back a well-deserved ass kicking with everything she had. Theia couldn't help rooting for her to fail in her endeavor to resist the impulse.

Lucy stared down at him, jaw clenched. "If anyone should go home, Hamilton, it's you. If you know what's good for you, you will get up and walk out of here right now before I do something I'll regret."

Carter rose with leisurely grace. "I can see that you're

upset, so I'll give you and Lucien some privacy. And some time to decide how to proceed with Edgar's health care. Just let me know if there's anything I can do to help."

After nodding to Lucien and Theia on his way to the elevator, he turned around to observe Lucien while waiting for it to arrive. "You look a little run-down, Lucien. You might want to take extra care with your archery. I assume it's also how you came by that fading black eye." He glanced at Theia, deliberately holding her gaze though he was still talking to Lucien. "You'll need all your strength for your other…pastimes. In my experience, the Carlisle women are absolute wildcats in bed."

The elevator opened before Theia could think of a snappy retort to put him in his place, and Carter stepped inside and faced them for one last parting shot. "But of course, you wouldn't know that yet, would you, Lucien? You've fallen for the delicate unspoiled fruit. Let me know how it goes if you manage to pierce that delectable untouched skin. Absolutely anything could happen."

Theia's face blazed, and Lucien launched himself toward the elevator with a snarl, but the doors closed in his face.

After giving Theia a disbelieving look, Lucy broke the awkward silence that followed. "If she's a virgin, what the hell did I walk in on the other day?"

Lucien turned to give her a sardonic, James Spader smirk, his eyebrows raised suggestively. "Creative chastity."

As Theia drove back to her place later, Lucien pushed the point of her bob behind her ear, letting his fingers linger at her nape. "Thank you for coming with me tonight. And for putting up with that odious piece of garbage."

Theia shrugged. "He doesn't bother me. His game is intimidation and trying to make everyone around him feel inferior. He's what would happen if an internet troll stepped out of the comments section into your living room. He deserves exactly the same consideration."

Lucien smiled at the thought of an in-person block button. "You know I'm not bothered about you being a virgin, either. I'm not concerned with…"

"Piercing my tender flesh? Being the first to pluck my delectable flower?" She gave him a quick sideways grin.

Lucien laughed. "Jesus. That guy. Who talks like that?"

"I was going to say a Neanderthal. But that would be an insult to Neanderthals." Theia slowed at the turn toward her apartment. "Rhea's going to look in on Puddleglum for me, so I was planning on staying in Flagstaff tonight. But would you rather be alone? Do you want me to drive you home?"

Lucien shook his head. "I most emphatically would not rather be alone. Lucy says she'll call me if anything changes, but the doctors don't expect it to. And for obvious reasons, neither do I."

Theia glanced at him. "Did you and Lucy talk about what you're going to do? I mean, are you…"

"Going to let my father live out the entire span of my life being spoon-fed pureed meat from a blender and wearing a diaper?" Lucien sighed. "I wish I knew the answer to that. It was his bargain to make. He sold his soul as surely as he sold mine. I have every right to live a full life before I pay the bill he racked up. I just wish that felt better to say than it does."

They climbed into bed with little fanfare, Theia in her underwear and a T-shirt and Lucien in his boxers, planning only to sleep. The splint and sling would make anything else difficult anyway. And making out didn't seem quite right with Edgar in the condition he was in. Although if Edgar remained in that state indefinitely, Lucien would have to get past that.

Despite their plans, Lucien couldn't help kissing her good-night, and the kiss turned into more. Not a lot more—he could tell she shared his apprehension about what might happen if they went any further—but he was content with moving slowly with Theia. Something he'd never considered in his life. He'd been other women's first—or other girls', anyway, in high school—but looking back, he was fairly sure he hadn't exactly been a great first experience. He wanted to do this right with Theia. Especially if it turned out to be the only time they could be together. If he was going to turn into some inhuman creature and join the seven-headed beast of the apocalypse afterward, he was damn well going to make it good for both of them.

He lay awake after she'd fallen asleep, his head too loud to find stillness, and got up to go to the bathroom after an aborted attempt to quiet it.

As he washed up by the glow of the electrical switch that served as a built-in night-light, Lucien glanced in the mirror over the sink. The shadows made his face look odd. Was his hairline receding? Laughing at himself for being paranoid, he switched on the light, but his laughter died as his eyes adjusted to the brightness. Two small, bony protrusions were erupting beside his widow's peak. Lucien touched the top of his head and confirmed his worst fear. He was growing horns.

Chapter 25

His hand, as he pushed back his hair to see closer, felt stiff and awkward. His fingers were hard to uncurl, as if he were an old man with severe arthritis. He brought his hand down in front of him. The fingernails were lengthening as he watched—long and curved and pointed. He was growing claws. He could feel it in the hand in the sling. As he nudged the fabric off his arm, his shoulders ached, and he rolled them back—and saw another protrusion at his shoulder blade. Lucien ran his fingers over the growth. It was leathery, and it was expanding.

Panic started to set in, and Lucien sat on the edge of the tub trying to breathe. There was a prototype of the anti-transformative at the lab. But how the hell was he going to get there? He couldn't risk calling a car and having something happen while he was in it that couldn't be undone. Maybe he could take Theia's car. He could slip out while she was sleeping, get to the lab and shut this whole process down in less than twenty minutes. The dosage hadn't been perfected yet, but they'd been successful in reversing the shift in the animals they'd bred for the lab. It was almost ready for human trials, and there was no time like the present.

But it was becoming quickly apparent that he was running *out* of time. He needed a thumbprint to get into the refrigerated case where the serum was stored, and his thumb was turning scaly. Maybe the retinal scan bypass would work. He rose and saw his reflection in the mirror. His eyes looked wrong. They were still the same pale blue, but the pupil was a vertical slit. The horns positioned above them were small but obvious. And from behind his back, a pair of leathery, webbed wings in brilliant blue were unfurling.

A loud crash woke Theia from a dream about the Carter-cockatrice gloating at Edgar Smok's bedside. Theia rolled over to see if Lucien had heard the noise, but he wasn't in bed. Across the hall, light was visible under the closed bathroom door. Maybe he'd dropped something.

"Lucien? Are you okay?" When she didn't get an answer, she threw off the covers and hurried to the door. "Lucien?" It was locked, and only silence emanated from behind it. Theia rattled the doorknob. "Lucien, answer me. Are you all right?"

Lucy's words came back to her. *And I suppose he told you about his suicide attempts.*

"Lucien!" Glancing around for something heavy, she spied the stone doorstop behind the front door and ran to grab it. With a few sharp blows, she'd broken the doorknob, latch and all.

Theia expected to find Lucien collapsed on the floor. Instead, the room was empty. A light breeze blew the thin window curtain inward through an empty frame above the bathtub, fragments of one of the sliding panes scattered in the tub. Theia scrambled onto the edge of the tub and looked out. There was nowhere he could have gone. They were on the fifth floor. The parking lot below them was undisturbed.

Lucien's clothes were still in her bedroom. So was his phone.

He was still using the same password, thank goodness. She selected Lucy's number, but the call rolled to voice mail after a single ring. Why would Lucy decline a call from her brother with their father in intensive care?

A moment later, a text message came through with the answer.

Sorry, Lulu, I'm exhausted. Edgar's condition hasn't changed. I've gone home to get some rest. Consider this permission to bone your girlfriend.

Theia quickly responded.

This is Theia. Lucien's disappeared. I'm worried.

She waited several minutes, but there was no indication that Lucy had read the message. Maybe she'd turned off her phone. After leaving a more detailed text about what had happened, Theia checked the contacts. Lucy's address at a luxury resort in Sedona was listed. Hopefully she didn't have more than one place she was staying.

After throwing on jeans and sandals, Theia took a quick walk around the complex before getting into her car to see if there was any sign of Lucien, but she found nothing. She drove by the lab first—where of course she couldn't get in—and checked the hospital, both in the ICU and at admissions to see if Lucien or a John Doe had been brought in. Nothing.

It was four thirty in the morning when she arrived at Lucy's resort. The room number was a villa with a private entrance. Theia expected her to ignore her knocking, so she kept at it until at last she heard movement inside.

"Lucy?" She shouted against the door as she continued pounding. "It's Theia. Lucien's missing. Open the door."

"Maybe he's just sick of you" came the reply from the other side.

"Can you just open up?"

"It's four thirty in the morning, Theia."

"And I'm going to stand out here pounding on your door until you open it, so you might as well get it over with before I wake the adjoining villas."

There was silence for a moment followed by the clunk of a dead bolt. The door opened, and Lucy peered through the crack, the security latch stretched across the gap, her face in shadow.

Theia squinted into the darkness. "I replied to your text."

"Yeah, I saw it."

"Aren't you the least bit concerned? Lucien went out a five-story window in his boxers without leaving so much as a broken twig at the bottom where he ought to have landed."

"Maybe he just climbed down. He's always been a good climber."

Theia sighed. "Lucy, you obviously know something. Is he here? Is he having some kind of a breakdown?"

"No, he's not here. I don't know where he is. But I wouldn't be surprised if he's having a breakdown. I'm considering one myself."

"Did you get some news about your father? I went by the hospital to see if Lucien was there. They said Edgar was sleeping and hadn't had any visitors."

"Edgar isn't sleeping. He's in a catatonic state. He will probably never sleep again—or do anything else—thanks to Hamilton and his amulet. And apparently we were all wrong about what that means."

"Wrong how? What do you mean?"

Lucy leaned her forehead against the door frame and sighed before unhooking the security latch and stepping back to hold the door open.

When Theia entered, Lucy went to sit on the couch. The lights were off, but the pale predawn glow through the sheer curtain illuminated Lucy's features. Her usual neatly styled hair looked tousled above her braid. Of course, she'd just been woken up at four thirty in the morning.

Theia sat on the edge of the chair opposite her. "So what did you find out?"

Lucy chewed on a cuticle. "You'll appreciate this. You're into genetics. Lucien and I are monozygotic twins, like you and Rhea. We're identical, not fraternal. But apparently, our original fertilized egg had an extra X chromosome, and when our tiny little blastocyst split, Lucien took the Y chromosome with him. Hence, identical twins but different sexes."

It was unusual but not unheard-of. "Makes sense. You two do have an extraordinary resemblance."

"The upshot," said Lucy, "is that it turns out we're both cursed by dear old Madeleine Marchant. And the amulet, it seems, has the effect of rendering Edgar effectively dead as far as the curse is concerned. So, lucky us, it kicked in early this morning."

"What do you mean, *it kicked in*?"

Lucy stretched her arm along the back of the couch to switch on the lamp beside her. In the glare of the compact fluorescent bulb, her pupils contracted. Into vertical slits. And what Theia had taken for tousled hair was the result of two small but distinct garnet-colored horns. It looked like a clever Halloween costume—novelty contact lenses and carefully applied spirit gum under latex horns. But Theia had seen enough magical transformation to know it wasn't.

"Yeah," Lucy agreed to words Theia hadn't said. "Kinda leaves ya speechless, doesn't it? Of course, my first reaction was a bit more audible. And I demolished my bathroom mirror." She held up her bloodied knuckles. "My martial arts training took over, and I tried to kill the mirror demon, but it punched me back."

"Shit."

"Yeah, that was the next thing I said. Plus a few other choice expletives."

"And this just happened to Lucien, too. In my bathroom."

"It would seem so."

"Did he come here?"

"No. I haven't heard from him, except a phone call I ignored because I was freaking out. But I guess that was you."

"Yeah." Theia pushed her hair out of her eyes, as if it would make Lucy's appearance go back to normal. "But how did he manage to crawl out my bathroom window and disappear from the fifth floor?"

Lucy sighed and stood. "I imagine with the help of these." A pair of ruby-red webbed wings unfolded at her back, extending from her shoulders at least three feet in either direction, bony segments between the webs terminating in black claws. "Ruined one of my favorite shirts. I'm not pleased."

"Well, this is—wow." Theia shook her head. "Lucien and I were afraid that if we—if I—if we consummated the relationship, it might trigger the transformation. Carter Hamilton intimated as much."

"And did you?"

"No. Now I'm starting to feel pretty stupid about that."

Lucy retracted her wings and sat back on the couch. "If it's not too personal—oh, hell, of course it's personal, but I don't really give a damn. Is there a reason you're still a virgin at age…"

Theia swallowed. "Twenty-two. For a while I thought it was because I was unfuckable." She dismissed the notion with a shrug. "But really, it was my dreams. My visions. I kept seeing an alliance with a dark prince, and it scared me, so I kept pushing guys away."

Lucy laughed. "And then your dark prince comes along and you miss your window of opportunity."

"I like to think the window's still open. I mean—you don't think he flew…to the underworld?"

"To hell? Well, *I* didn't. But maybe he's still the one who has to pay the soul price. He did grab that Y chromosome in the zygote lottery. Who knows? I have a feeling, though, that this isn't the final transformation."

"You think…"

"I expect the full dragon experience is yet to come."

"What about Smok Biotech's research? Lucien said the

lycanthropy suppressant was months away from clinical trials, but maybe it could inhibit your trigger."

"My trigger? And what do you suppose triggered this? Obviously, it was Edgar's collapse. I think it's a little late for suppressing genes."

"That's not what it does. I mean, obviously, much of the research was geared toward isolating the gene responsible for the shift and finding a way to shut it off. But what Lucien was working toward was developing a drug to manage lycanthropy. Like you'd manage diabetes."

"Turning into a dragon is not diabetes."

"No, but it's a condition that can be managed, and a response to a trigger that can be suppressed. Like inhibiting serotonin or norepinephrine reuptake in antidepressants. We just have to pinpoint the right neurotransmitter."

"God, no wonder Lucien's into you. You sound like a biology textbook. I'm pretty sure he jerked off to those as a kid."

"My point is that there may be a simple fix to this. But we have to find Lucien. Do you have any idea where he would go with no clothes and no wallet?"

Lucy shrugged. "I don't know. Maybe to Polly?" Lucy seemed almost apologetic, as if she cared whether the idea was hurtful to Theia. "That's where he's always gone in the past when he's been in trouble. Sometimes she gives people sanctuary at the Grotto. And she has contacts who could hide him. We've used them for safe houses. She doesn't like to divulge her list, but she'll hook people up with what they need. For a price."

There was always a price.

Rhea and Leo were asleep in Phoebe's room when Theia stopped by to grab some clothes. And Leo, apparently, slept in the nude. Well, they both did, but Theia had seen Rhea naked plenty. Facedown on the bed with his arm across Rhea protectively, Leo displayed a nice little half-moon above the sheets. Theia took a picture for trotting out later to mess with Rhea.

After tiptoeing to the dresser and sliding open the drawers as quietly as she could, Theia turned around with a pair of Phoebe's capris and a clean T-shirt to find she'd disturbed Rhea anyway.

Rhea rubbed her eye with a fist, looking crabby. "What time is it? What are you doing here?"

"I'll tell you when you wake up. Go back to sleep."

Puddleglum appeared and jumped onto the pillow above Rhea's head to announce that it was time for breakfast. Whoever slept in Phoebe's bed, apparently, was the designated server.

Rhea sighed and slid out from under Leo's arm. "I'm up, you philistine."

With her eyes half-open, Rhea fed Puddleglum while Theia brewed a pot of coffee.

Rhea shuffled to the breakfast bar and slouched onto a stool, yawning. "How's Lucien? What's the word on his dad?"

"That…is a complicated story."

"Of course it is."

"You can go back to bed."

"Shut up. Just tell me."

"Edgar is in a vegetative state. Probably thanks to Carter Hamilton. And Lucien…took off."

"Took off?"

The coffeemaker beeped, and Theia waited until she'd poured them each a cup. "He went into the bathroom in the middle of the night, apparently developed secondary dragon characteristics and flew out the window."

Rhea nearly choked on her coffee. "You pulled an Ione, didn't you? You screwed his brains out and turned him into a dragon. You little minx."

"No, I didn't."

"Of course you did. Just own it."

"I *didn't.*"

"Come *on.* What makes you think it wasn't you?"

"Because I haven't had sex with him."

Rhea nearly snorted coffee through her nose. "Right. Because you're saving yourself for marriage." Her mocking grin faded slightly as she took in the serious expression on Theia's face. "You… Theia… You've *had* sex before."

Theia didn't respond. Which was response enough.

Rhea set her mug on the bar with a bang, sloshing coffee over the top, her mouth hanging open. "You've never had sex and you never told me?" Her shocked expression turned to aggravation. "I can't believe you don't tell me things. Our whole lives, I thought we were open books to each other. We shared everything. Who *are* you?"

The equilibrium Theia strove to maintain, like an internal level that kept her on an even keel, not buffeted by the stress of other people's confusing emotions or intrusive visions, suddenly snapped.

"Do you realize that I've never had anything private, never kept a secret—from any of you—for most of my life? Everybody always assumed that whatever you did, I did, like I wasn't a whole person, I was just half of a twin set. I never needed to act up. I'd get in trouble in school—and at home—for things you'd done. People never asked my opinion on anything, just filled in what they thought

I was thinking. Thought I'd like whatever you liked. I always got birthday and Christmas presents in your favorite colors, books and video games that were on your wish list. Doesn't that bother you? Didn't it ever drive you crazy when people acted like we were interchangeable?"

Rhea, for once in her life, was at a loss for words. "I…got you in trouble on purpose, stupid. Because you were Miss Perfect. And now I find out I was living with a creepy pod person the whole time."

"Very funny."

"That's me. The hilarious one. See? People know that about me. We're totally different. No one thinks you're funny at all."

Theia growled and threw her hands in the air, dropping onto the stool beside Rhea to drink her coffee in resignation.

"Sorry." Rhea nudged her with her elbow. "It never bothered me because I was always trying to live up to your image. When people thought I was you, it made me look good." She took a sip of her coffee and muttered into it, "I *may* have given certain people the impression that you were a total slut in high school, though."

"Nice."

"So what are you going to do about Lucien? Do you want me to send Leo after him?"

"What is he, a bloodhound?"

"No, I just figured…" Rhea considered for a moment. "No, I guess he can't just automatically find magical people. He hunts down murderers and oath breakers."

Theia swallowed a sip of coffee. "I'm going to go talk to Polly."

Rhea swiveled on her stool to stare at her. "Are you sure that's a good idea?"

"You think I can't handle talking to his ex? You talked to Faye plenty of times, if I recall correctly."

"Polly didn't seem like that much of an ex the other night. And Faye's different." Rhea lowered her head over her mug. "We have an arrangement."

Theia paused with her cup halfway to her mouth. "*Have* an arrangement? What arrangement? I thought she released him from his bond when you broke the Norns' curse."

"She did. She just…sometimes we…the three of us get together and…"

Theia had tried to take another sip of coffee, and she nearly choked on it. "Oh. My. God."

Rhea sneaked a glance from the corner of one eye, a mischievous grin on her face. "You're such a prude. *Virgin.*"

"I am *not* a prude. I just don't… I thought you said you were just experimenting in college."

"You, of all people, should know how experiments go. You have to do it multiple times to see if you can duplicate the results."

"Wow." This was a whole new side to Rhea she'd never suspected. Apparently, Theia wasn't the only one with secrets. "Regardless, that is *not* happening with Polly. I don't need to conduct any research on that subject."

Rhea shook her head. "That's a shame. I mean, a *siren*, come on."

Theia concentrated on her coffee. "So, anyway, I'm going to go talk to her and see if Lucien sought sanctuary with her or maybe is hiding out someplace she knows about. Lucy says Polly keeps lists of information on people in the magical community."

"Well, that doesn't sound at all shifty."

"She also exacts a price for information, so I'm not sure what that's going to be."

"I can think of one."

"Enough with the threesomes, you perv."

"You just assume I was talking about a threesome."

"Weren't you?"

Rhea grinned. "Well, yeah, but it's rude to assume." She got up to refill her coffee. "In all seriousness, though, I don't trust this siren chick. Who knows what she's going to want? If she's going to be offering Faustian bargains, you're going to need backup."

"I don't think she deals in souls. Lucy would have said so—that's her thing, after all."

"I suppose there's that. But I'm going with you."

Theia sighed. "If we both go, she'll want a payment from you, too. She's not going to hand out information to whomever I happen to bring along."

Rhea set the pot on the warmer. "I'll stay in the car, and you can signal with a text if you need help."

"*No.* Will you just let me do this myself, please? Now I'm sorry I told you."

Rhea took a sip of coffee, looking sullen. "Keeping secrets, being all virginal, doing things by yourself—you are the worst twin. I want a new one."

"Oh my God. You pain in the ass."

Rhea smiled. "That means I'm going."

"Fine. You're going. But you *are* staying in the car."

"Cool. We'll take Minnie."

Theia hadn't considered the fact that she was going to face Lucien's super-hot ex-girlfriend when she'd chosen the navy capris and white T-shirt. She felt awkward as she got out of the car in the parking lot of Polly's Grotto.

For that matter, what if no one was here at this hour? It wasn't like Polly actually lived in the club. Was it?

The door was locked. Theia stood in front of the entrance, trying to decide what to do. Should she knock? Maybe she should call Lucy and find out what the protocol was. Or maybe she should stop being a baby and suck it up and try the door.

Before she could psych herself up, one of the doors opened on its own. Polly probably had a camera on it. No turning back now.

Theia took a deep breath and went inside. The door swung shut behind her.

Chapter 26

As her eyes adjusted to the dim interior, she realized the place wasn't empty. A woman with long platinum-white hair that clearly wasn't white with age was seated in a semicircular booth between two unearthly pale young men on one side—who seemed to be a couple—and someone Theia could only describe as a human tiger on the other. The naked tiger-man growled.

"Now, now, Giorgio. Don't be rude." The white-haired woman stroked his fur. "Polly's is open to everyone who finds their way in. Particularly tasty little demon-blood girls." She extended her hand toward Theia. "Don't be shy. Giorgio won't bite. Without my permission. And Raul and Rocco only bite boys."

Theia approached the booth, feeling decidedly underdressed. Polly was draped in a white silk gown that looked like it belonged to some femme fatale from the 1940s, designed to show off her curves.

Theia reached over Raul and Rocco, who were paying her no mind—and appeared to be giving each other hickeys, though Theia suspected they were sharing blood—and took Polly's hand to shake it, but Polly simply held hers with her fingertips, looking Theia up and down. "I'm Theia Dawn—"

Polly stopped her. "I know all about you, sweetheart. Even if I hadn't already met your twin—who's waiting in the parking lot to come to your rescue should I turn out to have an appetite for human flesh—I make it my business to know about everyone who matters. What I don't know is what you're doing here. If you've come to make a fuss over Lucien, I'm afraid you're wasting your time. I offered him my bed, knowing he wasn't getting his needs met with you—no offense—but he refused."

Theia wasn't quite sure what to say to that, but she breathed a little sigh of relief. "Nice to know I matter, anyway."

"You and your sisters have more power than you think. So long as that power doesn't threaten mine, you matter, but you're of little consequence to me. Now what is it that's brought you into my cozy grotto?"

Theia wanted to remove her hand from Polly's, but yanking it away seemed rude. "I'm generally a good judge of whether someone's lying to me or not, so I'm going to assume from your question that Lucien isn't here."

Polly's frosty-white eyebrows rose. "And why would he be here? Don't tell me you've lost him?"

"I think you know how I lost him."

"If you mean his transformation, yes, I am aware. But not because he's been here. What made you think he would be?"

Her fingers were really beginning to feel awkward in Polly's grasp. "I was told he might come to you for sanctuary."

"Sanctuary." Polly smiled, amused. "Lucien would never need to take sanctuary with me, though I would certainly give it if he asked." Her smile turned mischievous, and her eyes literally twinkled. "One must always ask the right question if one is to receive the right answer."

So they were playing word games. She supposed it made sense.

"Do you know where Lucien is?"

Polly's expression gave nothing away. "I do not." She'd answered in the negative, but Theia had the impression that there was more to it than the simple reply. And she was still holding Theia's hand.

"Do you know of anyone who does?"

"I know of someone who may have the answer." Now they were getting somewhere. Maybe.

"Will you tell me who that someone might be?"

The siren curled her fingers around Theia's and drew her closer across the table. "What's the answer worth to you?"

"What do you usually charge?"

Giorgio roared, and Theia jerked back on her arm and nearly fell sideways into the laps of Raul and Rocco when Polly didn't let go. But Giorgio, it seemed, was laughing.

"I don't *charge*. I merely expect. It's a courtesy. I see Lucien hasn't explained how I operate, so let me make it easier. I like shiny, pretty things." She held up her other wrist, a charm bracelet sparkling with gemstones of various shapes and sizes.

Theia bit her lip. "I don't think I have anything shiny."

"Oh, sure you do. Lots of shiny things. Everyone does. I once had a choker made of irises."

Theia thought she meant the flowers, but after a significant glance from Polly's glittering eyes, the meaning became clear. Her own widened. No way in hell was she giving this nutjob an eye.

Polly laughed. "Those were from desperate men, as I'm sure you can imagine. People generally pay what they're willing to give up. From you, I think…" She studied Theia intently, as if trying to decide, though it was clear she had something in mind from the start. "Yes, a drop of blood would make a lovely trinket."

This was starting to bring to mind monkeys' paws and Faustian bargains. "Where would the drop of blood be taken from?"

Polly laughed. "Smart girl. Just a finger prick. Nothing life threatening and no need to maim anything. You'll barely feel it."

"And what are you going to do with it?"

Polly's expression turned unfriendly. "That's a very rude question. Do you ask everyone you give a gift to what they're going to do with your gift?"

This wasn't exactly a gift. It was more like extortion. But Theia knew better than to say so out loud.

"Let me put it another way, then. Will this 'gift' give you any power to harm me?"

"Oh, you *are* a smart girl." Polly's affable smile was back. "No. It won't affect you in the least. It will simply be my trinket to do with as I please, when I please." She took a pin from her gown—which certainly didn't look as if it were holding any pins—and drew Theia's index finger toward her. "Are we agreed?"

"This is the only price you're requiring? No hidden follow-up or extras?"

"Nothing at all." Polly placed the pin against Theia's finger.

"And you'll tell me who knows where Lucien is?"

"I'll tell you the name of someone who *may* know. That's the best I can do. Not knowing where he is myself, I can't speak in certainties. I can only give you likelihoods."

This was starting to seem like a bad deal, but the pin had pricked her finger before Theia could back out of it.

Polly touched the drop of blood, transferring it from Theia's fingertip to her own, and released her. "Marvelous. I think I'll have to wear this one on its own. It's much too nice to be crowded by a bunch of ordinary charms." The red drop solidified on her finger into a sparkling, faceted gem. Polly tucked it away into her cleavage and glanced over Theia's head toward the door. "Your vivacious twin is getting anxious."

The door swung open in the same leisurely fashion as before, and Rhea, facing the parking lot, whirled around. She took a step inside, peering into the darkness.

"I'm over here, Rhe. You didn't have to come after me. I'm fine."

"You've been in here forever."

Polly laughed. "If she'd been in here forever, you'd have perished long ago."

Theia sucked at the still-bleeding finger and pressed it to her thumb to stop the blood. "The name, please?"

"Of course," said Polly. "Lucy Smok."

Theia blinked at her. "Is this some kind of joke?"

"Not at all."

"You don't think I'd thought of that? That Lucy wasn't the first person I went to?"

"It's hardly my fault you didn't specify whom you'd already spoken to. You asked me who would be most likely to know where Lucien is. And that is Lucy."

Theia wanted to strangle her. "Lucy is the one who told me to come see you. That's why I'm here."

Polly shrugged. "That's unfortunate. You might have led with that. Nevertheless, Lucy Smok is the most likely person to be able to tell you where Lucien is. If she chooses not to, that's her business."

Rhea marched toward the booth. "People like you love to play games of semantics. Come on, Thei, you're wasting your time with her." She grabbed Theia's hand and turned her toward the door.

"People like me?" Polly's voice hinted that Rhea had gone too far, and Theia tried to pull her toward the exit without saying anything else, but Rhea paused and turned around.

"You immortals. Like the Norns. Creatures above it all who like to mess with mortals, making sketchy deals where everything's fine print."

"Forget it, Rhea. Come on." Theia tugged her toward the door, afraid it might close on them at any moment and lock them in.

"For your information," said Polly as they reached the exit, "I do *not* make sketchy deals. I provide information honestly."

"Oh, really?" Rhea shook Theia's hand off her arm. "My sister asked you a simple question, and you gave her a bullshit answer because it fit the semantics of the question. That's not my definition of honesty."

"Your sister seems to have a pretty good grasp of semantics, and she considered her question carefully. Do you think you could do better?"

"*Rhea*." Theia shook her head, but once someone pissed Rhea off, there was no dissuading her.

"In the interest of *honesty*," said Polly, "Theia has already asked me directly if I know where Lucien is, and the answer is no. But if you have another question, I may have another answer."

"And what did Theia give you for it?"

Polly took the gemstone from her cleavage and held it up in the light. "A drop of blood. Isn't it pretty? I wouldn't mind a matching set. They would make lovely earrings."

Rhea glanced at Theia. "You gave her your blood?"

"It was just a drop. A finger prick. She swore it wouldn't give her any power over me or cause me any harm. What she said rang true."

"Fine." Rhea stepped forward, holding out her finger.

"Rhea, don't. She's just playing with us."

"I have a question," Rhea said stubbornly.

Polly smiled, producing her pin from nothing once more. "Ask first. Present your gift after."

"Are you working with Carter Hamilton to harm my family or Lucien's family?"

Damn. Rhea was good at this. It hadn't even occurred to Theia that Polly might be in cahoots with Carter. But it ought to have. She was the one who'd hooked Lucien up with his anonymous source.

Polly seemed to be trying to formulate an answer. Rhea had definitely hit on something.

Rhea folded her arms. "Are you going to answer the question or not?"

"It's not a simple question."

"I think it's a very simple question. Yes or no?"

"I would never do anything to harm Lucien." Polly threw a pointed look at Theia. "Or anyone he cares about."

"But you *are* working with Carter."

"I *work* with no one. I provide information. Carter Hamilton bartered with me for certain information that he was free to do with as he pleased. But if he's used that information to harm Lucien..." Polly frowned. "I would be extremely unhappy with him."

"Well, he has." Theia returned to the booth. "He made a deal with Edgar to become a silent partner of Smok International, promising Edgar an extended life. And then withheld what he'd promised until giving it to him would only prolong Edgar's suffering."

"Mr. Hamilton isn't known for his scruples, but Edgar did make the deal. Though I don't see how he's harmed Lucien."

"You don't see how? Because Edgar is in this limbo state between living and dying—this state that Carter drove him to deliberately—Lucien is transforming into a demon. You probably know Lucien better than anyone. How can you not see that as harm to him? He's been afraid of this happening his entire life. And if I can't find him, he'll probably end up in hell. If he isn't there already."

"And you have some magical means of keeping him out of hell?"

"No, I don't," Theia admitted. "But if anyone can, I would think it would be a direct descendant of Madeleine Marchant. And I intend to do everything in my power to find a way."

Polly studied her. "Being an inhuman creature isn't the worst fate. As you and your sisters have discovered, there are strengths in having unnatural blood. Lucien has always feared his power—trying to deny it, trying to run from it. I think that's a mistake. But if this transformation has been forced on him early and Mr. Hamilton is responsible, he's forfeited any remaining good will he may have had with me. I did, in fact, put him in touch with Lucien. I now regret that. At the time, I thought it would cheer Lucien up to have some new targets."

"Targets like my boyfriend," said Rhea.

"Another thing Mr. Hamilton misled me about. I wasn't aware that Leo Ström had been made mortal. I was led to believe that despite having been released from his mistress, he was still a Hunt wraith."

Rhea uncrossed her arms. "So let me get this straight. People come to you for information because you've got the goods on all things supernatural, and in the past week or so, you've let this one narcissistic, two-bit necromancer give you easily debunked information and use you to bring harm to someone who apparently means a great deal to you. Do I have that right?"

Theia cringed as Polly's glittering eyes began to smolder. Beside her, the tiger-man growled low in his throat, and they'd finally gotten the attention of the lovebird vamps. Raul and Rocco slid out of the booth without being asked, stepping back and giving Polly a wide berth as she emerged from it.

She came to stand face-to-face with Rhea, who, to her credit, didn't flinch. "Are you maligning my reputation?"

"I think you're doing a pretty good job of that all by yourself."

Theia put her arm out in front of Rhea as if to stop a physical fight. "Carter Hamilton is an expert at telling people what they want to hear. He's done his best to ruin more than one excellent reputation in this town. Just ask my sister Ione."

Polly narrowed her eyes at Theia. "And just what does that have to do with me?"

"You might consider that he's deliberately undermining your reputation for his own gain as part of his larger plan."

"What larger plan?"

"He envies everyone's power. He wants it all for himself."

Polly's expression softened slightly, and she laughed. "You think he has his eye on my little grotto?"

"And your good name. They go hand in hand, don't they?"

The siren's expression hardened again. "He's in for a big surprise if he thinks he can unseat me." Without warning, she grabbed Rhea's hand and stabbed her finger—to Rhea's squeal of surprise—taking her drop of blood. "You've gotten your answer. Time for you little witches to go."

Theia turned Rhea around and hurried her to the door before she could get them in any worse trouble. She suspected it was only the finger in Rhea's mouth that kept her from running it.

Polly spoke once more before they reached the exit. "Ask Lucy where Lucien would go if he didn't want to be found via electronic means."

Theia paused and looked over her shoulder.

"Electronic," Polly repeated.

Theia nodded. "Thanks."

Chapter 27

Rhea held her pricked finger off the steering wheel as she drove toward Phoebe's place. "What was that about 'electronic means'?"

"I think she meant somewhere without cell phone service or Wi-Fi."

Rhea's shoulders rippled in a little shudder. "Sounds like hell to me. Do you know someplace like that with meaning for Lucien?"

"No, but I think Lucy must." Theia glanced at Rhea's profile. "Thanks, Moonpie."

"Oh, God. I'm Moonpie again. What did I do now?"

"I think you riled her up to the point that she was mad enough to actually give me some helpful information."

Rhea grinned and gave her a sidelong glance. "By the way, did you see how riled up 'kitty' was? And I do mean *up*."

Theia groaned. "I'm never going to be able to look at Puddleglum the same way again."

Rhea couldn't stop giggling about "Bad Kitty" on the drive back to Phoebe's. She climbed into bed with Leo when they arrived, and Theia put in her ear buds to drown out any embarrassing noise that might ensue and dragged out Rafael Sr.'s archives, carefully rereading everything. She'd missed any hint of a curse the first time, so maybe she wasn't looking in the right place.

She combed through deeds and bills of sale in French, in which she was far from fluent but could get the gist of. Lists that looked like maybe instructions for household staffs and bills of lading—things she would have been fascinated by at any other time—and finally stumbled upon something promising after several hours of eye-strain: the declaration of Madeleine's guilt, attested to by Philippe Smok, Vicomte de Briançon.

Seeing the words on paper made her shiver. This was Madeleine's denouncement by her own employer, who, by Lucien's account, had done it for personal gain. It made it seem a great deal more real, even if she couldn't read much of it. Theia stroked her fingers over the ancient ink. At the bottom of the page was what she thought at first was a smudge. But on closer inspection, she was convinced it was the symbol of the black moon—the mark of Lilith.

She stroked the ink of her tattoo—one she'd gotten because of a dream. She'd thought it would protect Rhea from the danger the dream had foretold if she had the tattoo she'd seen on Rhea on her skin instead. Of course, Rhea had already tattooed herself with the symbol. And the dream had actually been about Leo and not danger at all. Trying to outsmart her dreams was a fool's errand.

Theia looked back carefully through some of the daily minutiae she'd skimmed over. Had she seen the symbol on something else? Sure enough, there it was on what she'd taken for a bill of lading—with what looked like a partial signature at the bottom that could have been "Madeleine." Were these Madeleine's own words?

The antiquated syntax was difficult to understand. Time for her translator app, even if it would only give her an imperfect understanding of it.

Painstakingly, Theia typed in one line at a time and copied the translations into her notepad. It seemed to be an exhortation of some kind. Theia pieced it together and came up with an approximation.

Mind what you have wrought. Seven daughters born and seven lost. The great lady will birth them again anon. And from every seven born and gone among your house will the Devil reap a son.

It was the curse Madeleine had spoken against the house of Smok.

After Lucy ignored her call and texts, Theia returned to the villa.

This time Lucy opened the door promptly and sighed. "What now? I haven't heard from him. I would have told you if I had."

Theia wasn't so sure about that. "I spoke to Polly. She didn't have any information except to tell me to talk to you and ask you where Lucien would go to avoid electronic communication."

Lucy squinted at her, obviously sensitive to the light. "Electronic?"

"Someplace off the grid. Is there somewhere you went when you were kids that might have special meaning for him? Somewhere he'd feel safe?"

"Around here?" Lucy reached up to scratch her head but stopped with a grimace as she evidently remembered what was making it itch. "We didn't spend much time around here when we were children. Although…"

"Although what?"

"There was this one time when Lucien said he was going to run away from home. Edgar was mad at him about something. I think it was right after our grandmother died. The family doctor had been at the funeral, and Lucien snuck into the back of her car. She was going to some vacation home she owned, and he ended up at her cabin. When she realized she had a stowaway, she let him stay for a day or two before she drove him back. Lucien never told Edgar where he'd been, and Fran didn't give him away. Lucien only told me about it later."

It sounded promising.

"Do you know where it is?"

"I don't, but I can get the address from Dr. Delano." Lucy was already dialing. "Hi, Fran. No new developments. I just wondered—this is going to sound like an odd question, but do you have the address of that place you used to have in the White Mountains?" Lucy listened for a moment. "You do? That would be great, thanks." She ended the call and glanced at Theia. "She still owns it. She's texting the address to my phone." Lucy forwarded it to Theia when it came through. "Seems like a long shot, but here you go."

"Thanks." Theia paused. "Do you want to come with me?"

Lucy laughed and partially unfurled her wings. "I

don't think so. Not until I figure out what to do about all this myself. Lucien may have the right idea."

It was just an hour before sunset by the time Theia reached the turnoff for Heber-Overgaard, but among the towering pines lining the two-lane highway that wound up into the mountains through logging country, it was already dusk. She was stuck behind a logging truck on the gradual incline, and it was nearly dark when she found the gravel road that led to the lakeside cabin. It was slow going after that, and Theia was starting to get the creeps driving so deep into the woods. Maybe she should have waited until morning.

But just as she was seriously considering finding somewhere to turn the car around, the headlights illuminated a log cabin in a small clearing—although "log cabin" seemed too rustic a name for it. It looked like a stately old homestead, as though someone had traveled west, stopped here before reaching the other side of the mountains and let the trees grow up around them until the place had been forgotten.

Theia stopped in the ruts of an old parking spot overgrown with weeds and got out, using the flashlight app on her phone to approach the cabin. Every horror movie cliché ran through her head. Why in the world had she driven here alone? She checked the cell signal. She'd definitely entered a dead zone.

There were no lights on inside the cabin. Theia tried the door and found it unlocked. She took a deep breath and opened it. The cabin smelled long unoccupied.

"Lucien?" Her voice came out in a raspy whisper, like she was trying to shout in a dream. The eerie feeling that maybe this *was* one of her dreams came over her. She cleared her throat and tried again. "Lucien, are you here?"

Something moved in the darkness. Theia pointed the light toward the sound, but whatever it was moved swiftly out of the beam. What if Lucien wasn't here and she'd startled some wild animal? Or an ax-wielding maniac? Just as she was about to call out again, the figure in the dark spoke, and the rough whisper made the hairs on her arms stand on end.

"Why did you come?"

"Lucien?"

"Not anymore." He squinted against the beam of light as she turned it on him, and she caught the flash of something bright blue before he rushed her and snatched the phone from her hand and shut it off. He was standing just inches in front of her now, and all she could see was the preternatural glow of his eyes. "You shouldn't have come."

"You shouldn't have run off without telling me what happened."

"Should I have come back to bed and touched you like this?" A claw stroked her cheek, and Theia jumped. "You see? I disgust you."

"No, you don't, you idiot. You're just scaring the crap out of me by hiding in the dark in a cabin in the woods and acting like you're an ax murderer."

"You should be scared."

She was beginning to adjust to the darkness. His dim shape in the shadows just looked like Lucien. Except for the wings peeking out over the tops of his shoulders, slowly rising and falling with his breath.

"Who are you, Jeff Goldblum? Stop being dramatic."

"*The Fly*. It's a good analogy. I'm not Lucien anymore.

I'm like Seth Brundle becoming the fly—Brundlefly."
He paused. "*Smokdragon.* Has a nice ring to it. Actually,
'Smok' means dragon in Polish." He seemed to be get-
ting his sense of humor back.

"Except the Brundlefly was a monster. You're not."

"Give me a few days." He stroked her with his claw
again, running it down her arm, but this time she was
prepared and didn't flinch. She might, in fact, have gotten a little aroused. "How did you find me?"

"I asked Lucy. She didn't have any idea where you'd
go at first, but then I...went to see Polly, and she told me
to ask the right question."

Lucien's eyes narrowed. "You went to Polly? What
did you give her?"

"A drop of blood."

"Theia." He shook his head. "God, I wish you hadn't
done that."

"She promised she wouldn't use it to hurt me, and I can
read people pretty well. Their emotions give themselves
away when they're lying. She was telling the truth."

"Of course she won't use it to hurt you. Because now
you'll never be able to hurt *her.* Any harm that comes to
her will be felt by you and all her gammon. You'll come
to her aid. That's how she protects herself. It's why she
surrounds herself with those creatures. They all belong
to her gam."

"Her...what? Her gam?"

"It's what they call a pod of whales or dolphins. A
gam. From gammon. That's what Polly likes to call the
ones who give her 'trinkets.'"

"Are you one of these...gammon?"

In the dark, she could just see the sadness in his smile.
"Of course I am."

And Rhea had given the siren a trinket, too. It was something Theia would have to worry about later. Right now she was more concerned with Lucien.

"So what are you planning on doing, hiding in the woods and living off squirrels?"

"I was thinking possum. More meat." His smile was less sad and more amused. "But as it turns out, Fran has a propane-powered freezer full of meat, and the pantry is fully stocked." Lucien stroked her arm again, seemingly unaware he was doing it. "If you're hungry, I can whip something up."

Theia's stomach growled to announce that apparently she was.

"I'll take that as a yes." His hand slipped down to hers, but he seemed to remember himself as she intertwined her fingers with his, and he let go with a jolt. "As you see, I won't be making anything complicated, but I think I can handle a spoon and a pot." He turned and moved swiftly through the darkness into the kitchenette, as though he no longer needed light to see.

Theia followed, feeling for furniture and banging her knees on the corners of things along the way.

She rubbed her arms as she watched Lucien fill a pot with water and light the burner under it on the stove. "So there's gas at least. No electricity?"

"There is, but it's shut off when the place is empty, I guess. Sorry. Luckily all the appliances use propane." He glanced at her after taking a box of couscous down from the shelf. "Are you cold?"

"A little bit, yeah."

He shook his head. "My senses are all out of whack. Maybe I can light a fire later." He slipped off the robe he was wearing and held it out for her. "Go ahead, take it. My core temperature is higher now."

Theia put on the robe. Though it had been snug on Lucien, it fit her well enough, but she had to roll up the sleeves. He was wearing nothing but his boxers, which made for a nice view of his abs as he stirred the spices into the water. It also gave her an excellent view of his brilliant blue wings when he turned around.

Lucien caught her staring. "Freakish, aren't they?"

"That's not the word I was thinking of."

"Oh? What would you call them?"

Theia smiled. "They're kind of sexy, actually. Lovely color."

Lucien laughed sharply. "Right. So sexy. Just like the scales on my fingers and the horns on my head."

"I don't mind."

"How are you going to feel when I get further and further from human?"

"How do you know you will?"

"It's how the curse works."

"I'm not sure you know how the curse works. Have you read it?"

Lucien stopped stirring and stared at her. "Have I *read* it?"

"Because I have. Rafe's father's archives on the Covent—they're magical. Every single item that's been tagged and inventoried over the centuries can be conjured up from its listing."

"And you *saw* Madeleine Marchant's curse? In writing?"

"I held it in my hands and touched the ink."

Lucien whistled. "So what does it say? Will the gates of hell open and swallow me up?"

"Well, that's the thing. It's not so specific about details. It's more...poetic. I think she meant for your ancestors to spend years trying to work it out until the first son was transformed."

The water had started to boil, and Lucien turned back to the stove to put the couscous in. "So it's useless, in other words."

"Not if we can figure out what the words mean. I saved the whole thing on my phone. We can take a look and try to decipher it."

"Theia, there's no magic cure. The drug Smok Biotech is working on might have done something to prevent this, but it's too late. It's happening." He put the lid on the pot and turned off the heat to let the grain absorb the water. "If you want to do something useful with your phone, set the timer for five minutes. Forget Madeleine's stupid poetry."

She decided not to push it and let the subject drop.

When it was ready, Lucien dished up the couscous and served it with a bottle of water. "Sorry. I may have misled you about my culinary skills. There *is* plenty of food in the freezer, but this is actually all I know how to make, to be honest."

Theia laughed. "It's fine with me."

They took their meal into the great room, and Lucien set about trying to figure out how to light a fire in the fireplace while Theia sat on the couch to eat. Lighting fires, it seemed, wasn't part of his skill set, either, and after the fifth or sixth match failed to do anything but incinerate the balled-up newspaper he'd tucked into the logs, he bellowed in frustration. Surprising both of them, his outburst expelled a blast of blue flame—luckily aimed right at the firewood. In an instant, they had a cozy blaze.

Lucien straightened and grabbed the bottle of water he'd given Theia and drained it. "That was…" He shrugged after a moment. "Weird."

"Did it hurt?"

"No, but it dried out my throat. I feel like I've been in a stadium all night screaming." He did sound a bit gravelly. Which only added to his allure. He sat beside Theia. "I forgot to ask you how Lucy was handling things. She and Edgar have always been—well, *closer* isn't the right word, because Edgar doesn't really do close, but let's say less acrimonious than Edgar and I."

"She's handling it about as well as you'd expect. I mean, she didn't run off and hide in the woods, but she's staying close to home."

"Why would Lucy want to hide?"

Theia paused with a forkful of couscous. "You don't know? I thought maybe you two had a magical twin connection, and you could feel it. But I guess you're a little preoccupied with what you're feeling."

"Feel what? What happened?"

"You're not the only one who was struck with the curse. Lucy assumes it's because you both shared an egg."

Lucien was stunned. "She's shifting? She's…" He indicated his horns and claws. "Like this?"

Theia nodded, eating the bite of couscous. "Pretty much exactly like that. Not so much with the claws but the horns and the wings. Only her color is red."

"It never even crossed my mind that something could happen to Lucy." Lucien tried to brush his hand through his hair and cursed as his claws hit his horns. "So I guess it's a package deal. Edgar sold both our souls, and he didn't even know it. I suppose we'll both end up in hell."

"Unless we can work out what Madeleine's curse means and see if there's any way around it."

Lucien frowned, contemplating his food. "I know you mean well, but I really wish you'd drop it. I've spent the last twenty-four hours trying to come to terms with the fact that this is actually happening to me. I don't want to think about magical cures or spend my time chasing false hope." He met her eyes. "I'd pretty much resigned myself to never seeing you again. And then you show up here. And I can't pretend I'm unhappy about that fact. As much as I dread losing my humanity and becoming something even more grotesque—and as horrified as I am at the prospect of you witnessing it—all I want now is to spend the time I have left with you. Just being with you. Not fighting this."

Theia set her bowl on the steamer trunk that served as a coffee table and reached for Lucien's hand. He hesitated, claws tightly clenched inside his fist, but finally relented.

"And I'm here for that. I won't bring it up again." Which didn't mean she wouldn't keep pondering Madeleine's secrets. She just wouldn't mention it.

Lucien leaned toward her and kissed her chastely, but Theia *wasn't* here for that. She'd had enough of chastity.

She moved her other hand to Lucien's neck, thumb against the rough stubble at his jawline, and kept him from pulling away as she deepened the kiss. He wasn't difficult to persuade. He also tasted of mint. Theia laughed softly against his lips, and Lucien drew back slightly, a puzzled smile on his face.

"What's funny?"

"You brushed your teeth before I got here. You heard me coming, and you brushed your teeth."

He smiled, a hint of color to his cheeks that wasn't reflected firelight. "Maybe I just like clean teeth."

Theia shrugged off the borrowed robe. "Be quiet," she murmured and climbed over his lap, knees balanced on the couch cushions. The fabric of the long skirt of Phoebe's she'd changed into before heading out stretched to accommodate the position, but Lucien pushed the hem up higher, his hands against her thighs, abandoning self-consciousness.

The luminescent blue of his eyes was almost white.

"You're bossy tonight."

Theia rested her forearms on his shoulders. "No, I'm not. I just know what I want."

"And what would that be?"

"To stop wondering what it would be like for you to fuck me."

Chapter 28

The unexpected bluntness of that word on her tongue, so matter-of-fact, so sensually charged, sent a buzz of electric energy through him, straight to his groin. He hadn't considered that she'd want this. Not now. Not when he looked like *this*. But the delivery of that little word had certainly said otherwise. And her eyes said she wanted him completely.

He hadn't realized his hands had kept sliding, gliding up along the smooth plane of her skin beneath the skirt. His thumbs brushed lace. Cautiously, he let his claws slip beneath the elastic at the crease of her thighs to see how she'd react.

A little gasp escaped her. Not shock. Arousal. She rose slightly so his hands could encircle her hips.

Lucien pulled her closer, settling her more firmly in his lap, where she couldn't miss the hardness of his erection inside the cotton boxers. Theia rocked into him. He could feel the damp heat between her thighs. He moved his hands from her hips and brought them up to her waist beneath the T-shirt.

"Do you want these hands on you?" His voice was rough with desire. "When they're like this?"

In answer, Theia pulled the T-shirt over her head and moved his hands up higher. "They're your hands. Why wouldn't I?" She hooked her arms around his neck and kissed him, and Lucien forgot about his hands and his horns and his wings.

Kissing Theia, as always, was like happily drowning. Tasting her, drinking her in, forgetting to breathe, her soft moans vibrating against his tongue like they were coming from him. He stroked his palms across the hard peaks of her nipples through the bra, careful not to snag his claws in the lace, and her little noises became more insistent in his mouth. He tried to unhook the bra anyway and got himself caught, but before he could ruin the moment with anger at himself, she reached back and unhooked it for him, tearing the lace away from his claw to slip the garment off.

Cock straining against his boxers at the touch of her skin, he moved his hands back to her breasts. Perfect and petite—he could cover them entirely in each hand. But he didn't want them covered. Lucien withdrew his mouth from hers, ignoring her moan of protest, and brought her up higher on her knees, dipping his head to circle one taut nipple with his tongue to the accompaniment of her increasingly melodic sighs of pleasure until she let out a breathless squeal as he sucked the nipple into his mouth. He loved making her breathless.

She returned the favor with a sudden dip of her hand

into the opening of his boxers to encircle his cock. The damp nipple slipped from his mouth as he let out a soft groan.

"Are we really doing this?" he breathed against her.

"Of course we're doing it."

It dawned on him that all he'd brought with him to the cabin were the boxers, taking wing in a panic as he'd thrown himself out her bathroom window, somehow thinking he might land on the ground. He'd soared high, exhilarated even as he was horrified, not knowing where he was going until he'd reached the pine forests of the White Mountains and remembered Fran's cabin.

"Theia." The word came out part groan of desire, part lament. "I don't have any condoms."

To his surprise, she just laughed. "Don't worry. I bought some on the way here."

Lucien's eyes widened, and he stifled another groan as she stroked his cock. "You came up here looking for me, knowing what you'd find…and you brought condoms?"

A sexy, self-confident shrug rippled downward from her shoulders with a little motion that jiggled her breasts. Here she was, sitting in his lap, skirt pushed up to her waist, topless, his cock in her hand, and she was nonchalant about the fact that she'd come prepared to lose her virginity to him despite the fact that he was becoming a monster.

He couldn't help but laugh, delighted and amazed by her. If he lost his humanity in the morning, at least he'd have this one ordinary, extraordinary night with her.

Lucien tucked her hair behind her ears with a stroke of the claws on his index fingers. "God, I love you." The last word caught in his throat as he realized he'd said it out loud. He drew back, mortified. "Sorry, I meant—"

"Lucien." Theia put her hands on his shoulders and held his gaze. "It's okay. Don't panic. I love you, too."

He kissed her to avoid looking her in the eye any longer. He'd never said those words to anyone. He'd been in love with Polly once, his first real love, but he'd known better than to tip his hand by saying so. Polly didn't do exclusivity, and she sure as hell didn't do love. And now he'd just blurted it out to Theia like an amateur.

And she loved him back. At least tonight.

Lucien slid her off his lap and scooped her up in his arms to carry her to the large sheepskin rug in front of the fire. "Where are the condoms?"

"In my bag on the front seat of my car."

"Be right back."

He dashed outside and found the bag, digging through it to find the box so he wouldn't have to fumble for one when he got back inside. With his prize in hand, he headed back into the cabin to find Theia casually naked and lying on her belly, ankles crossed in the air behind her.

Oh, what the hell. Why not say it again?

Lucien grinned. "Have I mentioned that I love you?"

"I think you may have, yes." She swung her feet and recrossed them.

"Good. Just checking. I might have to say it a few more times." He stripped off his boxers, and Theia watched with an approving eye. "You still want to do this?"

Theia laughed. "If you don't get down here and fuck me instead of asking me that question repeatedly, I'm going to start getting mad."

He dropped to his knees beside her and felt his wings partially unfold, tipping back to balance his new center of gravity.

Theia followed the motion with her eyes, and Lucien cringed, but she looked curious. "Can I see them? All the way?"

"Right now?"

"Will it affect...anything else?"

Lucien laughed. "I think I can maintain two opposing states." He rolled his shoulders and unfolded the new bones he hadn't had the day before, letting the wings extend to their full width.

Theia rose onto her knees to face him. "Can I touch?"

Lucien nodded, and she reached up to stroke the top edges of each wing, fingers following the curve of the bone as far as she could. It was a curious, energizing sensation, a new erogenous zone, making his abs tighten and his erection stand up even straighter. When she let go, instead of sinking back onto the carpet, Theia lowered her hips to sit on her heels and took hold of his cock. While he balanced on his knees with his infernal wings stretched wide, Theia took him into her mouth.

Lucien stroked a claw lightly along her shoulder, tracing the curve of her spine to the dip before her pert bottom, trying to breathe steadily and keep it together, but the touch drew a voluptuous moan from Theia that nearly made him lose it.

He grabbed her by the hair a bit abruptly and pulled back, inspiring a less sensual sound of protest from her as she let go.

"Sorry." Lucien softened his grip and brushed her hair back into place with a sheepish grin. He folded his wings behind his back and lowered himself to the carpet, drawing her with him, his mouth against her throat. "If you want me to fuck you, darling, we're going to have to slow down." It was the sort of thing he might have said a week ago—in an entirely different tone—to keep her at arm's length, like a verbal talisman to ward off emotion he couldn't handle. But this time the word *darling* was a little prayer of devotion.

He rolled her onto her back and kissed her mouth, making sure she'd heard it the way he meant it, before moving down to the hollow of her throat, her collarbone, the slope between her breasts. Teasing each nipple with his tongue until she was arching toward him and pulling him closer with pleading moans. Tracing the contours of her breasts with his claws and reveling in her delightful shiver as he made his way farther down. And at last parting her legs and coaxing her open with his tongue.

Theia whimpered as he teased her clit, her fingers curled in his hair and her hips tilting upward to give him better access. He wanted to make her come as he had the first time he'd tasted her, but her whimper had turned into whispered words: "Please fuck me, Lucien."

It was all he needed.

He scrambled for the condom packet and ripped it open only to realize he couldn't handle the latex with his claws. "Shit."

Theia saw his predicament and took it from him, sitting up to unroll the condom over his cock. "Teamwork," she said with a wink, and Lucien framed her face with his hands and kissed her, trying to understand how he'd gotten this lucky. If it was fate and blood and demons and curses that had drawn them together, he no longer cared.

He eased her back down to the carpet, still kissing her as he brought himself between her legs. Using his fingers was out of the question.

"You sure?" he asked one more time.

Theia rolled her eyes. "Jesus. Are you going to make

me sign an NDA?" She wrapped her legs around his hips. "I'm sure. And I'm not made of china, I'm just getting older by the minute."

Lucien laughed—something he'd never expected to do at a moment like this. Time to get out of his own head. Theia moaned softly as he entered her, her crossed ankles at his hips urging him on. Every motion of her body, every sound she made said she wasn't interested in his attempt to be gentle. He soon forgot to be, rocking and grinding with her as he pumped his hips, their bodies perfectly in tune, rolling with her after a moment so that she was on top. Theia rode him without hesitancy, hands beside his head as she tilted her pelvis to just the right angle to bring herself to orgasm.

He watched her nipples tighten as she picked up speed, soft moans rising in pitch until she arched her back and cried out, hips locked against his, the cry becoming soft and melodic and a little wistful as it died down. Lucien gathered her to him and kissed her throat.

"You're amazing," he murmured.

Theia gave him a shaky giggle. "I had a little help."

"A *little*?"

She laughed as he rolled her onto her back.

Lucien winked. "I'll show you little." He let go of all restraint and fucked her with abandon, letting himself vocalize while Theia crooned encouragement, hooking her ankles behind him once more. The heat of the fireplace warmed his back, and sweat was making their bodies slippery. The climax burst out of him joyfully, and without meaning to, he flung out his wings as he came inside her, dimly recognizing that she was reaching a crescendo of sound herself, coming again on the heels of his climax.

It didn't occur to him until they lay panting beside each other, relaxing in the afterglow, that her second orgasm had come with the spreading of his wings. He chuckled to himself.

Theia rolled onto her side, resting her chin on one arm against his chest. "What?"

"I think you're fetishizing me. You just want me because of my wings."

"Shut up. I can't help it if you're even hotter as a demi-demon."

"You're a wing freak. Admit it."

"Oh my God." Theia slapped his chest playfully. "I need to use the bathroom." She climbed to her feet. "Tell me it's not an outhouse."

"No, there's a genuine bathroom upstairs. Nicely appointed, too. First door on the right." He watched her go with a smile, admiring the way her body moved, perfectly at home in her nudity as she trotted up the stairs. He had to laugh at how stupid he'd been, fearing that she'd bring the demon out of him, that she'd entered his life to fulfill the curse. The curse had been triggered by something utterly unrelated to Theia—that Lucy was also affected was proof. And who knew? Maybe Theia was right. Maybe there was something in Madeleine's words that held the key to suppressing this. Maybe the Smok Biotech serum could control it. All was not lost. He'd had sex with a daughter of Lilith, and the world hadn't ended.

Lucien sighed with satisfaction. He'd probably better clean up. It would be awkward if Fran showed up, alerted by Lucy that he was squatting here, and found him naked on her sheepskin rug with a used condom discarded beside him.

A twinge went through his knuckles as he picked up

the condom to throw it away, and Lucien flexed his fingers. Had his claws gotten sharper? He didn't remember them curling over quite so much. A pang struck his gut just as another twisted along his spine.

"No." Lucien stared in horror as the scales that covered the tips of his fingers moved up his hands.

It was Theia, after all.

Chapter 29

Theia took her time washing up, savoring the ache between her legs. For an event that had been given such a buildup—the hype beginning before she'd even hit puberty—losing her virginity was remarkably unremarkable. She wasn't magically changed. *Nothing* was changed, really—thanks to her personal experiments with penetration, there had been no proverbial cherry popping to speak of—except that she now belonged to this not-terribly-exclusive club.

And yet it had been far better than she'd imagined. Feeling Lucien inside her, being physically closer to him than she'd ever been to anyone—as close as they could get—had given her a connection with him she couldn't explain. She still felt him there, nestled in the sensitive folds of her body. She could smell him all over her, could still taste the salty-sweet drop glistening on the tip of his cock.

She licked her lips at the memory, smiling at her reflection as she washed her hands, hair a little cockeyed, eyes shining. She was, as Rhea would call it, stupid in love. Theia dried her hands, leaving her hair mussed, and headed back down, looking forward to falling asleep in front of the fire in Lucien's arms.

She slowed on the stairs. Lucien stood facing the fireplace, wings half-erect and shoulders slightly hunched, staring at his hands.

"Lucien? Are you okay?"

He cringed visibly at her voice—*cringed*—and didn't turn. "You need to go." His voice was rough, as though he'd been stoking the fire with his breath.

"What do you mean, go? I'm not going anywhere unless you're coming with me. Why don't we just sleep here tonight and figure out what to do in the morning?"

"There's nothing to figure out. There's nothing to be done. I want you to leave."

Theia came down the last few steps, her chest tight with anger not entirely her own. "We are *not* doing this. Whatever you've fixated on, it's your depression talking to you."

"It's not depression, goddammit." Lucien whirled around.

Theia couldn't help but gasp. His hands were curled into reptilian forelimbs, blue scales covering his arms and his abdomen. And his face...his face was drawn and inhuman. Still a human-shaped mouth and nose, but no longer the pale ivory flesh—it was leathery and taut and brilliant blue.

"Lucien..."

"No. I don't know who I am, but I'm not Lucien anymore. There's no Lucien. I'm a monster. And I want you to go."

She moved toward him, reaching for him, and he snarled, making her hesitate. "Lucien, I'm not going. I love you."

"Then there's something wrong with you. And if you won't go, I will."

"No—"

He'd moved so quickly that she was still staring at the place he'd been, her hair blown across her face by the breeze he created as he passed by her. Theia turned, and he was at the door.

He paused, his hands too gnarled to turn the knob, and lifted his head. "Tell Lucy I'm sorry." The door exploded outward as he rushed it and leaped into the air, and Theia ran after him just in time to see brilliant blue wings flapping in the distance.

"No. No, this isn't fair." Tears rolled down her cheeks as she stared up into the empty sky, stars twinkling over the pines as if nothing were wrong. She couldn't even call Rhea for comfort, and she was freezing, and the ache in her cunt was compounded by its emptiness. She went back inside and found the robe, curled up in it on the couch and sobbed.

Eventually, her swollen eyes and stuffy nose forced her up in search of tissues, and she saw the wide-open gap where the door had been. Anything might get in. What the hell was she going to do now?

"Thanks a lot, Lucien, goddammit!" she yelled into the emptiness. "You could have just asked me to open it for you." But she wouldn't have. And he'd known it. She started crying again, and then got mad at herself and at Lucien and Madeleine Marchant and Edgar Smok—and why not throw God in, even though she didn't believe in him—and then really full of white-hot murderous rage at Carter fucking Hanson Hamilton.

A light appeared through the trees in the distance—two lights, headlights—accompanied by the rumble of an engine. Her heart leaped for an instant until she realized Lucien hadn't left in a car. So who the hell was this?

The car came closer, a silver Range Rover, driving a little too swiftly over the gravel for her taste. Theia stepped back inside, tightening the belt on the robe and glancing around for anything to use as a weapon. All she could find was the poker by the fire, and she brandished it as the Range Rover came to a stop in front of the house.

A woman got out, middle aged with short salt-and-pepper hair.

She stared at the broken door lying on the ground and back at Theia. "What the hell happened to my door?"

Theia lowered the poker. "Are you… You must be Fran."

"I know who *I* am. Maybe you'd like to tell me who you are?"

"I'm Lucien's…" The poker slipped out of her fingers and clattered onto the floor. She wasn't Lucien's anything.

"You're the Marchant girl." Fran closed the door of the Range Rover and came toward her. She stopped in front of Theia and took stock of her tearstained, puffy face. "Oh, honey. I'm so sorry."

Theia had effectively broken into her house, stolen her robe, eaten her food and had sex on her rug, but she flung herself into Fran's arms, undone by the sincerity of her emotion.

"Come on. Let's get you inside. Your feet must be frozen." Fran led her to the couch, and Theia sank onto it, unable to protest. The older woman produced a box of tissues from somewhere, and Theia blew her nose while Fran went outside and dragged the door upright to inspect it. She glanced at the hole in her house. "The frame is cracked, but I think I've got some extra screws in the kitchen. We can put this back up, at least overnight until I can get a carpenter up here."

She propped the door against the wall and went to get the screws, returning with a toolbox. "Come on, give me a hand."

Theia dried her eyes and came to hold up the door while Fran screwed the hinges back onto the frame. It closed, albeit with a little wobble.

"All right, honey. Let's get some hot chamomile into you and you can tell me what happened."

Fran listened as Theia relayed the events of the past twenty-four hours, frowning at the mention of Lucien flying away. "And I suppose his arm was no longer splinted."

"Splinted? No, it wasn't. I'd actually forgotten it had been. I guess the transformation healed the bone."

"It may have made him feel invincible, like a shot of adrenaline, but I doubt the break has healed." Fran sighed. "That boy is as stubborn as his father. Worse."

"You've known Lucien a long time, I guess."

Fran studied Theia's face for a moment, as though trying to decide whether to trust her. "You love him."

"Yes."

"He hasn't had much of that in his life, I'm afraid." She took a sip of her tea and exhaled. "I've known Lucien longer than anyone in his life. I was at his birth."

"You were the attending physician?"

She met Theia's eyes. "I'm his mother."

Theia blinked in surprise. "He didn't tell me."

"He doesn't know." Fran combed her hair back with her fingers with the same gesture Lucien used. "Edgar insisted that I sign a nondisclosure agreement."

"Oh my God. These people and their NDAs."

Fran smiled sadly. "I knew what I was getting into when I married him, but I somehow thought I could, I don't know, soften him. That fatherhood would soften him. When I realized what he'd done to escape the curse for himself—leaving it to Lucien—I was furious. I told him I wanted out. That I was taking my babies and leaving him. And he reminded me that I'd signed a prenup that relinquished any claim to his offspring. I tried to stick it out for a while, but I just couldn't. It was soul crushing. So I left, but Edgar's lawyer insisted on the NDA. If I ever wanted to see my babies again, I could never tell them who I was."

"That's barbaric."

"That's Edgar. I couldn't live with him, and I couldn't live without ever seeing my children again, so I agreed. And he 'graciously' hired me as the company's doctor, which included treating the children when they needed it. I lived for their bouts of croup and strep throat. Isn't that horrible?" She shook her head, remarkably unfazed by it. "But I tried to give them affection and guidance from the perspective of a caring family doctor. Especially Lucien. Lucy has always been pragmatic and resilient—not to mention headstrong. But Lucien feels things very deeply."

"He does," Theia agreed. "It's what I love about him."

Fran squeezed her hand across the table. "You may be the first person to see that about him outside of Lucy and myself. No wonder Lucy's impressed with you."

"Impressed?" Theia laughed. "She hates my guts. She

was going to drug me and wipe my memory to get me out of Lucien's life."

"She doesn't hate you at all. She just loves her brother. She's very protective." Fran shrugged. "She's had to be."

"I take it you know what's happened to her—that the curse has hit her, too."

Fran nodded. "But only partly. It hasn't progressed as it has with Lucien, and we may have some luck with the anti-transformative serum."

Theia looked down at her teacup. "Lucien's progression is my fault. It's my Lilith blood. We finally…" Theia blushed, waving her hand vaguely. "And then afterward, that's when it happened."

"No, honey. I don't think it had anything to do with you. It was Edgar. He's died."

"Died?" Theia raised her head, shocked. "I'm so sorry."

Fran pursed her lips. "I'm only sorry it hastened Lucien's transformation."

"But how? I thought the amulet was supposed to protect him."

"Someone removed it." Fran's eyes darkened. "And I'm quite sure it wasn't anyone on staff at the hospital."

"Carter Hamilton," said Theia.

"It would seem so."

"So it's too late. There's nothing we can do." Theia had lost him.

"There may be something. I remember Edgar talking about a loophole years ago. Beyond his personal cheat, that is."

"A loophole?"

"I've been through Edgar's papers at the office and the house, and so far I haven't found anything. But I know he had other places he kept things. Safes in other houses he owned. It could be anywhere. There's supposed to be something in Madeleine Marchant's own words, an addendum to her curse."

"You mean the riddle?"

"The riddle?"

"It's part of the text of the curse. She'd magically disguised it as a household list."

"How do you know that?"

"I found it," said Theia. "I translated it. At least as far as I could. I've got it on my phone."

She got up and found her phone in the great room. "Here it is." She showed Fran the first part she'd translated, the text of Madeleine's curse on the house of Smok. "I couldn't make out all the words that followed, but it seemed to be written as some kind of cipher, like she wanted someone to figure it out."

"'And from every seven born and gone among your house will the Devil reap a son.'" Fran sighed. "That's pretty much self-explanatory, I'm afraid. Every seven generations, the eldest son of the Smok family has inherited the curse and taken his place in hell."

"I know, but the part after—see here? I think it reads, 'The harvest will materialize…' But then I couldn't make out the next bit. After that, I got 'must the seventh son be bound to be free.'"

Fran took the phone from her and studied the original. "'The harvest will come to fruition when the *déesse*…the goddess…'" She chewed her lip. "The ink has smeared here. *Demande,* maybe?" She shook her head. "I'm not sure that's right. But the next is 'seed.' 'The seed of the…' I can't make out this word, but then it's 'of the first.'" She studied the illegible word again. "*Armure?*"

"Armor?"

"I'm not sure. Her handwriting is so stylized."

"So we've got 'The harvest will come to fruition when the goddess demands. To the seed of the armor of the first must the seventh son be bound to be free.'"

They both shook their heads. It didn't make any sense.

"Wait." Fran looked closely at the text again. "*Arbre*, not *armure*. Tree."

"The seed of the tree of the first… The family tree? Maybe the first is Madeleine. So the seed of Madeleine would be…" She glanced up at Fran as the meaning came clear.

"Madeleine's descendant." Fran set the phone down. "I've heard this before. Phrased a little differently, as a daughter of Lilith. It used to make Edgar pink with rage. No son of the house of Smok was going to be bound to a daughter of Lilith, as long as he was alive."

So a daughter of Lilith had to willingly bind herself to Lucien. Theia didn't have a problem with that. If it meant legally, well…that might take a little more convincing.

"But there's one more line," Fran pointed out. Theia had mistaken the stylized, repeating letters for the signature. "*Lié à l'enfant et lié à l'enfer.* 'Bound to the child and bound to hell.'"

That wasn't quite so promising. If she freed Lucien, it seemed to be saying, she'd end up pregnant and in hell.

Chapter 30

Theia waited until morning when Fran closed up the cabin to face the drive home. She had no plan for finding Lucien, and even if she found him, the loophole might not be a loophole at all. It might be a death sentence.

She responded to anxious texts from Rhea once she was back in range of a cell tower. That she'd found Lucien but lost him again was all she was willing to tell her. She wasn't about to go into the whole night. Rhea probably wouldn't tease her about it at a time like this, but she just wasn't ready to talk about the fact that she'd finally gotten laid. And she'd never hear the end of it if any of her sisters even suspected that she'd turned a guy into a dragon and sent him to hell the first time she ever had sex. That topped Ione's first time with Dev and Phoebe's sex tape combined.

There was also a message from Laurel. Once again,

she was the only sister Theia could talk to. After checking in with the TA who'd subbed for her biology final, she met Laurel for lunch downtown.

"I have news," Laurel said before Theia could bring up hers. "I got in touch with Rowan and Rosemary."

"You did? That's terrific." But Laurel's face wasn't saying "terrific."

"We met for lunch, and they seemed really happy to see me. There was hugging and reminiscing, and it was all great until I told them I'd been in touch with Dad's other daughters."

"Oh. No."

"Yeah, it didn't go well. They think I've joined up with 'the enemy.'"

"I'm sorry, Laurel. I know it's not the same, but you have us. Ione's open to getting to know you, and Rhea will come around."

Laurel laughed. "I'm not holding my breath, but thanks. Anyway, it's not like it's any big loss. I hadn't seen them since I was little. I barely remember them. But it was just one more childhood fiction bubble popped, you know? I used to imagine they'd come rescue me and we'd all be a happy family again."

Theia reached across the table and squeezed Laurel's hand, but Laurel laughed and brushed it off. "Really, I'm okay. It's you I'm a little worried about."

"Me?" Theia swallowed. "What did you see?"

"Carter's up to his old tricks, isn't he?"

"Oh." Theia breathed a little sigh of relief that it wasn't something horrible about Lucien. "Yeah, you could say that. He convinced Lucien's father to sign half the company over to him—they own Smok International—in exchange for an extra dozen years of life, and then he killed the guy."

"Oh my God."

"He was dying anyway, but Carter never misses an opportunity to make a bad situation worse." She wasn't sure how much she should say about Lucien's problem.

"And Lucien—sounds like you decided which way you were going to go with that."

"Yeah, I guess both our visions came true there." Theia concentrated on her food to keep from blushing furiously, which she knew she would if she saw Laurel's face. "That's what I wanted to talk to you about, actually. It turns out—"

"He's turning into a dragon?"

Theia's head shot up. "Shit. You do see everything, don't you?"

"To be fair, it's not much of a leap, considering the rest of your family."

"Ha. Yeah. I just didn't think… I mean, I figured I'd end up with the Prince of Darkness, not a full-on dragon who happened to *be* the Prince of Darkness. And here's the kicker—I think I can save him from being permanently damned to hell. But it might mean damning myself."

"By signing the contract."

Theia nodded. "Figuratively speaking."

"No, not figuratively. I saw an actual contract."

"But where would I get a contract that would involve selling my soul?"

"From Smok Biotech, I suppose."

"Smok…" Theia dropped her fork, and it clattered loudly on the ceramic-tile floor of the outdoor patio. "The fine print."

* * *

There was something to be said for being a monster. Lucien didn't have to care anymore whether what he was doing was right or wrong. He might not be able to pick up a pen and write a check from the bottomless Smok account to get what he wanted, but he could take what he wanted, when he wanted. And who cared if anyone saw him do it? They pissed themselves and ran away—or simply told themselves it wasn't real. Amazing what humans were willing to just *not see*.

The area around Heber-Overgaard in the White Mountains was known for UFO sightings—the *Fire in the Sky* abduction had allegedly taken place there in the '70s. So, really, what was one naked half man, half dragon breaking into the general market stockroom in the middle of the night and stealing a cheap pair of jeans, an oversized plaid flannel shirt—to wear over his tucked wings when he wasn't flying—and work boots? When they reviewed the security camera footage the next day, they'd probably find some way to explain it. Just another out-of-work logger on a bender. He'd grabbed a red ball cap for good measure.

Lucien had stayed close to the cabin, worried that he'd left Theia vulnerable. He'd seen Fran show up, and he'd seen the two of them leave in the morning. Who knew what misguided plan they were hatching together? Fran must have already known what had happened to him after talking to Lucy. But it didn't matter what they were planning. He was beyond helping. And he didn't give a damn how they felt about it.

Except that he couldn't stop smelling Theia on his skin. And every time he closed his eyes, he saw her perched in his lap, head thrown back in ecstasy, that one bead of sweat trickling between her pink-tipped breasts as she came.

Great time to have a pair of gnarled forelimbs for hands.

It was also infuriating that the transformation hadn't progressed any further. Hell needed to get it over with and open up and swallow him already.

He waited for nightfall again and kept to the forested mountain terrain as he flew until he reached the stunning red hills and zeroed in on Lucy's villa in Sedona. As much as he'd relegated himself to the realm of monsters and as little as he was sure he cared about what happened to anyone else, he'd shared a womb with Lucy. And she'd inherited his stupid curse by mistake.

He perched like a gargoyle on the rooftop of the building opposite and watched for any sign of her. But nothing moved inside. If it had, he'd have seen it. His eyesight was excellent. He could have used this when he was hunting things like him.

So if Lucy wasn't inside, where the hell was she?

A little while later, he spotted her car pulling into the lot. She'd driven somewhere? Looking like a freak? Except when Lucy got out of the car, she wasn't a freak at all. She was just Lucy. No horns. No claws. No wings. No scaly anything.

Lucien swooped down and climbed through the window of the kitchenette—shockingly easy to jimmy with a good pair of claws—and sat waiting for her in the dark.

She opened the door dressed in one of her tailored suits—nowhere to hide wings in that—and jumped when he moved in the dark. She didn't have his eyesight. Instead of turning on the light, Lucy dropped into a defensive posture, ready to kick his ass. And she probably still could, enhanced strength or not.

"Lu, it's me." The growl managed to sound like words.

She lowered her fists and straightened. "Lucien?"

"Don't turn on the light. I just wanted to see if you were okay. Looks like you're doing much better than I am." He moved in front of the window where she could see his silhouette against the streetlamp.

"Fran told me. Why did you take off again? Why not stay there?"

"And do what? I can't be with Theia." The words were ragged in his throat. "Her blood did this to me." It hurt that Theia had been the cause of it. Even though she hadn't known for certain it would happen, it felt like a betrayal.

Lucy interrupted his thoughts. "It wasn't Theia. Edgar's dead."

"He's…" Lucien blinked. "How?"

"Someone took the amulet during the night. He suffered total organ failure almost immediately."

He ought to feel bad about it. He *did* feel bad about it. But on a level so deep he didn't know how to touch it. Lucien was floating above it. Stoic. Monster. Whatever.

"That's why you're back to normal. The curse fully transferred to me."

"Sort of. Not entirely. If you hadn't run off, Fran and I could have helped you get the serum. She got some for me last night. It works, Lucien. It suppressed my symptoms."

"But it's too late for me now."

"I think it might be, yes."

"Why am I still here? Why hasn't my damn soul been harvested?" It occurred to him that maybe it had. Not having a soul would explain why he couldn't feel anything.

"I don't know. You haven't fully transformed yet."

"Maybe there's a backlog in hell."

She smiled in spite of herself. He'd always been able to make Lucy smile when she didn't want to.

"You know Edgar set up the trust to transfer to you on our twenty-fifth birthday. Maybe there was a reason for that. Maybe whatever effect Hamilton's meddling has had on the curse, it can't fully manifest until the time is right."

Lucien nodded. It made sense. Their birthday was in a few hours. It gave him a sense of finality even as it terrified him. He couldn't go on like this indefinitely. If he were his former self, he'd have hunted his new self down by now. But there were other things he could hunt down in the meantime.

"I'm glad the serum helped you, Lu. Take good care of the company. And don't be too quick to send me new souls." He smiled even though she wouldn't see it and turned away.

"Lucien, wait." Lucy crossed the room, holding something out to him. His phone. "At least take this with you so I can contact you if something changes."

He shook his head. "What could possibly change that matters?"

"Just take it, goddammit."

He showed her his claws. "How would I even use it?"

"I disabled your password and the thumbprint recognition. You can use your knuckles. I tried."

Lucien sighed and snatched it from her to avoid an argument. "Happy birthday, Lu." He leaped through the window before she could say anything else. He hated long goodbyes.

He went through his list mentally—rogue creatures and deserving half humans he'd kept in his sights. He supposed he didn't need the crossbow now, even if he could have wielded it.

There was a certain priest in the Phoenix area who'd been transferred from one parish to another for years to hush up scandals. The harm he'd caused to the young boys entrusted to his spiritual care had been bad enough while he was mortal. Now he fed on his victims as well after having been turned by a former parishioner in an act of revenge. He ought to have died, but he'd managed to summon Smok Consulting in time to save his pathetic life and allow him to continue it as a closeted bloodsucker.

Maybe that phone would come in handy after all.

It didn't take long to nail down the priest's current location. Lucien took to the air and soared over the desert with the night birds. They viewed him with idle curiosity. He had a good sense of direction, and he'd memorized the map on his phone. The grid of the metropolitan area was laid out for him in lights.

At the church, his heightened senses led him to the scent of blood. He found the priest in the darkened chapel. Far too late for mass, he was cloistered in "confession" with a child he must have kept after. Lucien tore the roof off the confessional, exposing the monster. He hadn't really thought about the standard problem with eradicating vamps. Wooden stakes were a Hollywood cliché, and burning them—with sunlight or fire—just made them angry. Though it did have the satisfying effect of making them experience a great deal of pain while they grew new skin.

But it turned out that Lucien's enhanced abilities included being able to bite a vamp's throat in two, taking the head clean off. Tasted disgusting, but it did the trick. The boy cowered on the floor of the confessional as Lucien tossed the priest's corpse aside. What could he possibly do to allay the child's fear? Nothing, he realized. He was the devil, and the devil had just killed a priest.

A familiar chill rushed into the church, the thundering of horses' hooves and raucous calls accompanying a hunting horn in the distance. Through the open chapel doors, Lucien could see the approach of the Wild Hunt. He straightened to face the chieftain.

Leo Ström swung off his spectral mount, sword drawn, taking in the bloody scene with cold calculation. He approached Lucien with his sword raised, his brown leather duster scattering the flurry of ice that seemed to emanate from the Hunt itself—ice in May.

"So this is how I get to hell," said Lucien. "Makes sense."

Leo drew up short. "Lucien?"

His growl was still mostly intelligible, but he was surprised that Leo recognized him. "You have a good eye."

"Just a good nose."

He wasn't sure how to take that. He imagined he wasn't smelling too good about now, and he didn't think he'd had a body odor problem before turning into a monster.

"Fair warning," said Lucien. "I can more than beat you in a fight now, and I don't intend to go easily."

"Go? I'm not here for you. I came for this piece of garbage." He kicked at the head and it rolled under a pew. Leo studied Lucien's condition. "Slept with Theia, did you?"

Lucien burst out laughing—though it probably sounded

more like a roar. It felt good for a moment to have a genuine laugh.

Leo sheathed his sword inside the duster. "I could use someone like you in my hunting party."

"That's a generous offer coming from a man I tried to kill, but I won't be around much longer. Just waiting for my soul to be collected."

"Sorry to hear that." And he actually did seem sorry. "But it won't be collected by me."

Lucien nodded and turned toward the shattered stained-glass window he'd climbed through. "Do me a favor," he said as he jumped onto the sill. "There's a very frightened boy in the booth over there. If you could get him some help, I'd appreciate it. He's lost a lot of blood, and he'll need some antivenin therapy from Smok Biotech. Give Lucy a call. She'll know what to do."

Leo nodded and tipped his hat. "Farewell, my friend."

Lucien hadn't expected that. Maybe he did have some capacity for emotion left in him, because it made him blink his eyes rapidly as he took flight. Maybe it was just the force of the wind.

As he pondered his next target, his phone vibrated in his pocket. Lucien ignored it. For all he knew, Lucy might have told Theia he had the phone, and he couldn't afford to let himself indulge in any communication from her. When it buzzed again, he decided to set down on a rooftop and turn off all notifications before he took a moment to figure out where he was headed next.

A message from Lucy showed on the screen, just Hamilton.

Well, that was a thought. He could take out that piece of shit as a gift to both Lucy and Theia.

But the next message was just as brief and cryptic.
Daisy.

Daisy? The shade that had possessed Lucy?

Painstakingly, he texted her back. Where are you?

He could see her typing, but there was a long pause
before the answer came—in three distinct texts.

Holy C
Holy holy holy
Holy shit, you are both so stupid. Enjoy rotting in hell.

Lucien let out a roar and shot into the air, his blood
boiling—and it didn't feel like a metaphor. He'd been
right about the incident with the shade. Carter Hamilton was controlling it, and he was using it to control
Lucy. But what had all that "Holy" stuff been about?
She'd started typing Holy C— but seemed unable to finish
whatever word started with *C*. Holy Cow? Holy Christ?

It could be the name of a church. *Holy Cross*. The
Chapel of the Holy Cross was a well-known landmark
in Sedona. Lucy had been trying to answer his question:
"Where are you?"

He arrived at the darkened church nestled between a
pair of Sedona's ubiquitous red buttes to find Lucy alone
in front of the chapel. She faced outward atop the short
brick wall that served as a tourist lookout point for the
desert valley.

Lucy turned at the sound of his approach and grimaced. "God, she was right. You really do look like hell."
Something glittered in the darkness, nestled in her cleavage. She saw him zero in on it and looked down, finger-
ing the gemstone. "Pretty, isn't it? They let me in any

time of day or night to visit Edgar. All I had to do was give him a little Judas kiss and take this with me."

Lucien chose not to respond to the taunt. "I offered to help you the other day. I could have freed you from the one who's controlling you. Lucy still can."

A hooded figure stepped out of the shadows beside the chapel. "Lucy will do nothing but join you in hell." The figure drew back the hood, and Lucien wasn't the least bit surprised to see that it was Carter Hamilton.

He took a menacing step toward the necromancer. "Lucy is stronger than you think. And I'm about to end you."

"Are you really? I highly doubt that."

Hamilton made no move to block him or even evade his attack as Lucien charged with demon speed—and nearly tumbled off the edge of the wall behind the spot where Hamilton had been standing. Just like at the reception, it was only a projection.

"Coward."

Hamilton smirked. "This from a privileged scion who didn't even have the guts to take his place at the table of one of the most prestigious and influential firms in the world. So now that place is mine." He glanced at Lucy. "And it can be your sister's as well if I choose to keep her in her body." He stroked his phantom hand over Lucy's breasts. Her face had gone blank. Daisy's autonomy within the body had apparently been suspended.

The idea of what Hamilton might do to Lucy when he was gone turned Lucien's stomach and made his blood heat with rage. "You keep your damn hands off Lucy's body. If you think I can't find you wherever you're hiding and tear your head off with my bare hands, just try me."

"And how are you going to manage that while you're

fending off my friends?" Hamilton nodded over Lucien's shoulder. Something in the desert night smelled even worse than Lucien.

He turned to find half a dozen shuffling revenants crawling over the rocks. But these weren't just revenants. They were *draugr*, resurrected in putrefying bodies to serve their master.

"I understand they find living women irresistible," said Hamilton. "Like a drug habit or a sweet tooth they can no longer satisfy while in their graves—and then, suddenly, they're presented with candy."

"You piece of shit," Lucien growled and turned, snarling, to face the advancing *draugr*.

Chapter 31

Lucy wasn't answering her phone. Theia had found her copy of the Smok Biotech contract, and she needed a legal interpretation of the fine print. If only Phoebe were back from the Yucatán. She'd stopped practicing, but corporate law had been her specialty in school before she'd gone to work for the public defender. Of course, this was more like infernal law.

While Theia was pondering what to do next, she got a call from a number she didn't recognize. With all that was going on right now, she figured she shouldn't ignore anything.

"Polly would like to have a word with you." The voice was oddly thick, as though it was coming from a larynx not built for human speech.

"Oh, really? And just who is this?"

"Hello, Theia." The caller had evidently handed off the phone.

"Polly."

"I've been alerted to a situation I thought you ought to be aware of."

"Oh?"

"Normally, I wouldn't discuss one patron's business with another, but when a patron betrays my trust, all bets are off. I thought you'd want to know that Carter Hamilton is currently employing necromantic means to put Lucien's sister at risk. And when Lucy is threatened, Lucien responds."

So that was why Lucy wasn't answering. Goddamn Carter, up to his old tricks.

"Do you know where they are?"

"The Chapel of the Holy Cross. You're likely to need reinforcement against Hamilton's magic. That's all I can tell you. It's all I know."

"Thank you, Polly. I won't forget this."

"I know."

Theia tried to reach Rhea on the way to Holy Cross but got no answer. Ione was equally unresponsive. What was going on? The clock on her dash said it was almost midnight. She hadn't realized how late it was. Maybe they were in bed.

She arrived at the road to the chapel with a sense of foreboding. The last time she'd been here had been under the hypnotic control of a century-old Nazi bent on stealing Leo's soul. She had zero memory of the experience, but Rhea had told her enough that she counted herself lucky.

A gray, bloated form scrabbled across the road in front of her. Theia swerved to miss it, but it was already gone. A terrible stench, worse than Mrs. Ramirez, seemed to seep in through the vents as she drove through the space it had occupied. Theia's stomach lurched. Rhea had described the undead thing that had been unleashed on them by the Nazi, Brock Dressler, and Theia was certain she'd just seen one. Another skulked in the bushes ahead.

As Theia parked the car in the lot at the top of the hill, it occurred to her that Polly might have been setting her up. Why should Theia believe she was betraying a confidence and not just helping Carter further his agenda?

An inhuman, gut-churning bellow came from the walkway to her left, followed by a slightly more human snarl and a thick sound, like something punching through gelatin. As she came around the corner of the lot, she tried to make sense of what she was seeing. The remains of several of the things were strewn across the rocks, but the severed parts were inching back toward one another, and in the center of the melee what looked like a reptilian lumberjack was ripping one of the things in half.

Theia blinked, holding her hand over her mouth and nose against the awful stench. "Lucien?"

The glowing eyes fixed on her for a moment, and he growled. "Dammit, Theia. What are you doing here?"

Trying not to vomit. Theia swallowed against the urge. "Polly told me you needed help."

"Of course she did." He tore the arm off the *draugr* advancing on him and hurled it into the brush. "Start grabbing up these things before they reassemble and toss them as far as you can."

Theia swallowed again. "Grabbing?" There was no time to be squeamish. Steeling herself, she plucked up a—God, she didn't know *what* it was—and flung it over the low wall into a clump of cactus before grabbing another and hurling it into the parking lot below. "Isn't there any way to kill them?"

"Not unless you're a necromancer or you know where their graves are. Best I can do at the moment is keep them in pieces."

Theia was pitching the things at a fairly even pace, keeping up with the ones creeping toward each other while Lucien battled the already reassembled. She tried not to look as he tore them to pieces. At least she'd forgotten to eat today, because she'd seriously be losing her lunch.

At a lull in the festivities, she realized someone was standing motionless on the top of the wall beside the chapel, facing out toward the valley. "Is that Lucy?"

Lucien hurled a bloated head up into the rocks, and it burst like a melon. Theia steadied herself against the wall, trying not to succumb to a convulsion of dry heaves.

"She's being controlled by a shade. Waiting for Carter to come back and give her the order to jump. I've been too busy fending off these foul things to try to get her down from the wall."

"A step-in?" If only Phoebe or Rafe were here. Phoebe was a talented evocator who'd been channeling step-ins most of her life, and Rafe, of course, had the power to command the dead. "Maybe I can get the shade to talk to me."

"Be my guest. Her name is Daisy." Lucien punched a *draugr* that had crawled over the parking lot wall, having apparently found all—or most, anyway—of its parts, and beheaded it with a kick to the jaw. "Wish I had that Viking sword of Leo's. Would make this work a lot quicker."

Theia approached Lucy carefully, sitting on the wall beside her and swinging her legs over the edge. The side of the butte below wasn't a sheer drop—more like a wide, sloping ledge. Lucy would have to take a running leap to fling herself over it.

"Daisy, can I talk to you?"

Lucy didn't move, but after a moment, she broke her silence. "What for?"

"I was just wondering if you could communicate with Lucy. Can she hear me when I talk to you? Can you hear what she's thinking?"

"She's asleep." Daisy gave her a quick sideways peek as if she was curious about this new person addressing her. "I can wake her up. But she won't be able to answer you."

"Would you, please?"

Daisy shrugged Lucy's shoulders, and her posture changed, becoming more tense and alert.

"Lucy, I don't know if you can hear me—"

"She hears you."

"Fran told me she'd given you something to control those symptoms you were having. Do you know if Carter is aware of your…condition?"

"I told you, she can't answer."

"Well, you can. Does she know?"

Daisy sighed and pondered for a moment. "She doesn't think so."

"And how long do you think the medication lasts? When do you need to take it again to keep the condition under control?"

Lucy's brow wrinkled—clearly not an expression that was natural to her—as Daisy tried to understand the answer. "Not long? I think that's what she said." Daisy turned to look at Theia. "Why? What are you trying to do?"

"I don't think you really want to do what Carter's telling you. I think Lucy can help you defy him."

"You don't know anything about it. *He* said he's got one of my bones." She threw a glance at Lucien, who was flinging the lower part of a *draugr* torso over the wall.

"And we can get it back and release you. I've done this before with my sisters. We bound the necromancer so he couldn't hurt anyone."

Daisy laughed, making Lucy sound hoarse. "Yeah. I see how well that worked out."

Theia shrugged in acknowledgment. "Well, we still have to find the source of his power, but we could certainly help you."

"The ugly one over there said the same thing. It's bullshit. You just want me to step out because all you care about is your friend. But even if I could, I wouldn't. Why should I? You'd just double-cross me as soon as I did. And then he'd make me pay."

"My brother-in-law is Rafael Diamante. Have you heard of him?"

Lucy's brows drew together in suspicion. "The Lord of the Dead? I don't believe you."

"What does Lucy say? Can you tell if she tries to lie to you?"

Lucy frowned. "I can hear what she's really thinking. She says it's true. She also says he's in the Yucatán. So how's that going to help me?"

"He can be here in just minutes using his *nagual*— his animal form." She hoped that was true. God, Phoebe was going to kill Theia if she interrupted her honeymoon. "His power trumps Carter Hamilton's."

Someone else spoke behind her. "That's what you think."

Theia whirled to see Carter looking overly dramatic in a hooded cloak.

"He's not really here," Lucien growled. "He's a projection."

"Am I?" Carter smiled. "Try me."

Lucien stalked toward him and flung the rotting forearm of a *draugr* in his direction as if he expected it to go through him, but a look of consternation crossed his face when Carter snatched it out of the air.

"You'd be wise not to underestimate me." Carter tossed the forearm aside and glanced at Lucy with a nod. "Daisy."

Lucy's face fell, and she looked up at Theia. "You see? You couldn't help me at all." Before Theia could stop her, she'd turned and stepped off the wall, tumbling onto the rock ledge below. Lucien's roar drowned out Theia's shout. Lucy was still crouched on the ledge, arms and legs scraped up but otherwise apparently unhurt, staring down at the sheer drop as though trying to psych herself up to jump.

Lucien had charged toward them, but Carter threw him back with some kind of necromantic spell. Whatever magic he'd tapped into this time was definitely stronger than before. It was up to Theia to stop Daisy from finishing what she'd been ordered to do.

While Carter was occupied with Lucien, she climbed over the wall and skidded down the rock face, digging her fingers into a crevice for purchase as she slid toward Lucy. With her fingers firmly in the handhold, she stretched out her other hand.

"Daisy, don't do it. Just take my hand."

Lucy turned halfway and glared at her. "You said the Lord of the Dead would come."

"I can call him right now if you promise to stay put for a moment." She put her hand in her pocket and took out her phone, selecting Phoebe's name one-handed. Rafe's cell phone number was third on the list under Phoebe's and her landline. Might as well go straight to the source and save time. Phoebe was going to murder her either way. It rang three times, and Theia was afraid it was going to voice mail when Rafe answered.

"Well, hello, Tweedledee. Phoebe says this better be good..." He paused. "And also 'why the hell is she calling you, Rafe, are you having an affair with my baby sister?'" Rafe laughed. "Just relaying the message. What's up?"

"I need your particular skills to stop a shade from killing someone."

Rafe's voice turned serious. "Of course. How can I help from here?"

Theia hit FaceTime and held out the phone. "Rafe, this is Daisy. Carter's controlling her, and he wants her to throw Lucy Smok off a cliff. I was hoping you could talk her down."

Rafe spoke from the video. "Daisy, can you hear me?"

Lucy's eyes went wide as she straightened. "It's really him."

"Listen to me, Daisy. The necromancer who's bound you has usurped my authority. I know it will be difficult for you to obey, but you must ignore the pull of his magic and do as I tell you. Come away from the edge."

The struggle was visible on Lucy's face. "I can't."

"Yes, you can. Come to me." He held out his hand as if he were actually standing there and she could take it. Maybe as a shade, she could.

Daisy took a halting step forward, looking as though the effort caused her physical pain. Theia inched toward her, pondering how to grab Daisy's hand and hold the phone at the same time without letting go of the crevice in the rock.

"That's it," Rafe encouraged her. "You can resist him."

Lucy was just a foot away from Theia now. Above them on the walkway, the sounds of conflict between Lucien and Carter were ramping up, rocks shattering and crashing. She let go of her handhold. What mattered right now was keeping Daisy from jumping. She could worry about getting back up once Lucy was safe.

Rafe continued to speak in a calm, authoritative voice. "Come to me. Take Theia's hand and let her help you."

As Lucy reached for Theia's outstretched hand, her face suddenly contorted. "No. No, it doesn't matter. You can't help me. He's taken my body away from me. What's the difference?"

"Daisy, don't," Theia pleaded, but in an instant, Lucy had taken two broad steps back. Theia lunged toward her with a shout as Lucy plummeted from the cliff. The phone tumbled from Theia's grip as she grabbed for a handhold once more, and it bounced on the rocks and skittered off to follow Lucy.

Chapter 32

Theia nearly skidded off the rock ledge with them, managing to catch herself with a sneaker wedged into a crack. She closed her eyes, in shock, feeling the currents of the brisk spring wind swirling around her in eddies. It was quiet in the chapel courtyard above. Crickets were serenading as though it were an ordinary May night. What had happened to Lucien?

Carter's treacly voice echoed down to her. "It's pointless to go against me, Theia. You and your sisters should have learned that by now. My devoted, if somewhat pungent, foot soldiers have defeated all of them. You can come back up here and face me like an adult, or you can follow Lucy. The choice is yours. But know that either way, I own you. You signed an oath of fealty to Smok International and its leadership. And that leadership is now me. The house of Smok is no more. I own it all."

Which meant Lucien was dead. Despair fell over her like a black cloak. Like darkness must feel if you could touch it. What was the point of resisting? Carter had won.

Theia worked her shoe out of the crack that kept her from sliding farther, resigned to letting gravity finish what it had started. As her feet dangled over the empty air, something stirred it, whipping her hair around her face. Out of the darkness, crimson wings swooped toward her, and a pair of talons grabbed her by the shoulders, carrying her up and over the wall and dropping her onto her feet.

Beside her, Lucy brushed off her suit as she folded her wings over the torn jacket, glaring at Carter, who stood speechless before her. "Wrong again, asshole. You forgot to wish me a happy birthday."

"So you inherited the curse as well." Carter's pale brows drew together in irritation. "But not fully. Not enough to open the gates of hell, as your brother has done. And not enough to cast out my little helper. Daisy, close her mouth."

Lucy had taken a menacing step toward him, but she stopped and stared blankly as Daisy took over her conscious functions once more. The unexpected shift had apparently only bought Lucy momentary control.

At the perimeter of the courtyard, the reassembled host of *draugr* hovered as if awaiting Carter's command. And against the rocks behind Carter lay an object that at first glance appeared to be a large, blue, crumpled tarp. But Theia knew what it was. It was the wyvern from her dreams. It was Lucien. She ran to the dragon and knelt beside it. It was still taking shallow breaths.

"He lives, for the moment," said Carter. "His transformation was very helpful in unlocking a source of power I've been seeking to acquire for some time. 'When the heir to the infernal throne rises, the gates of hell are opened, and when the heir descends, the gates are closed again for seven generations.' A little something I learned from Madeleine Marchant."

Stroking the dragon's neck, Theia was barely paying attention to him, but the last words sank in, and she raised her head. "You've been around since the *fifteenth century*? I'd have thought you'd be better at this by now. But I guess practice makes perfect, you fucking psychopath."

Carter laughed, though his eyes weren't smiling. "I didn't learn it from Madeleine directly. I learned it from the elder Rafael Diamante. He was quite the magical history buff."

"So where are these open gates you're so fond of? I don't see anything."

"It's not a visible manifestation. At least not for someone of your limited vision. It flows through the heir— *H-E*-I-R. In essence, he *is* the gate. I can't keep it open indefinitely, of course, but the longer it remains open, the greater the power I can absorb."

The wyvern stirred beneath her hand, its gem-like blue eye opening. Theia scrambled back as it struggled to rise. As dragons went, it was fairly small, but it was still easily twice as large as a man. The wyvern rose onto its jointed wings, using the forward joint like the forelimbs it no longer had to walk on the stone like a bat. The right wing was clearly broken, and it dragged beside the wyvern as the dragon hobbled forward, eyes fixed on Carter as though sizing his throat for its teeth.

"Still trying to win." Carter shook his head. "You can't win, Lucien. You lost before you were born—the moment Edgar sold your soul. You should know better than anyone that a soul price will always be paid, no matter how you attempt to avoid it."

A soul price.

Theia narrowed her eyes at him. "You killed that poor old woman. It was your people who gave Rosa Campos the overdose when Lucien went to take it back."

"*Lucien* killed the old woman when he tried to circumvent his own corporate contract. I didn't feel it was good business." Carter raised his arm and held up his palm toward the wyvern as if signaling "stop."

"I'd rather not strike you again. It would most likely hasten your death. The way I see it, I have at least another five or ten minutes of energy transfer from the gates if you just stay put." The wyvern continued moving toward him, and he shook his head. "Have it your way, then. I've gotten plenty."

As Carter lifted his arm, Theia darted forward and put herself between him and Lucien. "Over my dead body."

Carter observed her with amusement. "If you insist."

Theia threw her arms out at her sides as if to block Carter's attack from the wyvern and closed her eyes, bracing for impact, but as she did so, she seemed to feel her sisters' hands taking hers and the Lilith bond forming. They'd pooled their strength before, but never without physical contact. Maybe she was just imagining it. Or maybe Carter had been overconfident about the success of his *draugr* minions.

She closed her fists around the invisible hands, taking strength from them, and willed Carter's attack to be inert. Theia felt the strike, but a field of energy rushed out of her at the same moment, and the space between the two opposing forces seemed to warp for an instant, rippling like gelatin as her energy absorbed the blow.

She opened her eyes to find Carter's blazing.

"Stop wasting my time. You're only going to exhaust

yourself, and Lucien is in no condition to take me on. I have endless reserves of energy as long as the gates remain open, and you have the finite potency of demon blood."

He was trying to wear her down emotionally before he wore her down physically, but it was true. She wasn't going to be able to hold him off for long, even with the Lilith bond. Maybe if she had a binding spell from Ione, but without her sisters physically here, there was no hope of that.

As she repelled a second attack, the aura of a vision wavered at the perimeter of her sight. Theia clenched her teeth. What good was a vision now? It would only detract from her concentration. Lightning flashed in the distance, and thunder rolled around the edges of the surrounding mountains, circling the butte, echoing from rock to rock. The air began to ripple with the electrified energy of a monsoon storm, though it was too early in the season.

Theia watched the lightning fork beneath the clouds again, horizontal, a bolt of brilliant blue turning the night sky to daylight for an instant. A loud crack split the air directly over their heads, almost deafening her. The strike had been just feet away. She seemed to be floating within herself, unanchored but full of power—the power of the demon goddess.

She shouted something at Carter as he struck out at her once more, a word she didn't even recognize, old French. Carter jerked backward as if she'd stunned him. Behind her, the dragon was moving once more, taking a running leap into the air. Despite its broken wing, the wyvern barreled into Carter like another flash of lightning and toppled him to the ground. Carter lashed out, not with magic, but with a short blade. He slashed the leathery blue scales and drew blood.

The dragon stumbled, and Theia shouted again, more

words she didn't consciously know, and this time she could see her feet actually floating inches off the ground. Carter made a noise of pain, as if her words were hurting him, but lashed out once again with the desperation of a cornered animal. The dragon was limping as it tried to evade the blade, and it sank into scaly flesh.

Noise and chaos seemed to have risen up around the valley, stones and cactus undulating, as if the ground were fluid. And then Theia heard the unmistakable thunder and whinny of horses and the blast of a hunting horn.

Leo, in a cowboy hat and duster, led the party charging toward them across the sky. "For Freyja!" he shouted— or was it "For Rhea"?—and leaped from his mount with his sword drawn.

Theia was still muttering foreign words, and they trailed out in front of her like pieces of gold rope, forming unfamiliar curly letters she knew instinctively only she could see, and surrounding Carter Hamilton.

The wyvern pinned Carter against the stone with the thick joint of its good wing and roared. Fire blasted from its nostrils and curled around the hand that held the weapon, burning it until Carter shrieked and let the blade fall.

Leo stood over him, sword point at Carter's throat, and nodded to the wyvern. "I've got this, brother."

Electrical energy was still pulsing through Theia, but the Lilith bond was receding, and she stumbled as her feet touched the ground. She grabbed for Lucy's arm, and a startled noise escaped Lucy as Daisy's shade stepped out of her, visible to Theia somehow, looking as shocked as Theia felt. Both Theia and Daisy hit the ground, and Lucy turned as if waking from a trance.

"Theia? Are you all right?" She reached down and touched Theia's shoulder but recoiled, gripping her arm, as the dissipating energy snaked toward her in a visible static spark. "Shit. I think you've been struck by lightning."

Daisy seemed to look through them both, eyes wide, and Theia turned in the direction of her gaze to see an unusually large crow alight on the top of the wall. As it lowered its wings, the crow became a man—Rafe Diamante, his iridescent blue-green-and-violet-feathered wings half folded at his sides.

"The Lord of the Dead," Daisy whispered.

Rafe, wearing nothing but a pair of rather thin white linen pants, stepped down from the wall and came toward them, eyes taking in the entire chaotic scene.

He reached a hand down to Daisy and touched her lightly on the head in an almost fatherly gesture. "You're free, Daisy. Go where you will."

The shade, tears pouring down her cheeks, nodded and dissipated.

"Theia." Rafe sank onto his haunches. "Thank God. I thought you'd gone over the edge with…" He paused and looked at Lucy. "I thought you'd both—oh, I see." He nodded with approval. "Nice wings."

Lucy smirked. "Same to you." She glanced at Theia. "Theia's a bit…electrified. I think lightning struck her. I'll leave her in your hands. I need to see to Lucien."

"I'm fine," Theia insisted as Rafe looked her over with concern. "Although I could see Daisy. I thought for a minute I might have crossed over without realizing it."

"You saw her shade?"

Her head was starting to throb. "I think I was channeling my sisters. Maybe it was Phoebe's gift."

"Phoebe can't see them."

Theia shrugged. "I don't know. But really, I'm okay. Stop fussing." Around them, the *draugr* minions still hulked on the perimeter. "Maybe you can do something with them, though."

Rafe stood and nodded. "We had some in Cancún as well. I sent them packing."

"I think he sent them to Rhea and Ione, too," she said as Rafe helped her up.

"They seem to have lost their power." Rafe threw a smug look toward where Carter still cowered under the point of Leo's blade. He threw his arms out wide and stretched his wings. "Return to your graves, unnatural *muertos*. Your master is defeated."

The nasty things recoiled and shuffled backward, whining, and disappeared into the dirt as if they'd sunk into the ground.

In the corner, by the chapel doors, Lucy was engaged in an earnest discussion with the wyvern. As Theia approached them, Lucy turned and shook her head in warning.

The wyvern's blue eyes met Theia's for a moment, heavy with sorrow, before it turned and limped toward Carter. Leo stepped back as the wyvern grabbed hold of Carter by its foreclaws. It leaped into the air, taking Carter with it, and flew away.

Lucy blinked back tears. "The gates couldn't stay open any longer. I'm sorry. He can't survive in this realm. He had to go."

Madeleine's loophole no longer mattered. Lucien was gone.

Chapter 33

Theia rode back to Phoebe's place with Rafe—who had expended too much energy in translocation to return to Phoebe the same way—letting him take the wheel. In her lap were the torn garments Lucien had cast off with his transformation, including the stupid red cap.

After a few minutes of respectful silence, Rafe glanced over at her. "Those Lucien's?"

Theia nodded. "I suppose you think I'm an idiot for falling for him anyway after your warning. After reading your father's archives."

"Of course I don't. Nobody's an idiot for loving someone. And from what I saw, it seems I misjudged Lucien and his sister without even knowing them."

"They were both entangled in the darker side of Smok's business," said Theia. "But Lucien was trying to do the right thing. And I think, in her way, Lucy is, too. Of course, it's all hers now. Lucien inherited the *other* end of it."

"I'm sorry, Theia."

"Me, too."

He turned onto the semiprivate drive that led to Phoebe's place. Lined up on the side of the road in front of the house were two cars besides Rhea's Mini in the driveway. Among them was Ione's motorcycle, her not-so-secret secret.

"What's going on?"

Rafe shrugged. "I haven't been in contact with anyone. I left my phone in Cancún. Phoebe's probably going insane right now."

"Yeah, sorry about that."

He parked behind what looked like Dev's Mercedes. "Seems like the gang's all here."

Rhea threw open the screen door and ran out as Theia stepped from the car, and Dev darted after her to catch the speeding ball of Puddleglum fluff making a break for it.

Rhea bear-hugged her. "Why haven't you called or answered your texts?"

"I lost my phone."

Rhea glanced at Rafe. "So you did make it here. Phoebe's on the phone, and you're in big trouble."

Rafe grinned. "What's new?"

"Ouch. Trouble in paradise already?"

"Nothing but good trouble."

Rhea linked arms with Theia, turning her toward the house. "You're not going to believe who else is here."

Inside, Laurel was seated in Phoebe's living room, with Ione next to her. They looked remarkably civil.

"We pooled our resources," said Rhea. "Did you feel it?"

"I… The three of you? Together?" Theia shook her

head in amazement. "I certainly did. I just didn't realize—
I thought maybe Phoebe had somehow joined remotely."

"It was Laurel's idea." Ione rose. "She came to find
me. Said you were in trouble. She'd seen it, but she
couldn't reach you. So we formed the bond."

So it was Laurel's ability she'd been channeling when
she'd seen Daisy's shade.

Phoebe's exasperated voice came from the cell phone
sitting on the coffee table. "Is that Theia? Goddammit,
you guys! What's going on?"

Rafe picked up the phone. "I'll take care of her," he
said with a wink and headed for the bedroom.

Rhea snorted. "I'll bet you will."

Theia tucked her hands into her pockets, feeling awkward. "Carter said he'd sent *draugr* after all of you."

Dev nodded. "We handled it."

Rafe popped his head out before closing the bedroom
door. "He's finished, by the way. He won't be bothering
anyone anymore."

Rhea glanced at Theia. "Leo took him to Náströnd?"

Theia shook her head. "Lucien took him." She sank
onto the couch. "And he's not coming back."

"Oh, sweetie." Rhea enfolded her in her arms. "I'm
so sorry."

They stayed up talking until Leo arrived just after
dawn. Dev and Ione headed home, giving Rafe a ride to
his place, while Laurel headed back to Flagstaff despite
Rhea's insistence that she was welcome to sleep there.
Theia finally got to crash.

When she woke after noon, Rhea and Leo were gone.
Rhea had left her a box of her favorite sugared cereal.
Theia curled up in the papasan chair with the entire box,

eating it by the handful. She'd finished her finals, so she had the whole day to just wallow and be disgusting.

But someone was heading up the drive as she glanced out the window. Theia sighed and set the box aside as Lucy pulled up in front of the house. How had she gotten this address? She supposed Smok's database had everyone's information. She locked Puddleglum in the bedroom and opened the door.

"Theia." Lucy took off the dark shades that made her look like one of the Men in Black. "I wanted to thank you for what you did for me last night."

Theia shrugged. "You would have done the same." She held the door open. "Did you want to come in?"

"Actually, I came by because I knew I couldn't reach you by phone." Lucy held out a brand-new smartphone. "It's from Smok."

"Oh." Theia took it reluctantly. "I guess I'm still bound by the contract."

"It's not that kind of phone." Lucy made an attempt at a warm smile. "It's just a gift. The contract, well…that's what I wanted to talk to you about."

"Did you come to wipe my memory? Because I think you're going to have to use your flashy thingy on my entire family if that's what you have in mind."

"Flashy thingy?"

"*Men in Black.* Never mind."

Lucy shrugged. "I don't watch television. But, no, I didn't come here to make you forget. I talked to Fran this morning, and she mentioned the text you and she translated."

"It's kind of a moot point now. He's gone."

"It's not as if he's dead."

"Well, it's not as if I can just go to hell, either. Unless you came for my soul."

Lucy made her scoffing version of a laugh. "Not today." Well, that was encouraging. "I received a call from Polly. She said you should go see her."

Theia sighed. "What, do I owe her more blood for her help last night?"

"I think she has something for you, actually."

Polly might have saved Lucien's skin last night, but there was no way she didn't want something else for her trouble. Theia might as well get it over with. The sooner all of this was over, the sooner she could get back on track with her program and her classes. She hadn't even looked at the outline for her thesis in over a week.

Business was apparently already in full swing for the evening when she arrived at Polly's place. The bouncer seemed to recognize her, even though she was sure she hadn't seen him before. Maybe there was something about Polly's gammon that gave them away. Maybe he could smell it on her; he was big and bearded, and he looked like a werewolf. On second thought, maybe he was just a bear.

A waiter escorted her to Polly's table without asking who she was, and Polly, mercifully, was alone.

"You wanted to see me?"

Polly smiled, aqua-blue hair flowing in waves over her shoulders to rest on a teal gown that sparkled with red where her fingers brushed the nap. "Theia, darling. Have a seat."

Theia scooted into the booth reluctantly.

"Lucy told me what happened with Lucien, and I understand there was some prophecy about the two of you? That only one of your line can break the Smok curse?"

"I could have, but it's too late."

"Not necessarily. I know the words. I heard them many

years ago. And the key begins with the descent of the goddess."

Theia wrinkled her nose. "I don't even know what that means."

"It means, sweetie, that you couldn't have broken the curse before it came to pass, before Lucien's transformation was complete. It means you have to journey to the underworld to complete your 'quest.' It's one of the oldest myths. You can find it in many cultures."

"And how the heck am I supposed to journey to the underworld?" She'd already asked Rafe and Dev and even Leo about the possibility. Even if they'd been willing to help her enter it, there was no telling if Lucien shared a common underworld with them. It was all about perception—his. "The gates have to be opened, and only Lucien can do that. And I can't contact him."

"The thing about Polly's is that it exists in many dimensions at once, in many places and many times. If I choose, the doors can open virtually anywhere." Polly smiled darkly. "Even in hell."

It took Theia a moment to understand the significance. "Wait...are you saying you can get me into hell?"

"That's exactly what I'm saying."

"What would I have to give you?"

"Nothing at all, darling."

"You don't strike me as the altruistic type."

Polly laughed. "No, indeed. But Lucien is special to me, and I'd prefer for him to be able to travel in this plane and not be trapped in hell being miserable. Besides, I owe him one, and I don't like owing people. So if you'll agree to go in and get him, I'll open the door for you. It's as simple as that."

"And will you open the door for me to come back, or is this a one-way ticket?"

"Such a smart question. Two-way door. No strings attached."

She didn't need to think about it. "I'm in."

As busy as the Grotto was, she couldn't imagine how Polly was going to manage having a door that opened into hell, but Polly, of course, had a separate, private door. When she opened it, it was impossible to see what lay on the other side.

Theia took a deep breath and stepped through. But she was still in Sedona, golden-orange setting sun glinting off the red rocks encircling the little enclave where Polly's was tucked. The back door led to the alley. Polly was full of shit.

Theia turned around, but the door had disappeared. Great. She'd fallen for the dumbest trick in the book. She hoped the siren and her creepy friends were having a good laugh.

When she walked around to the front of the building, the parking lot was empty. The sign that said Polly's was still there, but the club looked dark inside. What was going on?

Theia yanked open the door, determined to give Polly a piece of her mind—and found Lucien, in his human form and looking absolutely devastating. He was seated in front of a fireplace in a leather chair with his feet up on a matching ottoman, intent on reading some leather volume.

Theia breathed in sharply, intending to say his name, but only a squeak came out as she choked on her own saliva. He'd taken her breath away. Again.

Chapter 34

Lucien glanced up at the sound, and his mind couldn't make sense of what his eyes were seeing.

"Theia?" He jumped up from the chair, scattering the delicate pages as he let the ledger fall to the floor. Maybe he was starting to hallucinate. She couldn't be here.

He crossed swiftly to her and peered into her eyes, hands at her shoulders, and Theia sputtered, eyes welling up as if she'd swallowed wrong and couldn't catch her breath.

Lucien pounded her on the back awkwardly. "Are you okay?"

Theia nodded, the moisture in her eyes a little brighter as she gazed up at him.

"What are you doing here? You haven't…"

"No." She shook her head. "I haven't crossed over. Polly opened a door for me."

"*Polly?*"

"She said she owed you one. When I went through the door, I thought she was pulling my leg. It looks just like home out there."

Lucien nodded. "It's merely a different plane. It's all about perception. Which is why you perceive me as myself, as you knew me."

"Stop talking like you're dead."

"I am, to the plane above. I can't come back, Theia." He tucked her hair behind her ear, pained by her understated beauty. "God knows, I wish I could." The irony of his choice of words wasn't lost on him.

"But you can. Fran and I deciphered Madeleine's message. The curse can be broken."

"Theia, it's too late. I'm not human anymore. If I went back, I'd be a monster. And I have a job to do here. It's all very bureaucratic and dull, actually. You can't even imagine. Nobody burning in a lake of eternal fire, no demons prodding people with hot pokers. Just a lot of people doing ordinary jobs. And a lot of creatures that have to be cataloged and managed in their proper zones to keep order. There are lower levels, of course. Personal hells. Like where Carter Hamilton will spend eternity feeling powerless and bitter."

"Lucien, listen to me. There's a way for you to return with me—at least part of the time. If you're willing to be bound to me."

"Bound to you?"

"Fran said it was a blood bond." Theia's cheeks went pink. "We might…have to have…offspring together."

"*Offspring?*" Lucien's hands fell away from her shoulders and rested at her hips. "Are you telling me you'd have my child?"

"Well, not right away. I mean, I have my master's to finish, and I was hoping to get my PhD—"

"You realize you're certifiable."

"Maybe a little." Her mouth curved up in a slight, mischievous smile. "All it means for the moment is that we'd agree to be bound by blood. Always. It would break the curse that keeps you from being able to retain your human form in the earthly plane—and it would tie me to hell along with you."

Lucien frowned, the little flicker of hope she'd ignited extinguishing. "I can't tie you to hell, Theia."

The flush of pink in Theia's cheeks took on the redder hue of anger. "You don't get to make decisions for me, Lucien. If I want to tie myself to hell, I damn well will."

Despite his misgivings, Lucien couldn't help smiling. "*Damn* well, huh?"

"Oh, shut up." Theia slipped her arms around his neck as he let his hands travel around her waist. "Just say you'll do it and kiss me."

Lucien did the latter, just to silence her, but their mouths together felt right—everything about her felt right. He'd forgotten how not touching her felt like he was deprived of air. And the idea of having a baby with her wasn't, as he'd always imagined, an unthinkable prospect. It wasn't anything he wanted any time soon, but he wouldn't mind the practice involved.

"This binding…how would it work?"

"Fran said it could be a finger prick and a vow. Or… other physical contact involving…fluid exchange."

Lucien laughed. "You're saying if we have unprotected sex, I can walk out that door with you and end up in the earthly Polly's."

Theia smirked. "That's the idea. And there's no rule

that says we can't use the morning-after pill. I've got some at home, in fact."

Lucien lifted an eyebrow. "Do you, now?"

"You never know when you're going to need it—or a friend or sister is."

He trailed his fingers down her arm, enjoying the little shiver the touch elicited. "I suppose they're all waiting for you now."

She shook her head. "They have no idea I'm here. Polly's offer took me by surprise."

Polly was *full* of surprises, it seemed. She never did anything without expecting something in return. But Lucien was thinking too much again. There would be plenty of time to find out what she wanted later. Right now, Theia was here, and he was flesh and bone, and he wanted her so badly his chest ached.

Theia was watching him intently, as though cataloging his emotions as he cycled through them. "So what do you think? Should a son of Smok and a daughter of Lilith be eternally bound by blood?"

"Is that a proposal?"

Theia colored. "I didn't mean… That's not exactly…"

Lucien laughed and kissed her, pulling her into his arms. "Doesn't matter, darling. For you? Whatever it is, the answer's yes."

Despite thoroughly enjoying the necessary ritual, Lucien maintained his skepticism until he walked through the back door with Theia, prepared at any moment to do a quick about-face and return to his den. But when the door opened into Polly's suite, he was still himself. Polly was nowhere to be found, and Lucien walked out the private door with Theia into the spring Sedona evening, and nothing changed. Crickets were chirping, Oak Creek was still running over its polished slabs of sandstone, and the full moon was unabashedly gorgeous.

Lucien drew Theia into the circle of his arms. "No claws or wings. It seems Madeleine's loophole works after all."

"Fran said you should come see her. There might be a time limit to how long you can stay, but the Smok Biotech serum might still be useful in setting your own schedule."

"Time enough to figure that out, though, I suppose. Right now, I just want to go home with you and do some more bonding."

Phoebe arrived home from Cancún the following morning, still a little cranky about having been abandoned on her honeymoon and a bit put out to discover that Ione and Dev had beaten her and Rafe to the altar. Rhea had conspired with Dev to throw Ione a surprise reception, and Theia helped distract Ione, taking her shopping and bringing her back to her house to find the entire place festooned with cream satin ribbon and balloons.

Lucien showed up looking gorgeous in a buff-colored silk suit. "You didn't tell me what you'd learned about Fran," he murmured as he wrapped his arms around her from behind.

"I didn't think it was my place."

"Lucy knew. For years, apparently. I asked her why she didn't tell me, and she said it wasn't her fault I was born stupid."

Theia laughed. "Yeah, I get that kind of thing from Rhea a lot. There's an evil twin in every set, I guess. So did she have any insight into how long you can stay?"

"She thinks it may be tied to the phases of the moon."

Theia turned in his arms and smirked. "So I guess we'll have to wait and see if we get PMS together."

Lucien grinned, but then his expression turned serious. "I also talked to Polly. Her comment about owing me one was evidently in regard to my circumstances solving a rather vexing problem for her. It turns out Carter Hamilton was actively trying to turn her patrons against her in his bid to control the unnatural world. That stopped, of course, the moment I took him with me through the gates. But what she said she owed me wasn't the opportunity to let you complete your rescue mission." Lucien winked. "That was for her own selfish purposes. What she wanted was to return this."

He reached into his pocket and pulled out a small, hinged red velvet box. Theia's hand flew to her mouth as he opened it to show her the most perfect, flawless diamond nestled inside.

"It was the price she asked of me that day you drove me to the Grotto. A tear. You showed me I could express them without shame. So I think it should be yours. It's just the stone, of course, at the moment. We can shop for a setting together."

Theia couldn't speak as Lucien dropped to one knee in his exquisite suit among the tea roses in Ione's garden.

"Theia Dawn, will you do me the honor of becoming *officially* eternally bound to the reluctant Prince of Darkness?"

All she could do was nod, happily. As usual, he'd taken her breath away.

* * * * *

We hope you enjoyed this story from

HARLEQUIN®

NOCTURNE™

Unleash your otherworldly desires.

Discover more stories from
Harlequin® series and continue
to venture where the normal and
paranormal collide.

Visit **Harlequin.com** for more Harlequin® series reads
and **www.Harlequin.com/ParanormalRomance**
for more paranormal reads!

From passionate, suspenseful
and dramatic love stories
to inspirational or historical...

With different lines to choose from
and new books in each one every month,
Harlequin satisfies the most voracious
romance readers.

www.Harlequin.com

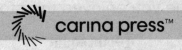
"Unless you stop me, I'm going to kiss you." He shifted one hand and gently dragged his thumb along her lower lip. "Do you want that, *mihara*?"

Want? Was he joking? *Want* was staring at your favorite dessert when your belly was already full of grade A fillet, tossing aside guilt and not caring how uncomfortable your waistband would feel on the way home. Feeling his mouth on hers was *necessary*. A primal connection she had zero experience knowing how to claim for her own, but knew on the most intrinsic level would re-chart every truth in her life.

"Elise?"

"Yes."

She was pretty sure the word made it past her lips. Tried to at least pair it with a dip of her chin. Whether either worked was hard to tell. Not with the prickling anticipation skittering across her skin and his hot gaze holding her rooted in place.

He slowly lowered his head.

Her heart kicked and thrashed like a frantic animal desperate to escape a trap.

But her lips parted.

Willing.

Desperate.

Ready.

His warm breath fluttered against her skin a second before contact, her lungs reflexively drawing in the unexpected gift along with his earthy scent.

And then was *there*. The full press of his mouth fitted perfectly with hers. The soft whisper of his beard. The teasing glide of his tongue along her lower lip, coaxing her to open. His soft groan as she gave him what he wanted, and the wet heat of their kiss.

She was lost. Floating through a riot of sensations she'd never dreamed existed. Drowning in all that was Tate. Absolutely nothing else mattered except the taste of him. In following where he led with each slick glide of his lips against hers. In savoring the decadent feel of his tongue sliding against hers.

He angled his head and deepened the kiss, sliding one hand to the back of her head and holding her firm as his other hand slipped around her waist and anchored just above her ass, pulling her flush against him.

So much muscle and heat. His arms banded around her. His muscled torso against her breasts and questing palms. His powerful quads pressed against her hips and—

She gasped and jerked away, the startling realization of what she'd felt hard against her belly knocking her headfirst back to reality. She staggered back a step. Then another. Willing her lungs to function despite the air thick with need around her.

A low growl surrounded her before she could take a third. "Don't run." Chest heaving and chin lowered as though he were seconds from charging forward, Tate pumped both his hands in fists. "I won't hurt you. Not ever. But you can't run."

Something in his tone suspended her fear. A desperation that put the brakes on all thoughts of distance and made every protective instinct fire bright. "What's wrong?"

"Just promise me, Elise. Whatever you do…*don't run*."

Find out what happens next when Rhenna Morgan's
Healer's Need *goes on sale October 22, 2018.*
Look for it wherever books are sold!

www.CarinaPress.com

CARRMEXP1018

Need an adrenaline rush from nail-biting tales
(and irresistible males)?

Check out **Harlequin Intrigue®**
and **Harlequin® Romantic Suspense** books!

New books available every month!

CONNECT WITH US AT:

Facebook.com/groups/HarlequinConnection

 Facebook.com/HarlequinBooks

Twitter.com/HarlequinBooks

Instagram.com/HarlequinBooks

Pinterest.com/HarlequinBooks

ReaderService.com

**ROMANCE WHEN
YOU NEED IT**

SGENRE2018

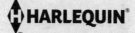

Love Harlequin romance?

DISCOVER.

Be the first to find out about promotions,
news and exclusive content!

Facebook.com/HarlequinBooks

Twitter.com/HarlequinBooks

Instagram.com/HarlequinBooks

Pinterest.com/HarlequinBooks

ReaderService.com

EXPLORE.

Sign up for the Harlequin e-newsletter and
download a free book from any series at
TryHarlequin.com.

CONNECT.

Join our Harlequin community to share
your thoughts and connect with other
romance readers!
Facebook.com/groups/HarlequinConnection

**ROMANCE WHEN
YOU NEED IT**

HSOCIAL2018